Distraught over the loss of her b
Pinkerton decides to follow in his footsteps—and prove the tragedy wasn't his fault. But when she's chosen as the first woman to fly the Air Force's F-35, her plan for a life that revolves around work is thrown off course by a handsome, mysterious stranger…

Thanks to Locke's seductive British accent, sweet nature, and one too many beers, Tink is soon inspired to throw caution to the wind—and herself into his arms. She thinks maybe love can heal after all—until she discovers Locke is her superior officer. Tink has no problem risking her life in the air, but with everything on the line, is she brave enough to risk her heart on the ground?

Visit us at www.kensingtonbooks.com

Books by Jamie Rae

Call Sign Karma

Published by Kensington Publishing Corporation

Call Sign Karma

Fight like a girl!

Jamie Rae

Jamie Rae

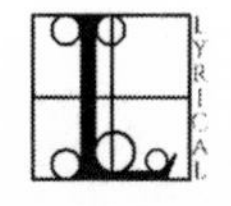

LYRICAL PRESS
Kensington Publishing Corp.
www.kensingtonbooks.com

Lyrical Press books are published by
Kensington Publishing Corp. 119 West 40th Street New York, NY 10018

Cover photo credit Scott Wolff

All Kensington titles, imprints, and distributed lines are available at special quantity discounts for bulk purchases for sales promotion, premiums, fund-raising, and educational or institutional use.

Special book excerpts or customized printings can also be created to fit specific needs. For details, write or phone the office of the Kensington Special Sales Manager:
Kensington Publishing Corp.
119 West 40th Street
New York, NY 10018
Attn. Special Sales Department. Phone: 1-800-221-2647.

Kensington and the K logo Reg. U.S. Pat. & TM Off.
Lyrical Press and the L logo are trademarks of Kensington Publishing Corp.

First Electronic Edition: January 2015
eISBN-13: 978-1-61650-670-4
eISBN-10: 1-61650-670-9

First Print Edition: January 2015
ISBN-13: 978-1-61650-671-1
ISBN-10: 1-61650-671-7

Printed in the United States of America

To my husband and children, you are my life.

and

To the brave men and women who wear the uniform working endless hours to protect our freedoms.

Acknowledgements

Thank you to my favorite fighter pilot, my husband, Mike. I love you for not only being an extraordinary man but for believing in me more than I believe in myself. Thank you for encouraging me to follow my dream even when everyone else thought I was crazy.

Thank you to my amazing children, Jake, Josh, and Jordyn. Your beautiful smiles keep my heart overflowing with joy and your love inspires me to never give up and to strive to be a better person.

Thank you to my parents who instilled in me at a very young age that the sky was the limit and with hard work I could achieve anything and everything.

Thank you to my friends, critique partners, and beta readers--Katrina, Cindy, Fiona, Taeya, Kelly, Lizzy, and Caleb. Thank you for dropping everything to read, offer incredible feedback, and for delivering a barrel full of hugs and laughs when I needed them. You've each made my writing process fun in your own unique way, while keeping me sane!

Thank you to my agent and friend, Michelle for believing in this story and for your countless hours of hard work to find Call Sign Karma the perfect home.

Thank you to Renee, Jennifer, Lyrical Press, and Kensington Publishing for taking a chance on a debut author and her feisty fighter pilot.

An extra thank you and shout out to my incredible editor, Jenn for challenging me to dig deeper and raising the bar. Because of you, this story is one that I am proud and eager to share with the world. It's been an awesome and incredible experience working with you. In the words of Tink…Holy hell, you rock!

To my readers, I hope that you will love this story as much as I do!

Thank you for giving me the opportunity to dream, write, and inspire!
Keep your circle positive.
XXXOOO
Jamie Rae

Chapter 1

There was zero chance of survival—for either of us.

The thought caused my insides to twist as I stood, paralyzed staring at the blazing inferno. I watched in shocked horror from the window of the control tower as the jet-fueled flames fed on his body, still strapped inside of the cockpit.

Tonight the distant flames were from a bonfire that danced happily in celebration of a holiday, but their flames were close enough to ignite the memories. Memories that still fueled my nightmares. A familiar chill skated down my spine.

I slammed down the beer bottle on the table next to me and looked away from the flames. Sweet honey lager splashed out and onto the cover of my tablet that sat on the edge of the table.

The tablet called to me. I couldn't help but reach for it. My shaking hand nearly knocked over the beer bottles that surrounded it. My index finger hovered over the screen. The damn arrow glowed as if challenging me to touch it.

Go ahead Tink, watch me one more time.

I swallowed the boulder-sized lump in the back of my throat as I accepted the dare. My finger tapped the start button and instantly dropped me in the middle of the nightmare that had consumed and wrecked my life.

"Altitude. Altitude. Pull up. Pull up." The unemotional, mechanical female voice of the jet's warning system rang out.

Her words rattled in my head like a pinball looking for its escape. I studied the altimeter screaming toward two thousand feet.

"Pull up," her empty voice commanded. Each time she repeated those words, my stomach lurched. That voice, that command, still haunted me.

I squeezed my eyes closed unable to stop from reliving that day in the tower and how her robotic tone had sent everyone into a panic. I stood frozen, unable to do a damn thing as the jet continued its nosedive.

My own weight crushed me as if I were being pushed down by the forces of a hard turn in the cockpit. I gasped for oxygen, my lungs rebelling as the image of the jet pitched down. I began counting between breaths to keep from passing out the way they had taught us in pilot training.

Three.

The sound of calm breaths from video filled the air. The ground rushed closer as the jet blitzed toward fifteen hundred feet.

"Pull up," the voice repeated. "Pull up."

Two.

I leaned forward and my lips parted as if I were going to retch, but nothing spilled out. I forced each breath to prevent me from blacking out like Colin. His calm, sleeplike breaths seeped from the tablet's speakers, haunting me in its wavelike rhythm. I held the tablet tight in my hands. The breaths were the last sound that I'd ever hear from him.

"Pull up! Pull up!"

A giant green arrow flashed across the video. It acted as a forewarning of the jet's impending impact. My entire body shuddered as adrenaline thrust through my veins.

I wanted to choke the aloofness from her tone. To the jet's warning system it was just another jet. To me, it was my world coming to an end. She may as well have tacked the word 'idiot' onto her feeble attempt of a warning.

The military Humvees scrambled on the screen like cockroaches escaping the light. I was paralyzed. I couldn't do anything to prevent it from happening then. Why did I still hope I could stop it now?

"Pull up!"

I closed my eyes.

It was too late.

"Pull up!"

One.

I opened my eyes. The ground rush on the display was exactly how they described it in pilot training; the world blossomed as earth ripped through to meet you in the cockpit.

Her vacant voice instructing him to pull up was the last thing to ring out right before my life shattered. Everything exploded into a bright blinding haze on the screen with a blaring detonation. The blood cooled in my veins.

I flipped the tablet cover and traced my still trembling finger along the lines of the worn material. I had stolen the video from my father's files the night after the funeral. I had watched it a thousand times, each time reliving the horrors of that day.

But tonight, once was enough.

Tonight, I had to figure out how the hell I was going to climb into the cockpit and fly the jet that killed my brother.

* * * *

The annual Fourth of July fireworks filled the sky right on cue. Red sparks showered down as the blue lights twirled across the backdrop of an onyx sky. It used to be our favorite family tradition.

A wave of guilt washed over me then pooled deep in the pit of my belly. How was it fair that I was standing here watching the fireworks, while Colin was buried six feet deep?

The reflection of the flashing lights off the ocean blinded me. High pitched screams and loud blasts shook the windows behind me as I leaned on the banister of my deck, watching the show, alone.

The silver ones that whistled were Colin's favorite.

My heart pounded at the thought of my tenderhearted brother. I squeezed my eyes tightly together to try to force out tears, but nothing fell. Not a single drop. I had cried so much that I had become numb to the pain.

My phone vibrated in my back pocket, interrupting the fireworks display. The ringtone of magical chimes followed. I sighed loudly. This was not a call I wanted to take.

Ignoring my mom wouldn't make her go away. It would only make her more determined. It was like she had a beacon implanted in my brain to know when I was thinking about my Colin's accident. I pulled my phone from the back pocket of my cutoff jeans and growled.

Pink 1 flashed across the screen.

My thumb hovered over the 'Off' button, but I couldn't bring myself to press it. She would know that I had dismissed her call. My mother knew everything, except when I didn't want to talk, or maybe she knew, but that still wouldn't stop her until she 'heard my voice'. It had gotten even worse since Colin's death.

A chime alerted the arrival of a new text message.

I forced myself to look at the screen and read the words;

He loved you.

I let out a long drawn out breath. Her words were always the same.

I picked up the bottle of sweet brown lager and gulped it. All of it. I reached for another. I twisted off the lid, and spun the tiny metal cap across the deck.

I wanted to feel Colin's pain and grief for a life he'd never have. But I couldn't shed any more tears. I was empty. Broken. There was nothing left of me. The only thing that kept me putting one foot in front of the other was the determination to prove that his death was not due to pilot error. I would prove it, or die trying.

The phone buzzed again.

Pink 1.

I swallowed another drink before I surrendered and answered the call.

"Hey, Mom," I said, my voice higher than usual in a failed attempt to mask my misery.

"You okay?" she asked with her usual cautious tone.

"Yeah, I'm great. I'm heading to Krusty's for dinner," I lied. "Can I call you tomorrow?"

"I wanted to hear your voice, sweetie, and wish you luck."

Luck? I needed a helluva lot more than luck. Tomorrow, I started training to fly the jet that cremated my brother.

"Thanks, I'm excited," I said as another lie slipped off my tongue.

It was becoming easier to fib to my mother. They just popped out one after another. I was never dishonest as a child, but now it felt like I never told anyone the truth.

"I'm looking forward to getting started." The words sounded sweet, but I'd need another lager to wash out the bitter taste. So much for being a pillar of honesty.

"Oh, Tinklee, you are such a liar," my mother said. "I know you're nervous. Who wouldn't be? I'll be there, in spirit, and so will he."

Her voice was warm and tender, as if she were smiling through her tears. She sniffled loudly. She was okay with her tears.

"Okay, I'm losing the connection. I gotta go."

"I can tell you don't want to talk so I won't keep you. I'll see you soon. And remember sweetie, keep your circle…."

"Stop Mom, I'm twenty-two, enough with the positive affirmations."

She ignored my plea. "If you keep your circle positive, you'll attract good Karma."

I rolled my eyes and held back a sigh out of respect to the woman who spent thirty-six hours in labor for me.

"Besides, age doesn't matter. I love you, baby girl. You'll always be my little Tinklee," she said. Her voice danced when she emphasized 'little' and 'Tinklee.'

I couldn't help but cringe. She'd screwed me with that one.

A blond-haired, blue-eyed fighter pilot trying to make it in a man's world couldn't be taken seriously with the name Tinklee Pinkerton.

Good job, Mom. You rock.

Chapter 2

If only I could drown the pain. I grabbed the last bottle from the cooler and hopped the deck rail into the sand. The grains were warm, baked under the hot July sun all day and retaining the heat well past sunset. I wiggled my toes, cracked open the bottle and tossed the lid over my shoulder onto the deck.

I loved this beach almost as much as I hated it. My parents bought this house when my dad was stationed here and kept it as a vacation home when he retired from the military. My mom insisted I stay here during my training, but being here just trudged up memories of Colin and me watching the jets fly over the beach. We dreamed of the day that we'd be in the cockpit flying side-by-side. And now, like him, those dreams were buried.

My chest tightened and I stifled a short breath. I wasn't ready for tomorrow. I was going to need something a hell of a lot stronger than the honey lagers that were going down like sweet tea. Taking a drink, I strolled toward the ocean's edge and stepped into the water. The coolness washed over my ankles and the current tugged at my feet. Everything in my life seemed to be pulling me in a direction I didn't want to go.

I wanted to be a fighter pilot from the first time I'd held onto the pant leg of my father's flight suit and breathed in the pungent scent of jet fuel. But now, as I moved another step forward to achieving my dream, nothing about it felt right.

I was selected to be not only the first female, but also the youngest pilot to ever fly the Air Force's prodigy, the F-35, Joint Strike Fighter. Not to mention doing it right out of pilot training. All that glory on top of the fact that my head was so screwed up over Colin scared the shit out of me.

Still, I plastered a smile on my face and told everyone that I was 'fine.' I had tits in a testosterone world and showing any sign of weakness was not an option. I. Was. Fine.

Only the best of the best would fly the Air Force's awesome creation. It could fly from D.C. to L.A. without showing up on radar if it wanted. But what were the chances of my being selected to fly it? I wanted a Viper and avoided the F-35 because of our messed-up history. I made sure I graduated top in the class of Undergraduate Pilot Training to be able to choose any other jet. But as it always did, my plan came back and bit me in the ass. I gambled and lost. Vegas style.

It wasn't fair.

"Why have you taken everything from me?" I screamed into the sky and kicked an incoming wave. "Leave me the hell alone."

I stumbled as a another wave rolled in. A light pressure appeared behind my eyes skewing my vision just a little. I realized that I may have drunk a little too much, but I was beyond caring.

The ocean spray soaked my clothes and hair. I steadied myself against the current. A chuckle escaped my lips. It sounded dark and slightly crazed. A rage, like I had never felt before swirled inside me like tornado looking for its target. I swallowed the last sip of lager and shook the bottle toward the star-filled sky.

"Here's to you, Karma," I shouted. I closed my eyes and twirled in a circle.

I spun until I was so dizzy that I could barely stand. I roared and launched the bottle with enough force that I nearly fell face first into the water. I steadied myself.

"Bloody hell, Karma's a bitch!"

My eyes opened to see a tall, shadowed man with broad shoulders towering over me. His arm was raised as he rubbed his forehead. I gulped as I spotted my bottle a few inches from his foot.

I stepped backwards and my heel dug into something sharp. A shooting pain launched up my leg and knocked me off balance. I swore, flailing backwards and fell into the ocean, landing with a big splash. Shock was quickly replaced by mortification. Heat traveled from cheeks to my ears.

Something, cold, smooth, and scaly swept over my legs. I shrieked and prayed a creepy crawly wouldn't bite off one of my limbs.

With about as much grace as a pig on ice, I scrambled to the shore. Adrenaline pumped through me, but it only made me feel more woozy. Just as I swallowed a gasp of air, a blunt object smacked into my head. Rays of light blurred my vision and I shouted as a blistering pain radiated from my head.

I balled my fists with the thumbs on the outside, like Colin had taught me. Did this guy just attack me? Did he have any clue who he was dealing with? Sure, I was tipsy and not steady on my feet, but I wouldn't go down without a fight. I was a frigging fighter pilot.

I pushed wet strands of hair from my eyes and squared my shoulders preparing to counter attack, but he waved me away as he held his nose. Blood speckled his shirt and dripped from the bottom of his hand. I softened my fists slightly still prepared to defend if needed.

"Blast it girl. You're dangerous," he said in a British accent that made my insides awaken. I pressed my lips together and prayed that I didn't just kick off another Revolutionary War.

Holy shit, it was time to go. The last thing I needed was for him to call the cops or the county mental health department. And as badly as I felt, apologizing would only be an admission of guilt in a court of law or worse, land me standing at attention in front of my commanding officer for an ass-chewing.

I bolted, teetering like a penguin, to the house and hauled myself up the side stairs of the deck, dripping wet. Mom's voice echoed inside my head to take off my sandals. The image of bloody, sandy footprints in my hall seemed almost as horrifying as the stranger's ass I just accidentally kicked.

"Damn it," I cursed under my breath.

I grabbed a towel on the deck chair and rushed for the outdoor shower stall on the side of the house. The water was ice cold, but it rinsed the blood from my foot and thinned a few lagers from my brain. Of course, it did nothing for the two pounds of sand in my underwear weighing me down like a sagging diaper.

I ditched the clothes and wrapped myself in the towel, shoving on the door to the inside of the house. Damn, it was stuck. I'd have to go back the way I came. I gripped my towel tighter and swung open the outside door.

Thud.

"Ouch. Bloody hell!"

I leapt backward, my hand slamming tighter into my chest. Oh my God! This could not be happening.

The guy from the beach collapsed back onto the ground, grasping at the newest wound on his head. The second I had caused in less than five minutes.

I didn't stop to apologize, just wrapped the towel over my chest, and sprinted back into the house, locking the door behind me. There was a pair of shorts and a tank top crumpled in the corner. They were as good as anything to wear. It's not like I wanted to dress up for my stalker, but if his knocking on the back door turned into kicking it down, it'd be nice to wear some clothes for the crime scene pictures.

Crap, where was my phone? My heart thudded in my ears. If I just ignored him, would he go away? If he didn't take the hint, my father kept a baseball bat in the hall closet.

Three quick knocks rapped on the back door.

As I ran for my weapon, I caught a glimpse of the man standing on the deck. He peered through the glass of the French doors. I swung open the closet, pulled out the Louisville slugger, and limped toward him. I may have played soccer instead of Little League, but I still knew how to swing a bat.

"Go away. I called 911," I shouted.

I flipped on the outside deck light so I could get a better look at the man. I'm guessing the detectives, FBI, and office of Homeland Security would need a description.

He was six foot, possibly two, with short, wavy blond hair and lightning blue eyes that were squinted from the porch light. He held a handkerchief to his nose and wore a light blue, bloodstained, linen shirt that was partially unbuttoned revealing his ripped abs. I hesitated until I remembered I was in danger.

He had on khaki shorts, flip-flops, and a tattoo on his ankle. I scanned back to the top of his body. Muscular, tan, tall, and wow, those electrifying eyes. Holy hell, this guy was freaking hot. He was going to have a *really* good mug shot. If only we had met under different circumstances, I might actually offer him a beer.

A soft smile tugged at his lip as he dangled my smartphone in his hand. My wet, sand-covered smartphone.

"Son of a bitch," I moaned as I remembered that it was in my back pocket when I fell into the ocean. I had to get it into a bag of rice and fast. It had my music, my schedules, and all my passwords. I was lucky if I remembered my own number, let alone everyone else's.

"Leave it on the deck. And go."

I tightened my grip on the bat. Mr. Tall, blond, and handsome removed the handkerchief from his nose.

A tiny flutter tickled in my chest. My head tipped slightly to the side. He didn't look threatening. Minus the blood, lumps and cuts, he looked like he just stepped off the front cover of GQ.

"Sorry, Miss Nutter, but do you think I could trouble you for an icepack?"

"No," I replied.

"Please?"

He sounded and looked like a real life Prince Charming. The only thing missing was his white horse. Maybe the Karma gods had sent a peace offering? I shook my head. No. My house was built of stone and there was no way I was letting a freaking wolf in, no matter how smoking hot he was.

I needed to protect myself.

But why did I need protection? I looked at the bloodstain drying on his shirt. If anything, he needed protection from me.

As if he had read my mind, he shook his head and laughed. He sat my phone on the bench, raised his hand in the air in a non-threatening manner and turned to walk away. Where was he going?

I dove forward and gripped the door handle ready to pull it open, but I stopped as my father's stern, no-nonsense voice boomed in the back of my head—"*Don't ever let strange men into the house.*"

But when in my life would I meet another crazy beautiful man with a British accent that twisted my lady parts into a knot? His hand rested on the railing as he was about to walk down the steps and out of my life forever. I cursed under my breath and prayed that I wouldn't wind up on the news.

"Wait," I called to him as I swung open the door. He stopped and turned to look at me. "There's ice there in the cooler. There, by the chaise." My voice cracked as our eyes met.

"Thank you," he said. His steps back toward the house were hesitant. His eyebrow rose as he pointed to the bat in my hands. "Are you planning on hitting me with that?"

His lips tugged into a smirk. It was the most incredible half-lifted-top-lip smirk I had ever seen. And that damn accent. Holy hell it was getting hot in here.

"I didn't do a good enough job before," I said and I couldn't help but smile.

"You are a bit of a *nutter*, aren't you?"

"I guess it would appear that way, wouldn't it?" I wasn't sure of the exact definition of nutter, but the way it sounded rolling off his tongue and the way his shirt gripped his muscles it didn't matter what he called me as long as he didn't leave.

I handed him a towel that I'd left out earlier. "Here's a peace offering."

"With a smile like yours, your mental state is forgiven."

In a bar, that line would've earned an eye roll and a sigh, but with his alluring accent, I'd let it slide. His smile widened as he accepted the towel and wrapped the ice from the cooler inside. He pressed it on his forehead and winced, his smile replaced by a scowl. A sexy scowl. Damn, I was so going to need another cold shower

"Thanks," I stammered and glanced down. My cheeks burned. "I need to get my phone into rice."

I scooped up my cell from where he'd left it and nearly dropped it with my shaking hands. I turned to head inside but stopped. "Can I get you anything? Maybe something to drink?"

I wasn't sure what I was doing. He needed to go, but I liked the way he looked me over. Maybe a drink wouldn't be so bad. It wasn't like I had anything else to do. The Fourth of July and all I had planned was screaming at the ocean. A cute guy's company sounded like a fun, sane option.

"Is it safe? You don't plan on finishing me off with a poisonous pint, do ya?" he asked.

I was just about to laugh at his comment when he winked and it stopped me short. My breath hitched in my chest. What the hell was it about this guy that made me react like I was in heat?

Take control, Tink.

"You'll have to decide if you want to take your chances," I replied with a slightly flirty tone.

"Something tells me to run like bloody hell, but something else tells me to take my chances. I think that might be the head trauma talking."

I fought a smile. He was charming and witty and I couldn't help but want to know him better.

He kicked off his sandals and tucked his handkerchief in his back pocket before sitting on the chaise lounge. He held the ice to his nose. His eyes reflected in the moonlight. I knew nothing about this strange man, yet his presence had made me remember how good it felt to smile again.

I took my phone to the kitchen and caught his reflection in the window. He continued to stare at me with a smirk. My insides stalled and hit a free-fall.

I opened up the pantry, and rummaged through the container. The closest thing to rice was quinoa. It was a grain, wasn't it? I shrugged and dropped the phone in the bag. It was close enough.

Out the window, my stranger remained sitting on the deck with his icepack. At least it gave me a little time to run to my room and scope out my reflection.

My hair was drying into a natural beach wave and I tousled it to add a little volume. I breathed into my hand, then squirted a blob of toothpaste onto my toothbrush and quickly scrubbed my teeth. After adding a little mascara on my lashes, I swiped my lips with lip balm. Oh my God. What was I doing?

I didn't understand how this guy could make me feel so crazy. I didn't know a single thing about him—not even his name. I was acting like a high school girl with a crush. This wasn't me. Were an accent and a panty-dropping smirk all it took to ground me?

I was having a horrible night before he came along and tomorrow was going to be a shit day. I had enough to drink and I didn't give a damn. Tonight, I would allow myself to feel something—anything. For one night. Then, tomorrow he would go back to wherever he was from and I would continue onto my path of hell.

After all, it was a holiday, a day to celebrate independence. It used to be my favorite. Maybe, just maybe, it could be once again.

Chapter 3

One hot Brit and a cold beer coming right up.

Thankfully, I had another six-pack stashed in the back of the fridge. Swallowing my nerves, I tucked it under my arm and limped outside.

"Are you all right?" he asked as he stood up.

"Yeah, I think a crab bit my foot in the water," I replied and shrugged to downplay it, but my foot hurt like hell.

He reached out, took the bottles and placed them in the cooler.

"You should prop it up," he said folding a towel on the chaise.

I nodded. I sat and elevated my foot as he opened two of the bottles and handed me one.

"Cheers," I said and lifted mine with gratitude.

He flinched.

"Really?" I choked out, but I couldn't blame him after our initial meeting.

"Sorry, it was a bit of a knee-jerk reaction," he said. "Round one was a bottle to head. Round two was a nut to the nose, and round three, the door smashing. Who knows what round four holds?"

"Nut to the nose?" I asked and fought a grin. "What the hell does that mean?"

"A head butt."

I laughed, trying to shake the first visual from my mind.

"Yeah, really funny," he said with a smile. "You injured me three times, then left me to die."

He raised three fingers, but then laughed. I liked the rich baritone sound.

"You caught me off guard," I said and took a swig of my beer.

"I caught you off guard? Hell, I didn't know what hit me. Literally."

"I'm sorry," I finally admitted out loud. I shrugged and chewed on the inside of my lip. "This is a private beach. There aren't people around very often. Or at least not anyone close to my age."

At least he looked close to my age but something about him seemed more mature. The way he held my eyes when I spoke and the way he'd folded the towel beneath my foot, even the way he handed me my beer and waited for me to take the first drink seemed more reserved than most of the guys I'd known.

My curiosity peaked. "How old are you anyway?"

He shrugged a shoulder and leaned forward, answering me in nearly a whisper. "It's impolite to ask a person their age, you know."

"It's impolite that you never told me your name," I responded.

His smile widened to show straight, white teeth. "Locke," he said. "And I'm twenty-six."

He extended his hand to me and I leaned forward to accept.

His grip was firm. Confident. Assertive. He locked onto my eyes. There was something about the way he watched me, observed me that made me feel comfortable, yet vulnerable.

I broke the stare and nodded at his tattoo. It was an intricate design, richly colored in burgundy, navy and gold with what appeared to be a lion holding a tiny gold circle.

"You don't seem like the tattoo type," I blurted out. Not that I knew what this stranger's type was.

He ran his fingers across the design. I shivered at the thought of those fingertips running down my body.

"It was done on a dare," he said as his gaze locked on mine. "It's my family's crest."

"Family crest? Wow, how very British," I responded, giving him my best British accent.

"Yes, it is very British. Unlike your accent."

"What's wrong with my accent?"

"It's Australian," he said with a teasing smile on his lips.

"No, it's clearly British." I pronounced 'British' with the accent and waited for his response. He raised his eyebrow as if he realized that he was not going to win this argument. I couldn't help but smile.

"Where did you go to college?" I asked.

He took another sip of his beer before he answered, "I attended Cambridge."

Warmth spread through my body. Locke was hot and well educated.

"Cambridge University," I said, attempting to correct my accent.

"That was Jamaican."

I swatted at him and tipped from the chair. I swung my foot down to catch my balance and winced. Damn, my foot throbbed.

"You okay?" he asked.

"I'm fine," I said, adding another lie to the long list that continued to accumulate.

"Is there a first aid kit inside?"

"I don't know, maybe in the bathroom," I said with a shrug. "It's not necessary, I'm okay." I tossed back the last of my beer. Alcohol could numb any pain.

"So are you going to tell me why you were shouting at the ocean?"

I closed my eyes and took a deep breath. For the first time in what felt like forever, I was enjoying myself. A fun, flirty conversation was what I needed.

His eyes narrowed as if he were studying me. "I can see that you've been terribly hurt," he said with a soft, understanding expression.

There was something in the way he spoke—I'm not sure if it was the tone of his voice or the genuine expression of care on his face, but it made me feel protected from my demons. I wanted to talk to him.

I opened my mouth to tell him about Colin, about the jet, about everything, but stopped myself. This was ridiculous. I barely knew him. I pressed my lips together with a silent reprimand and reached for another beer in the cooler. I wasn't sure how many I'd drank, but there were a lot of empty bottles on the ground and my cheeks were beginning to numb.

"Besides being a great punching bag, I'm a decent listener."

"I lost someone very close to me and very suddenly," I confessed. My voice cracked as I admitted the truth out loud to someone other than my own reflection in the mirror. "It's been rough."

Shit. I definitely had too many beers.

"A breakup?"

I shook my head. I wish. A break up would've been easier.

"A death?"

I nearly choked on the lump that immediately formed in my throat. I dropped my head down and nodded once. A few seconds of silence passed. He slid down the chaise toward me.

"I'm sorry."

I was, too. I stared at my bottle, ready to crumble. Damn it, I couldn't do this. I couldn't open this wound I struggled to keep sealed up. It was too much of a risk. I needed my head in place for tomorrow.

"Thanks, but I can't talk about it."

He took the beer from my hand and placed it on the table next to us.

"I'm a firm believer that life will never give you more than you can handle," he said and leaned toward me. I glanced up into his eyes. "You seem like a survivor."

The words stung like someone had poured a carton of salt into a large gaping wound. In a sense, he had. He'd called me a survivor. I was a survivor, but Colin wasn't.

"Well, looks are deceiving," I muttered and looked to the side.

His hand touched my cheek and directed my face to look at him. I forced myself to meet his eyes. He held my stare, imploring me to hear him. It was ironic that a total stranger believed in me more than I believed in myself.

The back of my eyes burnt, I needed to change the subject before my heart dove into a tailspin. I shifted my leg and a pain jolted through foot. I hissed.

"Here let me take a look," he said as he scooted forward. I bent my knees closer to my chest. My foot was red and it hurt, but medicating with alcohol dulled most of the pain.

"It looks wicked."

He lifted my foot into his hand as if caring for a wounded bird. Delicate. Gentle. His touch spun my world into another universe. He looked at me with a mixed expression of shock and desire. His grip—the strong, lithe fingers and muscular forearm—tightened its hold.

For a moment, I sat frozen in silence, not breathing, only hearing the pounding of my heart. I wanted to pull away. No one had touched me like this since college, before Colin's accident. And even then, no one had touched me, especially my foot, like that before. Apparently, I'd been missing out.

His palm glided upward toward my ankle, and my skin blazed along its path.

His hand wove a path up my leg until it reached my hip. His fingers grabbed the belt loop of my shorts, pulling me closer. I gasped and he smiled. The sexy half-lip smile and my whole body shuddered with excitement. His gaze never faltered and I didn't dare blink, afraid he would disappear if I closed my eyes even for a second. He was too good to be true.

Locke leaned in and the smell of honey lager and the warmth of his breath invited me closer. I licked my lips lightly and parted them. His kiss was soft and playful and I felt as if I had been kissing him my entire life.

I never believed in fairytales, but this had to be how 'Once upon a time' felt. I shifted my body without breaking our embrace, straddling my legs around him and sitting on his lap.

Locke's hands rested gently on my hips. His fingertips pressed into my lower back and sent heat spiraling through my body. He sighed softly.

Nervous chills traveled down my spine. I was kissing a stranger. A charming, sexy stranger. My mind raged in a tug of war against my heart. Just a few hours earlier I'd been ready to call the police and now I was considering inviting him into my bed. I'd never done anything like this before, but it felt too good to quit.

I opened my mouth slightly and his tongue entered, swiping against mine. His soft moan gently vibrated against my lips.

"What's your favorite color?" a breathy voice asked. I sucked in a gulp of air. Was that my voice?

"What?" he murmured and pressed his lips back against mine.

I pulled my face inches from his. "What's your favorite color?"

"Blue."

"What's your favorite football team?"

"Manchester United."

"That's soccer."

"No, darling, it's *real* football." A wicked smirk crossed his lips.

Holy hell, if he called me darling like *that*, he could tell me the sky was green and I'd agree.

He pressed his lips against mine as his hands tangled in my hair. I didn't want to stop, but I barely knew anything about him. My heart raced. I pulled away. Again.

"When's your birthday?"

He leaned back and raised an eyebrow.

"July 31st. My favorite movie is James Bond, Goldfinger." His smile spread as if he realized what I was doing. "I love dogs, but don't have one, and I hate orange juice."

I like James Bond. Good enough.

My fingers ran through his hair and I pressed my lips harder against his. He chuckled then nibbled my bottom lip. A flurry of anticipation erupted as I wondered where he would nip next. His lips traveled slowly below my ear and I tipped my head back slightly and lightly purred. His breath warmed against my skin, as his hands explored under my tank and up my back. An electric pulse ignited as his fingers traced along my spine. I slid my fingernails gently down his arms. Bumps rose upon his skin and I knew he wanted me as much as I wanted him.

He stopped kissing me, and my body fell into instant withdrawal. I wasn't ready for it to end. I leaned into him. His tongue traced along the pulsing vein in my neck and I resisted the urge to cheer out. And when his lips brushed against my cheek and his breath tickled my ear, I shuddered.

"Bloody hell. You take danger to a whole new level," he whispered and nuzzled into my neck.

Amused, I stifled a laugh.

"You have no idea how happy I am that I hit you in the head with that bottle," I said softly into his ear. I traced my finger along his face and gave a nibble to his earlobe.

My lips moved toward his and brushed them softly. He stood, lifting me. My legs found their rightful spot, tucked around his waist.

He carried me into the house. I stopped kissing him for a few, short, raspy directions on how to get to my room and to make sure he had protection, or a Johnny as he called it. Once he stepped into the doorway, his lips found mine.

He sat me gently on the bed, never breaking the mind-blowing, world-silencing kiss, even as I unbuttoned the remainder of his shirt and pushed it off his shoulders.

My heartbeat thumped loudly in my ears as the reality of what was about to happen diluted the effects of the alcohol. His beautifully tanned and toned muscles flexed as he hovered over me making me wonder if everything about this man was too good to be true. I lay back and shivered as he joined me. He brushed a loose strand of hair from my eyes.

"We don't have to do anything you aren't comfortable with, darling," he said gently and held me firmly at arm's length.

My eyes traced slowly across his right arm and then his left. I wanted him, but more importantly I needed him. Throwing caution to the wind, I touched my hand to his face.

"I've never felt more comfortable in my entire life."

Chapter 4

It didn't seem fair for the angel and the devil on my shoulders to gang up against me last night. I didn't know whether to hug them or smack them. I squeezed my eyes closed and my pulse thumped loudly in my head. A low moan escaped my lips as I pulled my pillow over my face and rolled over. The rich spicy scent of his cologne lingered causing my heartbeat to quicken. I slowly peeked from under the pillow. Disappointment tugged at my belly.

Locke, my stranger, was gone, but a glass of water awaited me on the nightstand with two Tylenol, a first aid kit, and a paper airplane. It was just one night, I reminded myself. I picked it up and unfolded the note, to read:

I can't believe I don't know your name. Or did you tell me and I suffered from amnesia due to my head injuries? Either way you owe me a date to make up for the way you treated me last night. I'll pick you up after work around 6:30.

Locke.

Okay, maybe two nights.

I popped the Tylenol into my mouth and downed the entire glass of water. After rereading the note, I folded it into its plane form and sailed it into the air. Ironic.

As I swung my legs out from under the sheets, I discovered an expertly dressed bandage on my foot and I wondered how he didn't wake me. Especially since every time he touched me my body erupted like a volcano. My face lit fire as a satisfied grin tugged at my cheeks. I should hate this day. I had dreaded its arrival for so long, but I intended to enjoy this moment while it lasted.

For the first time in over a year, I felt alive. I hadn't allowed anyone that close to me, but Locke felt different. Just the thought of him made my stomach bottom out. Feelings equaled pain and I promised myself that I would never allow my heart to be broken again after Colin's death. I couldn't risk losing someone that I loved ever again. Locke was danger. Serious danger.

I tugged the blankets over my head and rolled over. The sandalwood scent sent my heart into a flurrying panic.

After a shower and breakfast, I stepped into my flight suit and laced up my boots. The pain in my head was replaced by an ache in my foot. I pulled my hair back in to a ponytail, then wrapped it into a bun.

I took my phone from the plastic container. A text from *Pink 1* wishing me luck again and a calendar alert that read 'doomsday' lit up the screen. I regretted saving the damned phone's life.

I tossed a bottle of water into the passenger side of my jeep and climbed in. The sun was shining and it looked like the Karma gods had taken pity on me and given me enough time to drive through Starbucks.

As I pressed the cup's lid to my lips the image of Locke entered my mind. Just the thought of him reignited the feelings from last night.

Warmth spread deeper in my belly as I replayed our extracurricular activities. His strong hands on my bare skin, his soft lips pressed against mine....

The concrete walls of the base flanked by the Forty-fourth wing's blue and gold insignia smacked me into reality. An uncomfortable tingle started at my cheeks and shot through my body as I neared the barriers that staggered the entrance. I handed my identification card to the security guard and blinked several times waiting for my dream to end.

"Have a good day, ma'am," the young airman at the gate said with a salute.

I sharply returned his salute and realized that doomsday had arrived, but maybe it wasn't as bad as I anticipated.

Taking a deep breath, I donned my game face. A stupid sunny smile would not win me any points among the most fierce and competitive group of guys in the Air Force. I rolled my shoulders back and stood up straight with a brief pep talk. For the next eight hours, I was a woman on a mission.

* * * *

I ignored the slight shake in my hand and punched in the code to the squadron door. I walked in with a few minutes to spare. Our brief would begin on the hour so I didn't have time to mingle with guys, who most likely didn't want to gab with me anyway.

It didn't matter how many of them I could take down with a single shot, I didn't have a dick, which seemed to be required for membership. I wasn't here to make friends or be in their club. I was focused on a single objective: clear my brother's name.

A guy named Freak leaned against a wall. He was a senior at the academy during my freshman year and flew the A-10 Warthog after pilot training. He might have been decent to me at school, but this wasn't the academy anymore. This was a completely new monster.

Another guy nodded as I walked by. I didn't know him, but he obviously knew of me.

"Aw, look guys," he said as he leaned back in his chair. "Tink just floated in with her magic pixie dust. Maybe she'll sprinkle some around and we'll all start to fly."

He waved his hands in the air. If he was trying to pull off the look of a fairy he failed. He looked more like a deranged duck. I decided that he'd be the first one I'd crush in the air.

Freak playfully punched him in the chest. The chair clamped back against the floor.

"Knock it off, Mojo. She earned her spot just like the rest of us," Freak said and crossed his arms.

I caught sight of the Weapon's Officer patch on his arm, which spoke louder than his words. The patch wearers were in the top one percent of the Air Force. It signified that they were the best of the best. It was something we strived to become. And here I was, just a kid from pilot training. Big difference. Still, I took a mental note; Freak—cool; Mojo—ass.

I ignored the others' stares and strode to my seat in the conference room. Thank God my phone worked. It was a lot easier to deal with the whispering and laughter with a phone to offer a distraction. I bit my lip as my blank stare reflected back at me.

I flipped through the news and heat spread across my cheeks as I read that Manchester United had won last night.

Loud footsteps pulled my attention from the news, but I didn't bother to look up. I sat quietly and kept my head down. It was my plan—head down, mouth shut, and fly the damn jet. A hand tapped on the table in from of me. I glanced up to a familiar face.

"Hey, Stitch," I said with a genuine smile.

His family was friends with ours and he was a few years older than me. He was Colin's best friend.

"Surprise!" he said and winked at me. "I got a last minute spot in the class. Maybe my dad can start talking to yours again."

"Yeah, well he wasn't the only one pissed at my dad when I was selected. We all know he played a hand in the selection, if not, I'd be sitting pretty learning how to fly a Viper," I said with a sigh.

"You deserve to be here, Tink. Don't ever doubt it."

I pressed my lips into a soft smile. "At least now our dads can go back to fighting over their golf games," I said with a shrug trying to lighten the mood.

Stitch chuckled and patted me on the arm before sitting down.

I felt better knowing Stitch was here. At least there was one, maybe two people who weren't going to hate me.

The room was called to attention for the Wing Commander's arrival. The sleeves of his flight suit were pushed past his elbows and his lips were drawn into a thin no-bullshit line. His long career to service with sacrifice were etched in the creases around his eyes and stamped in approval with three navy blue stars lined up across his shoulder.

"At ease!" he shouted and my heart leapt when he smacked his hands together.

I scanned the room as I sat. There were twelve of us and I couldn't help but wonder who would be the first to go. I wanted to stand back up and volunteer, but I didn't.

I needed to clear Colin's name.

My father would lose his shit if he received the call that the entire fleet of F-35's was grounded due to a faulty environmental system. The thought made me smile.

"Am I amusing you, Lieutenant?"

Shit. This was not the way to keep a low profile.

"No, sir," I answered and pressed my hands on the table in front of me.

"Good, because there is nothing funny about any of this training you are beginning. You were each hand picked for a reason, don't make us regret it."

"Yes, sir," I answered, folding my hands into my lap. I watched as the moist outlines of fingers faded from the table.

The room was called to attention again and as he left, the next commander came in to brief security. I wiped a drop of sweat from my brow. It was turning out to be a long morning. Learning about the base and safety briefs were as boring as watching the grass grow.

Where were the jet systems and air space briefs? Something flying related. I hadn't been paying much attention and I was thankful we only had one more set of academics before lunch.

I twirled my pencil around on the desk and tried to keep from dozing off. My stomach growled desperately in need of food. My lack of sleep and too many beers was catching up with me. The pencil spun off the table and hit the floor. I bent down to pick it up when I noticed my boot string tied to the table. What were we in, kindergarten? Stupid fighter guys. They were all the same. I pulled on the lace, but it was knotted.

The door opened and two sets of boots came into the room. One was the Director of Operations, Major Rex, or T-Rex. I recognized his voice without looking up. His scruffy tone was one that a person wouldn't forget. I'd spoken to him on the phone during the selection process.

I tugged on the knot, but it was too tight. I wiggled the tip of the pencil into the tangled mess. I didn't want to cut the stupid lace. Freaking boys.

"The Joint Strike Fighter will not only be flown by our guys, but some Allied Forces are joining the fight as well. Flight Lieutenant Sinclair has flown over five hundred hours in the Eurofighter and two hundred hours in the F-35. He has flown in combat with RAF Corningsby and has an extraordinary record with the Brits," T-Rex said as I continued to work on freeing my damn boot. "We are fortunate to have him here and look forward to his expertise. Flight Lieutenant Sinclair. Call sign, Duke."

I tugged on my string almost freeing the knot so I could sit back up and see. I gave it another jerk.

"Thank you Major Rex. It's awesome to be here," said a male voice laced with a British accent.

A too familiar British accent. It couldn't be the toe-curling, heart-flipping, cause-me-to-lose-all-good-sense, British freaking accent.

My heart skipped a beat or twenty.

"No," I mouthed silently to myself as my eyes widened. It couldn't be....

I lifted my head up to see if my ears had deceived me, prepared to drop and army crawl the hell out of here.

I sucked back a breath and instinctively jerked up. My head cracked on the bottom of the table. Shooting stars clouded my visions.

"Holy shit," I muttered and grabbed for my head.

Through the haze, I could see well enough to recognize my perfect stranger standing in Flight Lieutenant Sinclair's boots. All six-foot-two of him. Hot, gorgeous, and neatly packaged in a well-fitted flight suit.

I needed to get out of here. Now. He was staring directly at me, ghastly white and shell-shocked. I knew the feeling.

I gulped and jumped to my feet, forgetting that my foot was still tied to the table.

"Shit!" I cursed and fell backwards.

My head cracked against the ground. I lay flat on my back with my eyes closed, head pounding, foot tied to a desk and very vivid images of my instructor, naked in my bed. The calendar was right. It was doomsday.

Chapter 5

The only one laughing at my cringe attack was Karma.

Stitch was by my side within seconds, grabbing my hand and looking me over. My boot tugged as a tearing sound ripped through the air. Damn. They cut the lace. With a fuzzy mind and throbbing head, I couldn't help but regret that I didn't cut it myself. *Stupid.*

"Shit Tink, are you okay?" Stitch steadied me as I sat up.

"Yeah, I'm fine."

Lie. Of. The. Century. I wanted to die, but first I wanted to kick someone's ass.

I threw a pissed off glance in the direction of Mojo then snuck a quick peek at the Brit instructor, still praying that it was all a mistake.

Nope. He stood above me, looking the same, but so different. He had a bruise under his left eye—a stark remind of last night. The sexy smirk and quiet confidence were gone, replaced by thinly drawn lips and dark cold eyes.

"Take *her* to Major Rex's office," Flight Lieutenant Sinclair commanded. He dropped his hands to his hips and sighed loudly without a glance in my direction. "The flight doc is on his way. The jackasses that tied the boot can join her."

The way he looked past me hurt worse than the damn crack to the head. I knew he couldn't show any outright affection because of his position. Sleeping with a student was definitely taboo, but was it really necessary to have me removed like yesterday's trash?

"I'm sure as hell not letting these dumbasses take her alone," Stitch said as large hands gripped my elbows and helped me to stand. The two guys who were sitting in front of me joined him. They were shadowed next to his burly frame.

"I'm fine. I don't need to see the doctor," I replied and pulled my arm away. No weakness.

"It wasn't a request," my knight-turned-asshole said. He turned and walked to the front of the room without a look in my direction. "All right, Yanks. Get your heads out of your arses and back into the game."

I had been dismissed.

With my pride trampled, I stormed out of the room. I saw stars, first from what was probably a mild concussion, and second from my anger. I wanted to faint and throw up. Simultaneously. And that would have looked even more fantastic then my head banging, ass-crash I performed. This circus act was ready for the road.

"Tink, stop. Just wait. You look like you're going to faint. Let me help you," Stitch pleaded.

He was visibly upset. I didn't want to look into his overprotective eyes or have him show me any kindness because I feared I would cry. I needed to stay angry and driven. I needed my poker face.

There was no way in hell that I would cry on my first day and definitely not in man's town.

I swallowed back my emotions and shot him a look, and thankfully he got it. He stayed close, but didn't touch me. Two sets of footsteps echoed behind us. If the jokesters thought their stunt was funny earlier, they were no longer laughing.

T-Rex's neck was beet red and his nose flared like a bull as I entered his office. He ignored me and waved to a guy who had just walked in. He was a bronze-skinned guy whose hair was definitely not regulation.

"Hey Doc. Check her out and keep me posted, let me know if she needs to go off flying status," he said and snapped his fingers, pointing to the two knuckleheads. "You two assholes follow me. Stitch, back to academics," he ordered jutting out his thumb.

Stitch looked like he might argue, but his lips pressed together. He nodded and disappeared.

"Off flying status? You can't keep me from flying," I argued as my eyes widened in panic. "I'm fine."

"Shut the hell up Pinkerton, the doc will decide that, not you." T-Rex left the room before I could argue.

Fully pissed, I swallowed back a growl. He would have told anyone else to grow a pair and get back to class.

"Dude, you're off to a great first day." The doc patted me on the shoulder as he closed the door halfway. He was a little taller than me with deeply set dimples and shaggy blond hair. He needed a surfboard instead of a stethoscope.

If I wasn't so enraged, I may have actually smiled when he called me dude. For once, I was just another pilot, just another dude. His nametag read Captain Fisher and his sandy hair waved with unruly curls.

"I'm Bodhi," he said as he reached out his hand to me.

I accepted the gesture. "Hey, Bodhi."

"All right, dude. Squeeze my hand."

I fought a grin.

"Did you think I was going to say pull my finger?"

"Something like that." I struggled to stifle a smile.

"It's okay to laugh. It's good for you. Releases endorphins and all that good stuff," he answered and glanced at my nametag. His lips twisted into a smile, not one that was laughing, but one that was genuine. "Tinklee Pinkerton. Cool name. Are you related to that lobbyist from Virginia? The one that's always around the squadron?" He reached for my other hand, and I squeezed harder than I intended.

"You're crushing my hand," he said with wide eyes.

"Sorry," I apologized in nearly a whisper. I lessened my grip.

It wasn't his fault that I thought my dad was an asshole. Most people liked him. Hell, I liked him at one time, before a fleet of F-35's replaced Colin and me as his children.

Bodhi clicked on a penlight and shined it into my eyes. I followed the beam as he moved it around. "Well?"

"Well, what?"

"The lobbyist? Is he your dad?" He pressed and moved closer to me and stared into my eyes. The distinct scent of salt water confirmed my suspicion that he held a surfboard as often as he did a stethoscope. Probably more.

"Yes."

"So you're Thor's lil' sis?"

I dug my nails into my leg and gave a sharp nod. Bodhi moved around behind me and parted my hair where I hit my head. Not once, but twice, in the same damn spot.

"Sorry for your loss. Thor was an awesome dude. It crushes me to even think about it."

I swallowed what felt like a dry cotton ball that scratched all the way down my throat. I couldn't answer even if I had wanted to.

Bodhi patted my shoulder as he stepped away. I appreciated his sincerity, but my dead brother was not something I was going to discuss.

"You're not going to take me off flight status are you?" I questioned. I held my breath and waited for him to answer. I couldn't be grounded on my first day.

"You just cracked the heck out of your noggin, I need to make sure you're okay to fly," he responded and turned his back to me. He pulled open the door and hollered down the hallway. "Dude, grab me an icepack from the bar."

A second later, he was back standing beside me.

Normally, I would shut my mouth and figure another way around the situation, but I trusted him for some reason and I thought he would understand.

"Please," I said trying to keep my voice even and unemotional. "I don't want to draw any more attention to myself."

"Yeah, I get it," he replied with a shoulder shrug. "Stand up. Let me see you walk." He propped himself on the edge of on the desk and folded his arms.

I stood. The blood rushed toward the bump on my head and it pulsed. Fighting back a wince, I limped toward the other end of the office. My foot ached as much as my head and as a reminder of last night, my heart joined in on the pain.

"Did you hit your foot, too?" he asked when I turned around.

"I got pinched by a crab. It's fine."

"Dude, you're totally axed. Sit and take off your boot. We better make sure it's not infected."

I sighed as I followed his orders and sat on the chair. I hated people fussing over me. Bodhi sat down on the desk in front of me. I lifted my foot and he undid the laces, pulling off the sage green boot followed by my sock.

"It has a bandage on it. Did you use antibiotic cream?" he asked as he loosened the wrap. Heat seared my cheeks as I scrambled to think of a lie.

"I don't know," I muttered since I hadn't put on the bandage.

There was a knock on the door and a guy dressed in gray camouflage walked in holding a can of beer.

"I couldn't find an icepack, so I grabbed a beer," he explained.

"Way to improvise, man, I like it." Bodhi fist-bumped the guy, then handed me the can. "Put this on that gnarly knot."

I placed it against my head. The coolness felt good, but after last night I was steering clear of beer. The bandage fell. My foot was red, but didn't appear swollen.

"Yes," he said.

"Yes, what?"

"Yes, *someone* put antibiotic cream on it," he said with a grin and winked.

The heat traveled south as I remained quiet. Things couldn't get any more embarrassing.

"Why the bloody hell are you examining her foot? She hit her head." The British voice startled me.

I jumped as I pulled my foot away. I didn't bother turning around. I couldn't bring myself to have him look past me again.

"I'm just being thorough. I was about to start the breast exam when you decided to cock block me, dude."

My eyes widened and I wasn't sure if I should laugh or kick him in the groin. Maybe both. My prior bedmate roared in laughter before I could decide. Locke's laugh made me want to growl and possibly hit him in the head again with a bottle, only harder this time.

"Duke Sinclair." Bodhi stood and to my shock, they man-hugged. "Dude, I haven't seen you since that night in Australia when we got inked."

"I'm still trying to forget that night and so is my ankle. I can't believe I let you talk me into getting a tattoo," he said and his accent irritated me.

Bodhi chuckled. "At least yours has significance. I ended up with a…" he trailed off and glanced at me. "Never mind. How've you been, dude?" He returned his attention to Locke.

"I'm good, man. It's great to be here."

I rolled my eyes.

"When did you get in?" Bodhi continued as he sat on the desk.

"Just a couple of days ago. I signed in at the base, found a house and went straight to work."

He didn't go straight to work. Not so admirable now was he? They continued their exchange. I sat unacknowledged with a can of beer on my head.

"Ahem," I said and cleared my throat.

Bodhi glanced back at me.

"Dude, you need to stop abusing your students. The lieutenant is pretty banged up," he said.

I choked causing my eyes to water. Bodhi shot me a sideways glance.

"Are you okay?" He asked as he patted me on the back.

I nodded and wiped my eyes with the back of my hand.

"Is *she* off flight status?" Locke's voice went cold.

His use of pronouns when referring to me torqued me. Apparently referring to me as Lieutenant Pinkerton was too hard. I ignored Locke and instead, stared with pleading eyes at the doc.

"No, she's good. Nothing a dose of ibuprofen won't fix. And a prescription to stay away from you," Bodhi teased as he flicked his gaze between us. There was a dark undertone to his voice that caused my gut to tighten.

"At least she can fly," he said.

I glanced in Locke's direction. He was looking at me, but his eyes were cold and distant as if the Locke from last night no longer existed. I now knew that our perfect first night was definitely our last.

"Dude, she almost got a concussion in your class, first day even. You need better control of your students," Bodhi said and hit Locke in the arm, breaking our trance.

Locke looked away before he answered. "I have to get back. I only wanted a report on her status as the incident occurred under my watch."

Another pronoun. And now I was an incident. Sounded about right. My throat thickened as I tried to swallow.

"Sure, man, she's good. I'll package her up and send her back to you in just a bit." He reached up and slapped hands with Locke. "Good to see you."

"You too. When you're done, send her to lunch. We start back at 1400, Lieutenant."

Without another look in my direction, Locke walked out. If the doc hadn't been sitting there I would have flipped him the bird. Last night, he really was too good to be true, and my so-called perfect man turned out to be a more perfect asshat.

Thank God we were inside and I didn't have to salute him.

Bodhi picked up my foot and reached into his medical bag. He cleaned off my wound, put on fresh ointment, and redressed it.

"There you go. I can bandage you up way better than any red coat."

A string of curses shot through my mind. My Starbucks coffee churned in my stomach…he was referring to Locke. How could he know?

Bodhi scribbled something on a pad, ripped off the paper and handed it to me along with a wink and a smile. He patted me on the shoulder then strolled from the room.

"See ya around, Pinkerton."

I stared at the notepad. The prescription was short and direct: "Cleared for flight status. Good luck."

Chapter 6

With the way today was going, I was certain Karma and Lady Luck had teamed up to destroy me.

I wanted to kick myself. Who was I last night? I never had a one-night stand, but secretly I hoped it wasn't going to be just one night. But that was no longer an option. We could both destroy our careers.

I kept my head down and when *he* appeared in class or in the hallway, we acted as if we were complete strangers, which is what we had once again become.

I needed to forget it and forget him. There was no room in this program to be unfocused. I was about to get my ass handed to me in the Joint Strike Fighter. Conquering this beast needed to be my sole focus. Nothing else. No distractions.

I tossed a binder into my backpack as Mojo, one of the guys who had tied my lace stepped in front of me. And if short, dark and handsome assholes with hazel green eyes were your type, then Mojo would be your man.

"How's your head?" Mojo asked as if he really cared. He was only a few inches taller than me and held his arms like he was ready to push over a house.

I walked around him.

"Listen, I'm trying to apologize," he said as he followed.

I kept walking.

"Come on, I didn't mean for you to get hurt. It was a joke. An initiation."

I stopped and turned back, getting into his face. "Would you have done it to one of the other guys?"

"Yeah."

"What would you have done when he cracked his head on the ground?"

"Laughed my ass off," he said with a smirk.

My mood lifted a hair knowing he would've done it to one of the guys too.

"Good, then laugh your ass off, dickhead." Shoving him, I headed toward the door.

"Pinkerton?"

"What?" I stopped and glanced over my shoulder.

"Let's go, we're meeting at The Debrief Bar." Mojo smiled. He would almost be handsome if he weren't such an ass. I hesitated and considered his offer for a truce.

The shoelaces tied together was just a joke. They would have done it to anyone—boobs or no boobs.

He opened up the door and punched me in the arm. I tried not to flinch. It was a good kind of pain and in spite of myself, I smiled.

* * * *

I needed more alcohol like I needed another crack to my head, but it was nice to be a part of the brotherhood so I couldn't refuse. I tossed my bag by the door of the bar. Stitch held a beer in my direction and I joined him.

"Cheers to the first day down," he said.

We clanked our bottles. One day down, lots more to go.

I took a drink.

Mojo told a story about shitting his pants during a flight after eating bad sushi in Okinawa. The bar erupted in laughter when he mimicked the expression of the crew chief when the jet's canopy opened.

It was way too much information, but I was one of the guys and this is what guys did. Talked about gross stuff, laughed, and scratched themselves. I wasn't about to scratch my ass, but I could if I wanted to, and it felt good. I felt good. Until *he* walked in.

The first thing I noticed was his lips, and instantly remembered how he tasted like honey with a touch of spearmint when we kissed. The thought made me want to touch myself first and then smack myself upside the head. Hard.

British slurs where thrown out while others patted him on the back. I tried not to notice when he smiled and joked with a few of the guys before strolling to the bar to grab a beer. But it was hard not to, especially when I caught his spicy scent as he walked by.

My stomach twisted into a giant-sized knot. His ass looked incredible in his flight suit, which was not easy to pull off. I silently scolded and reminded myself that we couldn't be together. Not now, not here, not ever.

But last night was too fresh in my mind and I needed to get out of here. I took the last gulp of beer and stood. I couldn't watch him anymore.

"Where are you going? It's only 1730," Stitch said.

"I need to run errands," I replied and the knot in my stomach tightened. I was going to burn in hell for all these little lies.

"I'll walk you to your Jeep." He had taken on the role as my guardian. And though it was nice of him, I didn't need protection. I could take care of myself.

"I'm good."

He nodded with a patient look of understanding. I grabbed my bag and almost ran into Bodhi.

"Dude, how's the noggin?" he asked as he knocked on my head.

"Fine."

"Cool. Let me know if you need anything," he said and fist bumped me on the way out.

I shot a quick glance to the bar. Locke didn't even notice that I was leaving. What did I want him to do? Kiss me and tell me he'd be there for our date? It wasn't going to happen. It couldn't.

I swung my legs over the Jeep's door and tossed my bag in the back. My fist collided with the dashboard. I muttered a string of obscenities and pounded on the steering wheel.

"Easy girl, that's not how you get that car to start." A male voice startled me.

I glanced in my side mirror. It came from a dark haired guy in camouflage donning a burgundy beret that declared him a Combat Rescue Officer with Special Forces.

"Sorry, I didn't mean to scare you. You might have heard me coming if you weren't abusing your poor Jeep." He rested his hand on my door as if I were inviting him for conversation.

I wasn't.

I wanted to get the hell out of here and go home. This was not a time for conversation.

"Bad day?" he asked.

Did he realize I wasn't participating? I stared at him deciding to see how long he would talk to himself.

"What's your name?"

He leaned in and looked at my chest. My eyes narrowed.

"Lieutenant Tinklee Pinkerton," he read out loud. "Pinkerton, that name sounds familiar. I know we've never met, I would have remembered."

He smiled, and if he wasn't so annoying, I might have paid more attention to his perfect jaw line and dark eyes.

He continued, "Well, Tinklee Pinkerton, hope tomorrow's a better day." He tapped my door and walked away.

I watched. He was strong, fit, rugged, and confident. He couldn't care less that he'd had a completely one-sided conversation. He glanced back over his shoulder. I couldn't believe it—he pushed his luck.

"Great talking to you," he said with a wink.

The last thing I needed was another arrogant ass toying with me. He jogged up the stairs and punched in the door code to the squadron. The door swung open and he disappeared inside.

"Asshole," I said to myself.

I put the key in the ignition and started the Jeep when the door opened. My pulse quickened and I locked eyes with my monumental mistake.

I shifted the Jeep into gear and reversed. I did not want to see him and I definitely didn't want to be alone with him. He held a motorcycle helmet in his hand and started toward me.

"Lieutenant," he yelled.

I put the Jeep into drive as he continued rushing toward me.

"Wait!"

Not a chance in hell. Accelerating way too fast, I peeled out of the parking lot without looking back. Adrenaline pumped through my veins. I turned the corner a lot faster than I should have and a security forces policeman flashed his patrol lights as a warning.

I slowed and drove the twenty-five mile an hour speed limit. The way my blood pumped, I could have gotten out and ran faster than I drove. I heard the motorbike's buzz before I saw it. Locke was behind me. I wanted to slam on my brakes and see how far I could launch him into the air. He'd need his own jet to get down.

Once I got off the military base, I threw it in fifth. The motorbike had no problem keeping up with me. I pulled into my driveway, cut the engine, jumped over the door, and stormed to my walkway. He was off his bike and at my side before I made it to the porch.

"Wait!"

I ignored him and trotted up the first few stairs to the porch. His footsteps followed.

"We need to talk."

My key sank into the lock.

"Tinklee," he said with a thickened accent.

I swung around, resisting the urge to push his ass off my property.

"So you do realize I have an *actual* name."

"What did you want me to do?" he asked with a deep-set crease between his brows. He was visibly upset. "You shocked the bloody hell out of me. Why didn't you tell me you were a JSF student?"

"I don't know, why didn't you tell me *you* were a JSF instructor?" I questioned and threw my hands in the air.

"You didn't tell me your name, which by the way, might have been good to know. I read the student roster. That would have saved us both from this *mistake*."

I jerked my head like his words slapped me across the face. It was too late. It was out there. I knew it was a mistake, but saying it out loud cut deep.

I turned back toward the door.

"That was a daft thing to say," he said in a gentle, caring voice. "I didn't mean it like that. Listen, last night was incredible."

"Just go," I replied. I turned the key and I tried to swallow the lump wedged in my throat.

He grabbed my hand and sparked that fire that made me want to forget who he was and what it meant. My perfect stranger was back with all his tenderness. I wanted to kiss him, hold him, and not have any of the rules matter. But I knew it was impossible. He knew it, too.

"Tinklee, please. I understand now. The pain, the hurt in your eyes." He paused. "I read the report about your brother's accident today. I know what you weren't saying last night."

"You need to go," I said and pulled my hand away.

I couldn't do this with him. He was my instructor. If he knew how messed up I truly was, he could end me.

"We need to talk," he said.

"You're my instructor. I think that says it all," I whispered as I stared into his eyes.

The muscles around his jaw tensed and I watched in silence as he walked down the stairs. He sat on his Harley, revved the engine, and held his helmet by its strap. He made me feel like my old self last night. It was something I thought would never be possible.

Locke pulled out of my driveway and turned into the drive next door. He shut off his bike and got off. What was he doing?

With a glance in my direction, he strode to the front of the house. He unlocked the door and went inside.

Oh. Hell. No.

Locke Sinclair was my *neighbor*?
Freaking Karma.

Chapter 7

I wouldn't be borrowing a cup of sugar anytime soon.

The only thing worse than my new neighbor was the gauntlet of work the training squadron forced on us. At least it kept my mind off Locke. There was no room in my head for him. My brain overflowed with so many systems, instruments and advanced handling characteristics that it would malfunction if I tried to add any personal drama into it.

I shoved my air-to-air binder into my backpack and grabbed a bottle of water from the refrigerator. I twisted open the cap and chugged it. This course was more intense than I ever imagined. Several guys had already washed out of the program, setting all of us on edge. But I held my own. I wouldn't accept failure.

I tightened my bootstraps and grabbed a banana from the counter before jogging down the front stairs to my jeep. I was tired from the hours training in the simulators, exams, and being drilled by our instructor pilots.

There was one more simulator ride before it was go-time. No more practice; it would be the real deal.

Just thinking about it freaked me out. It was easier to face your demons in a simulator than in the actual jet. In the simulator your heart flies into your throat and you drip in sweat, but it wasn't giving me the answers that I needed. Neither were the endless hours of studying. I needed to climb into the cockpit to discover the truth about Colin's accident.

I pulled out my tablet and tapped the videos. I wondered how many times I could watch this footage before it or I self-destructed. I scribbled down more notes about the times, sounds, even movements of objects in the distance.

Everything was normal about the flight. The sound of his voice created tightening in my stomach. Air-to-air fighting. He was engaged—winning.

I stared at the screen and watched him break free from the other jets and listened to the sound of his breathing.

Soft, shallow breaths. Then the airwaves were filled with the warning system. I could mouth the words along at the same time.

"Altitude! Altitude!"

"Pull up! Pull up!"

"Pull up! Pull up!"

"Altitude! Altitude!"

"Pull up! Pull up!"

"Pull up! Pull up!"

Giant green arrow. Full explosion, then darkness.

I pushed out a long breath. Don't doubt the jet. It wasn't just on the syllabus; it was practically tattooed onto your skin. But the jets *were* dangerous. The JSF's malfunction killed my brother. The thought of climbing into its cockpit made me ill.

* * * *

Cold, sterile, and impersonal. The simulator's building matched my mood. The large concrete building smelled of electrical wiring and was shockingly chilly, a stark contrast to the muggy dampness that persisted this time of year. The machine itself was tucked away in a secluded room. Not that it mattered. The simulator did a damn good job at making you feel alone. Just you, the machine…and Mr. Gumpbert, the retired F-16 instructor pilot who ran the program.

"So it's just you and me today," he said in his thick southern drawl. He was so lanky that he reminded me of a daddy longlegs when he moved.

His call sign was Forrest, for obvious reasons. He patted me on the back, then pulled out a comb and smoothed what was left of his thinning gray hair. He was a good ol' boy and loved hanging out with the squadron, reliving his glory days in the cockpit.

"I think there's more coming. Our first flight is Monday," I said as I twisted my ponytail into a bun.

"Nope, just you. Hop on in that saddle, young lady. Put that on." He flipped a few switches then pointed at something before he sat in the old worn out chair in the control box.

My helmet. What the hell? Where did that come from? Usually we wore a pair of headsets for the SIM. I picked it up and did as he asked without argument. The mocked up cockpit stared back at me with its myriad of blinking lights and screens. I strapped on my helmet and performed the required checks.

My hands shook, but he didn't seem to notice. What the hell was bothering me? I had done this a hundred times over the last few weeks. Sure it sucked, but when the guys were around I just did what I had to do. I didn't know why this was any different, but I felt like a cow being led into a slaughterhouse.

I took a deep breath and gave the thumbs-up. The simulator closed, surrounding me in darkness. The walls came to life, lighting up to display the Florida greenery to the north and the blue open water of the gulf to the south.

"All right, you've finished the ground emergency procedures so you're going to start off right away in the air. Ready?" Forrest spoke as if his mouth were full of rocks.

"Affirm," I stared ahead and bit my bottom lip.

"I have you set up at twenty-four thousand feet, straight and level. You're cruising at 450 knots. You have the jet."

The earth dropped away and my view from the cockpit skyrocketed into the air. In the matter of a second, I sat four miles above the earth's surface motionless.

"I have the jet." My voice held steady.

The jet suddenly sprung to life in my hands. The smallest input to the control stick began to roll and sway the aircraft. It rocked with the turbulence and the wind's rush and static crackled in my headset from radio calls in the background. The systems chirped and buzzed with alerts and messages. The room around me transformed from cold and sterile to a flurry of movements and inputs.

Sweat began to trickle down my neck as my eyes automatically transitioned to quick and rapid scans around the instrument panel.

Attitude, altitude, airspeed. Fuel is good. Engine in the green. Systems are in the green. I repeated the mantra to myself as my crosscheck quickened.

"All right go ahead and set yourself up for an advanced handling profile. Take it through the normal progression, High-G turn, Loop, Split-S, Immelmann, Max-sustained turn, and so on. Make sure you have the right parameters before you start and be disciplined executing the maneuvers." Forrest ordered. "You fly the jet. Don't let it fly you."

"Roger that." I swiped my hands on my legs and gripped the stick, ready to show him what I could do.

The jet accelerated to five hundred and fifty knots in mere seconds. The airframe buffeted as the airspeed climbed.

"Five hundred and fifty knots, twenty-four thousand feet. Starting the High-G turn," Forrest instructed.

I dropped the nose five degrees below the horizon, quickly snapped the wings ninety degrees to the skyline, and pulled the stick back with a smooth and steady pull. The horizon spun by in a blur.

I completed a full circle in the sky. The cockpit screens erupted in a flurry of blinking red and yellow lights. I scanned the displays to determine the problem.

"I have a fire light with fluctuating engine indications," I reported and craned to look back over my shoulder to see thick black smoke trailing from the aircraft. "I have both visual and engine indications for a fire. Executing the engine fire-failure bold face."

I sprung to action pushing buttons and flipping switches around the cockpit, all the necessary steps to shut down the engine and put out the fire. The SIM stilled, the horizon froze, and the instruments stopped moving and flashing. My face scrunched with frustration.

"Not a bad job hitting the boldface, but look at your aircraft attitude," he warned.

I darted a look toward the Attitude Direction Indicator. I fell into a lazy thirty degree nose low dive. Not screaming at the ground, but not getting away from it either.

"Remember, maintain aircraft control, then analyze the situation and take the appropriate action. You shouldn't be in a slow descent—you're going to need that altitude when you look for a suitable airfield to land with just your auxiliary systems."

Damn it. I had to be better than this.

"But like I said, not a bad job getting the boldface done. Let's keep going. New jet. New day. You're back at twenty-four thousand feet, straight and level, four hundred and fifty knots. You have the jet."

In a blink, the cautions and warnings disappeared and I was flying a good aircraft again as if nothing had happened. For the next hour, I ran through the emergency procedure wringer. One emergency after another; one on takeoff, one on landing, one over the water, small indications to major problems. I was mentally and physically exhausted. I had to be near finished.

"All right, go ahead and execute one more High-G turn for me."

I dropped the nose five degrees, pushed up the throttle, and snapped the wings to ninety degrees.

"Smooth on the pull, here come the G's. Here's a three-sixty."

The screens showing the outside world went gray and the panels in the cockpit went black. The aircraft shook and the wind rushed. Disorientation consumed me.

"I don't understand this one. I can't see anything," I said as my breathing shifted into shallow gasps. Sweat poured down my back.

"Fly the jet," Gump ordered.

"Altitude! Altitude!"

The familiar voice—her words made by blood run cold.

The jet was in a dive, but I didn't have any references. I slammed the throttle back to idle and pulled back on the stick to what I thought would be the horizon. It exacerbated the situation. The aircraft rocked and the wind rush rang in my ears.

"Altitude! Altitude! Pull up! Pull up! Pull up!"

I gripped the stick tighter as fear spread through me. Oh my God. I had watched this video a thousand times and now it was happening to me. My eyes burned as I stared at the screen without blinking.

The horizon and my instruments flashed on. I pointed at the ground. My eyes darted to the altimeter. Two thousand feet in a flash. My breaths quickened. We were going to die. My hands shook and I squeezed the stick tighter.

"Pull up! Pull up!"

I couldn't. I froze, just as I had that day in the tower, watching the earth blossom up to meet me. The screens went red as the simulator jerked to a stop.

Soaked in sweat and ready to vomit, I pressed my hands to my lap, regaining my composure. Crushing anxiety pinned me to my seat. If I could eject right now, I would. I would launch myself far away from this demon that was screwing with my mind.

"All right Lieutenant. You passed the operational test. How's the head?"

For the first time since the simulation began, I looked over at the control box. Several familiar and unfamiliar faces stared back at me. I stared into each of their eyes. Pride, arrogance, satisfaction, doubt, then *his*...the one that I wanted to avoid most. I forced myself to face him. The electric blue shade burned into my soul and tortured me. Pity? Regret? Sorrow?

No. He didn't get to feel sorry for me.

The hair raised on the back of my neck as perspiration trickled down my spine. My legs shook as my bottom lip quivered in pure rage. I struggled to maintain my wall.

They were screwing with me. They took me to the brink of crashing, and forced me past my impending doom. The last simulation was an exact replica of my brother's crash. It wasn't a coincidence. It was a test. They made me relive Colin's death so they could assess my reaction. They were trying to break me. I was their lab rat under dissection. Arrogant sons of bitches.

And *he* stood shoulder to shoulder with them.

I dug my fingers into my leg to keep from tearing off my helmet and hurling it at them. Every fiber of me wanted to launch it so that it would ricochet and take more than one of their smug asses out. Bowling for bastards. But I wouldn't give them the satisfaction. I had something more important to do.

I pushed up my sleeves, lifted my chin and jerked out my hand giving a thumbs-up. It was all I could manage without losing my freaking mind. I unhooked my helmet and harness, and climbed out of the simulator.

"Good job with the 'standard' emergency procedures, Lieutenant. Looks like you're ready for Monday's flight," Shatter, my commander, said.

"Yes sir," I replied and pulled off my helmet. I stood at attention with it under my arm. A million thoughts swirled in my head, but the loudest was the one shouting for me to get the hell out of there. I was careful not to look anyone directly in the eyes. I knew it would be my tipping point and it wasn't going to happen, not today. I planted my heels firmly into the ground.

"Good. What do you think fellas, she good to go?" a major asked and my left eye began to twitch.

Oh hell. They were not going to do this in front of me. I shifted my weight and blurred the voices in the room. I stared at a smudge on the wall instead of at the lineup of asshats determining my fate. I counted back from one hundred.

"Pinkerton!"

"Yes, sir," I answered and stopped counting, wondering if I was using my outside voice.

"You're dismissed," T-Rex barked.

I saluted, spun, and walked toward the door. Once outside, the muggy air flooded my lungs as if I were surfacing from underwater. I inhaled and rushed to the equipment room to drop my gear and get off this base as soon as possible.

* * * *

They tricked me into the jet with my brother. They tried to rattle me on purpose, to break me. But they didn't know I had been in that cockpit with him before. I was there on that day in the tower and I was there *every day* since it had happened. I couldn't count the number of times I watched that video, how many times I relived that explosion, or how many wishes I had made to change what had happened that day.

Colin was my big brother, my protector, my knight, my best friend, and my world. I lost my security when I lost him. I was so broken that it frightened me. I fought hard to hide the tears and bury the pain. It left me feeling like an empty shell in a life without emotion. It was the only way I knew how to move forward so that I could clear his name.

I pushed through my life for my brother because deep down I knew it was what he would want. Colin was proud that I was going to be a fighter pilot. He was my biggest supporter, my biggest fan, and, even though I felt so alone without him, I wasn't going to let him down. Not again.

The drive home was a blur. I threw my bags on the floor, went to my room, and changed. I needed to run. Whose idea had it been to relive the scenario? My commander? T-Rex? Locke? Damn, maybe I really knew nothing about him after all. Shoes laced and about to burst, I jogged down my stairs off the back deck and toward the shoreline.

The salty air from the water stung as I breathed. The voice in the simulator, warning of impending doom, echoed in my mind. I pounded my feet harder against the ground trying to shake the panic, the fear, the feeling of coldness that lingered in my veins. Was that how Colin felt? Did he know he was about to die? Was he frightened? Did it hurt?

I fell to my knees at the water's edge panting. I picked up a handful of sand and tossed it into the ocean. Flying was our dream—together. It would never happen now.

My throat burned.

"We said we'd do this together," I shouted, choking back a sob. "We said we'd do it together." I whispered, my bottom lip trembling.

Something moved in the water and startled me. I stood up to get a better look, brushing the sand from my hands. It was probably just a dolphin. My heart raced as the sea creature broke through the water. It was a shark. A shark with blond hair, iced-blue eyes, and six-pack abs. A shark named Locke.

The water sparkled across his tan chiseled abs and he dragged his hand threw his thick blond hair. A familiar storm of rage, desire, and disgust brewed inside. I bit my lip and turned back to the house.

"Tinklee!" he called out.

I picked up my pace, hurrying up the stairs and inside. Why did he have to make me feel like this? Like I wanted to kiss him then punch him. It pissed me off that this was the reality of my life. The truth was simple—reality sucked ass.

Chapter 8

I tossed and turned as the crash flashed through my mind like lightning bolts. I rolled over and pulled a pillow over my head.

The familiar sting in the back of my eyes burned as the nightmares taunted me. I watched myself drift down the aisle behind the casket in the church with a twisted expression pulling at my face. A long line of people with extended hands and solemn stares drifted in and out of the haunted dreams as I knelt, sobbing at Colin's grave wanting to join him. My shaky fingers traced along his scripted name on one of the many lined rows of tombstones at the Academy burial ground. The images, like the stone that marked Colin's grave, were cold and hard. And just like that horrid day, I desperately prayed for an escape out of this suffocating hell.

I jerked up blinking rapidly and gasped for air as my pillow fell to the side. I buried my hands deep into my hair and squeezed my eyes shut.

I slammed my foot on the mattress as the back of my eyelids burned. That freaking episode in the simulator had brought back the nightmares. Avoiding the tears, I pushed off the bed and stared out the window. I knew none of this would be easy, but I didn't expect it to make me feel so out of control.

I didn't know how long I stood there but I was grateful when the sky began to warm and even more grateful for a shower. Steam filled the room as the scent of vanilla verbena filled the air while I lathered my hair. My scalp tingled and my lids felt heavy. Zombies were more alive than me.

A car door slammed, startling me.

A female laughed. The giggle was followed by Locke's masculine chuckle. I shut off the water and wrapped a towel over me, swinging the curtain back so I could climb up to the window to eavesdrop. I hoisted myself up, gripping the edge of the sill with my fingertips.

I smeared the condensation from the window. My heart stopped. Locke stood beside a white Mercedes convertible, shirtless and barefooted, holding a mug of coffee. That was a freshly fucked smirk if I ever saw one. I bit my lip as heat traveled up my neck and spread to my ears.

A Megan Fox look-alike with morning-after hair and a snotty smile sat in the driver's seat. He laughed again. What the hell was so funny? I wanted to pound on the window and interrupt, but I resisted.

I kicked the wall with a swift and powerful sweep. My other foot slipped. I dug my fingernails into the windowsill, but it did nothing. My arms flailed as I tried to catch my balance. I caught a hold of the shower rod above me just in time. *Phew.*

The metal rod buckled causing me to crash to the ground.

I lay flat on my back inside my bathtub. I closed my eyes wishing I had the ability to turn back time.

A magical ringtone interrupted my misery, but I didn't have time to talk. She would leave a message if it were important. The voicemail alert blinked onto my screen and I rolled my eyes. I'd get to it later along with the mess in the bathroom.

Yawning, I finished getting ready and left for the squadron. I needed coffee. It was a necessity and worth being late. Luckily the drive-thru was quick and I ducked in only a few minutes tardy. I kept my head down. Maybe if I didn't see them they wouldn't see me.

"Is everything okay?" Mojo whispered as I slid into the chair next to him.

"I slept in."

"You look like shit," he said.

"You smell like shit," I fired back as I stared straight ahead. I took a sip of my coffee.

Mojo chuckled and left me alone. I looked up after a few seconds and everyone was focused on the speaker, everyone except Locke. He stared at me. Our eyes connected for a second. Looking away, I fixed my gaze on the table. I felt his gaze bore into me. So what if I looked like hell, it was rude to stare.

His expression revealed something more. Something else. Guilt? He didn't know I had seen him with her. And we weren't dating. We had sex. Big flipping deal. It was one time and even though it was the best sex ever and I thought about it more often than not, it didn't matter. He was free to do what he wanted, and so was I.

He moved on, and I would do the same with someone else. That was my answer. I had created that perfect night in my head. I needed to knock that night off its championship pedestal and throw my hat back in the ring. I needed to have sex. Now.

Well not now, but tonight. I needed to have mind-blowing sex with someone else and move on. Another one-night stand.

Shit. My shoulders slumped. Who was I kidding? It wasn't me, not to mention I'd already learned my lesson. The hard way.

"Lieutenant Pinkerton, please stay. I need to speak to you." A British accent interrupted my thoughts.

Really? He was going to corner me in the squadron?

Mojo patted me on the back. "Start crying. It makes guys uncomfortable and he won't say anything about your being late."

This wasn't about my being late. At home, I could avoid him when he said my name, but here, he was my instructor. I had to follow his orders.

The room emptied. Locke closed the door, and came over to my seat. His leg brushed mine as he sat. Heat filled me in places that I was ashamed to admit as my heart swooned. I hated that he had this effect on me.

He rubbed the legs of his flight suit. Was he smoothing the wrinkles, or getting the sweat off his palms? Either way it made him look nervous. I waited it out. This was his meeting, not mine.

"Are you okay?" he asked.

There it was again—the scent of sandalwood. I tried to focus on something else, but all I could do was nod.

"Are you sure? You don't look okay." The kind tenor of his voice brought me back to our first kiss, not what I wanted.

I nodded again as I forced his lips from my mind.

"Have you eaten or slept?" He leaned closer.

"I'm fine. Is that all you wanted? I don't want to be late again."

"Tinklee, listen, I handled things poorly. I'm so sorry about your brother's scenario. I should have come to you first. I wanted to warn you, but we had to know where your head was before you climbed into the jet."

My eyes threatened to pop from their sockets. He *was* in on the plan.

He reached for my hand.

A shock bolted through me. I jerked my hand from his and narrowed my eyes. I couldn't think straight when he touched me. The electricity shorted out my already barely-functioning brain. He should have warned me, but he hadn't. He chose to be my instructor, not my lover. His betrayal burned.

"Well, now you do," I answered and folded my arms.

"I know it's going to be difficult to climb into the jet after what happened with Colin. I can see your hurt…I feel your pain. I want to help you. Please talk to me."

A boulder wedged itself in my throat. I couldn't do this. I wouldn't. It was clear what could break me. I wouldn't let it happen. Not for a guy, not even *this* guy.

"We had sex, once. That doesn't make you a tuning fork for my emotions. Stay out of my head, and stick to teaching me how to fly the jet," I replied and shoved my chair back. I avoided his stare as I walked from the room.

I was knocking him off that pedestal, tonight.

Chapter 9

Nothing like a good mind fuck to zap your energy. I was so physically and emotionally tapped out that I was face down and out cold before I could take off my boots.

A car horn woke me. I rolled over and peered out the window. It was a white Mercedes with Miss Thing in the driver seat fixing her gloss in the mirror. A few minutes later, Locke got into the passenger side. He looked wickedly handsome in a white shirt that highlighted his tan. He leaned over, hugged her, and kissed her on the cheek.

I frowned. It stung to see him with someone else. Growling, I went to the spare bathroom to shower then tried to find something in my closet. I pulled out my standard cut-offs and T-shirt. Then tossed them back on the ground. What if Locke was there with Brunette Barbie? I needed to find something to wear that made me look more like a girl.

Finding an outfit gave me chest pains. I finally settled on a blousy tank that was revealing even for my not quite B-cups and my favorite cut-offs. It wasn't as suggestive as Locke's bimbo's outfit, but it might make him regret his betrayal.

I closed my eyes and growled. I was beginning to get on my own nerves.

It was the perfect evening to sit on the deck at Krusty's overlooking the water. I pulled to the side of the building and slid my keys under the mat. A white Mercedes was parked in front. Maybe I shouldn't go in.

I caught my reflection in the window of a car and adjusted my boobs in my bra. I had this. Locke wouldn't ruin my night.

It didn't take long to find the guys. A gaggle of local girls surrounded them. Stitch, Mojo, and Freak chanted my name as the rest of them made comments about my tits. I rolled my eyes. The local talent glared in my direction. They didn't want the competition. They didn't know I wasn't competing.

"Time for some birthday shots!"

I turned to see where it was coming from. Brunette Barbie. She had barely enough fabric to cover her tits or ass. Compared to her, I looked like I was on my way to church. She passed a tray of shots. I didn't see Locke until I felt a hand brush against my back. Did he mean to touch me?

My cheeks flushed. I turned away, but then felt his thumb moving up and down the small of my back, causing a new layer of goose bumps that had to look out of place in the warm evening air. He was close enough to smell the whiskey on his breath. That's when it hit me. July 31st. It was Locke's birthday. I stepped forward, forcing his hand to fall. This night was already tailspinning out of control.

Thankfully someone else held the tray of shots by the time it reached me. I grabbed one and slammed it. The tequila burned. I grabbed another and turned to face Locke. His commanding blue eyes bore a familiar hunger. I couldn't tell if the fire blazing inside me was from the tequila or his eyes but I needed to get out of here.

I turned to walk inside. A guy stepped in front of me, blocking my path. I moved to the right and he did the same. I moved to the left and he followed. I was about to throw a jab to his trachea when I glanced up. The Combat Rescue Officer. The one from the first day of class. I didn't have time to chat. I needed to get out of here.

"Hey there, Tinklee Pinkerton," he said as his brown eyes sparkled.

Damn it. Not now. I tried to move around him. He blocked me again.

"How's the Jeep?"

Dimples formed as his lip curled into a grin. I was usually a sucker for dimples. Any other time maybe, but not now.

"Are you ever going to talk to me?"

"I am going to ask you to move," I said and slammed my hands on my hips.

"Why, you just got here?"

"I'm meeting someone, somewhere else." Drop another one into the lie bucket.

"No, you're not."

I stepped to the left and he followed. I slid to the right and he did the same. This dance was tiring. And I wasn't impressed or in the mood.

"What are you doing?" I asked and tried to keep my voice calm.

"Trying to buy you a drink," he replied with a smile.

"I'm not thirsty, and I'm leaving."

"You don't have anywhere to go and you know it. Come on, let me buy you a drink."

I shook my head at him without an answer.

His smile widened as he bent down on one knee. I gulped, immediately feeling people's eyes focusing on us. My cheeks warmed.

"Stand up," I begged between clenched teeth. "People are staring."

"Say yes."

I leaned down and grabbed for him. "Stop, they think you are asking me to marry you."

"Say yes!" Someone shouted.

"Get up," I said and reached out to tug on his arm.

"Yes! Yes! Yes!" The bar chanted.

He stared up at me with an adoring look on his face. He was basking in the attention. I wanted to die, but first, I wanted to kill him.

"Yes! Yes! Yes!" The bar continued to cheer.

He winked.

I glanced toward the bar, immediately spotting a frowning Locke leaned against the bar. His green-eyed expression gave me the nudge I needed.

"Fine. Yes," I shouted and decided to play along. "Yes!"

"She said yes!" He raised his arms like he scored.

The entire bar applauded, everyone except Locke. I couldn't hold back the smirk that crept across my face. I wanted him to feel the pain. To hurt the way that I'd hurt.

The crazy guy dipped me back and pressed his lips to mine. I gasped. The crowd went wild. He grabbed me by the waist, swung me around, and carried me to the bar. I would kill him as soon as everyone stopped congratulating us.

"Give us another round," he said and winked at a small redhead. She looked like she might erupt into flames.

I scanned the room and I didn't see Locke anywhere. I hoped that I ruined his birthday.

"Do you always make guys work that hard to buy you a drink?" His dimples returned.

"Do you always have to work that hard to buy a girl a drink?" Looking at him, I knew the answer. He looked like an artist had chiseled his muscles from stone.

"Oh come on, Tinklee Pinkerton, that was funny. And besides, it worked. Look who's having a drink with me." He winked.

I wouldn't give him the satisfaction of agreeing.

"Here's to the future missus, and many years of keeping you barefoot and pregnant in both the bedroom and the kitchen." He toasted with a raised shot glass of Jack Daniels.

I raised my glass. "Here's to the future mister and his many bottles of lotion and frozen dinners."

I swallowed the amber liquid. It burned. He chuckled as he reached up and wiped a drop of whiskey from my lip. A light tingle lingered where he touched.

"By the way, I'm Ash."

Though rugged around the edges, he was annoyingly charming and funny. Special Forces. Definitely more than I bargained for, but hell, if I was pseudo-engaged to this guy, then why not have some fun. I'd already decided against my one-night stand plan, but I liked irritating Locke, and Ash was easy on the eyes.

He winked and slid me another shot. I smiled.

"Hey, Tink. I wanted to make sure you didn't actually go get married," Stitch said as he approached. His head shook, but there was a hint of smile.

"Oh God. Did you see that?" I gasped and covered my eyes.

"Everyone in the whole bar saw it. Nice work, Walker." Stitch joked and shook Ash's hand. "You coming back outside? The guys were ready to send out a search and rescue team for you, but then we realized it was a para-rescue man that had actually taken you."

"Sure, I'll meet you out there. I need to use the restroom first." I shifted my weight and Ash slid my chair back. "Can you grab some waters?" The shots were sneaking up on me.

"Sure. Meet you on the deck." His hand brushed my back as I walked away. There was something about him. He wasn't Locke, but I liked him. And he had definite potential to make Locke miserable.

* * * *

I'm not sure if it was the heat of the night or the heat of the company I was keeping, but I suddenly needed to get the hair off my back. After my stop at the restroom, I went out to the Jeep to get myself a hair band. I stumbled on the gravel in the parking lot.

Whoa, I definitely need to stick with water when I go back inside.

I leaned over the seat to grab an elastic band from the gearshift when a hand gripped my waist.

"Ash, you couldn't you wait until...." I turned around and gasped.

"Until what?" Locke's eyes blazed. He was totally jealous.

His scent and proximity consumed me even though I was pissed at him.

"You scared the shit out of me."

He stepped closer, his gaze meeting mine. My legs weakened and I reached back to grip the door of my Jeep so I didn't fall. He touched my hair and gently tucked it behind my ear. I closed my eyes and tried desperately to keep it together.

"What are you doing out here?" I asked, breathier than I hoped for.

"Looking for you."

I opened my eyes and held his stare. I hated the thought of him holding anyone else.

"You found me," I replied lost in his gaze.

"I hate this."

The rasp of his voice told me he was hurting too. He wanted me as much as I wanted him. He leaned forward and placed his arms around me. My face was beside his neck. I tried to breathe as the closeness of his bare skin made my nipples harden. I pressed forward needing to be closer to him. His breath on my hair set my nerves into overdrive and I wasn't sure if I would survive. It was like my heart had forgotten to beat without him and every part of me needed him. I wanted to explode and rip his clothes off. I needed him to rip *my* clothes off. And I bit my lip trying to remember why we couldn't. I struggled to regain control to be rational, but with the desire building inside, I was losing the battle.

He placed his hands on mine and when he pressed against me, I felt his desire, too. His lips brushed against my cheek and once they reached my lips, my head dipped and I moaned.

"We can't," I whispered as our lips parted.

He pressed his mouth more firmly to mine, ignoring my pathetic attempt at refusal. He tasted just as I had remembered, but with a hint of tequila and lime. He tasted good. So damn good.

"We need to find a way. I can't stop thinking about you," he said with a deep exhale.

"What about Barbie?" I asked.

"Who is Barbie?" His words brushed against my lips as his tongue moved gently inside my mouth as his fingers tangled in my hair.

Exactly. I pressed harder against him and his hands gripped my thighs, he lifted me to the edge of my Jeep. I wrapped my legs around him and I felt his hunger as he pushed against me. Our lips pressed harder with a panicked intensity. I placed my hands under his shirt and my nails gripped his skin. His sigh made me grip tighter. I wanted him and needed him now, before I caught fire.

"Ahem."

My heart stopped as suddenly as our kiss. I hesitated for a moment before pushing myself to fall back into the driver seat. I focused straight ahead, trying to regain control of my breathing.

We were busted.

"Dude, Kassie's looking for you."

Holy shit, that was Bodhi's voice. I'd know his 'dude' anywhere. He'd already suspected us, but this was proof. We got caught.

I wouldn't look at Locke. I didn't want to see his expression. I buried my head in the steering wheel.

"I'll be right there," Locke said in a shaky voice.

"Cool. See you inside," Bodhi said. "Hey, Tink."

I couldn't respond. I just nodded and refused to look him in the eye. He chuckled and disappeared, with only the fading sound of his footsteps crunching in the gravel. Too bad we hadn't heard that as a warning when he approached.

Locke kicked up some pebbles and growled. I glanced over as he plowed his hands through his hair. What the hell were we thinking? We may have ruined both of our careers—mine before it even got started. I turned my head back and stared at the dashboard.

"Bloody freaking hell," he cursed. He leaned against the Jeep.

"You need to get back inside," I forced myself to say. I wanted to stop the words as they came from my mouth, I wanted him to stay here with me, but I couldn't. We had been careless.

"Shit." He slammed his hand against the door and dropped his head, hesitating.

"Happy Birthday, by the way."

"Yeah. It's been naffing brilliant." He pushed himself off the Jeep.

Maybe not.

* * * *

I hadn't meant to leave, but I couldn't bring myself to go back in. I was only a few miles away and the walk would hopefully help clear my mind. I wouldn't watch him with her and act like what happened in the parking lot hadn't and I couldn't face Ash again. He seemed like a nice guy, persistent as hell, but it wouldn't be fair to him.

Locke was both my best and worst mistake. As much as I wanted to knock him off his pedestal, I knew it would be impossible. He was like an addiction that I couldn't break. I was drawn to everything about him. His looks, his accent, even the fact that he was my instructor and off-limits made my thighs tingle. Freaking Karma was upping her game.

I went home, ate a bowl of cereal, and went to bed praying I could sleep then figure out a way to stay away from Locke Sinclair.

* * * *

The sound of footsteps pulled me from my sleep. At first I thought that I was dreaming, but the hallway creaked with the sound. I jumped out of bed. Someone was in my house. My thudding heartbeat drowned out the footsteps.

I slid down on the floor beside my bed, the blanket still covered me. I threw a quick glance at the clock. It was 0700, who the hell broke into houses at this hour, on a Saturday?

There was a soft rap on the door that launched my heart into my throat. I closed my eyes for a second and tried to remember where I had left the bat. My head ached, a brutal combination of the alarming wake-up and the damn shots.

I blew out a breath prepared to meet the intruder head on. Hopefully I had the element of surprise on my side. I dropped the blanket and rounded my bed, padding silently across my bedroom floor to the door.

I held my breath and peered down the hallway. He disappeared into my bathroom. I slid down the wall and rested on the floor.

"What the hell happened in here?" a booming male voice questioned.

Dad.

My headache jolted from an ache to crushing blindness. Why was he here? A magical ringtone filled the air. Shit. I growled. Sneak attack.

"What the hell happened in this bathroom?" His tone was curt and as usual, he made me feel like a five year old.

"I thought you were an intruder."

I narrowed my eyes and wished that I had dead bolted the door. I'd welcome an intruder, instead of my father.

"On a Saturday morning? That doesn't even make good sense. Where are those bells coming from?" My father asked as he scanned my room.

"Mom's calling," I said with a sigh. I reached for my phone to silence it. Its sound seemed out of place in the present mood.

"Maybe if you answered it when she called you wouldn't be surprised at my arrival." He nonchalantly entered my room and flipped open my shutters. "Get off the floor and start your day, it's after seven."

He shook his head and walked out.

I grabbed my phone to retrieve my messages. Mom had sent a text last night. Damn, I had been so upset that I hadn't checked.

Tinklee,

Dad will be there in the morning. Try to get along with each other... please. Love you baby girl.

Mom

I snorted and reread the message—"try to get along". There was a better chance that it would start snowing in hell. As usual we were off to a stellar start. I blamed him for Colin's death and he didn't care as long as the F-35's reputation remained untarnished and in flight. We'd never see eye to eye about anything, ever again.

I fell back onto my bed and read the other missed texts. A few of the guys had checked in to see where I had gone and if I was alive.

There was a text from Locke. My pulse quickened. Damn recall roster. I'm sure it was not intended for personal use.

Sorry.

Sorry…really? How do I even respond? Was he sorry he screwed with my mind at work, at home, and everywhere I went? Or sorry that we got caught?

"Are you planning on staying in bed all day?" Dad questioned as he came back down the hallway with a bunch of tools clanging at his side.

He couldn't leave the mess in my bathroom as I had, it would drive him crazy until it was fixed. Once the sound of hammering filled the bathroom, I safely escaped. Coffee. It smelled wonderful. I grabbed a protein bar from the pantry and poured myself a mugful then moped outside onto the deck.

I groaned. The last thing I needed to deal with was the complication of my father. A dolphin leaped from the water and I wished I could join it and swim away. Far, far away.

I bit into my bar and listened to the waves. The calming sound of the water was replaced by a high-pitched laugh.

I glanced over toward Locke's deck. Brunette Barbie laughed at Locke. Her clothes were barely covering anything and a familiar knot twisted in my stomach. Locke turned his head and our eyes met for a brief moment. I sighed and walked back inside.

My dad was in the kitchen. I was trapped. I needed to get out of here. I changed into workout clothes and sprinted for the door.

"Tinklee," my dad called.

I moved toward the large island.

"Sit," he ordered without looking up from the newspaper.

"I was going to go for a jog."

"Good idea. You need to sweat out whatever is seeping from your pores," he said and flipped the page not bothering to look at me.

I grabbed a bottle of water from the refrigerator and leaned against the counter.

"I said sit," he repeated and pointed to a chair in front of him.

I was twenty-two years old. Old enough to ignore lectures and orders. I didn't sit, but I gestured for him to speak. His attention shifted from his newspaper to me. He stared down his nose through his reading glasses. His lips pursed.

My father wasn't used to people challenging him and when they did, they always lost.

"How's the jet?" he asked and folded his paper. His eyes, a reflection of mine, cut through me.

I shrugged. His eyes narrowed as he folded his arms, his muscles flexing. He was athletic and fit for sixty-seven.

"Any problems I should know about?"

Translation meant, was there anything I need to smooth over with the politicians in D.C.?

I shook my head. Lines formed between his brows.

"I didn't hear you," he said in a general officer's voice. I narrowed my eyes at him. I wasn't seven years old anymore. "Are there any problems?"

"Nope."

He cleared his throat. If he thought he was getting a "no sir," he could clear his throat raw. He lost that respect when Colin died.

"Are you flying on Monday?" he inquired as he lifted his mug and sipped the coffee.

I nearly snorted. He already knew the answer. "That's why you're here, isn't it?" I shot back and slammed my water on the counter. I stood. "For a photo-op?"

He'd shown up for Colin's first flight too, then spread the news around to everyone who would listen. But when Colin died, he buried the story deeper than he'd buried his son.

"You need to change your tone."

I opened my mouth to argue, but stopped myself. I turned and bolted from the kitchen, letting the front door slam on my way out. I was in a full on sprint as I jogged down my driveway into the road.

Brakes squealed. I flinched and prepared for impact. I pulled myself together and glanced at the driver. I sneered at the Karma gods. Of course, I'd run right in front of Brunette Barbie's Mercedes.

"Oh shit! I almost hit you!" Barbie said in a snooty voice and fake accent that she'd apparently developed overnight.

"It would make your life easier, wouldn't it?" I had developed an accent too. A Bitchish accent.

"What's that supposed to mean?" she asked, her perfectly arched eyebrow lifted.

"If you ran me over then you wouldn't have to worry about your boyfriend's tongue being down my throat when you aren't looking."

It was unfair for me to attack her, but I wasn't in a sugar-coating mood. The words just came out like vomit.

"What the hell is your problem?"

"Why don't you ask him?" I said nearly shouting and pointed to Locke as he approached.

I jogged away. I had sent him to the gates of hell, but I didn't care. It served him right.

Chapter 10

I spared my charm and avoided everyone for the rest of the weekend, spending every second preparing for my first flight.

I sat in my bed reviewing take off and landing data when the phone rang.

"Hey, it's Fantom." His voice boomed in my ear.

I gulped before answering. "Hello, sir."

"I'm the flight lead tomorrow so I wanted to breakdown the flight."

It was a no-bullshit call. I listened without speaking, or breathing, I just scratched down notes.

At the end of the call, his humanity surfaced and he added, "You've got this, Tink. You're gonna be fine," he paused as if unsure if he should offer any more support. "You wouldn't be in the program if we didn't think you could make it."

It was these the moments that freaked me out. None of these badasses wanted me to fail, but I wondered if deep down they worried I would. That sucked the most.

I got dressed and picked up my watch and strapped it on. It had been a gift from Colin when I graduated from the Academy. Wearing it would be like having him with me in the cockpit. It was a double-edged sword that brought me happiness and pain.

I polished the watch face with my sleeve and stared at my reflection in the glass. I'd give up my wings to see his warm, boyish grin one last time. I swallowed the lump in my throat and slung my backpack over my shoulder. I rushed out the door before my dad could ask for a ride.

He would be there because of his job, photo-op or whatever other bullshit reason, but I didn't want him or his work connected to me. I needed to wear a disclaimer: I am Max Pinkerton's daughter, but my thoughts, opinions, and flights are my own.

My stomach growled. I wasn't sure how food and nerves would mix, but I needed to try. I pulled into the coffee shop outside of base. It was way too early to go to the squadron and I didn't want to sit around dwelling on this first flight. Once I got past this one, I would be fine. At least I hoped to be. Would I ever be comfortable flying the beast that spurred my demons?

"Miss?" A high-pitched voice interrupted my thoughts.

"Sorry, Venti Americano and an old fashioned donut," I stammered. I hadn't had time to think about what I wanted.

"Can you add two waters and a protein plate?" A strong hand slid a twenty-dollar bill across the counter. My stomach twittered with butterflies as I recognized his voice and remembered his hand on the small of my back.

"No, I got it," I replied and fidgeted with my wallet, irritated that my brain went fuzzy when he was around.

The cashier's face turned red as she stared into his eyes.

"Please, take it from the twenty."

The brunette giggled. I rolled my eyes. It was that damn accent.

"Thanks."

"My pleasure," he said as he flashed me a gentle smile. "How are you feeling?"

I shrugged.

He reached for my coffee. Holy hell, he had a death wish.

"Miss, could you bring over the rest?"

Of course she would, I thought bitterly.

Locke turned to me. "I have your coffee, so I know you won't run away from me. You really shouldn't have it, but it looks like you might need it."

I had to give it to him, that was a clever plan. I followed him to a table in the back corner of the shop and he pulled out a chair for me.

"What's that supposed to mean?" I reached out my hand for him to hand over my liquid gold.

He held up the cup and motioned to the chair.

I wouldn't normally negotiate with terrorists, but he was holding my coffee hostage. I growled and dropped into the chair.

He sat next to me and slid me the cup. "I was merely suggesting that you look a bit frazzled, but still lovely."

I snatched it and took a gulp.

"I'm not frazzled."

I was hoping to convince him and myself. The brunette server delivered the rest of our order. I waited for her to move out of earshot before adding, "And don't flirt with me."

Locke chuckled then opened the water and slid it to me. "Here." When I shook my head, he reached for my coffee. I gripped it tighter.

"Drink the water. You're going to puke if you drink that. Water and protein, that's what you need."

Locke removed the plastic from the plate and slid it toward me. He took my donut and bit into it.

Locke was right, but I didn't want to admit it. I grabbed the donut from his hand and took a bite.

I sipped my coffee and he shook his head.

"You're so bloody stubborn and obviously pissed. Point made. Eat your donut and drink your coffee."

Could he blame me?

I picked up the water, drank it, and grabbed a piece of cheese from the plate. I was trying to be difficult, but I realized that I had fallen into his trap and done what he suggested at the beginning.

I resisted smiling as the corners of Locke's lifted into a grin.

"I'm sorry about the other night. It was daft of me to put both of our careers on the line."

I shrugged and glanced down at my watch. My first step into the cockpit was approaching at lightning speed. I had to get my head in the game. I twisted the pilot bezel on my watch.

"Bodhi won't say anything. So please don't worry," Locke said quietly. I hadn't been too worried about Bodhi blabbing, he was a good guy. "You have to relax if you are going to function in the jet."

The mention of the word jet and I worried my breakfast would make a reappearance. I pulled down my sleeve and polished the face of my watch.

"You're wound as tightly as that watch you keep staring at," Locke said as he tapped my foot with his.

"It was a gift when I graduated from the Academy," I whispered.

He leaned forward and placed his hand on my leg under the table.

"From Colin?"

I flinched at the sound of his name.

He rubbed his thumb along my leg.

"I should have realized by the way you've been looking at it."

"Yeah, it probably isn't wise to have my ghosts haunting me in the cockpit." I reached for the latch to undo it.

Locke's hand covered mine. "It's brilliant. Allow his memories to bring you strength."

I looked up into his eyes. They were full of trust, encouragement... understanding. He believed in me.

"You're ready Tinklee. I've watched you in class and in the simulator. You've got this."

It gave me the confidence I needed to face the jet, but it frightened me that he had stolen another piece of my heart.

Chapter 11

It was time to kick the tires and light the fires. I repeated the familiar phrase in my mind as I walked into the briefing room. Bodhi sat at the table messing on his phone. I felt awkward since he was the one who had busted Locke and me, but I didn't want to mention it.

"Dude, you ready for today?" He asked and held out his hand for his signature fist bump to greet me.

Bodhi's grin widened. My shoulders slumped as my embarrassment dissolved instantly. He wasn't that guy to judge me. Thankfully.

"What's the flight doc doing here for the brief?"

"I'm supposed to check your internal noggin," he said. He raised his hand and knocked his head. "Don't worry, I'm not a shrink and everyone is normal compared to my family, so you're good as far as I am concerned."

"Are they having you check everyone?"

"Sure," he answered and shook his head no.

"This stupid game they're playing is making me crazy."

I tried to swallow back the anger.

"Yeah. I get ya. It's best to play along. They'll move on soon enough." He unzipped his pocket and placed his phone inside.

Fantom walked into the room and tossed his bag on the ground. He fist bumped Bodhi and pointed to me. "She's good. Right?"

"Yep. Just as normal as the rest of us," Bodhi said before he strolled out of the room.

"Good," Fantom said as he rolled up his sleeves. His wedding ring clanked against the table as he smacked his hand for emphasis. "Let's go over the plan for today."

After Fantom finished the brief, he asked if I had any questions. I shook my head. My mouth was too dry to speak. I followed him to Life Support to get our gear, but as we hit the hallway, the flash of cameras and murmured voices stopped me in my tracks. The sound of my father's voice caused my chest to constrict. And suddenly the calm me was ready to come out swinging.

Someone grabbed my arm and pulled me into an unused room. The door shut, but whoever it was didn't turn on the lights.

"What the hell is going on?" I questioned.

"Shh. They'll pass in a second," a familiar voice whispered.

"Stitch?"

Fantom shushed me.

This was ridiculous. I couldn't see anything, but by distinguishing several different aftershaves, there were at least four of us.

The clicking sounds of cameras became more prominent and I heard voices outside the door.

"Sir, are you confident the JSF is ready to go? Besides the basic test flights this will be the first time the jets will fly in a training environment. And with students no less." The words were quick and eager.

"Greg, I assure you, the jets are and have been ready for everything and anything." My father's voice was smooth and calm as always, but he could never hide the underlying condescension in his tone.

"What about the oxygen concerns, the ones related to your son's accident. Are those all corrected?" Greg pressed.

"I am not certain why you would ask," my father said and cleared his throat, which signaled that Greg had pushed one of his buttons. There was that slight pause before level of condescension increased. "There aren't, nor have there ever been any concerns with the jet's environmental system."

The reporter continued, "But your son's death was a highly publicized incident, and still many questions remain about the exact cause."

"The cause remains, as it was ruled," my father paused. "Pilot error."

Those two words—pilot error had me fighting not to bust open the door and slap him hard across the face just as labeling my brother's death as pilot error was slapping Colin in the face.

"But the…."

My father interrupted him with fake enthusiasm. "Let me ask you, Greg. Would I allow my only daughter to fly the JFS if it weren't safe?"

Now he'd gone too far. My blood hit instant boiling as I grabbed for the door. Fingers tightened around my arm as a hand covered my mouth.

I struggled against whoever held me, but six hands forced me into stillness. I said I didn't want the photo op, but right now, I wanted nothing more than to be on the front page of every newspaper in the country, choking my father.

My father wanted to use me. He'd erase any doubt of the jet's safety by sending his only daughter up in it. Picture perfect proof. It didn't change the fact that his son died in this jet, and he did everything to push it as a pilot error instead a mechanical failure. All so he could lobby for his own agenda. He had been a military advisor for the F-35 and then hired to lobby for its funding and sales. The JSF was his baby. He loved it more than he loved my brother and me. My dear old dad already offered one of us up as a sacrifice and he wouldn't have a problem offering me up too.

Finally, the voices passed. I was too enraged to hear any of the remaining conversation. It didn't matter. It was propaganda. I chomped down on the hand that covered my mouth.

"Ouch!" Stitch yelled. "You bit me."

The lights came on and my eyes adjusted to see Stitch, Woodstock and Fantom standing before me.

"You're lucky that's all I did," I said and spun around.

Fantom opened the door wide enough to pop his head out to check the hallway.

"We were trying to avoid a scene before you went up. Talk about lousy timing," Stitch said as he shook his hand. "You bit me."

"You heard the shit he said. You really want to bitch about getting nipped?" I asked and poked him in the chest.

I didn't want to fight with Stitch because I knew his intentions were good. He was my brother's best friend and Colin's death hit him hard too, but my dad couldn't get away with it anymore. I was sick of his pilot error bullshit that desecrated the memory of my brother and sullied every award and accreditation he received for being a badass pilot. It was time for me to defend him.

"Tink," Stitch called out to me.

"Stop," Fantom said. "We don't have time for this shit. Are you ready to fly or do you want to cancel out?"

My eyes flicked to him. "I am *not* cancelling out."

"Are you sure? I'm not going up there and risk you losing your shit. I've got a wife and kids," he explained. "My oldest has a soccer game tonight, and I'm not missing it because I died over some screwed up family politics."

His shiny bald head was blazing red and I didn't blame him. This was crap. All of it. I needed to get this stupid flight over with.

"I'm good," I answered. I placed my hands on my hips and nodded. I could do this.

An awkward silence filled the room. Woodstock snorted.

"What the hell is so funny, Woodstock?" Fantom growled.

"Dude, you pulled the kid card. That's messed up," Woodstock said as he laughed harder. "I don't want to die because my kid has soccer tonight."

Stitch and I stood, not sure how to react.

"Screw you, Woodstock." Fantom flipped him off with a hint of a smile.

The universal gesture only made Woodstock laugh louder.

Fantom's color softened. "You're an asshole. Let's go, Tink."

* * * *

Five minutes later and thirty pounds heavier from my gear, I was ready to take flight. Fantom and I approached the operation deck in silence. I prayed my legs wouldn't buckle from the shaking and tried to calm my breathing while the Director of Operations reviewed the weather, airfield advisories, and aircraft status.

This was it.

Fantom glanced sideways every few seconds but he didn't speak. A crew van waited for us outside. The shaking spread from my legs to my hands. I pressed them flat against my body hoping to avoid detection or raise doubt in my capabilities. I could do this. At one time, I believed that I was born to do this.

The short ride to the flight line felt like an eternity and when I arrived at my jet, I leaped and tripped out of the van. An airman caught my arm.

"Thanks," I said.

"Sure, ma'am," he said with a smile and saluted.

"Talk to you at check-in," Fantom shouted over the noise.

I gave him the thumbs-up and walked to my jet. Another young airman waited with aircraft forms. I approached him when he saluted smartly and reached out for my gear. The forms were a log of any maintenance issues and the corrective action taken to fix the problem. Everything was in order and multiple supervisors signed off the work. I started my preflight inspection of the jet's exterior. I walked around ensuring everything was sound and configured.

Once satisfied, I met the crew chief.

"Ready, ma'am?" he asked.

I swallowed hard wishing the lump in my throat would go away.

"Yes," I replied.

I climbed the ladder, each step more hesitant than the last. I shouldn't be feeling like this. I needed to feel focused and confident. Maybe Fantom was right. Maybe I should postpone this flight.

I swung my leg over the side of the jet and settled into the reclined ejection seat anyway. The crew chief helped me secure my shoulder harnesses to the latches. He watched me, and I think he suspected he was about to be showered with vomit.

"Are you good, ma'am?" He questioned.

His eyes locked on my eyes as if looking for some warning signal that I shouldn't go up. Part of me wished he would see something.

I forced a swallow and stared back at him. He seemed familiar, though I couldn't place him. I looked down at his nametag—Sergeant Wilson.

The harness clicked. I was now attached to a parachute contained within the seat itself. Wilson? I studied his face as he continued to adjust my straps. Why was the name familiar? Then I remembered. He was the airman at my brother's service. The one who handed me a flag. I was too catatonic to remember much else, but I recall looking into his eyes and his nametag that day. Wilson. He knew Colin.

Wilson finished then firmly shook my hand. He held my gaze and I held onto him. His grip tightened and a smile spread across his face. "You're good, ma'am."

I exhaled. He was right. I released his hand as he walked back down the ladder. I was good.

I strapped on my helmet, flipped the switches to the electrical system and the jet awakened. Everything proceeded normally as I started up the engine and ran all the necessary systems checks. Once I had the cockpit set up the way I wanted it, the crew chief disconnected from the aircraft and waited for me to taxi.

I looked at my watch. 0938. Two minutes to check in. At exactly 0940 the radio came to life. "Gambler Check!"

"Two," I said sharply.

"Any issues with your bird?" Fantom asked from his jet.

"Everything is in the green," I confirmed.

"All right, let's taxi."

I glanced back at my wrist. This was the closest thing I'd ever have to my dream of flying with Colin.

"It's you and me big brother. Let's do this," I whispered.

Fantom made a radio call to the control tower that we were ready and I signaled to the crew chief to pull the chocks. I eased the throttle forward and yanked it back against the stop as the jet eased forward. We approached the runway and Fantom radioed the tower for clearance.

"Gambler flight, you're cleared for takeoff, Runway One. Three. Right. Switch to departure," the tower advised.

"Gambler flight's cleared for takeoff, switching," Fantom responded. "Okay, you got the lead, run 'em up."

We lined up on the runway together and I eased out in front. My palms were sweaty and I wished I'd worn my gloves. I smeared them across my pant legs then pushed the throttle up while checking the engine and the status lights. Everything looked good. I released the brakes, took a deep breath and slammed the throttle into afterburner. The G-forces of the acceleration pushed me back into the seat as the JSF leapt forward. My speed ticked higher in preparation for takeoff. I eased back on the stick, and the plane soared from the ground and my heart joined in. The landing gear retracted and power reduced while I ran my post-takeoff checks. The jet was sensitive, but surprisingly comparable to the simulator.

And if the JSF hadn't killed my brother, I might have thought she was awesome. Just thinking about movement seemed to make her respond. We were in our assigned airspace over the ocean in a matter of seconds.

"All right, set up your profile. I am going *'loose chase'*. If a maneuver isn't going as planned, stop, reset, and we'll try it again," Fantom radioed.

I leveled off and got oriented for the "G" exercise of intensive turns. Once I hit my speed I pulled the stick, rolled 90 degrees to the left, and pulled back.

The gravitational force crushed me into the seat as my suit inflated and squeezed my legs and chest. It was shocking and I tried to recover from my surprise while remaining conscious. I ran through the profile and before I knew it I had burned through half of my fuel. An hour had passed yet it seemed like mere minutes.

The jet was starting to talk to me and it was feeling less foreign in my hands.

"Let's take it back and do a few practice approaches before we land for real." Fantom's voice crackled in my headset.

I turned back toward the coast and ran the pre-landing checklist. I lined up with the runway and shot three practice approaches pulling up each time before touching the ground.

"Are you ready to land this one?" Fantom asked.

"Affirm," I answered.

"Make this one a full-stop," he instructed.

I set up for another approach. As I made my way down the glide path, I continuously checked the airspeed, altimeter, and attitude. Gear coming down. Lined up. On airspeed. I got over the runway, reduced the power, and let the jet slowly settle. My body stiffened as the wheels returned to land. I exhaled. I did it.

"Real nice," Fantom's voice sounded relieved and proud.

His jet pulled high into the sky maneuvering to land behind me. We taxied and I swallowed a celebratory yell. I was no longer a JSF virgin. I was soaked from sweat and the sun beamed through the glass with intensity.

When the canopy opened a rush of air hit me in the face and though it was hot and muggy, it felt refreshing. I conquered my first flight. I finished my checks to shut down the jet. When the crew chief unstrapped me, I resisted grabbing his face with both hands and kissing him.

"Everything good ma'am?" He asked and worked to free me from the cockpit.

"Yes. Everything is great, Staff Sergeant Wilson," I answered not able to hide my excitement. "Just great."

I climbed down the ladder and walked over to the jet. I touched its warm, smooth belly. I still hated this jet, but now I loved it just as much. I patted it and turned back walking toward the van.

Staff Sergeant Wilson handed me my gear and I hugged him. It was totally inappropriate, but I didn't care. If it weren't for him, I may have aborted my first flight.

"Thank you." I beamed. My arms squeezed him tighter.

His body was stiff, but he whispered in my ear. "I'm sure you made him proud."

I got into the van and Fantom held his head in his hands. I wondered if he wasn't feeling well, or if I had screwed up something and hadn't realize it.

"You okay?" I asked after a few minutes of silence.

He looked up with wide, angry eyes. My heart stopped. His bald head was crimson again.

"I was until a few minutes ago," he said and blew out a sigh. "Tink you can't fucking hug a crew chief. Tell me you know this and you temporarily lost your freaking mind."

My cheeks heated. "Sorry, sir. It won't happen again."

I shouldn't hug a crew chief for all sorts of reasons. It was a breach of protocol and didn't help to cultivate my badass image, but I wasn't sorry.

I hugged a person that knew my brother and helped me over the edge of quitting. It could've been worse.

Fantom ran his hands over the top of his scalp but didn't say anything else for the quick ride back. I followed to Life Support to get out of our gear.

I was famished and eager to get something of substance in my stomach before I passed out. T-Rex and Mojo were in the squadron when we walked in.

T-Rex and Fantom reached out and smacked into a fisted handshake. "How'd it go?"

"Good," Fantom replied, but didn't mention my final mishap. "How about you, Mojo?"

"All right, I guess." Mojo replied and shrugged. He looked at the floor.

"It wasn't bad for first time up." T-Rex responded and hit Mojo on the back.

The door opened and guys filed in, both students and instructors.

Our commander, Shatter, came out of his office and smacked his hands together.

"Everyone here?" He asked and scanned the room.

"Yes, sir," T-Rex answered.

"Good. Freak, close that door." He pointed and continued. "We have contractors, reporters, and generals up in the main bar. They've provided lunch. Whether we agree or not with why they are here or what their true intentions are, now is not the time to address it." He paused.

"Shut your mouths, eat your lunch, and when they say smile for the cameras, just do it." Towering at six-foot-four with a stern voice, it was clear not to screw with him. "Let's get them the hell out of here as soon as possible so we can get back to business. Got it?"

"Yes, sir!" Everyone answered in unison.

His hazel eyes landed on me and my heart raced when he raised his left eyebrow. "That especially means you, Pinkerton." I nodded as my heart raced. "Smile for the cameras and shut your damn mouth."

"Yes, sir." I responded with my outside voice while my inside voice was shouting, No way in hell.

"I'm serious, Tink. This is not the time or place to fight this battle. I am not going to risk losing funding or get buried under a shitload of paperwork and red tape because of a snarky comment to Daddy." His facial expression softened. "Save it for Thanksgiving dinner. Not my squadron."

"Yes, sir." I repeated. It torqued me, but I got it.

"All right, carry on!" Shatter ordered then ducked into his office.

I glanced around the room. Where was Locke?

"How did it go today?" Stitch asked as he caught up with me in the hallway.

"Good," I answered and shrugged. The mention of my dad deflated my previous excitement.

"Awesome." He swallowed me under his arm and squeezed me.

I shook my head. He couldn't resist.

"I need to stop in here." I ducked from under his grip and pushed the door open to the ladies room.

I needed to buy time before seeing my dad. Why couldn't he have waited a month, a week, or even a day? Why did he have to show up today? But that's how my dad rolled. The moment the Air Force selected me for this jet; I predicted this day. My stomach twisted.

I leaned against the sink and closed my eyes. This was bigger than me. My actions could affect others. The boss was right. Today was not the day to settle differences with my dad. Not to mention how it would make my mom feel and she'd already cried enough.

I opened my eyes and stared at the girl in the mirror. I focused into the depth of sea-blue and watched as my pupils dilated. I leaned closer and tucked a strand of blond hair behind my ear.

"This isn't about you. Keep it together." I spoke to my reflection. "Keep. It. Together."

A toilet flushed. I jumped.

I wasn't alone.

I bent down and saw a pair of tan high heels with red bottoms. I straightened up and rushed to the door but it was too late. The door to the stall had opened and her voice cut me like a dagger.

"Sounds like good advice," Brunette Barbie said with a coy smirk.

What the hell was she doing here? It wasn't "bring a slut to work" day. Why would Locke bring her here, especially after this morning? Hurt and shock turned to anger. I spun around.

We glared. She looked like a lioness in a business suit about to jump her prey. She even licked her chops in preparation. A tag was attached to her lapel of her jacket. Press. It was a perfect opportunity to be snide. It was pinned over her fully augmented left breast, but the true meaning of the word press crushed my opportunity to be snarky.

Shatter's words swarmed in my head, *Keep your mouth shut.*

"Are you keeping it together for Daddy or for Locke?" She asked with a wicked grin.

I pictured myself standing in front of Shatter defending why I slugged her and arguing she had started it, but I knew it wouldn't work.

"I thought I was alone." I responded and turned to leave.

"That's not an answer."

"I don't need to give you an answer."

"Just wondering, is it against squadron policy to be sleeping with an instructor?"

My body tensed as my hand froze against the door handle.

This chick could ruin me with one accusation. And the worst part was that I gave her the ammunition. The clicking of her heels closed in on me.

"I don't give a shit about you," she said. "But I do care about Locke. You could ruin everything he's worked for."

My knuckles blanched as I squeezed the door handle. She had me. My instinct was to counter. I wanted to knock her on her ass, but I couldn't because she was right.

I looked over my shoulder and stared as she applied her gloss in the mirror. She won this round.

I swung open the door and rushed into the hall. I collided with Locke's chest. He raised his hand to my arm.

"Everything okay?" he asked.

I jerked my body away from him as he reached for my hand. The warmth from his fingers traveled like a burning arrow piercing my heart.

I looked into his eyes, searching for answers, as I struggled not to lose it. This was the worst possible place for any of this to be happening. We were exposed. It was dangerous.

"Tinklee, what's wrong?" He questioned clearly upset. The thickness of his accent was always a sign. He was *my* Locke right now, not my instructor.

This was the Locke that I dreamt about every night since we first met. A pain raked deep in my throat. I tried to choke it back.

There couldn't be *my* Locke. That guy didn't exist. He was playing a game and I needed out.

The ladies room door swung open.

"Hey gorgeous," she said and winked at him.

Locke frowned. "What's going on?"

"Locke, relax," she sneered as her shiny lips smirked. "We were just getting to know each other better."

I clenched my fist, wanting to knock that grin from her face, but I wasn't going to give either of them the satisfaction of stooping to their level.

Besides I had another shit storm that required my attendance.

* * * *

I plastered a smile on my face and pretended that everything was great. The bar was full and buzzing in conversation. Flashes went off every few seconds and I ignored them. I lost my appetite, but my stomach growled reminding me that I had to eat.

I reached for a plate when I heard the voice.

"Tinklee, congratulations on your first fight in the Joint Strike Fighter." My dad's tone was more polished than his perfect-toothed grin.

Bright lights blinded me as Dad's arms wrapped around me. It was the perfect photo opportunity.

My chest puffed up ready to push off his bullshit attempt at a fatherly hug, but T-Rex shot me a warning glare. I sighed. This was ridiculous.

"Thanks, Dad." I said between clenched teeth. I forced myself to reciprocate the embrace.

The hug was unnatural. I stiffened as a wave of his cologne flooded me with memories of my eighth birthday. A pancake breakfast and a trip to the jewelry store in my prettiest dress. I was a princess. He told me to pick out anything in the store and I chose a pretty necklace with a delicate circle. It was special and he was my white knight. Until one day I woke up and realized he wasn't.

After a few more pictures and fake exchanges, I finally excused myself to get some food.

"Hello, sir," a British accent said.

I spun back around. My Dad and Locke shook hands.

"Hi, there young man," my dad said. "You're from the British Royal Air Force."

"Yes, sir."

"Young man, I have to disclose to you that I am quite familiar with your story. I may have been the one who dropped your name to come here. You have very impressive records and exactly the right man for this job."

My dad was responsible for Locke's being here? Of course he was. Fate seemed to be laughing in my face lately.

"Thank you, sir."

"Are you taking care of my daughter?" My father said followed by a laugh. He patted him on the back.

If he only knew. Locke avoided my eye contact. In perfect timing, Shatter approached with a tall pilot with black hair and Locke's bed bug.

Time to go. My dad rested his hand on my arm as if he had read my mind. I was stuck as more flashes went off around us.

"Shatter," My father greeted them. "Kassie, wonderful to see you again." He reached for Brunette Barbie's hand.

What the hell? How did he know her? I looked at her badge again reading the word, *Press Kassie Callahan.* The tall pilot's arm reached around her waist. I glanced at Locke to see if he noticed.

"You too, Mr. Pinkerton. Thank you for your letter of recommendation." Her voice was sweet. She was a fraud.

"Of course. You were my favorite intern."

My eyes widened and a calculated grin spread across her face as the pilot next to her rubbed her back. This was crazy. Locke was standing right beside them. Although he didn't notice because he was too busy focusing on me. Again. He needed to stop.

"Mr. Pinkerton, I would love for you to meet my fiancé, Sean Kraven." She gestured to the man beside her.

Oh my God. Locke was sleeping with an engaged woman and her fiancé was right here, right now in front of us. No wonder he was staring at me. He was afraid that I was going to rat them out. This was a hot mess.

"Yes, Major Kraven. *Clash* Kraven," my dad said with a nod. He shook Clash's hand.

I wished I had my Dad's staff to keep me current on everyone's status.

"And future Standardization officer of the JSF operational squadron," Shatter said.

Oh wow. The fiancé of Locke's bed buddy was going to be the new Stan Eval officer. Those were the guys that you avoided in the hallways. This just got better and better.

"Kassie, remind me how you and Locke are related." My father's finger swiped back and forth between the two.

"Locke's my cousin. Our moms are sisters," she said and glanced at me smugly.

"Locke introduced me to Sean. They were stationed together in England," she continued then she turned toward me with a smirk. "I met your daughter through Locke as well."

Chapter 12

This was bad. Really, really bad.

My head spun as I realized just how wrong I had been. I dragged my hand across my face trying to shield my shock. She wasn't sleeping with Locke. But I accused her of it and pretty much let her know I had hooked up with him.

And damn it. Her fiancé was Locke's friend and soon to be Stan-Eval officer of my next squadron. Adrenaline pumped in my veins and my mind darted trying to figure a way out of this.

"You okay, Tink? You look like you're about to pass out," Shatter said.

"Yeah, I am, I just haven't eaten anything." And I just had the shit shocked out of me.

My father's hand gripped my arm. He leaned down and whispered in my ear, "You need to get out of here before you pass out and the press have a field day."

I clamped down on my molars to keep my mouth shut. Damn my father and his never-ending obsession with keeping the press happy.

Locke reached out for me. "I haven't eaten anything either. We'll get something together."

"No," it came out more abrupt than I planned.

Bodhi. Now Kassie. Too many people knew about us.

Everyone quieted. Shatter raised his brow.

"I mean, thanks," I answered in a calm voice. "But I left something in the squadron. I have to go get it. I'll be right back."

My dad peered down his glasses at me. "I'll see you at the house tonight. We have dinner plans at 1800," he said. "And why don't all of you join us?"

Oh. Hell. No.

I had to get out of here. I wasn't joining this group for supper. I was too worried they would be serving my head on a platter once Barbie started blabbering.

I rushed away without hearing their replies. Once I rounded the corner, I gripped the wall trying to steady myself.

"You're white as a ghost," a voice said as my head jerked up to see Ash standing at my side. He gripped my elbow to help keep me balance. I had never been so happy to see someone.

"I just had a freaking out-of-body experience."

He chuckled.

"And I'm starving," I said. "I *really* need to eat something."

He reached in his bag and tossed me a candy bar.

I ripped open the wrapper and took a bite. It tasted like sweet heaven.

"Better?" he asked, smacking me on the back.

I nodded.

"Thanks," I mumbled through my mouthful of chocolate.

"How come you always look so pissed off or like you're running from something?" he asked as he tossed me a water bottle.

I caught it and twisted off the lid, chugging the entire bottle before I answered.

"Probably because either I'm pissed off or running from something," I replied and wiped my mouth with the back of my hand.

"Or running from something that you pissed off?" he asked as his dark eyes sparkled as the corner of his lip lifted, his dimples appearing. He was so clever twisting my words. Quick-witted and handsome.

"Thank you for the candy and water," I said.

"And?"

My ears warmed as embarrassment washed through me. "And, I'm sorry I bolted from Krusty's."

"I accept your apology, if you let me buy you some real food."

My stomach growled. How could I say no?

"Let's go. I'll drive." He followed me as I walked away.

When we reached my Jeep, I climbed over the driver side door. Ash got in and adjusted the seat. I let down my hair and shook it out. The tight bun was starting to give me a headache.

He reached over and patted my leg. "First flight that bad?"

"How did you know I was flying?" I asked and shifted my leg away from his hand.

"I was on the range. I heard your voice a few times on the radio."

I shrugged. "The flight went really well."

"What the hell happened to you then?" he asked.

"Don't ask," I said and rolled my eyes.

We pulled into the parking lot of a tiny Mexican restaurant right outside the gate. My stomach growled with anticipation.

"All right. Let's eat."

We walked in. There were only a few booths and a couple of chairs set up in the center. The lady behind the tiny bar waved and pointed to the booth in the back.

She brought over chips and salsa and took our drink order.

"One margarita, and an extra shot of tequila on the side," I ordered.

Ash laughed and leaned closer to me. "My kind of girl. Make that two, plus a couple waters."

I picked up a chip and shoved it in my mouth. "Thank you."

"Don't thank me. This is my lucky day."

I half smiled. "Thanks."

"No problem. Glad I could be there to give you some sugar."

He was impossible.

The margaritas came and we placed our order. I lifted my glass. "Cheers."

"Here's to popping the cherry."

I choked on my tequila. I coughed so hard that I had to blink back tears that were forming in my eyes. Ash chuckled and patted me on the back.

"You have quite the way with words. I'm assuming you are referring to my first flight," I replied.

He winked.

The waitress brought more chips and our waters. "Gracias, Maria."

She blushed. Man, he was good.

I sipped my water when my phone buzzed. I unzipped my flight suit pocket and looked at the screen. Fantom. Everything was cancelled this afternoon so they could continue with the tours. He said we would debrief tomorrow.

"It looks like I'm done for the afternoon."

My phone buzzed again with a text from my dad. I frowned. He was reminding me of the dinner and instructing me not to be late.

"Bad news?"

"What?" I asked and put the phone down on the table. "It's nothing."

Ash watched me, but didn't push for information. I was glad. I didn't want to talk about my dad.

"What time do you have to go back?" He asked erasing the awkward silence.

"Not until 1800. So I have a few hours."

We talked for a long while, avoiding personal topics and goofed around. I beat him in a several rounds of thumb war. Speed and agility were the keys to my advantage.

"Twenty questions!" he challenged.

"No." I hated this game.

"Come on, we'll keep it impersonal."

"Fine," I said. "Let me think."

"I'm first."

I pushed him playfully. "No, me first."

"Fine. Stubborn chicks first."

I smirked.

"What's your sign?"

He cracked up. "Isn't that a song or something?"

"That's 'Here's your sign.' I mean your astrological sign."

"My sign? Hell, I don't know."

"Oh my God! Are you serious? When's your birthday?" I rolled up a straw wrapper and threw it at him.

Ash swiped his hand in the air and caught it. "November 28th."

I picked up my phone and typed it on my app. "You are a Sagittarius."

"Okay. What's that mean?"

"I think it means you are a centaur looking thing." I enlarged the picture and showed it to him.

"Okay, what else does it mean?"

"I don't know. I think it means you are…" I paused then read out loud from the screen. "It says you are the life of the party."

"Well hell, I could have told you that," he replied with a sheepish grin. "So you wasted your question."

"No," I said with a frown.

He raised one eyebrow at me and I smiled.

"Okay, I wasted a question."

"Are you dating anyone?" he asked.

I shifted against the seat. "You said nothing personal."

"Hmmm," he paused. "I struck a nerve."

"No, you didn't," I choked out. Locke's face flashed into my mind. "No, I'm not dating anyone."

He didn't look convinced. "Are you sure?"

"Yes, I'm sure. I am not dating anyone." Technically it wasn't a lie. "My turn. What is your worst habit?"

"Your questions suck." He shook his head. I pushed him. "Okay, fine. I bite my fingernails."

I picked up his hands and he waggled his fingers. He was right.

"My turn. Most admired person, living or dead."

"My brother," I answered without hesitation.

"Shit, Tink. I'm sorry. I'm a dick. I wasn't thinking." He reached for my hand.

"No, it's fine." I lied and pulled away.

"No really, I'm sorry."

"It's okay. Really." I forced a smile to try to alleviate the uneasy look on his face. I reached out and swatted at his hand to soften the mood. "Now, I think we can both agree that your questions suck the most."

An annoying buzz interrupted yet another one of Ash's raunchy comments. He pulled it from his pocket and glanced at the screen. Then tapped it.

Trying to give him space, I took a sip of my melted margarita and glanced around. I jumped back as Ash's hand brushed against my lip. There was a light tingle where he'd touched, but no warmth in my belly.

"Salt," he said with that wide grin that showcased his signature dimples.

I nodded unable to respond. I liked him, but he wasn't Locke.

"We have to get going," he said. His hand rested on his side of the table. "Sully is going to swing by and pick me up so you don't have to go back to the base."

I nodded not bothering to hide my disappointment. Ash was a cool guy. I was enjoying myself.

A twinge of remorse flushed over me and Locke entered my mind. I didn't know why this felt like cheating but it did. Ash led me out of the restaurant and to my Jeep without suspecting my guilt.

"Thanks for today." I reached over and pulled on my seatbelt.

"You're welcome, but how about a real date?" he asked, drumming on top of the door.

My stomach bottomed out as I glanced at Ash leaned against the door of my jeep. He was as close to perfect as men came and every girl's dream. As much as I enjoyed hanging out with him, I was not going to bring anyone else in the middle of my mess.

"Ash," I said prepared to let him down gently.

"I'll take that as a yes," he said cutting me off. I opened my mouth to object, but he bent down and gave me a quick peck on the cheek.

Only Ash would take that as a yes. The only word to describe him was relentless.

Chapter 13

The images of both Locke and Ash tormented me. What was I doing? Neither Locke nor Ash would get me any closer to clearing Colin's name.

I changed and grabbed the quilt from my bed, my tablet, and headed to the beach. The scent of the salty air was refreshing and it was warm, though summer was winding down. I crossed my feet at the ankles and studied the fading scar. The memory of that night haunted me as it always did.

Sighing, I picked up my tablet. The familiar video filled the screen. I watched my brother's crash three more times. He was fine then he wasn't. I tried to figure out what he was doing when it happened.

I placed myself back into the cockpit, closed my eyes and hit play. The sound of his breathing drew me in deeper. I dropped the nose five degrees, pushed up the throttle, and snapped the wings to ninety degrees. I sucked in a breath preparing for the upcoming G's. I could almost feel the aircraft buffeting and the wind rushing through my hair. His and my own breathing shifted into shallow gasps.

"Altitude! Altitude!"

I squeezed my eyes tighter.

We were in a dive. The aircraft rocked and the wind rush rang in my ears.

"Altitude! Altitude! Pull up! Pull up! Pull up!"

I rocked with the movement and strained to hear something new, something different.

"Pull up! Pull up!"

The explosion echoed across the ocean until its sound disappeared.

Everything was exactly the same but I had to be missing something. Again, I had failed Colin.

I flipped the cover shut and tossed it on the blanket.

It had to be a problem with the air system. My dad could cover and say whatever he wanted to make himself look good, but I wouldn't let my brother's legacy go down that way. I just had to figure out a way to prove it.

I fell back and stared at the sky. The sun began to set as the soft shades of pink against the blue sky mixed into soft lavender. I closed my eyes exhausted from the day. I was on the verge of sleeping, but not quite there yet.

Locke had gotten to a place that no other person had ever been able to connect. The way he watched me silently as if he were guarding me, made me feel safe. And he seemed to be there in the moments that I needed him the most even when I didn't want him to be.

I traced my finger along my skin remembering how it felt when we touched. How his fingers drifted along my skin like they were melting into it.

After Colin's crash, I shut off that part of me. But somehow Locke was chipping at those walls and it frightened me. It was something I didn't understand.

My mind absorbed the memory and sweet earthy scent of his aftershave. My skin warmed as I remember the closeness of our intertwined bodies becoming one. I turned my head to the side and struggled against the weight of my eyelids. Locke. He was lying beside me, watching as if he were studying me.

"I hope you don't mind that I joined you," he said in a low voice with a hint of a smile that faded. "I'll leave, if you want."

His pinky finger touched my hand and sent shivers through my body and caused my pulse quickened.

I stared back at him and interlaced my fingers with his. God, this felt so right. It wasn't what I should have done, but his touch felt too good to be wrong. I craved him.

"I needed to talk to you. Alone. Without anyone interrupting us." His voice was tormented, as if he was fighting the same internal battle that I was. "I had to touch you."

I rolled over to my side and leaned closer. He was incredibly stunning and my body raged in awareness. I stared at his lips wishing they were exploring my body rather than requesting a chat. I didn't trust myself laying this close to him especially now that I knew he wasn't sleeping with someone else, but he was right. We needed to talk.

"It's torture seeing you and not being able to be with you," he said.

I wanted to erase the hurt from his expression, but I needed to hear what he was going to say.

"It's even worse to watch you with another guy," he said.

Was he talking about Ash?

He continued, "Someone who can be with you that way. I want that." He fingertips traced down my arms until they reached my hand and he interlaced his fingers with mine. I stopped myself from leaning closer and instead focused on his lips as he spoke. "I want to be the man you go to when you need someone. I don't want you with anyone else. I know that makes me a selfish ass, but that's what I want."

I wanted him to be that guy, too. I wanted to tell this beautiful man that he would always be that guy. I wanted to beg him to kiss me and make love to me; to make me feel safe. But I couldn't.

"You can't," I whispered and released our fingers.

"I know it's wrong and I play by the rules. I *believe* in the rules. But when it comes to you, all bets are off." The depth of emotion in his blue eyes struck me like lightning. "We can be careful. No one would need to know."

"If they found out, we'd both lose our wings," I argued. "They'd send you back to England and we'd both be flying a desk until they pushed us out, permanently."

"We'd need to be careful, but it would only be for a few more months," he said sitting up and reached for my hands. "And then after the course when we are in different squadrons and I am no longer your instructor, we can do whatever we want."

I shook my head. "There is only one deployable squadron here. They aren't going to keep you in the training squadron when we only have one that's operational. You're too valuable."

"You're probably right." He let out a loud, drawn out sigh. He dragged his hand through his hair thinking things out. Hopeful. Soul-crushingly handsome. "It will be different. You won't be a student, and I won't be your instructor."

"What about your cousin?" I asked. "She knows about us. She'll tell her fiancé. You know, the new Stan-Eval guy of the operational squadron."

"She won't say anything if I ask her to stay quiet. The new squadron goes operational in the next few months. I'll put in for an immediate transfer. We'd only have to hide it for a short while longer."

I hesitated. It was impossible to tell him no. My heart screamed at me to say *yes* though my voice retracted in fear. I respected everything about him. I studied not only his words in the classroom, but his actions.

He was strong, fierce, and committed to the mission as much as he was committed to me.

For now, with him so close, his emotions so raw, my heart would win the battle. At the hint of my smile he grabbed me and pulled me on top of him. My hair cascaded around him. His hands rested under my shirt on the small of my back. My body tingled wildly in response to his touch. I pressed my lips to his as he pulled me closer. There was nothing sweet and soft in his kiss. It was rough and full of desperate passion. He needed me and I wanted him.

"Is this a yes?" His voice was raspy.

"It's whatever it needs to be for you to continue."

He rolled me to my back and leaned over me. Our lips met again. I couldn't stay away from him. He consumed every part of me, heart and soul. He was still my instructor and with my missile-launching emotions, I wasn't sure it was possible to keep our relationship under the radar, but I needed to try.

"I've missed you," he whispered into my hair.

I had missed him too, though I resisted saying so. We held each other and listened to the ocean's waves. It felt comfortable and it frightened me because it felt so right.

"Things with your dad seem tense," he interrupted the silence after a few minutes.

"They always are." The last thing I wanted to do while in Locke's arms was talk about my dad.

"It sounds like I have him to thank for this assignment." He smoothed my hair. "I'm sure Kassie played a hand when she was his intern."

It would be more soothing if he didn't mention my major point of contention. "She's your cousin?" I asked.

"Yes, she's my mother's youngest sister's only child," he said.

No wonder she was such a brat.

"You don't like her."

"Why would you say that?"

"Lucky guess," he teased.

"I thought you were sleeping with her."

"What?" He choked.

He sat up and I patted him on the back. He cleared his throat and wiped his eyes.

"Why in the bloody hell would you think that?"

"I saw her at your house." I shrugged. "And Krusty's. Hell, I don't know. You never introduced us. What was I supposed to think?"

"Not that." He coughed again then raised his eyebrow. "So wait. Are you telling me that you thought I invited another woman into my bed after I was with you at Krusty's?" He frowned. "Is that what you think of me?"

He looked like I had punched him in the gut.

"No, I mean, yes. I mean, it is what I thought had happened, but it confused me because it seemed unlike you."

He took my hands. "I would never hurt you."

I wanted to believe him, but Colin would never have wanted to hurt me either, just as I never meant to hurt him. Yet he was dead and I was broken.

He wrapped his arm around me.

"We should plan a weekend away from here," he said. "Take a break from it all. That way we can definitely be free without anyone knowing." He reached for my tablet that was lying on the blanket. "Where do you want to go?"

He flipped back the cover. My brother's video lit the screen.

"What's this?" He dropped his arm from my shoulder.

My chest tightened.

"Flight footage," I muttered.

"Whose?" He pressed play.

I sat motionless as he watched it. Around minute 6:46, awareness flushed over his face as he continued to watch it. The video ended.

"How do you have this?" He looked up.

My mind raced. I wanted to tell him the truth but I couldn't.

I shrugged. I was a thief. Stole it from my dad's files, but I wasn't going to let him in on that.

He tapped the screen. A noisy breath escaped his lips. "Why are you watching this?"

This was restricted air space. I would always keep my emotions buried on this matter, except when I had too many beers.

"It says that this has been viewed nine hundred and twenty-four times. Those aren't all from you, are they?"

Yes. They were all from me and I deserved to watch it another nine hundred and twenty-four more. I had to find out what caused Colin to crash.

His eyes widened. "It was awful what happened to your brother. It was. But you can't do this to yourself." He reached out and lifted my chin until our eyes met. "It's torture."

I pulled back and looked away. "I don't want to talk about it, Locke. I'm sorry, but I just don't." I took the tablet from him and flipped the cover shut. "It's getting late. We need to go in for the night."

He touched my cheek. "You're upset."

"No, I'm fine." I leaned in and kissed him. "I'm really tired."

"I'm here for you." He tucked my hair behind my ear. "I wish I could spend the night with you."

"So do I. But Dad's here." I sighed.

"And Kassie and Clash are staying with me," he said. "They'll have their own place soon."

"I better go before my dad gets back."

Locke helped me shake out my comforter and we walked up to the house holding hands. It was an almost perfect evening. Once we reached the bottom of the deck, he pulled me close and captured me with his eyes.

"We'll make this work, I promise." He kissed me.

Everything about this could end in disaster, yet somehow I agreed.

* * * *

"I didn't know you were back." My father's voice startled me causing me to jump.

It must have been later than I thought.

"I just got home a few minutes ago." His arms were folded across his chest. "You missed dinner."

"Sorry. I got held up in a debrief." I lied and walked past him.

"He missed the dinner, too." He nodded toward the beach to the spot where Locke and I had kissed goodnight just moments ago and paused. "Was it the same debrief?"

The hair lifted on my nape and arms. I stopped walking and turned. I felt the color drain from my cheeks. His expression confirmed it. We were busted.

"You've always been reckless, Tinklee, but *that*, that is a sure way to get your wings taken away," he said and pointed outside. "*And* his. That boy has done a lot of great things. You could ruin his career with your lack of regard."

I felt a vein pulse in my neck. This wasn't about my wings. It was about embarrassing him. It was always about him. I opened my mouth to argue. But there wasn't anything I could say that would justify our behavior. Nothing would make him understand. I walked into the kitchen for a glass of water.

"How did the jet handle?"

I spun and glared at him. His brows were pulled in and his lips were pressed together in a slight grimace. My expression melted until it matched his. Was he asking for his own benefit or trying to communicate on more common ground?

"Good," I said with a shrug and leaned against the counter.

"How close was it to the simulator?" His voice was softer and he sat down on the edge of a chair by the counter.

"It was very similar. I was shocked how smooth the transition was from one to the other."

I tucked a strand of hair behind my ear. We were having an actual conversation. Weird.

"Great. That's good to hear." He nodded.

"I'm tired. I need to get some rest."

"Me too." He swallowed hard.

"Good night." I turned to walk away. A twinge of remorse struck me. I glanced back at him. "Sorry I missed your dinner."

He swiped his hand. "You would have been bored anyway."

A hint of a smile? It was time to quit while we were ahead.

In my room, I showered and got ready for bed. It had been an interesting day.

I survived my first flight, Locke and I were going to try to find a way to be together, and I had a semi-civilized conversation with my father for the first time in over a year.

My phone buzzed and I reached for it.

Ash.

Thanks for the great day

I fell back onto my bed. Why couldn't anything ever be simple?

Chapter 14

Thankfully over the next few weeks a personal life was impossible. My dad had gone home to Virginia. Kassie and Clash were still staying with Locke and Ash was out of town on a planning exercise. The training was becoming more intense and I was going to sprout my own set of wings with all the hours I had spent in the air.

I toyed with the jet and its air system every chance I got. I searched for any signs that something was off, but it kept coming up clean. Though the maintenance reports showed nothing out of the ordinary, I studied everything I could get my hands on. I knew the jet and its quirks intimately.

I was scratching notes inside my Moleskine when the door swung open to the classroom. The scent of sandalwood filled the air. I fidgeted with my pencil hoping the dreamy reaction from my heart hadn't spread to my face. Locke was more disciplined and maintained his composure when we were in the squadron but he was also smart enough to avoid eye contact with me.

He pushed the sleeves up on his flight suit but all I could picture were his hands unzipping my flight suit and his lips teasing my neck. I brushed my pencil eraser softly across my lips and pretended not to notice how the muscles in his forearms flexed as he scribbled on the smart board. And when my eyes continued to trace down to his broad shoulders then traveled south to his tight ass, I struggled to smother the flame that was dancing happily along my thighs.

Mojo punched me in the arm, startling me and instantly doused the flame.

"Do you have an extra pencil?" he whispered.

My eyes darted around the room as I reached into my pocket sleeve and slid a mechanical pencil across the table to him. I shifted awkwardly in my chair.

His eyebrows drew closer. "You okay?"

No, I needed a change of panties. But I wasn't going to tell him that. I nodded silently and pulled at the collar of my flight suit. Damn, it was hot in here.

"Alright Yanks. Let's continue with air-to-air combat tactics." Locke's voice commanded our attention. My lip tugged upward.

The air-to-air combat phase came easy to me. The instructors knew my brother was the best at this type of flying and they took extra care to avoid pointing it out to me, but it was something I already knew well. Things were falling into place and I was holding my own in the jet. I started looking forward to the next time I would go up.

After an hour the brief ended and Locke lingered behind.

"Want to grab a quick beer at Krusty's?" Stitch asked as he leaned forward and tugged at my ponytail.

I shoved my pencil into my sleeve and grabbed my backpack.

"Not tonight. I'm going to take a nice hot shower and stay in for the evening." I said it loud enough for Locke to hear, hoping he'd take it as an invitation.

I glanced back at the podium as I followed Stitch and Mojo from the room. I fought a smirk as Locke licked his lips.

* * * *

Three quick raps on the door set off a nervous tickle of hope in my belly. I flung open the door to a large, handsome man with a short mustache and beard. He was attractive in his crisp, starched uniform.

He scooped me into a bear hug.

"Ash!" I exclaimed and hugged him back. It was a natural reaction, and I surprised myself.

"Phew! I wasn't sure if you'd be pissed that I just showed up." He lifted me.

"When did you get back?" I asked as my feet returned to the floor. My eyes darted past him toward Locke's house and a wave of relief fell over me when I didn't see his bike.

"Twenty minutes ago."

Guilt tugged at my stomach. It wasn't fair to him, now that Locke and I were sort of together. We needed to talk. He was kind to me. I wouldn't lead him on.

"Come in. I was making a sandwich. Do you want one?" I asked. Locke always jogged as soon as he got home. Ash had some time.

"That would be great. I'm starving." He removed his beret as he crossed the threshold.

"So where were you? Or can't you say?"

He was growing a mustache and a beard, which usually meant deployment on the horizon. Special Forces needed to blend in plus they were in the field so long it was difficult to shave. Or maybe he was simply trying something new.

He sat down on one of the high stools as I pulled out the meats and cheese from the deli drawer.

"D.C." He folded his hands.

Oh no. He *was* planning for a deployment.

"When are you leaving?"

I cut the sandwich in half and put some chips on his plate. I poured him a glass of sweet tea and waited for an answer.

"Friday."

"As in two days, Friday?" My voice pitched higher as I held up two fingers.

He took a bite of his sandwich and nodded.

"How do you feel about it?" There was no way I was telling him now.

Besides, it didn't matter. He was deploying.

"The timing sucks. I got you to agree to a date, and now I'm leaving."

"I'm a lousy date anyway." That was the truth.

He chuckled. "How about a rain check? If you're not spoken for by then."

My throat tightened and I nodded. This was not the time to say anything that could mess with his head. Not before a deployment.

"Where you going?" I asked.

"Africa," he said.

"The conflict between Tunisia and Algeria?" I tore off the crust from my bread.

He watched me and smiled. I continued to amuse him for some reason.

"Add Libya, Morocco, and the other surrounding countries to the cluster."

"How long?" Any length would be too long.

"I'm not sure."

I filled our glasses.

"Want to sit on the deck?" he asked.

I hesitated then nodded. "Sure."

He stood and carried his plate to the sink.

"So where are you from?" I asked as we walked outside.

"Colorado." He scooped up a football that was lying on the bench.

He tossed the ball at me, and I reflexively caught it with one hand.

"Good catch." He flashed a perfect grin. The tiny scar above his lip suited him. "Come on."

My brother was an All-American quarterback in college so I knew how to handle a football. I followed him down the stairs and threw him a spiral.

"Whoa. Nice. I'd expected you to throw like a girl," he said as his hands swallowed the ball. He caught it and I kicked sand at him. He chuckled. "How about you, Where are you from?"

"Do you have a big family?" I responded without bothering to answer his question.

"I have two older brothers. One's an attorney and the other one's an oral surgeon. I have two nieces and a nephew." His face lit up when he mentioned them. "Dad's a pediatrician and Mom's an English teacher. They're flying in tonight. And by the way, awesome deflect on the question about you."

"Where did you go to school?" I was the queen of deflection. I lifted my hands into a 'V'.

"Colorado State." He tossed an easy spiral. "Family tradition."

"Major?"

"Pre-med."

"Really?"

He nodded.

"Dr. Smooth Moves," I taunted and pointed the football at him.

He ran over, swung me around and playfully tackled me to the ground. He hovered over me.

My breath hitched as my belly warmed. His flexing biceps and clean scent of sports soap was too way too close for my body not to react, no matter how involved I was with someone else.

"How's that for smooth? I've got you right where I want you."

I wiggled out from under him and he chuckled.

"Are you ever going to tell me anything about you?" he asked.

"Nope." I sat up and brushed the sand from my elbows.

"I'll let it go for now. But I warn you, I'm persistent." He reached over and brushed the sand from my hair. It made me more nervous than it should have and not just because Locke lived next door.

"I hadn't noticed," I said.

He laughed then helped me to my feet. We walked back up to the deck and sat down.

"So is it just your parents coming to see you?"

"And my brothers, and sisters-in-law, and my nieces and nephew. They all want to be there for my send-off," he explained. His dimples appeared and he pulled my chair out for me to sit.

"That's really sweet of them."

His family life was such a stark contrast to my own. It was hard to imagine a family event that didn't revolve around the media. I missed the days when our family was like that. It was before my father retired from the Air Force and began lobbying for the F-35.

"Yes, but it's going to be total chaos until I have to leave." He touched my hand. "I love my family, but I would have been happy to spend my last few in-country days with you."

"You're lucky. I don't think anyone would show up if I deployed. Well, maybe my mom."

Footsteps clicked on the deck stairs. Locke. And though we'd done nothing wrong, my pulse quickened and my mind raced. He stopped when he realized I wasn't alone.

I pulled back my hand.

"Hey, Duke. What's up? You live near here?" Ash stood up and broke the awkward silence.

"Yeah, next door." His expression was unreadable as he lifted his chin in the direction of his home.

Ash shook his hand. "Cool. This area's awesome."

"Yeah, it is. I was just going for a run but...I wanted to tell you that I saw a warning that the undertow was bad, in case you were planning on swimming later."

His eyes darted between Ash and I. His face had reddened and he dragged his hand across the back of his neck. Locke was a horrible liar.

"I usually swim for a workout." I winked at Ash. "Thanks for letting me know. I had a note from the Homeowners Association on my door earlier, too."

"Good," he said as his eyes flicked to Ash. "Sorry, I didn't mean to interrupt."

"Ash was out of town, and he just got back," I said.

"Maghreb?" Locke asked.

Thank goodness. Shoptalk.

Ash leaned against the railing. "Yeah, met with the United States-Africa Command team. It's getting bad." Ash leaned against the railing.

"Are you heading over there?" Locke asked.

"Friday," Ash said while he looked at his watch. "I hate to leave, but I have to go to the airport."

I stood, hoping I wasn't speaking too quickly. "It's okay. You need to get your family. I'll walk you out."

Locke shook his hand again. "Godspeed."

"Thanks, man, but it's all good. Do me a favor though, make sure she stays single." He dipped his head in my direction.

Shoot me now. Locke's lips drew into a straight line.

I walked Ash to the front door. He hugged me and bent down.

"Hopefully, I'll see you again before I leave." His lips brushed my cheek before he walked out the door.

I nodded afraid to say anything. I watched as he got into his truck. When he smiled and waved I felt a sense of loss. He was an awesome guy. I wanted to be nice, but I didn't know if it was right letting him think he had a chance.

"What was he doing here?"

Shit.

"He stopped by to tell me that he was deploying. What was I supposed to do?" I turned afraid to look at him.

"You like him," he said with sadness in his eyes.

"He's a great guy. A great friend." I clarified. "Locke, I'm sorry. It was wrong. But I didn't know how to handle it. I didn't want to lead him on, but he's leaving. I didn't want to make his departure worse. I suck." I walked over to the stairs and sat burying my head in my hands.

"You don't suck, but you *are* leading the bloke on. And that sucks," he said and sat beside me. "He's going away thinking you will be waiting for him. What happens when he gets back? Then what?"

"It will be easier when he gets back. Hell, he'll be gone for almost a year. He knows a lot can happen in that time." I tried to defend what I had done but I didn't know if it was for Locke or my benefit.

He wrapped his arm around me. "Sorry, I don't want to argue. It brasses me to see you with another guy."

His arms felt right. But I didn't care what he said. I did suck and that's why bad things happened to me.

Locke touched my face with his fingertips and my heart shot into afterburner. I forgot what we were even talking about. His lips pressed against mine. I wrapped my hands around his neck and climbed onto his lap. He playfully bit my bottom lip as I pressed my body harder against his. His kisses deepened.

"I thought you were going for a jog," I said in between breaths.

"I wanted to workout. I think this qualifies." His voice was rough.

All the naughty thoughts from earlier in the classroom resurfaced and spread southward.

I tore my shirt over my head and tossed it to the ground. He let out a low hungry growl as his fingers gripped my belt loops, pulling me closer. His lips traveled along my neck, to my collarbone and finally between the swells of my breast.

I shifted my hips pushing into him. "Are you marking your territory?"

Locke easily lifted and spun me around so that he was hovering over me. I gasped.

"You better believe it."

He reached down and unfastened my button then slipped off my shorts and panties with a single sweep before unsnapping my bra.

He wasn't kidding.

"Do you know how bloody hard it is to concentrate during a brief when my mind is spinning over how much I need to make love to you?" Locke's voice was deep and full of hunger.

I pressed my lips roughly against his. Stopping only for a moment to pull his shirt over his head and answer breathily. "Trust me, I know."

His hand rubbed my thigh and I trembled as my nipples hardened.

My hand traveled beneath the elastic on his shorts. His lips pressed firmly against mine as his hands traced along my skin as he lightly cupped my breast.

"God, Locke, hurry." I begged lifting my hips. He slid his body until his hips met mine and I gasped when he pulled me closer. He held me tighter and our hearts pounded wildly as he guided me into a steady rhythm.

"Damn, Tinklee. I've missed you." His breath blazed against my skin.

I buried my head into his neck and dug my nails into his back and my toes curled when he took me, all of me. I would never be able to climb these stairs in the same way again.

Locke's lips returned to mine, kissing me gently. "Are you okay?" he whispered softly.

I nodded trying to slow what felt like a swarm of bees buzzing through my body,

"I needed you. That was long overdue." He caught my bottom lip between his teeth.

"No kidding." My voice was breathless. "I was getting close to jumping your bones in the brief today," I said as I curled comfortably under his arm and rested my head on his chest.

He held me, carefully tracing his thumb up and down my back. "You seemed uncomfortable when I was discussing heat-seeking missiles."

"You have no idea."

"Yes, well thank God for podiums. My movement around the room has become restrictive lately."

I laughed.

He covered me with his T-shirt and stroked my hair. This was perfect. It was everything that I had remembered and more. Much more. I had fought with everything I had to keep from caring about anyone or anything ever again after my brother died.

"What are you thinking?" His breath tickled and I shivered.

I was thinking that I never wanted to let him go and it scared the living shit out of me. But I didn't say it out loud. Thank God, I was sober.

"I like the way you workout."

Locke leaned back and smirked, accepting it as a compliment.

"Time to hit the showers?" He raised his eyebrows.

A smile crept across my face. There was no way I could refuse that offer. We gathered our clothing and rushed to my room. I tossed the clothing on the floor and stepped under the steamy spray. He stepped in behind me and rested his hands on my hips. I leaned back. I was naked in a shower with an amazing man. I had never been happier or more frightened.

Locke picked up a bottle of body wash and read the label.

"What in the bloody hell is vanilla verbena?" He flipped open the lid and the sweet aroma filled the air. "Just for the record, I'm addicted to it."

I giggled. He poured the soap on his hands rubbed them together into a thick lather. My body tingled as they glided along my back and lower. He leaned down and kissed my neck pulling me closer. His fingers curved down along my sides and continued along the outside of my thighs and back up again. I arched my back and looked up into his eyes.

Locke smiled then leaned down and covered my mouth with his. We lathered, kissed, and held each other until the water ran cold. Neither of us said a word, yet so much seemed to be spoken. He shut off the water and I reached for the towels, handing him one.

"Your houseguests are going to send out a search party for you," I said as I tied the towel around me.

"They went to a movie, but they should be home soon." He wrapped the towel around his waist.

I studied him as he ran his hand through his hair resisting the urge to trace his six-pack abs with my tongue. His lip curled up and he winked at me. My eyes darted away as my ears warmed and the heat pooled south. I needed to stop. This was ridiculous.

He looked down at his watch and his jaw tensed.

"Everything okay?" I hesitated, not certain if I wanted to hear his response.

"Yes, but there was a reason I stopped by earlier." He rubbed his thumb across the face of his watch.

It wasn't like him to fidget.

"What's wrong?" I asked.

"There is a safety briefing in the morning."

I sighed. So what? We always had safety briefings.

"I saw Clash's report," he explained frowning.

"Is it that boring?" I teased.

"We are in the air-to-air phase." He paused. "It's related to the phase."

My stomach bottomed out.

"He's going to review my brother's crash," I said grabbing a t-shirt off the ground and yanking it over my head.

He nodded.

"Son of a bitch. He's going to use it as an example of pilot error, isn't he?"

Locke scrubbed his hand down face. "I tried to talk him out of it, but he is adamant about covering it. He said it is important. It has to be reviewed."

The hair on the back of my neck stood up.

"This is bullshit, Locke. Is he going to give the party line or will he tell the truth and say that the cause of the crash is still unknown?"

"I only saw part of the brief. I am supposed to review the rest in the morning before the main meeting. He talked to your dad about it the night they all had dinner. His office sent him the documentation from that discussion."

What was I going to do? Everyone had an agenda when it came to this jet.

"There is no way around it," he said.

A pair of headlights shined along the wall and gravel crunched in the driveway next door.

"They're back," he said.

"You'd better go." I chewed the cuticle on my thumb.

"No. I'll stay. I don't want you to be alone. I meant to tell you when I first got here." He took my hand away from my mouth.

I pulled it away and turned my back.

"I'll be fine. I'm tired and I just want to go to sleep."

A car door shut and I reassured him. "I'm fine. You need to go."

"I didn't want you to walk in tomorrow not knowing."

I nodded.

Locke rested his hands gently on my arms. My body tensed. He leaned forward, and kissed me on top of the head then sighed.

It was impossible for me to stay happy. Impossible.

Chapter 15

My body begged for sleep, but my mind wouldn't give in. I studied my brother's video twelve more times, looking for a good defense against the accusations I knew were coming, but I couldn't find anything. I had no idea how to prove that the accident wasn't his fault.

I considered calling in sick, but that was a coward's way out. I would be stoic for Colin.

The morning's rays warmed my skin and brightened the room. It was way too bright for the thoughts swirling in my head. I forced myself to prepare for battle. I wouldn't go down without a fight. I had to prove that my brother's crash was not due to pilot error, even if it killed me.

We had several academic classes to go through before *the* brief. I didn't pay attention. Stitch asked me at least twenty times if I was okay. Several others followed suit by telling me that I looked like hell, death warmed over, and my personal favorite from Mojo—dog balls.

I needed to pull my shit together. I sat out on the back patio and gathered my thoughts. Bodhi's walked around the corner.

"What's up, Tink?"

He greeted me with his signature fist explosion then held the door as I walked through.

"Are you going to the safety brief?" I asked, as I wasn't sure why Bodhi would.

"They want me there in case any of the medical stuff needs to be translated. Dude, I just found out which scenario, this has to be sucksville for you."

"You can say that," I muttered.

"You're strong. You can handle it." He swatted me on the arm.

"I guess we're about to find out."

Soon after I took my seat, the instructor pilots and Clash filed into the room. They sat in the front row. They usually scattered around the room wherever they wanted. Where were T-Rex and Shatter? A few minutes later, the door swung open and the room was called to attention. Shatter entered. An image of me jumping to my feet and shouting *I object* ran through my mind. I prayed it was anxiety and not a premonition.

Clash stood, and I fought the urge to scream. Maybe it would be fine. Maybe he would be the one to raise the bullshit flag on the pilot error argument.

And maybe little green Martians would float in and share their secret to living on Mars.

"We are in the air-to-air phase of your training," Clash said. "It's important to review specific scenarios experienced by others to help you recognize and correctly react to similar issues and situations you may encounter. We have chosen several examples. We will breakdown and discuss each one as we go. This is a closed discussion with only leadership and instructor contribution. If time remains, we will open for discussion at the end."

Clash stood with his hands on his hips like Captain America.

I glanced sideways as someone sat next to me. T-Rex. They placed a guard on me.

I looked forward ignoring him.

The first case was a landing gear issue. It was quick and easy. The second one was about abnormal engine fluctuations. It took a little longer because there were some small disagreements. But they quickly resolved. The third case lit the screen.

The title read, "Pilot Incapacitation."

I snapped my pencil in half. T-Rex cleared his throat signaling for me to behave myself.

The room fell silent.

"I'm sure most of you are familiar with this scenario as it created quite a media buzz when it happened," Clash said folding his arms.

"Sir." Stitch stood up.

My throat ran dry.

"Sit down. I said there would be no discussion until the end," Clash ordered.

"With all due respect, sir."

Shatter snapped his finger and pointed. "Sit your ass down, Stitch."

"Sir, I agree." Freak said and pushed his chair back and rose to his feet.

The room rumbled as a few of the others guys turned to look in my direction. I didn't move.

The lights flipped on. Clash's face had turned the shade of a steamed lobster.

"It seems some of the students have lost their goddamn minds."

Mojo stood also. "Sir, this is messed up."

Four more of the guys stood in solidarity.

They were putting themselves at risk for me. I had to do something.

I stood.

"I said this was going to happen," T-Rex growled and lowered his head to the table.

"We should review the scenario," I said. "It will be good to cut through the bullshit."

Everyone stared at me like I had asked if this flight suit made my ass look fat.

Clash split the awkward silence. "Thanks, Lieutenant. I'm glad we have your goddamn blessing to continue." A single vein protruded from his forehead. "I am going to say this once and only once, you jackasses better sit down and shut your mouths without interruption. Got it?"

Shatter cleared his throat and stood.

"All right. Let's all calm down." He snapped his fingers and pointed for us to sit. Everyone followed his command. "This is personal to everyone in this room, some more than others." His brows pulled together as he dipped his head in my direction in an apologetic nod. I didn't move. "No one wants to talk about it. I know. But let's face it; we should talk about it. We *need* to talk about it. So let's be professional and learn from this. What we discuss today may save someone's life tomorrow." His thick Texas accent was the voice of reason.

He sat back down.

"Go for it, Major." Shatter ordered and smacked his hand on the table.

He stretched his neck to one side then cracked his knuckles before speaking.

"The engagement was a two-versus-two dissimilar air combat training mission. The fight parameters followed all of the established procedures with standard altitude deconfliction between the 'Blue' fighters and 'Red' aggressors."

He took a sip from his water bottle and continued.

"The mishap pilot was a twenty-four year old male, excellent physical condition without any abnormal external conditions that could have contributed to the accident."

I pressed my palms against my legs.

"Standard toxicology testing was accomplished to determine if the mishap pilot was using any illegal narcotics or under the influence of any controlled substances at the time of the accident. The results were negative."

I felt my foot begin to tap.

Clash changed slides. "The cause of death was determined as extreme blunt force trauma consistent with an uncontrolled flight into terrain at high velocity. At the time of death it is surmised the mishap pilot was incapacitated due to a G-induced loss of consciousness."

My blood ran cold. The words should have set off a volcanic eruption instead a creepy calmness flushed through me as I listened.

"At approximately five minutes and thirty-seven seconds into engagement, five seconds into the High-G turn, the mishap pilot loses consciousness due to an improper G-strain maneuver. The board classified the loss of situational awareness as pilot error due to a G-induced loss of consciousness, more commonly known as a G-LOC. Let's play the last two minutes starting with the High-G break turn."

He hit play.

A chill ran down my spine as goose bumps traveled along my skin.

"Altitude! Altitude!"

"Pull up! Pull up!"

"Pull up! Pull up!"

Saliva pooled beneath my tongue and my throat ran dry.

"Altitude! Altitude!"

"Pull up! Pull up!"

"Pull up! Pull up!"

I dug my fingers deep into the cold metal underneath the edge of my seat.

Giant green arrow. Full explosion then darkness.

My insides shook uncontrollably.

"Shit," T-Rex whispered.

I didn't blink or breathe. I was afraid to move, unsure of what it might set into motion. I just sat frozen staring at the blank screen.

"Again leadership, this was ruled pilot error. Let's open the floor." Clash stepped back and waited.

Blood pumped to my arms and legs as adrenaline rushed through my body. I searched my mind for anything to annihilate those two words. Pilot error.

A few guys shifted, but no one spoke. The silence was eerie.

"No one? I know each of you have reviewed this extensively, so come on, let's hear it." He folded his arms.

Silence. He turned to Locke.

Every single nerve ending stood on edge.

"Duke, let's hear what you have to say. You made some valid points I think should be shared."

My pulse echoed in my ears.

Locke didn't answer.

This was unlike him.

"Duke," Clash ordered.

Locke rose. I couldn't breathe.

"This was difficult. There was evidence for both sides of the argument." His voice was direct.

I listened as sweat trickled down my back.

"At that last break turn, he is in full control of the jet, then it starts to point," Clash said. "Do you think he was fading due to the G-force? Put that back up there. What point was it?"

"5:27," Locke said.

I swallowed hard. He had it to the second.

"Let's put it up there. 5:27." Locke repeated.

The screen came back to life. A loud repetitive beep came from the jet's audio system. The high-pitched sound mixed with rapid breathing and grunting from the pilot fighting off the G's.

The video stopped.

"Assess," Clash ordered.

"I think he loses consciousness due to the G-forces pulling the blood from his brain."

A sharp pain tore through my chest as my mind stretched. Son of a bitch. He was just like the rest of them. I had heard enough and stormed from the room.

"You win Karma. Now please, leave me the hell alone." I muttered as I left him and the bullshit behind.

* * * *

The doorbell woke me, followed by frantic pounding.

"Tinklee, open up! I need to talk to you," Locke shouted.

I ignored him as he continued to pound. After a few minutes the pounding stopped but began again on the back door.

He could pound his knuckles raw. I hated him.

"I'm not leaving until you let me explain," he said and pounded on the door. "Tinklee! Come on."

A female's voice interrupted the banging. I walked down the hall and peeked around the corner through the window.

Kassie. I didn't trust her or her fiancé.

"You need to leave her alone," she replied in a gentle voice. She tugged on his arm. "She doesn't want to see you right now."

"You don't understand. She thinks I betrayed her. I have to explain."

The banging continued. Louder.

"Locke, Sean is almost home. You can't let him see you this way."

"Screw him."

"Give her time. She's angry, and she isn't going to hear anything you'd say now anyway. Let her cool off." Her voice softened. "You need to cool off, too."

"Tinklee!"

He was going to break the glass if he didn't stop.

"Damn it, Locke. Listen to me." Her voice cracked. "I love you, and I don't want you to do anything stupid. This is not the right time!"

He stopped pounding and turned to her.

"This is bloody brilliant. You keep Clash away from me. This is his fault. He did this for his own personal agenda."

He stalked away. She wiped a tear from her cheek then followed.

I gripped the wall to keep from chasing after him. I needed to hate him but the anguish in his voice pulled me. No. I couldn't. Locke betrayed me. He betrayed us. I slammed my hand against the wall. A photo in a small alcove fell over. My fingers shook as I reached for it. Colin smiled from the frame.

My throat burned as I touched his face through the glass. He was hugging me and I was looking up at him, adoringly. It was taken the night before he had left for war.

I tried to remember exactly what he had said to me that night, but I couldn't. I squeezed my eyes tighter and my bottom lip trembled. His memories were fading, just like the scent from his old gray t-shirt I kept carefully tucked in a zip-locked bag in my closet.

I ran to my room and tore through a stack of t-shirts until I felt the cool smooth plastic against my shaking fingers. Ripping open the seal I pulled out the soft worn cotton and closed my eyes. His familiar clean sporty scent rushed through me as I gripped it tighter in my trembling hands, struggling to breathe as I remembered…

..."Dad says the jet is unmatched. He's never seen anything like it." I handed Colin the article, pointing at the picture. The edges had already been worn as I had looked at it a dozen times since the magazine had arrived

Colin slid the magazine to the side and tossed his football in the air. "I'm not leaving the F-22."

"But look at it," I said and waved the picture in his face. "Look what it can do."

"You fly it then. You can be its first female pilot. Dad would love it. His golden child flying the air force's prodigy."

I snatched the ball from his hands.

"I'm gonna fly it. But you should too. You'll need a head start if you want to keep up with me." I challenged.

"That's awful big talk for such a tiny little girl," he teased.

I threw the ball to him and he caught it with one hand.

"I learned to smack talk from the best." I sat in front of him on the floor. "You need to accept the match. It will make Dad happy," I said.

"I don't want it. I'm happy in the jet I'm in." He sat down beside me. "Besides, it would be for the wrong reason. I don't want to be Dad's poster child. I just want to fly."

"That's not fair," I said. "You'll get promoted sooner. It will fast track you for sure."

"You're starting to sound more like him every day," he said with a sigh and rolled his eyes.

"Dad just wants what's best for us. Besides, you'll be helping the Air Force. You are the best of the best. The Risner winner. Come on. It makes sense and you know it," I pleaded my best case.

He lay back on his bedroom's carpet and stared at the ceiling.

I reached for the picture from the desk and waved it in front of his face. He snatched it and sat back up. He looked at the image and back to me.

"Don't do it for Dad. Do it for me. You promised that one day, we'd fly together. Side by side." I gave my best puppy dog eyes. "Come on. The JSF can be our jet."

He laughed. It was a contagious laughter that made others want to know him.

"That's not fair, Tink."

"Why not?"

He pulled me into a headlock and ruffled my hair.

"Cause, you're my little sis'. I would do anything for you."

I slid down the wall and buried my face in his t-shirt. My shoulders shook uncontrollably as my tears resurfaced. A sob escaped my lips. I begged him to fly the JSF. It was my fault that he was gone.

"I'm so sorry, Colin."

* * * *

I zipped the bag shut and swiped back the remaining tears from my cheeks. I dragged myself into my room and turned on my computer and selected the best man-hating music I could find. I lay back on the floor, closed my eyes and listened to the chorus. It described my loathing of men right down to the final twangy word.

I pulled a blanket from the bed and over my head. I wished I could stay hidden.

A knock rapped on the door. Not again. I didn't want to talk to him. The doorbell rang and I looked at the time. 2330. I pulled the blanket back over my head.

"Tink, you in there?"

It wasn't *him*. It was Ash.

I turned off the music but didn't move.

He knocked again.

I wondered if everything was okay. His family was in town and he was deploying in the morning. My stomach tightened. I couldn't blame him for what Locke did.

Ash greeted me with a pizza, and a six-pack.

"What are you doing here?" I asked and opened the door, but it didn't mean I had to let him in.

His smile faded. "You look like hell."

"Isn't your family in town?" I sighed.

"Yes, but everyone is sleeping so I thought I might be able to sneak away to say goodbye. What happened to you?" He repeated.

I stepped back and invited him in. He followed me to the kitchen and the smell of the pizza made my stomach growl.

He flipped open a can and handed it to me. "You look like you need this."

I took the can from him.

"I hate seeing you upset," he said.

"Every time you see me I'm upset." I grabbed some plates and handed him one.

He folded his arms. He wasn't going to give into my lack of humor.

"It's okay. It was just a bad day. You're the one who's deploying. I don't want to talk about me, let's talk about you. How are you?" I sipped my beer.

He didn't look convinced, but he let it go.

"I'm fine but my family's a disaster. I was happy they went to sleep finally."

"They're just worried. They love you," I said.

"I know. But none of them are military. They don't handle deployments very well. This is my third one. You'd think they'd get used to it."

"I don't think you get used to saying goodbye to someone you love. Maybe you should cut them some slack," I said with a shrug and took another swig of my beer. "I remember when my brother deployed; I stayed glued to the news and the Internet. It was great when he called but it was always hard to hang up. When he came back, I couldn't run fast enough to greet him."

"You're probably right," he said. "I know it's harder for the families that are left behind. We're too busy and too focused on the mission to have time to really miss anyone."

I stared out the window.

"The worst is the panic you feel every time you see a dark car coming up the street. You pray they don't stop in front of your house to deliver the news," I said softly to my reflection in the window.

"Did that happen when your brother died?" he asked.

I sighed and turned around shaking my head. "No, I was in the tower that day." I sat on the counter next to him. "I had just graduated from the academy and was heading to pilot training. I begged Colin to get me a pass."

"You were there when the accident happened?"

I nodded.

"That's awful."

"A living nightmare." I couldn't believe I was sharing this with him.

"I am so sorry," he said.

I nodded appreciating the words yet knowing no one would ever be as sorry as I was.

"They reviewed my brother's flight in the safety briefing today."

Ash's hand clenched over his beer. The can crinkled in his grip. "Why would they do that?"

"It was a great opportunity to learn from a known *pilot error*," I said. "It made for a really shitty day."

He glanced at his watch. "It's 0030 and the start of a new day."

He reached over and clanked my can.

"But you're leaving today." We headed to the living room, and I cleared a blanket off the couch for him to sit.

"No complaints. My send-off has started out great."

"Thanks for listening." I rested my head on his shoulder.

"I didn't really have a choice. You just kept going on and on and on."

My mouth fell open as I looked up at him. The corners of his lips curled into a smirk.

"You jerk!" I grabbed for the pillow and hit him, spilling his beer down the front of him.

The front of his shirt was drenched. He glanced down then grabbed the pillow and whacked me.

"No! Not that one. It's torn."

Feathers exploded everywhere and I yelled in surprise, waving them from my face.

"Hell. I'm sorry!" He swatted them from the air.

I glanced down. My hair was full of feathers.

"Oh shit." I looked like a half-cracked chicken.

He erupted into laughter. It was contagious. I joined him until it left me gasping for air.

"I needed that," I said in between gasps.

"You're an interesting woman."

He studied me with uncertainty.

"Is that good or bad?"

Ash reached up and picked a feather from my hair. It felt more comfortable than it should have.

He leaned forward. I didn't move.

Ash's lips brushed against mine. I hesitated for a moment before leaning closer, inviting him to continue. His hand touched the side of my face. He kissed me more deeply, and my mind shouted for me to stop. I broke away, looking at the ground.

"Sorry," he said.

"Don't apologize." I backed away. "It's me. It's not you."

He chuckled.

I frowned. "What's so funny?"

"It's me. It's not you." He mimicked. "That is the worst let down line in the world."

"Shut up," I said rolling my eyes. "Your shirt is soaking wet. Take it off."

"Now you're asking me to take off my clothes? Make up your mind, woman!"

"You're impossible. I'm going to get you something dry."

He pulled his shirt over his head exposing his bronzed, chiseled chest and abs. A slightly raised scar traced his shoulder. I hesitated. Dimples formed in his cheeks.

My face lit fire. I left to grab one of my dad's shirts from his room.

A few feathers stuck in my hair. I searched for the few stragglers and picked them out. I frowned. Kissing Ash wasn't going to make my problems with Locke go away. Someone knocked on the door.

"Are you expecting anyone?" Ash called from the other room.

"No," I responded and grabbed a shirt from the dresser.

"I'll answer it."

Locke shouted from outside. "Tinklee, open the door!"

Oh my God! It was Locke. And Ash was going to open the door. I looked down at the shirt in my hand. Shirtless! Shit. I ran after him but it was too late. The front door was open.

"What in the bloody hell are you doing here?" Locke slurred as he stepped forward.

"Hey Duke, I think you've had too much to drink." Ash pressed a hand against Locke's chest, preventing him from entering. "You need to leave."

Locke knocked his hand away and both men stared the other down. I hesitated in the doorway.

"What the hell is he doing here?" Locke demanded ignoring Ash's warning and moved toward me.

Ash grabbed his arm. "You really need to leave."

Locke's eyes turned glacial. "Get your bloody hands off me."

"Not until you leave."

My voice shook. "Locke, please. Just go."

"Not until you tell me what the hell he's doing here." His stare could chisel ice.

"She doesn't have to explain anything to you. You're her instructor, not her goddamn boyfriend!"

Ash's face twisted as his eyes widened with a sudden comprehension. My stomach dropped.

"Shit." His shoulders tensed.

I dropped the shirt. "Ash—"

Then it happened. Locke's fist connected with Ash's jaw. Ash stumbled backward, his hand gripping the injury. His expression darkened. Before I could stop him, he charged at Locke. Punches flew as rapidly as the profanity. I shouted, but they ignored me. I dodged the thrashing fists and jumped away as they overturned a table on the porch. A flowerpot shattered against the floor.

Ash's fist connected with Locke's face. I shouted as Locke tumbled down the front steps landing on the ground.

"Locke!"

I bolted down the stairs. The punch looked vicious but he jumped back to his feet ready to go again. I stepped in front of him and pressed my hands to his chest.

"Locke. Stop!"

His jaw clenched.

I turned back to Ash. He watched me in silence, rubbing his cracked and swollen knuckles. He turned to go back inside. I didn't know what to do. What the hell had I done?

Ash held his shirt and keys in his hand as he rushed to the driveway.

"Wait! Don't go." I raced to him reaching for his arm.

"Why? Do you want to tell me I'm wrong?" He was calm, but his eyes were dark. Hurt.

"Yes. I mean no." I tried to explain. "Ash, please. It's complicated."

"It always is." He pulled his arm from me. He didn't give me another look, just got into his truck and left. I watched dragging my hands through my hair. This was a disaster.

I turned back to Locke. There was a gash below his eye.

"Are you okay?" I asked.

"Yeah."

He wiped the blood with the back of his hand.

"Good. Then get the hell off my property."

I walked up my stairs, then slammed and locked the door.

What a fucking shit-show.

Chapter 16

I needed to try to clean up at least one of my messes. Ash's departure was set for 0800. His family would be there and the last thing they needed was for me to ruin their goodbye, but I didn't want him leaving with the way things ended.

I walked toward the hangar where everyone met for the send-off. I wasn't sure what I was going to say. I'd just have to wing it.

I saw him standing in the middle of the hangar as soon as I entered. His family hugged him. He had a small dark-haired boy on his shoulders and two cute little strawberry blond girls attached to his legs. A young woman with the same shade of blond as the two girls in her late twenties was taking pictures. A guy that looked like Ash reached up for the little boy and lifted him off his shoulders. They took a picture together. The rest of the family rotated with Ash, and as an older man with a receding dark-gray hairline, who I guessed to be Ash's father, hugged him. I smiled.

This was his family time. I shouldn't intrude. I walked out of the hangar. He seemed fine. It was for the best, I told myself.

"Tink."

I spun around. Ash stood with his hands in his pockets and a small bruise below his eye.

My stomach dropped. "Ash, I am so sorry."

"I shouldn't have left like that last night," he said.

"Yes, you should have. You had every right."

"I'm glad you're here."

He pulled his hands from his pockets. His knuckles were cut and bruised. I winced when I saw them.

"I'm sorry, I didn't want to interrupt your family time, but I didn't want to leave things the way we did last night," I explained.

"It was a pretty awesome night until your boyfriend showed up."

"He's not my…."

"You don't need to explain. But I do want you to be careful. You're playing with fire. I don't want anything to come back and bite you in the ass." He shook his head. "Hell Tink, even I know better than to get involved with my instructor."

"Your instructors are all men."

"Good point." He laughed and the sound of it made me grin.

"You'd better go," I said.

"Are you sure you don't want to come in and meet the Griswalds?" Ash asked and chuckled.

"Thank you, but this is their time." I hesitated. "Are we good?"

"We're good." He bent down and hugged me.

"Be safe." I squeezed him back.

I glanced up at him and donned a veil of strength. These were the moments that you etched details of their faces, captured their scents, and memorized the way it felt when they touched you in case these memories would need to last you for your lifetime.

He nodded and winked before disappearing back into the hangar. I watched as everyone said goodbye. He picked up his green duffle bag and hugged his mom while she wept.

"Mothers spend their lives protecting their children from danger. It's difficult to accept when they volunteer for it. You'll understand one day, when you have children of your own." My mother's words swept through my mind. It's what she told me after Colin's send-off when I teased her for being a hot mess.

Ash's farewell felt like déjà vu. Especially when Ash, like Colin, waved one last time before walking out to the plane.

I closed my eyes and said a prayer for his safe return.

* * * *

Target practice was the perfect way to blow off some steam. Once I got to the range for my nine-millimeter requalification, I found a grassy area and sat. The sun warmed my face as yesterday's events filled my mind… the brief, Locke, Ash, the brawl on my front porch. It was too much.

"Hey!"

A voice startled me.

I blocked the sun from my eyes and looked up. It was Mojo.

"Hey," I responded and tried to keep my tone non-bitchy.

"How's it going?' he asked.

"I'm ready to blow shit up."

"Atta girl. Let's go," he said as he reached out his hand and pulled me to my feet.

The others guys were already setting up near the equipment. The instructor explained last minute safety instructions. Once he finished, everyone loaded the weapons. I holstered my gun and walked toward the target. Fantom stood next to me, talking to the other guys.

"...We were hammered. We were at Krusty's so he walked home. I don't know what the hell happened."

"His cousin stopped by to see if he made it home, and she found him on the sofa bloodied and ticked off. She called Bodhi to come over and when we got there, he was on his back deck," Woodstock said. "Dude, he was pissed, but he wouldn't talk to anyone. Bodhi finally convinced him to let him fix his cheek and put some ice on his swollen hand, but he didn't say what happened."

I pulled the safety glasses over my eyes and removed my weapon.

"Did anyone stay with him?" Fantom asked.

"Kassie," Woodstock answered.

I unloaded my weapon, annihilating the bull's eye. My ears rang.

"Lieutenant! You must wait for my signal," the instructor shouted. "And put in your earplugs."

Mojo chuckled. "You weren't kidding about blowing shit up."

I shot him a sideway glance as I reloaded my weapon and holstered it. He shook his head and pulled his safety glasses over his eyes.

"I wonder what the other guy looked like?" Woodstock continued his conversation with Fantom. "Bodhi thought Duke's hand might be broken. He told him to come in for an X-ray today."

Shit. If it were broken he wouldn't be able to fly. It would be my fault.

I slipped in my earplugs. I removed my weapon and I waited for the instructor to give a thumbs-up. When given the sign, I emptied my round, dropped my clip, loaded another and continued. After several targets were shot up, and the instructor called, "cease fire," I flipped the safety and returned to the holding area.

I didn't feel any better, like I had hoped I would. I felt worse. Locke and I destroyed everything that we had in a single stupid day.

"Can you give me a ride?" Mojo asked patting me playfully on the back.

"No," I said tossing my gear on the table.

"Why not?" He grabbed me by the shoulders and shook me. "Come on."

I walked to my Jeep. Mojo followed and got in even though I never answered him. He reached down and turned up the volume on the radio. I had been listening to a song about never getting back with your loser boyfriend. I turned it off.

Mojo glanced over his aviators. "Would you rather talk instead?"

I reached down and turned up the volume.

He laughed. "You're a funny chick, Tink," he said with a snicker and reached over and shook my shoulder again.

"Stop shaking me."

I swatted him in the chest.

Mojo was like an annoying younger sibling that wouldn't go away. He left me alone for ten seconds then poked me in the side.

"You okay after yesterday?" he asked.

I didn't answer.

"What did you think about Duke's argument?" He leaned back anticipating another smack.

"I think Duke's an asshole," I spat out gripping the wheel tighter.

"He's a badass. Duke's got skills. He thought your brother did too," he said. "He played ball at the academy, didn't he?"

"What are you talking about?" I was confused.

"Your brother. He was a running back, wasn't he?"

"No, quarterback. And why would you say Duke thought that my brother had skills?"

"Because of everything he said about him. Serious bro-love going on there."

"What happened?"

"Did you leave?" he asked.

"Obviously. What happened?"

"Duke has balls of steel. He brought up a classified argument concerning some of the contracted subsystem failure rates."

My pulse raced. Locke brought up the environmental systems and I'd stormed out before hearing what he had to say.

"Then he talked about how your brother was capable of pushing the jet and himself beyond what other pilots had before," Mojo explained as I stomped down on the pedal, driving faster. "He thinks he may have G'd out but not for the usual reason. The General requested the investigation be reopened."

I felt like someone sucker punched me.

Locke risked so much for me and how did I repay him? By acting like a spoiled brat. I was the asshole, not him.

Mojo handed me his water bottle.

"I'm sorry, I thought you knew. I didn't realize you left."

"No, I didn't know."

"Reopening the investigation is good, right?"

"Yeah, it's good."

Thankfully, Mojo didn't speak for the rest of the drive. When we got back to the squadron, we finished our briefs and the day finally ended after what seemed like an eternity. Everyone was planning to go to the Debrief Bar. I had to find Locke and talk to him.

I scanned the bar for him, but he was nowhere to be found. My next stops were the halls and offices, but they were empty. Maybe he'd taken the day off. I swung open the back door to leave and my heart stopped.

He and Bodhi were coming up the stairs to the squadron. A fresh wound highlighted his eye and his hand was wrapped in a white cotton bandage.

"Locke!"

His gaze narrowed. He continued to the door as if I were invisible.

"Locke, we need to talk." I grabbed his arm.

He yanked it and walked inside.

I tried to follow.

Bodhi stopped me.

"Just let him go," he said. His tone was different and he didn't call me dude.

"What? No, I need to talk to him." I knocked his hand away.

"He needs space."

"But I didn't know what happened after I left yesterday." The desperation in my voice made me cringe, but I couldn't change it. I just wanted Locke to hear me.

"He tried to tell you last night, but you wouldn't listen. And when he tried again, he found you with another dude and almost got himself a one-way ticket out of the cockpit."

Bodhi knew what had happened and he'd chosen a side. It clearly wasn't mine.

"I thought he betrayed me."

"Well, now you know how he feels," Bodhi said.

His words felt like a dropkick to the chest. I drew in a long, deep breath and leaned against the wall.

"How's his hand?" I asked quietly.

"Sprained. Nothing's broken." Bodhi leaned beside me. "Listen, I know this is none of my business. Duke's my friend." I stared down at the ground as he continued, "But I consider you a friend, too. And from one friend to another I need to be honest."

I looked at him.

"Just because you want to be together doesn't always mean that you should."

He patted me on the shoulder before he went inside.

I rubbed the back of my neck and growled.

Bodhi made sense, even if his words were difficult to swallow.

Chapter 17

"Ready to take on the man today?" Mojo smacked me in the arm.

"Screw off Mojo," I responded reflexively before his question registered. My eyes widened and I tugged on his arm. "Wait, what are you talking about?"

A wide grin spread across his face. "Yep. Clash fell out of the scenario, so Duke got pulled in," he explained.

I threw my head back and moaned trying to muffle the sound of my heart pounding from my chest. Locke and I had avoided each other for weeks, but if we were flying against each other today, the avoidance would have to end.

Mojo chuckled. "Sorry girl, but you're going down. No one can beat the man."

"Stop calling him that," I said and smacked him in the chest.

It annoyed me how Locke was the instructor who had set the bar. The pilot that every student achieved to be. Why did he have to be so damn perfect at everything? And why did I have to get thrown into a flight against him today, without notice? I frowned.

"Watch it girl, or your call sign is going to end up being Grumpy." He lifted his fists then ducked and weaved like he was avoiding my next punch.

I cursed under my breath. Following the Aggressor flight, there was a naming ceremony. Those of us who didn't have call signs were going to be named. It was a big day, and night, that I was suddenly dreading.

I sat in the back for the brief, trying to replay today's aggressor scenario in my mind. I was flying in a four-ship with T-Rex, Woodstock, and Stitch. Shatter and Locke were the enemy bandits.

Woodstock was the lead. He reviewed our setup. "Our mission today is Offensive Counter Air. The name of the game is aggressively flying, finding MIGs, and killing them."

Locke sat off to the side with his arms crossed.

A flash flood of anxiety crashed through me. It was bad enough battling him on the ground, but now I'd have to do it in the air too. I pressed my hands firmly against my knees as my legs began to shake.

"We'll start the engagements with a beyond visual range split then press in as required for a visual fight in order to achieve a kill." Woodstock zoned in on Stitch and I. "This is an extremely demanding environment so you need to be on your game."

We nodded.

"Remember, a lot of aircraft will be in a small amount of airspace. This is a physically exhausting profile, so everyone watch your environmentals. Duke will brief the Aggressor admin so we're all on the same sheet of music for altitude blocks, kill calls, and kill removal procedures."

Locke tossed his pencil on the table and stood. I jumped. He hesitated for a split second, his top teeth denting into his lower lip. He swallowed hard then reviewed how the aggressors would be integrated, careful not to divulge any of their aggressor tactics. They'd be flying the same jets, but red pods hung beneath their jet to mark them as enemy MIGs. Shatter was Red One and Locke was Red Two.

His eyes were narrow, his attitude focused, and his voice was curt. There was something frightening about him.

He asked if there were any questions. He looked directly at everyone in the room, skipping over me.

Woodstock clapped his hands. "Let's do this."

We geared up and headed to the jets. The van shook with excitement and adrenaline, but Locke stayed quiet and so did I. It was the closest we had been for some time. He stared out the window.

The van stopped in front of my jet, so I climbed out over the seats. It was a tight fit, and I had to pass within inches of Locke's face to get out. I stared at the faded scar below his eye and resisted the urge to reach out and touch it. The scent of his aftershave filled the van. I inhaled and lingered for a moment.

An airman saluted me and I returned the custom, handing him my gear. I went through the standard flight procedures and soon I was strapped in. Ready to go.

"Kick their asses, ma'am," my crew chief shouted. I gave thumbs-up as the canopy encased me.

Locke got into his jet a few hundred yards away. I couldn't help but notice the way his muscles flexed as he climbed into the jet. He was great at his job and fiercely in control. Watching him prepare for the flight made me want him. I missed the way he used to watch me, and how his stare made me feel guarded. Now he just looked past me. I shook out my hands and stretched my neck side to side. Wrong mindset. I was a freaking fighter pilot tasked to kick his ass, not check it out.

The crew chief motioned me to move. My headset came to life. Air Traffic Control directed me to the runway. I was number four and I filed in behind the others. Shatter and Locke approached from behind in their Aggressors.

He was the enemy. It was my job to defeat him.

The takeoff, departure, and entry into the airspace were standard, only they happened in a flash. I was completely zoned in and geared up for the fight. I scanned the horizon, focusing my eyes searching for the small black specks that would close on me at over 800 miles per hour.

The radio crackled to life as our controller checked in. The air battle manager was a critical piece of the choreographed chaos. He fed us information and helped keep us alive.

"Disco, Gambler Flight is established in the North." Woodstock radioed.

"Disco copies, Aggressors are calling that they are ready in the South." The controller replied.

"Gambler copies Aggressors ready in the South, Disco/Gamblers. Fight's on!"

"Disco copies fight's on. Gambler hostile contacts south of your position, maneuvering."

"Gambler copies, Gamblers action!"

The flight spread out into a spread formation to search and find the Aggressors on radar. Woodstock picked them up.

"Gambler One contact bearing one-eight-zero, thirty miles, twenty-seven thousand feet."

"Gambler One hostile," came the controllers reply.

Both Woodstock and Stitch took simulated long-range shots. The aggressors maneuvered and survived the attack. We were committed to a close, visual fight. I rapidly scanned the horizon looking for the Enemy MIGs.

There it was!

Below the sun, on the horizon line, the slightest movement and what looked like a mirror flash. I continued to scan. Tiny drops of sweat formed above my lip. Two small black specks flew toward Woodstock and T-Rex's element. My fingers tingled as I gripped the stick tighter. The Aggressors.

"Gambler One. Break right. Flares! Bandit your right three o'clock for three miles." I yelled a warning into the radio.

The two bandits closed in on my wingmen.

I broke the jet toward the two MIGs and slammed the throttle forward trying to chase them down as quickly as possible. In a matter of seconds I was racing at over six hundred knots toward the two enemy aircraft.

"Red One. Kill the lead F-35." Shatter called on the radio.

"Copy kill," came Woodstock's dejected call. He was out.

"Red Two. Kill the trailing F-35." Locke reported cool and calm.

"Copy kill," T-Rex sharply replied. It was two against two.

Shit! I gritted my teeth.

I closed the distance and uncaged my short-range missile, locking up the lead MIG. I double checked all of the weapons parameters and simulated taking the shot.

"Gambler Four. Kill the lead MIG. Northbound."

"Copy Kill." Shatter barked as he rolled the jet to the right and exited the fight.

He rolled the jet to the right and exited the fight.

Adrenaline rushed to my fingertips. One down. One to go.

I repositioned and pointed the jet onto the trailing aggressor. His fighter violently pitched back and it seemed like his aircraft came to a dead stop as the nose quickly rotated toward my aircraft. I snatched back on the stick to avoid his yet-unlocked weapons. I rocketed up into the sky and cleared behind me. Locke came out of his maneuver and positioned his jet to chase me down.

I set my jaw. Not in this lifetime.

I stomped on the bottom rudder, pulling the stick back toward me, corkscrewing the jet around to get the nose back on the aggressor. Anticipating my move, he already had his nose jacked high in the air and zoomed high above my canopy in a high rolling reposition, fighting to get behind me.

Not gonna happen.

I matched his maneuver by ratcheting my nose straight up as I fought to stay behind him. I panted as sweat stung my eyes.

Don't stop!

He updated his rolling maneuver to get behind me where he could employ his weapons. I matched his motions turn for turn, fighting to get an advantage. He exited out of the trick.

I had held on to every word he'd said in the classroom. Studied every one of his tapes. He was skilled and focused. I understood why he chose his maneuvers and anticipated what he'd do next. He taught me well and if I wanted to defeat him, I had to hit him with the unexpected. My pulse quickened. I saw my opening.

I aggressively dug toward his jet, pulled my nose onto his spinning aircraft. As my nose approached, I sweetened up my weapons solution and squeezed the trigger. The simulated gun data peppered Locke's jet for a full two seconds as he desperately tried to escape.

"Gambler Four. Gun kill on the second MIG."

A drumming rattled in my chest.

"Gamblers, knock it off!" T-Rex officially ended the engagement. "Gamblers, safe it up, let's return to base."

Hell yeah! I shook my fist in the air. I was the freaking air-to-air queen. This girl just handed two of the best guys their asses. If there were ever any doubts about my earning my spot, today's flight would erase them.

I landed my jet and struggled to play it cool. I had to lose the shit-eating grin and be humble but I couldn't. Not yet. I wish I could have seen the expression on Mr. British hottie's face.

The man. I scoffed. *This American girl owned your ass!*

I struggled to hide my smile as the canopy opened.

The crew chief gave me a thumbs-up as he climbed the ladder.

A small grin gained control of my face.

"I won fifty bucks on you today, ma'am. Guess I should give you a share."

"Keep it Sergeant Wilson. You earned it for betting on the underdog." I shouted over the noise from the other jets taxiing in.

"I don't think anyone would ever refer to you as a dog, ma'am."

He was sweet and he had a knack for the right words at the right moment. I almost hugged him, but remembered Fantom's reaction the last time it happened.

I gave him a quick pat on the arm and climbed down to the ground. After finishing my post-flight paperwork I headed to the van. Stitch and Woodstock were inside waiting. They high-fived me when I got inside.

"You kicked ass out there! Shatter was tough, but Duke, man, he had me running for my life," Stitch whooped.

"He had everyone running for his life. Holy shit, that dude's skilled. I thought he was locked in on me during that furball. When I heard Tink call the MIG kill, I damn near screamed like a girl," Woodstock laughed.

"Maybe you should have, it was a girl that *owned* them!" T-Rex chuckled as he got in the van, "Hot damn, that was the most fun I've had in a long time." He high-fived each of us.

I was trying not to smile, but it was hard not to as I remembered the radio call, "Gambler Four, gun kill on the second MIG."

Locke and Shatter were still finishing up post-flight checks so we went back to the squadron without them. We dropped off our gear and finished our paperwork and I headed to one of the briefing rooms to review the film.

An hour passed and it was time for the group to debrief. Feeling just a bit cocky with the flight, I was excited for the first time in a very long while.

Everyone else was already in the briefing room. A bottle of Jack Daniels sat on the front table. Friday evening festivities were starting early. Stitch let out a whoop when I came in and I tried not to gloat. Locke scrawled something on a notepad. I watched as he picked up his glass and drank from it. Maybe he'd be a good sport, but then again, I didn't care.

Woodstock handed me a Solo cup of whiskey and I topped it off with Diet Coke. Our four-ship cheered as Woodstock shouted, "Here's to handing the MIGs their asses. Especially you, Duke. This American girl kicked your Redcoat ass."

Locke ignored him and kept scribbling. Shatter pushed up his sleeves and crossed his arms over his chest.

"Okay, so the engagement was a standard four-versus-two engagement. Blue game plan was to take max range missile shots then press into a visual engagement only if required and with mutual support," Woodstock said. "Shatter, what was your MIG game plan?"

We continued through the debrief discussing important aspects of the engagement. Locke gave feedback for Stitch and Woodstock, ignoring jabs and snide comments along the way. He sat without acknowledgement that I kicked his ass. Just like everything else lately, I guess we were supposed to act like it hadn't happened.

"Duke, any comments on the Gambler Four kill?"

Here we go. I wonder if I should turn around to make it easier for him to pat me on the back.

"It was dangerous." His tone was cold, his voice blunt.

What? My mouth fell open. He avoided my stare.

"Dude, don't be a sore loser," Woodstock razzed.

Locke pushed his chair back and strolled to the smart board. He quickly drew the diagram for the kill.

He turned back and stared directly in my eyes. "You performed some of the best maneuvers I'd ever seen, but that last move was unnecessary and dangerous. If you hadn't gotten the advantage during your last maneuver, then what?" He paused as if waiting for an answer. I opened my mouth to defend myself, but he continued his rant. "What was your follow up? Or, where was your out if you needed it? Was that risk worth the overall mission?"

"I was ready to accept that risk and make that sacrifice." To win. I crossed my arms.

"Sure, you may be willing to risk your life, but what about Woodstock's? What about Stitch?" He pointed to them. "Were you willing to sacrifice their lives for your gamble?"

I narrowed my eyes, but he didn't back down.

"You had two other aircrafts in your flight that were ready to engage, but you were out there trying to win the war all by yourself. It's not about you."

I felt my cheeks warm and I wanted to look away, but his eyes commanded my attention as he leaned forward and pounded his finger into table. "We push the envelope to accomplish the mission, but if you fail, then there will be thirty warriors out there risking their lives trying to save you," he said sharply. "Risk and sacrifice aren't just free words we throw around. When it is time to cash in those chips it better be for a good reason…and that last move of yours wasn't one." His voice trailed as the briefing room fell silent.

Way to piss on my parade. T-Rex interrupted the awkwardness.

"I think that is a pretty fitting point to end on. If there aren't further questions then it's time to sacrifice our livers and get to our roll call," he said as he clapped his hands together.

I glanced at Locke as he gathered his notepads. The back of his neck was flushed. My throat felt full of cotton as I tried to swallow. I hated the truth that surrounded his words.

"Are you coming?" Stitch asked.

Locke's jaw set hard as he shoved his pen into the pocket on his sleeve and walked out of the room.

My shoulders slumped. Damn it. Everything he said was spot on. I was so focused on winning that I had forgotten that this wasn't a game.

"You're getting named Tink, you don't want to be late and give them any more ammunition." Stitch reached out and patted me on the arm.

My stomach fluttered in nervous anticipation. This was huge. It was almost more important than choosing your mate. "I'm sure they're full of ammunition," I said shoving back my chair. "Please don't let them name me Tits or Fairy or...." I smacked my head, "Maverick."

He wrapped his arm around my shoulder. "The call sign chooses you."

"No, a bunch of drunk guys choose it."

He chuckled.

"Promise," I pleaded and smacked him in the chest.

"I promise I'll come up with something good to throw out there if they want to name you Tits…because that would just be awkward." He opened the door and I ducked under his arm.

It was standing room only in the squadron bar. Woodstock had on a Las Vegas dealer's outfit and was wielding a giant craps stick for retrieving dice. We were in trouble if Woodstock was leading this charge.

Stitch lifted his chin toward him and shouted over the noise. "He's the overseer and mayor for the event."

I nodded as I bit my thumbnail.

"This roll call of Gamblers shall now come to order!" Woodstock yelled at the top of his lungs.

He covered a long litany of rules then pointed the craps stick around the room as he continued speaking, "If any of the rules are broken, you will be punished by taking a 'shot.'"

He paced around the room twirling the stick then tucked it under this arm.

"Shatter," he shouted then paused.

"Here." Shatter barked.

"T-Rex."

"Yep," he said and raised his stein.

"Duke." My eyes darted in the same direction as Woodstock's. Locke was leaning against the back wall with his arms folded. He lips were drawn in a thin line and he gave a quick flick of his chin. I bit the inside of my cheek.

"Fantom, Crash..." Woodstock continued shouting out the call signs, taking roll. Cheers went out for those present and boo's and f-bombs for those who were missing. At the end of the "formalities" Woodstock cleared his throat.

"In combat, under stress, it may be difficult to remember the name assigned to your flight or other flights in your strike package," he explained. "In these stressful situations it may be easier for pilots to remember the names of their comrades, but we all know we cannot compromise security by calling out our real names over the radio," Woodstock paused for a moment then finished in a dramatic tone. "In this practice the *call sign* was born." He emphasized the word 'call sign' with air quotes.

Whoops and cheers interrupted him. The excited anticipation filled the room.

"Fighter pilots could now call out to their comrades in life or death instances, and without fear of compromising their true names," Woodstock said. "There is no quibbling, arguing, or changing your call sign. If you execute an act of buffoonery, the squadron may decide to rename you." He raised his finger. "However, once you have flown with a call sign in combat, it is your call sign forever." Woodstock wafted his hands. "Without further ado, the Fucking New Guys."

The crowd called out, "Fucking New Guys!"

He then lowered his hands to quiet the room and finished. "FNG's, clear out of the room—we will call you back in when we're ready!"

I walked out of the bar with the two other guys who were being renamed and waited by the operations desk. In the squadron bar the muffled razzing passed back and forth as the instructor pilots discussed our new names, followed by loud cheers, thunderous boo's, and roaring applause. One by one they called us in. I was the final naming.

I walked into a room not sure of what to expect. Sitting in the chair I searched for some reassurance that my name would be cool. Or, at least, tolerable.

Woodstock reached over me and handed me a large bullet casing filled with God knows what. I cringed waiting for my story.

"I have to say that we went round and round on yours. You were not easy. So to speak."

Everyone in room cheered at the reference to my sex life. Except for Locke. He leaned against the wall holding a beer. His grim expression never changed.

"We took pride in naming our first comrade with tits."

Shit.

"Good news travels fast and bad news travels even faster in these parts. So when one of our brazen warrior leaders was defeated by our resident fairy, the news spread like wildfire." Woodstock swiped his hand in front of him. "She made her warrior brothers proud, and we decided that her name should reflect this story as it is written in history."

Cheers erupted as I tried not to choke on my heart.

Woodstock quieted the room.

"Lieutenant Pinkerton, you kicked a royal MIG's ass!"

I could barely hear or comprehend was he was saying. Kicked a royal MIG's ass. They were referring to the flight today and Locke. He was the royal MIG. My mind swirled. But how in the hell did that translate into a call sign? I tried to piece together the first letters of the words. Kicked. A. Royal. MIG's. Ass.

"From this day forward, and for all eternity, you shall be known as KARMA."

Chapter 18

I needed a beer to wash down the frigging irony. I walked behind the bar, grabbed a bottle from the fridge and opened it as I glanced back at Locke. His hair was a little longer than usual and lighter. His helmet had twisted it into a natural wave and my fingers burned to run through it.

His head remained locked straight ahead and his eyes didn't pass my way. The expression on his face was emotionless, completely unable to read. I couldn't help but wonder if he still craved me the way I craved him.

Locke still consumed my thoughts and my body reacted so strongly, even when he was a bit of an ass during the debrief. There was something about the flight, the thrill of the chase and the competition that rocketed my desire. Damn, I wanted him badly.

Stitch hugged me and I gasped. "Do you like it?" he asked squeezing me tightly.

I blinked at him and muttered, "What?"

"Karma. Do you like your call sign?" he asked.

"Yeah, it's cool," I answered.

"We had the most fun choosing your name. Duke took some serious shit-talking," Stitch said with a grin on his face. I couldn't help but smile too. "I'm glad I was part of it."

His smiled softened into a sappy grin. The effects of the Jack were kicking in.

I wrapped my arm around his waist and rested my head on his chest. "Me too, Stitch."

I knew he felt obliged to step in for my brother. Though no one would ever be able to replace Colin, Stitch was the next best thing. Colin would have approved.

I told my mom I would text her and let her know my call sign. I reached in my pocket for my phone. Of course it wasn't there. Damn. I must have left it in the squadron.

"I'll be right back, Stitch. I told my mom I'd call. She'll be sitting by her phone," I said.

"Tell Miss Lilly I said hi."

Colin's friends all loved my mom. They even stayed in touch after his death. It meant a lot to her. I shut them out to avoid the pain though having Stitch around had been comforting.

I nodded to him, gave him a quick wave and headed for the squadron. It was dark, but the emergency lights gave off a soft glow. I grabbed my phone from my bag.

Good Luck. I can't wait to hear what it is.

I knew it.

Karma. I typed.

She didn't even give me enough time to grab another water.

Cool. Are you having fun?

I sighed. That was a loaded question and any answer would open a can of worms. The last thing I needed was more questions.

Call you tomorrow.
Keep your circle positive, Karma ☺

I held back an eye roll. Standard mom.

I snuck another bottle of water out and shouldered my bag. Locke stood in the doorway as I turned. I shrieked, grunted, and grabbed for my chest. I must have looked like a kid who found a spider under the covers. At least my heart hadn't pounded out through my rib cage.

"Holy hell," I said. "You scared me!"

He didn't speak. His expression as always was indecipherable.

"I needed to get a drink, something unfermented." I shook the bottle, but my nerves were setting in. He stayed quiet. I offered him the water. "Want it?"

Locke reached out for it. I missed the warmth in his eyes, the tenderness, and the way he made me feel protected when he watched me. It was gone. He pushed up his sleeves on his flight suit. His forearms were perfect. His body was perfect. Everything about him was perfect. Even the way he walked away and avoided my gaze as he leaned on the desk.

Why wasn't he saying anything?

Locke rubbed his face with his hand. He seemed uncomfortable and I didn't know what to bring up first because there was too much that we needed to discuss.

Thankfully, he took the lead.

"I can't figure out where in the bloody hell to begin," he said with a sigh.

My heart banged against my ribcage. I wanted to find a way to shield it from the pain of whatever he said next.

"It's like watching a jet tailspinning out of control and not having a goddamn clue how to stop it."

I remained quiet, chewing on my lip. I was defensive, but I wasn't stupid enough to argue. I knew my life was screwed up. But that was for me to say. Not him. Except that he was deep in the middle of all of it. If we were ever going to fix anything, we were going to have to chip away at the problems one by one.

I nodded. "I know I took a risk today."

He ran his hands through his hair.

"This isn't just about today and it's not just about you, it's also about me. It's about everything. All of it."

This was going to take a while.

Bright lights blinded me and I blinked trying to adapt to the sharpness.

"What the hell are you guys sitting in the dark for?" Locke's future douchebag-in-law, Clash asked in his normal asshole tone. "Are there any sodas in there?"

Locke didn't answer. I licked my lips.

"No sir, there's only water."

He cursed but took the water anyway, guzzling half the contents and wiping his mouth on his arm. He shrugged.

"So what are you guys talking about? The headache and paperwork Locke created for all of us a few weeks ago?"

Clash was clearly irritated at Locke. I wanted to tell him where to go and how quickly to get there, but resisted.

"No sir, we were talking about the naming ceremony," I said. Drop an extra token in the lie bucket.

"It must be in your blood to be a superstar," Clash said and from the look on his face, he wasn't meaning it as a compliment.

"Sir?"

"Your brother was a showman too. He loved pushing the limits also." He lifted his right hand and punched his fist toward the ceiling. "Thor."

Hatred bubbled inside my belly as I glared at Clash. The way that he had said Colin's call sign had made me want to wipe the arrogant smirk off his face.

"Knock it off," Locke said as he pushed off the desk.

"It was dangerous. You even said so." Clash turned to me before Locke could answer. "Did you hear from your boyfriend?"

"My boyfriend?" I choked out.

What the hell was he talking about?

"That Special Forces guy," Clash answered. "I saw you sending him off a few weeks ago."

"He's a friend, not my boyfriend."

I swallowed and tried to nonchalantly glance at Locke. His expression had returned to stone. So much for mending things.

"I saw you hug him," Clash continued. "I just assumed."

I gritted my teeth at his assumption.

"Has he said anything about what's going on over there?"

Ash e-mailed me when he first got to Tunis. He let me know he arrived and thanked me for coming to see him off, but I wasn't about to share that with Clash. Or with Locke.

Fortunately the door opened again.

Unfortunately, it was Kassie.

"Lucky me," she exclaimed in her fake voice. "I found my two favorite guys in the same room."

Kassie looked like a rock star and was scented with expensive perfume. I looked like a green bean and smelled like a sweaty sock.

I threw in the towel and walked from the room. This was a losing battle.

Chapter 19

I couldn't shake Locke from my mind. I hoped he would stop by after I got home so we could continue our talk.

He didn't.

Why couldn't I turn off my feelings when it came to him? I thought I could keep my emotions separate but I couldn't.

I woke up early and went for a jog to clear my mind. Clash screwed with me when he mentioned my brother. And his bringing up Ash only stirred up more problems. Locke and I might have worked through some things if he hadn't interrupted.

Five miles later and still pissed off, I glanced at Locke's house hoping he would come outside. I could go knock on his door. But the image of him shutting it back in my face put that idea to rest.

I picked up my phone and texted my mom.

What's the number for girl that does your hair and nails?

I poured a glass of sweet tea and reached for an apple.

Less than a minute later, my phone buzzed with a text from Mom,

She said if you come now she can squeeze you in. Booked hair, mani and pedi.

Of course she called her already.

I continued reading,

You'll love her. Already paid, tip included. Enjoy.

I smiled softly knowing she couldn't help herself.

Thanks mom. Wish you were here.

I actually meant it. Today, more than ever, I really needed a girl friend.

Everything okay? Want me to book a flight?

I knew she would hop on the next available flight if I typed 'yes' and I seriously considered it for a split second.

No, I'm good. Thought I would try a 'me' day. I typed.

You need to do that more often. Coming for a visit soon and we will do an 'us' day.

I wondered if that meant Dad was coming back. The last visit ended okay, but I wasn't sure I was prepared for another so soon.

Can't wait. Congrats on your call sign. Love you baby girl. Keep your circle positive.

I could use a little more positive.

* * * *

Kiss of Karma.

Of course.

I jogged up the stairs toward the colorful sign by the door.

The spa was an old refurbished house in an eclectic part of town. It was mom's favorite place to buy flowers and candles. She was a flower child at heart but being in the public eye with Dad convinced her to tone it back over the years

A girl with long platinum blond hair and a single streak of pink in the front greeted me from the front desk. She wore a tiny delicate daisy headband across her crown, and I fought the urge to greet her with a peace sign.

"You must be Tinklee," she said in a friendly voice.

I nodded.

"Cool beans, I'm Lyric." She struck a match and lit a stick of incense on her desk. "You look seriously scared."

Lyric had green eyes and was just a little taller than me. Same size, same light sprinkle of freckles. It was a little freaky. She looked like my alter ego.

"I don't really do this kind of stuff," I said.

"What kind of stuff? Dude, this is just an incense, not weed."

I smirked—could Lyric be a female version of Bodhi?

"I mean pampering stuff."

"You're kidding," she said as if she were appalled. "You're Lilly's baby. She didn't teach you how to relax?"

"We are very different."

"You look like her, too."

"Actually you look like her." I liked her.

She picked up a teapot. "Want some chai?"

"And act like her. Maybe we were somehow switched at birth."

Lyric laughed. "That's sweet. I love Lilly."

She handed me the tea. The scent was odd and I tried not to make a face as I looped a finger through the tiny porcelain handle. The cup shifted, and the tea rocked over the lip of the Victorian pattern. I clutched at the base with a grimace.

"Relax," she said. "I won't color your hair pink, even though your mom suggested it."

"Seriously?"

"Yep. Dude, your mom's a hoot."

I sipped from the cup, unsure of what to do with my pinky.

Lyric lifted an eyebrow. She took my cup and poured the tea into the large ceramic mug then handed it back to me.

"Thanks."

She winked and waved for me to follow.

"Am I the only one here?" I asked.

"For a little while. We don't open until noon today. Some of the girls went to a Bikram workshop this morning," she said.

"That sounds awful."

She smiled. "Not the yoga type?"

"Not really, bending like a pretzel in a sauna sounds like torture," I replied and plopped down in the pedicure chair. She turned on the water, poured in a purple liquid, then dropped lavender and rose petals in the water. The air filled with the sweet fragrance.

"It's fun," she said. "You should go with me sometime. I'll show you a couple tricks. It'd help you unwind a bit."

She sounded like she genuinely believed yoga was fun. And the offer was sincere. None of the guys would ever dare try yoga, but Lyric seemed nice enough to risk crunching all of my vertebrae in some half-moon, doggy-style, inverted backbend.

"Sure, why not? I need a change," I said.

She filled a bowl with the same mixture and placed my hand in it.

"Why do you say that?"

The massage chair revved to life. I settled in as she awaited my answer.

"I just do."

"Okay treat this like Vegas. Whatever you say here, stays here. Promise." She lifted her fingers into a Girl Scout promise and I laughed.

"Careful, once I start spilling, I may never quit," I warned.

"Duly noted," she said.

I picked up my chai and took a sip. Then I filled her in. Her eyes widened as I described meeting Locke and Ash, and she squealed with all the gritty details in between. When I'd finished, I was shocked that I'd reveal so much to someone I had just met.

"So there you have it," I said as I wiggled my feet in the water. "I am all sorts of messed up."

"Are you kidding me? You are my freaking hero! I'd be psyched to have your problems!"

"Really?"

"Seriously, most girls would die to be in your shoes. You have *two* guys tripping over themselves to get with you?"

I shrugged still not convinced that there was anything good about my current situation. Lyric's shoulders dropped and she tipped her head to the side. "Dude, you are twenty-two, not married, and you are in a sea of hot men in uniform. You got it bad for one guy, care about another, and you're just dodging all the crazy in between," she said trying to convince me.

I stared down at my toes. They were pink with a perfect little daisy on my big toe. I had officially stepped out of my comfort zone.

"Everything happens for a reason," Lyric continued. "You were destined to meet both of these guys at this time in your life. You may not see it now, but someday, you'll look back and understand."

She stood up and grabbed a brush from the counter. "Let's start your hair."

I was feeling a little better. Maybe there was something to this spa thing.

"What about you? Do you have a boyfriend?" I asked.

Lyric shrugged. "Nah, nothing serious. I was dating a guy a few months back but he turned out to be a jerk." She adjusted the seat and I sat down. "So no pink?"

I shook my head. Hell no.

She spritzed some water into my hair and ran her fingers through the knots. "You need to cut yourself some slack. Everything will work out the way it should."

"I wish I had your confidence," I said.

"If you want good things to happen, you have to believe they will."

Lyric handed me a towel.

"Not sure what I believe anymore," I said.

"Believe me, everything happens for a reason. You decided today that you were finally going to do something with those atrocious cuticles." I chuckled as she continued, "And it just so happened I was here when your mom called. You came in and bam!"

She flicked the waterspout and water sprayed everywhere. I shrieked as she continued. "Instant besties. That's how fate works."

The brush worked through my hair while I considered her words.

"Your face squished," Lyric said. "Spill it."

"What about Karma?" I asked.

"What about it?"

She offered me a steamy towel, and after I held it in my hands for a long moment, she leaned me back and placed it over my face.

"What do you think about it?" My voice was muffled through the towel.

"Well, the concept is easy. What goes around, comes around, whether it be good or bad. Do you believe it?"

"I'm not sure," I said. "I keep seeing references everywhere. I feel like my life has been spinning out of control since my brother's accident. The jet, my dad, Locke, Ash…" I said with a sigh. "I have bad Karma."

"I'm really sorry about your brother. I remember talking to your mom when that happened." She rubbed my arm. "But as far as Karma goes, you are being way too analytical. Your brother? The jet? That's just what life does to you, sucky as it is." I squeezed my eyes tighter, glad my pained expression was hidden under the towel. "Karma is how you choose to deal with life, and the energy you put back into the world. If you really want to break it down, Karma is how your actions in this life will affect your next life."

It made sense, sort of.

"So, in this life, you're good." She paused. "It's your next life that's going to suck."

I sat up from the sink and pulled the towel from my face. Lyric had a huge smile and I hit her with the towel. She roared in laughter.

A tall, thin girl with black spiky hair peeked around the corner.

"Your next one's here," she said. "Kassie something."

"Callahan?" Lyric asked.

"That's it," the woman replied.

"Shit," I hissed.

"What's wrong? Do you know her?" Lyric questioned.

"More Karma. *Bad* Karma."

"Tell her I'll be right there, Kimmie," Lyric said. "What are you talking about?"

"Kassie is Locke's cousin. The one I told you about."

"Eek. Should I shave her head?"

I seriously considered my answer.

"No," I answered. "Do you have a back exit?"

"Don't you want me to fix your hair? I wanted to try curling it."

"No, thanks. I need to get out of here," I said.

The last person I wanted to encounter on my "me" day was Kassie.

"Her being here isn't Karma. At least not for you. It may be bad Karma for her. She messed with my new BFF and I'm about to cut her hair."

She faked an evil mad scientist laugh.

I smirked. "Thanks for the help."

Lyric hugged me, "This was fun and I was kidding before. Hell, Tink. You're a good person. I can see that. You'll be fine in any life. Let's grab dinner one night next week. Give me your number."

We exchanged info and I thanked her again.

"Don't worry. I'm like a priest, I won't repeat a thing. Except from her, I'll tell you everything."

I opened up the back door and slipped around the front. When I got to my Jeep, I realized we weren't being very sly. Kassie's Mercedes parked next to me. She had to know I was there and probably realized I went out of my way to avoid her. Figures.

I swung by the bookstore and a few other stores in the area. I bought a candle that smelled yummy, and some of the lotion and body wash I loved. I smelled it when I got back in the Jeep and it reminded me of my steamy shower with Locke. I was certain this scent would always take me back to that memory. I closed my eyes and remembered the way his hands felt as they glided along my skin. My heart ached as I realized that might have been our last time together.

Lyric's words rang in my ears—*It is what life does to you.*

Chapter 20

Lyric texted me later. I was right—Kassie saw me there. Her "client" asked about the Jeep, but she had played dumb. Lyric told me not to worry and promised to take me on a girl's night out later in the week. I was actually looking forward to it.

It was a rainy day and I planned on snuggling on the couch to catch up on reading, studying and movies. I even brewed myself a cup of herbal tea.

My painted fingernails surprised me every time they caught my eye. I wasn't used to such a pinky shade. Or any pink, for that matter. But I didn't *hate* it. I decided to head out and buy a pink shirt this week.

My e-mail *dinged.* I grabbed my tablet and opened the app to see a message from Ash.

Hey Tink,

I might be going dark for a few weeks. Things are heating up. I wouldn't be surprised if they asked for more birds to come over. I know in my last e-mail I thanked you for sending me off, but I wanted to tell you how much the night before I left meant as well. It may not have ended in the best way but everything else was pretty much perfect. Sorry for the sap. I just wanted to be certain you knew.

Ash

It sounded like a "just in case I don't see you again" letter.

He was going dark. Translation, he was going on a mission. Of course he was, that was why he was there. But the thought of the danger scared me and the thought of never seeing him again scared me more. I tapped on the attachment.

His face was darker in just the few weeks of being there and his beard had grown in. He looked strong and fierce though he was smiling. I enlarged the image and stared into his eyes. I sighed and copied the image to my photos.

I picked up Colin's Air-to-Air training binder from when he was a student and flipped through some pages. Tucked between the pages were some of Colin's old notes. I traced my fingers along his familiar handwriting. It still resembled his script from when he was twelve years old and we would make handmade cards for our parents.

"Dad. There is something wrong with the jet," Colin said.

I pressed my ear against the door of Dad's study.

Dad sighed. "It's been checked. Many times."

"It's dangerous."

Dad was irritated. His voice was stern and commanding. "All the jets are dangerous. That's why you're trained to fly them."

"There's something wrong with the environmental system."

"Damn it, Colin. I am sick of this," he yelled. "I have wasted more money and interviewed countless people over this. It has passed every single inspection. There is nothing wrong with the system."

"You're not flying it," Colin responded with a louder voice. "I am. And when one of the pilots says something is wrong, don't you think you should listen?"

"Not when the pilot wants the jet to fail so he can go back to the old jet."

"That's bullshit and you know it."

"You have been given every courtesy because of the name Pinkerton. Enough is enough," Dad said with a pause. "Your job now is to shut up and support the mission. That's it."

"What's it going to take? Does someone have to die before you'll listen?"

No. Not even then.

Chapter 21

My phone beeped alerting me to a missed call. It was Mojo. Why was he calling at…I blinked…0400 on a Monday morning? Panic and fear flushed through me. I hope there wasn't an accident. The phone buzzed in my hand. It was Mojo again.

"Everything okay?" I answered. I held my breath and waited.

"Recall. Bring your deployment bag."

My stomach dropped. "Is it an exercise?"

"I don't know. They started the phone chain and all they said was bring your deployment bag."

"Okay. See you there."

* * * *

The weight of my bag and the stress of the unknown felt heavy on my shoulders. I tossed my duffle in my backseat, thankful to be able to dump at least a portion of the burden. Locke's bike was parked by the squadron entrance when I arrived. I'm sure he grabbed his bag and left, unlike me. I showered and stopped for coffee. He was perfect, as usual.

I sipped my Americano. Locke was a rules guy, I wasn't.

Freak walked up and reached into the back seat of my Jeep. He lifted out my bag.

"Thanks," I said.

"Sure," he replied. "Any word if this is an exercise or for real?"

I shrugged.

Headlights pulled in beside my Jeep.

Mercedes headlights.

Kassie hurried out of the passenger seat and ran over to the driver side. She wore pajamas. Teeny tiny pajamas.

"Can you send Locke out? I want to talk to him," she said to Clash as he stepped out of the car.

"We are going straight to brief," Clash answered sounding annoyed. "If we leave today, I'll call you and you can meet us at the hangar."

His words, 'if we leave today' caused my breath to catch in the back of my throat. Maybe this was the real deal, not just a training exercise.

Clash bent down and kissed her and she handed him a mug out the window. The back hatch popped open.

"Freak, grab my bag," Clash ordered as he snapped his fingers. "I don't want to spill my coffee."

Douchebag.

I took my bag from Freak so he could grab Clash's deployment bag. The trunk slammed and we walked into the squadron.

Bags were lined against the wall and everything and everyone was buzzing. It looked like an exercise, but felt like something more.

Stitch rounded the corner and pulled me aside.

"My dad called me this morning. It looks like we are shipping out today. You might want to call your mom in case she wants to hop a flight and say goodbye."

My eyes widened. "Seriously?" My voice pitched higher, uncertain if it was even what I wanted.

He nodded.

My throat felt like I'd swallowed a handful of sand.

I reached in my pocket for my phone. It buzzed in my hand.

My flight gets in at noon.

Good news travels fast. Bad news travels even faster.

I held up the phone to Stitch.

"She's on her way."

He smiled."Mine too." Then hooked his arm around my neck and whispered in my hair, "You'll be glad once she's here."

A twang of guilt hit me for possibly thinking otherwise.

Shatter clapped his hands.

"Let's go. Briefing room two."

* * * *

"We're deploying to Tunis," Shatter said.

The room shifted. Most of us knew it was coming. We just didn't know it'd be so quick.

"Our intelligence states they are nearing completion in producing several weapons of mass destruction. Their intent is to distribute those weapons to terrorist networks for attacks against the United States." He twisted the ring on his finger.

"To complicate matters, the Liberated Republic of Algeria has been provided with incredibly sophisticated surface to air missiles to protect its airspace. We're talking SA10's, SA20's, and the new S300's."

I wrung my hands together as he continued. "We are to strike the production facilities before the weapons are completed and distributed. The mission is too high risk for conventional fights. That's why we need every fifth generation fighter available. Every F-35 and F-22 is essential for success, even those flown by students."

I curled the end of my ponytail around my fingers. He smacked his hands together and I jumped. I felt my ears warm.

"Once your paperwork is in order and you've been cleared by the docs, get out of here and get your personal things in order. We are shipping out at 1800. Duke...." I bit the inside my lip. "Woodstock, Freak, Stitch, Fantom, Karma...." I bit harder this time a sweet metallic taste filled my mouth. "T-Rex, and Mojo. Fall back."

Shatter motioned for us to come up front.

"You're flying the first wave of jets across the pond. The rest will fly out tomorrow. Go home and get some rest. Be back by 1500 to get cleared."

"Sir, how long are we going for?" Mojo asked.

"Six months for now. But in reality, we are the only active F-35 squadron. We'll stay as long as they need us."

That was fine for those of us who didn't have families, but the pilots also known as dad couldn't hide their anguish.

Shatter dismissed us. "Go get some rest, if you can."

* * * *

The hum of a motorbike followed me into my driveway. Locke pulled in beside me.

"Do you need help getting anything ready?" Locke asked.

I shook my head. "My mom's flying in. She'll take care of it. How about you?"

"Kassie has a key."

I resisted an eye roll. He smiled.

"How are you feeling about deploying?"

I shrugged. "This is what we train for."

"No amount of training prepares you for the real deal."

He was speaking from experience. I remembered when Colin came back from the war. He was different. Something had changed and a little of that special spark had faded from his eyes. The harshness of the world had made him a little more jaded. I was already past jaded. What would I be like when I returned? If I returned?

I bit the inside of my cheek and looked down at my boots.

Locke reached over and took my hand. His touch sent my heart into a barrel roll. I'd missed his touch.

He rubbed his thumb along the shiny pink polish.

"I'm trying something new."

With everything that was going on, he noticed this tiny change.

"It's nice."

He let go of my hand and started his bike.

"Get some rest," he said. "It's going to be a long flight."

I felt like I should talk to him and finish our conversation from that night in the squadron. Just in case one of us didn't make it back home. Instead I nodded and turned as he drove away.

I climbed the stairs and walked to my room. Morning rays of light shined through the windows. I pulled the shades and collapsed on my bed. This morning was surreal. I would put on a brave face, but it wouldn't erase the anxiety that was building inside. It was happening.

Today, I was going to war.

Chapter 22

"Wake up baby girl."

The scent of vanilla and my mother's soft voice woke me.

I yawned then blinked my eyes trying to focus on my mom's long blond waves.

"What time is it?"

"A little after 1:30. Your phone alarm was going off, but it didn't wake you. I thought I should try."

She rubbed my arm and her silver bangles jingled like a tiny bell.

"Thanks."

"I heard from Lyric. It sounded like you two really hit it off."

I sat up and shook my hair.

"She's cool."

"I think...." Mom sniffled and pulled a handkerchief from the pocket of her long cotton skirt. "I think she'll be a nice friend."

She dabbed her eyes. Not now. Please.

"Mom, I'll be fine," I said.

"You will be, if you want to be." Her voice sounded as if she were pleading and deep set wrinkles formed between her brows.

I frowned. "What is that supposed to mean?"

"I know you are a capable pilot, but I worry about you, Tinklee," she said as her lips drew into a thin line. "You're driven and strong. You were always passionate with everything in your life. But you hardened when Colin died. It was like your spirit turned to stone."

I climbed out of bed. I didn't need this now.

"You harbor anger and guilt over his accident," she paused and I chewed on the inside of my lip wanting her to stop speaking. "You've let it consume you and change you as a person. You closed yourself off to fully living, fully loving. You let people in, but only so far before you drive them away."

"Wow," was the only that came out of my mouth. I grabbed my flight suit. This was not what I wanted to hear before leaving for frigging war. "This is unbelievable."

"I'm not trying to hurt you. I am trying to save you. I've prayed endless hours that you'd find something to live for again." Tears rolled down her cheeks.

"Oh my God. This is ridiculous," I said and spun to face her, my voice rising as the words spilled out. "You hid in your room and cried for *months.* Then you plastered a smile on your face and rejoined society sprinkling your fairy dust. Your son is *dead.* You should never smile again."

She winced as she looked down, smoothing a wrinkle from her skirt. I looked away instantly regretting my outburst. She didn't deserve it.

"I was grieving, but I slowly healed over time," she explained her voice jagged and filled with anguish. "The pain doesn't go away, it lessens so that you can cope. Moving forward isn't betraying your brother. He wouldn't want this for you."

"We'll never know what he wanted, will we? He'll never be able to tell us. We'll never be able to hear him, ever again. Because he's dead!" I shouted as my voice cracked. "He's dead mom. I watched him die. I heard my brother take his last breath right before he burned." My entire body shook.

My mom took a step toward me. I raised my trembling hand to stop her from getting any closer. "How, mom?" I choked back a tearless sob. "How do I move on from that?"

I collapsed at my desk and buried my face in my hands.

The scent of vanilla swirled around me as she kneeled down in front of me. Her hand rested gently on my knees. My throat burned.

"He loved you." Her voice was gentle yet firm.

They were the three words that hurt the most.

"He would want you to be whole again," she said softly.

I lifted my head and bit my lip to keep it from trembling. I shook my head slowly. "I don't know how."

Mom gently touched my cheek and pulled me into her arms. She whispered into my ear. "That's because you've buried the part of you that allows you to feel, to hurt." She squeezed me tighter. "And you fight against loving because sometimes it hurts to love."

My mother leaned back and smoothed my hair. Then she lifted my chin until her wet eyes met mine.

"The will to live comes from having something to live for." She moved her hand until it was resting on my cheek and a sad smile crept upon her face. "I am sending my baby off to war." Her breath hitched as more tears trickled down her face. "I desperately need her to have the will to survive."

* * * *

Nothing like a good psychological analysis and emotional breakdown before you're shipping off to war. I wanted to climb back in bed, but I had to get moving. I needed to get to the base and get my clearance before take-off.

After lunch and a "not-so-crazy" talk with my mom, she gave me a ride to base. She dropped me off and said she would meet me in the hangar. My dad was coming in and she needed to pick him up at the airport. Just what I needed.

I walked into the main squadron offices. Bodhi waved me over to his table. He slid me three pill bottles. One had a red sticker on it and the other green. The other was plain.

"This is simple. If you want to fly, take the "Go" pills that are marked green. If you need to sleep, take the "No Go" pills that are marked red. And these are the anti-malaria pills. All the instructions are on the bottles."

He seemed tired as he glanced down at a sheet of paper.

"All her immunizations are current except anthrax. Sorry dude, this one is gonna leave a mark."

I unzipped my flight suit and pulled out my arm. Bodhi's airman assistant rolled up the sleeve to my T-shirt and wiped off the area. I closed my eyes and he stuck me. The cool liquid spread inside my arm.

"Is that it?" I asked with a grin. "It didn't hurt at all."

Bodhi ignored me while the airman placed a Band-Aid over the area. I put my arm back in my flight suit and zipped it. He lifted his fingers to count to three, and then pointed at me.

I grabbed my arm and hissed. It felt like someone hit me with a blowtorch.

"Holy shit," I said bending forward and pushed a breath out.

Bodhi chuckled. "Same reaction all day. It's gonna be sore tomorrow."

Mojo sat down and laughed. "Don't be such a girl."

"I am a girl. I have tits in case you haven't noticed," I said.

He wagged his eyebrows. "Oh, I noticed."

I smacked him in the chest with the arm that didn't feel like it was on fire.

"Let's see, he needs small pox, tetanus, and anthrax," Bodhi said to the airman.

Mojo frowned.

"Good luck with that," I responded with a wink.

I walked to the operational desk to grab the flight plan. The departure was so sudden that we didn't have time for a traditional brief. We were making two stops. The first was on a small island in the Atlantic, the second Germany, and then we would finish the last leg to Africa. I made my way to Life Support. We were leaving in less than an hour.

Stitch and Freak were finishing up placing their gear when I walked in.

"Did you get some rest?" Stitch asked as I grabbed my gear from the hook.

I nodded. "Did your mom make it?

"Yes, but she is driving me nuts. She won't stop crying."

"What about you, Freak? Was anyone able to make it here on such short notice?" I asked.

"No, they're all on the West Coast. It would have been too expensive for just a few hours. We video chatted instead."

He shrugged.

"How about I give you my mom?" I said and laughed, but I sort of meant it. I didn't want to go through the crying thing again.

"You can have mine, too." Stitch joked. "We ready?"

I swallowed hard.

"Let's do this."

* * * *

The sun was setting and it shadowed the hangar, matching the mood. There was a much bigger turnout than I expected.

I spotted my mom's hair and signature long skirt and flowing blouse. Lyric was next to her, looking like mother and daughter. I didn't know she was coming, but I was glad to see her.

Her eyes widened when she saw me.

"What's wrong?"

"You look totally badass. You've elevated my pride for women to an all new level," she replied.

"I'm glad you're here," I said.

"Your mom asked me, and I wasn't sure if you only wanted family."

"Actually, I would have preferred to only have you," I said.

She frowned. "Don't say that. Your momma loves you."

"I know," I said and blew out a sigh. "We had a rough day."

"She's sending her baby to war. That messes with your internal balance."

My mom strolled over and hugged me.

"Let me get a picture of you two." My mom held up her phone, while Lyric and I posed.

"You next," Lyric said and reached out for my mom's phone.

"Where's your dad? Max, come over here."

She waved her arms. He was with Locke and they were both headed straight for us.

"Happy Buddha. Who's *that*?" Lyric asked.

My body awakened as it always did when he was around. I tried not to meet his gaze. "Locke."

"Dude, I'm not above sloppy seconds," she whispered.

"There's nothing sloppy about Locke," I said.

"And who is this good-looking young man?" My mother asked.

"This is one of my instructors, Flight Lieutenant Sinclair." I looked down. "This is my mom and my friend Lyric."

"It's a pleasure to meet you," he said shaking their hands.

"Oh my. Your accent. Please, keep talking," my mom said and giggled.

Oh my God, I wanted to zip my flight suit over my head.

"Tinklee, I don't know how you can concentrate with him as an instructor."

"Can we just take the pictures and get them over with?" I asked wishing there was a way to disappear at Mach speed.

My mom grimaced. Everyone else looked at me like I had kicked a puppy.

"Let's get you and your parents first," Lyric said recovering for me. "Tink in the middle. Squeeze in there, Papa Pinkerton."

She took several different pictures and angles.

"Let me get one of you and your instructor," she said waving her hand at Locke.

I was going to kill her. If I said no everyone would give me sulking faces again. Locke hesitated waiting for my approval. I gave a quick nod and he moved closer.

"Squeeze in," Lyric ordered in a sing-song voice and gestured, pushing her hands together.

She was enjoying this. A little too much.

Locke rested his hand in the small of my back. My body stiffened to his touch. He rubbed his thumb up and down slightly. The intimacy ignited a fire inside of me. My face flushed. A tiny smile crept upon Lyrics face.

"How did you end up with the U.S. Air Force?" My mom asked.

Was it time to go to war yet?

"I have your husband to thank for that ma'am," Locke said.

"Nice work, Max," she said and patted my dad on the shoulder then turned back to Locke. "I guess your family wasn't able to make it today."

"My cousin Kassie is here, but no ma'am my parents are in England. They're going to meet me at our stopover in Germany," he said.

"You remember Kassie. She was one of my interns last summer," Dad said.

"Oh, yes. What a small world. She's a sweet girl."

Sweet my ass. I looked at Lyric. She rolled her eyes.

Bodhi walked up and smacked Locke playfully on the shoulder. He smirked at me.

"Dude, how's the arm?" he asked as his gaze quickly shifted to Lyric.

"It hurts like hell, thanks for asking," I said.

Lyric looked similarly interested. I should have known.

"Dude, you've been holding out," he said. "I'm Bodhi."

"Lyric," she answered smiling.

He reached out his fist. "Cool name."

She bumped it and they blew it up. There couldn't be two people more perfectly matched. I glanced up at Locke and we shared a smile.

"Looks like they're rounding everyone up." Locke dipped his head toward the center of the hangar.

It was time.

A hand grabbed my elbow.

"I need a second with you," Dad said.

Every muscle in my face tightened.

The others migrated away. I waited with Dad. He rubbed his face.

"I know things are complicated with us and you blame me for Colin's accident," he said.

Here we go. My parents sucked at send-offs.

"I hope somehow, some day, when you're ready, you'll hear what I have to say," he finished.

His eyes turned misty, and I wasn't sure how to react so I looked down at my boots. I did blame him for Colin's accident, but the last thing I needed was to get into that now.

He reached for my hand and placed something cool in it.

My mouth went dry. It was a necklace. The one he had given to me on my eighth birthday. The one that I had never taken off until I had ripped it from my neck and dropped it in the trash the day I took Colin's video and accident report. He must have found it and kept it.

I bit the inside of my cheek and ran my thumb along its chain. He repaired the broken links and polished the metal. The delicate round circle shimmered back at me. I squeezed it in my hand and swallowed hard. Then I handed it back to him.

My dad lowered his head and closed his hand looking defeated.

"Can you help me put it on?" I asked.

He looked me in the eyes as his bottom lip trembled. I turned around and he placed it on my neck and fastened it. I hadn't forgiven him. I knew I never would, but something inside of me told me that when I was ready, I needed to listen to what he had to say. We didn't say anything else. I hurried to catch up with the others.

"You are never allowed to play photographer ever again," I hissed at Lyric.

She giggled.

"What'd you think of Bodhi?" I asked.

"He's sweet." Her face lit up. "We're going to keep in touch while he's gone."

"I'm glad. He's a good guy."

"Everything okay with your dad?" she asked.

"Yeah." I reached up and touched my necklace. "He was just giving this to me."

"Karma," she said.

"What?"

"The tiny circle. It's the symbol for Karma," she explained.

Of course it was. I shook my head.

"Here, I have something for you, too," she said and reached into the small bag strapped across her.

She pulled out a tiny pouch and a card and handed to me. Inside was a smooth, green stone.

"It's jade. It's for protection. The card will explain it more."

I rubbed my thumb across the stone. "Thank you. It's awesome."

Her arms wrapped around me and she squeezed. "Be safe."

I hugged her back. My mom and dad walked over and my mom rubbed me on the arm.

"I have to go," I said.

My mom nodded and handed me a soft white handkerchief with a pink heart in embroidery I had given to her for mother's day when I was young.

"I love you, baby girl," she said.

Tears spilled, streaking her cheeks.

My eyes began to sting. My mom had already shed so many tears for the loss of one child and barely lived through her grief.

I reached up and caught it with the handkerchief she had given to me.

"You're gonna get your pixie dust all soggy," I said.

She smiled then embraced me. My father cleared his throat and I glanced at him. Our eyes met and he dragged his hand across his mouth as tears wetted his eyes. I swallowed the giant ass knot that was blocking my airway and offered him a gentle smile. I squeezed my mom one last time needing to get out of here.

"Find your will, Tinklee." She glanced toward Locke then back to me. "Whatever it may be. Find it."

Chapter 23

The eight of us made our way to the jets in silence. Locke kept glancing sideways at me but he kept his distance. I walked taller, hoping it would make me appear more in control than I actually was. I broke off to the fourth jet and my legs felt gummy as I climbed the ladder. I blew out a deep breath as I strapped on my helmet, flipped the switches and prepared the cockpit. The crew chief disconnected from the aircraft and waited to taxi.

The radio came to life. "Strikes, check!"

My pulse quickened as sweat beaded on my brow. I gripped the stick.

"One," Locke answered.

"Two," Woodstock said.

Freak clicked on. "Three."

My voice was sharp. "Four."

"Four any issues with your bird?" Locke asked.

I shifted in my seat. Shit. He was checking on me. Only me.

I pushed the call button.

"Everything is in the green." I confirmed.

I released the button, readjusted the strap on my helmet and stretched my neck shoulder to shoulder.

"All right, let's taxi."

Locke made a radio call to the control tower that we were ready and I signaled to the crew chief to pull the chocks. I eased the throttle forward moved the jet toward the runway. Locke radioed the tower for clearance.

"Gambler flight, you're cleared for takeoff. Switch to departure." The tower advised.

"Gambler flight's cleared for take-off, switching," Locke responded.

We lined up. I watched the three jets before me lift from the runway. Adrenaline thrust through me.

I pushed the throttle up, gave the instruments one last check, released the brakes and slammed the throttle into afterburner. Within seconds I was in the air. Deployed for war.

* * * *

Eight hours later my eyes burned from exhaustion and my bladder screamed for relief. When the canopy opened and the crew chief unstrapped me, I wiggled uncomfortably and prayed I wouldn't have an accident.

"The bathroom is in that building over there, ma'am," he said.

I looked at him and arched my eyebrow.

"I've seen that look before." He smiled.

"Thanks."

I jumped from the jet, climbed down the ladder and ran for the small stone structure.

I vowed not to drink any more liquids until I arrived in Africa. I had never needed to pee so badly in my entire life.

"Feeling better?" Mojo teased when I found the others.

"Shut up, Mojo. You have a piddle pack if you have to go. My only choice was a damn diaper."

"We have another leg midmorning with only enough time for eight hour crew rest," T-Rex said interrupting our banter. "They made up meal packs for us to take back to the rooms."

We took off our gear and grabbed our packs before getting into the vans that would take us to our quarters. We rode in silence. I thought about my send-off with my parents in the hangar. For the first time since Colin's accident we almost felt like a family. I closed my eyes. I sighed and pushed the thought from my mind.

The sound of mumbled voices woke me. I blinked and glanced around the room. The walls were constructed of sterile white concrete blocks and a tiny metal desk sat against the wall. I had slept so soundly that it took me a second to realize where I was. There was a light tap on the door.

I got up to answer. Then I realized I was still in my T-shirt and panties. I was too tired to shower or change when I got to the room. There was another rap on the door.

Damn it. I figured I'd just see who it was. I stood behind the door and cracked it open slightly.

It was Locke. He was already dressed in his flight suit.

"You awake?" he asked, raising his eyebrow.

"Yeah. I just got up. Why? What's wrong?"

"You slept through breakfast so I wanted to bring you something to eat and make sure you were okay."

Locke lifted up his hands to show me the baggie. I opened the door wide enough to let him in. I yawned. His gazed swept slowly across my body.

"Sorry," I said closing the door behind him. "I fell asleep last night before I could get changed. What time is it?"

"0830. You still have an hour," he said. "What if I were someone else?"

"I wouldn't have let you in." I hauled my duffle bag onto the bed and rummaged inside.

"What are you doing?" he asked.

"Finding something to put on."

His hands brushed under my shirt against the bare skin of my waist. My eyes rolled back slightly as tingles traveled wildly through my body before finally landing south.

"I'd rather help you take it off."

I turned around and looked up at him. He brushed my hair back from my face.

"What happened to *I'm tailspinning out of control* and all our other crap?" I said with added snark.

"None of it changes the way I feel about you or how bloody attracted I am to you. You can't expect me to see you this way and not react," he said.

His lip lifted on one side. We were taking off in an hour and I needed to eat, shower and suit up. I had to ignore my heart *and* my body, and listen to the clock ticking.

"You can react, but not act," I said and smiled pulling on a pair of sweats.

He sighed as his gaze shifted to my neck. He reached out and lifted the tiny chain.

He rubbed his thumb along the chain. "This is new."

"It's actually old. I just got it back," I replied and turned back around to get my toiletries.

"From where?"

I sighed. Locke was jealous.

"My dad got it for me a long time ago. He found it before I left."

We were already dealing with enough, and as much as I wanted to tell him I wasn't about to throw more of a mess into the mix.

"Your dad is an interesting man," Locke said.

I shrugged.

"Do you know why he requested I come to the squadron?"

"Your cousin suggested it," I said.

I didn't want to talk about my dad or his motives for anything. He probably had a deal or agreement with some British diplomat. I was pretty sure he didn't make a decision unless there was a lot of money to be gained.

"She suggested it was because he was looking for something specific," he said crossing his arms. "Because I have experience as a test pilot."

His eyes never moved from me.

"He wants to increase the foreign sales primarily to the UK," Locke said.

No big surprise.

"Your father called me a few weeks ago." He paused.

I leaned against the desk to listen and he continued, "To review the findings of your brother's accident."

Locke watched me cautiously. I didn't know how to respond. My anger for my father began to resurface. What was he up to? I racked my mind trying to find an answer, but I came up empty. There had to be more to the story.

"Did he say why?" I finally asked.

Locke nodded. "He wanted an unbiased, fresh perspective. Someone who wasn't familiar with the accident, but was capable of pushing the jet to a specific limit."

He was still watching me in anticipation of an explosion.

"But why?" I asked. "The findings were conclusive. Why would he want to reopen it? It would hurt his sales if you found something."

Locke didn't answer.

"Do you have a theory?" My voice was laced with more sarcasm than I intended.

He frowned.

"Well?" I pressed.

"I think he is doing it for you."

"For me?" I said with a dark laugh. "You don't know my father very well. He only does things if it benefits him or his agenda."

"I don't want to overstep my place, but I disagree in this circumstance," he said.

The hair stood on the back of my neck. I balled my fists and narrowed my eyes as I waited for what he was going to say next.

"He knew you wouldn't give up until you found what you were searching for, no matter what the risk."

"For once, maybe he was right. Or maybe he asked you because he wants you to convince me to let it go." I grabbed my things. "I need to get showered."

"That's not the way to handle it," he said.

"Don't tell me how to handle it," I replied and pointed my shampoo at him. It wasn't the most threatening gesture, but my voice stayed hard. I didn't care how much I ached for him, he had no right to butt in where my family was concerned. "He wasn't your brother. You know nothing about my family."

"I'm not trying to upset you. I want to help," he said.

I could feel my temperature rising as a vein pulsed in my neck. He couldn't. The jet flew like a dream. Not a single maintenance issue. I knew it and so did Locke. Only now he was going to prove it and drive the final nail into my brother's coffin.

"You're my instructor." My voice thickened. "The only thing you should help me with is the damn jet. That's it." I walked into the bathroom and shut the door.

A few seconds later the front door slammed.

Chapter 24

I couldn't wait to escape from everyone and hide in my room when we touched down in Ramstein. I knew they would be going out for one last evening of drinking. Once we hit Africa the tap would run dry.

Base lodging was full so we had to stay in nearby local hotel. The tiny chateau lobby smelled of warm pretzels, making my stomach growl. Fantom handed out room keys. I clutched the fob in my fist.

"Are you okay?" Stitch asked and nudged me.

I nodded.

"You don't seem okay," he said.

"I'm fine, just tired."

"Are you going out tonight?" he asked.

I shook my head. "I think I'm going to call it an early night."

"Want some company?" he asked as we walked to our rooms.

"Thanks, but no thanks. You have fun. I am going to grab one of those big-ass pretzels I saw on the way in and call it a night."

I slid my key into the slot of the door. It didn't work. I tried it again. Nothing. I cursed.

"Do you want me to run down to the desk?" Stitch asked.

"No, you go get ready. I'll go back," I said.

"Okay. See ya in the morning."

I walked back to the front desk and waited for assistance.

A man in a smartly tailored charcoal-colored suit waited at the desk tapping his fingers against the top of the counter. The clerk came around the corner and instantly straightened his posture when he noticed the man standing next to me.

"Good evening, sir. We've been expecting your arrival," The clerk said and waved to another worker for assistance. "Please retrieve the lord and lady's bags."

My eyebrow rose. I wasn't sure how *lordship* translated, but the clerk had a skip to his step. I leaned against the counter. It looked like I wasn't getting my replacement key until the nobility's needs were met.

A petite lady wearing a black fitted suit and matching pumps strolled through the door. She carried a Chanel bag in one hand and a tiny dog in the other. The man next to me turned as she approached.

"There's a Ritz just down the street," she said. Her voice was a perfect blend of British and bitch. "I don't know why we're staying here."

"Because *he* is staying here," the man answered. He was British too, but he acted more reasonably. He rubbed his face, suppressing a yawn. They both looked exhausted.

"Well, he should be staying at the Ritz as well." She pursed her lips. The dog wiggled and barked in my direction.

I probably smelled like a dog treat. Lady Bitchy Britches turned in my direction. She scanned me from top to bottom before smiling. Fake smiling.

"This must be one of his group. Ask her."

I raised my eyebrows.

"He's right there." The lord pointed behind me.

I turned. My jaw almost hit the ground. It was Locke.

He frowned as he approached us.

"What are you doing here?" Locke asked. "I thought you were staying at the Ritz."

His pants and shirt were perfectly pressed. How did he pull that off? My clothes were rolled in a ball in a duffle bag and one big wrinkle.

"So did I, but your father wanted to stay where you were." The lady lifted her chin as Locke leaned over and pecked her on the cheek. He patted her dog on the head. She turned to her husband. "Let's move to the Ritz then. Make that happen, dear."

"We're fine here, Maggie," he said as he reached out and shook Locke's hand.

I stared, desperate to see what happened next. Locke glanced over at me and his jaw tightened.

"Did you meet my parents?" he asked me.

I shook my head and straightened my posture suddenly aware that I smelled like jet fuel.

"Tinklee, this is my mother and father."

His mom cleared her throat. Locke glanced back at her. Her eyes narrowed.

He straightened, a catch in his voice. "The Earl and Countess of Huntingdon."

Chapter 25

Was I supposed to bow? No one wanted to see a curtsey in a flight suit, but standing here with my mouth hanging open wasn't making anything less awkward.

Locke's father extended his hand.

"It's a pleasure to meet you, Tinklee," he said.

"Thank you, sir." I accepted his hand.

His mother kept her distance, surely afraid to get dirty.

"Forgive me, but you look quite young and delicate to be heading off into a warzone," his father said.

"I'm twenty-two, sir."

"And she can be ruthless," Locke said with a twinkle in his eye and a slight smile.

"Only when I need to be," I responded and shot him a look.

The Duchess raised her eyebrow as her eyes narrowed. They were the exact shade of Locke's, but that's where the resemblance ended. The furball yipped.

"It was nice to meet you. I need to get a key for my room," I said.

I turned back to the counter.

"Would you like to join us for dinner?" his father asked.

My palms turned sweaty. I prayed he was speaking to the clerk. I glanced back. Nope. He was looking at me.

"Thank you, sir, but I'm going to go to sleep early."

"Have you eaten yet?" he asked.

"No, sir."

"Well, then. We needn't have you starving before your big flight. You must eat. Please join us."

"I didn't bring anything suitable to wear," I said.

Locke's mom wore Gucci on top of Versace on top of labels I couldn't even recognize. The only designer I wore was Fruit of the Loom.

"Nonsense," he pressed and nodded toward the door. "The restaurant across the way will accommodate us. They'll even welcome Bentley. Come, I insist. Consider it our duty to improve foreign relations." He punctuated the request with a scratch to the tiny dog's ears.

I looked at Locke. He shrugged.

"Yes, sir. Thank you."

"Wonderful, we'll see you in thirty minutes."

* * * *

I wasn't sure of British customs. Was declining their dinner invitation a faux pas that translated to flipping them the bird? Just to be safe, I accepted.

I dressed in the nicest thing I could find. Since I had packed for a war, the best I could do was a pair of jeans, my favorite worn cotton shirt, and running shoes. Lady London was certain to take issue with my attire.

Locke and his father shared a drink at the bar when I arrived. They stood to greet me, and even though Locke upset me yesterday, his eyes lit up when he saw me coming and that nearly melted me along with my anxiety.

"What can I get you to drink, miss?" his father asked politely. He was a head shorter than Locke, and his hair was darker, but they had similar facial features. I couldn't believe I hadn't noticed the resemblance in the lobby earlier.

Their large stein of beer looked frothy and cool. When in Rome.

"Whatever you're having is fine. Thank you."

"Wonderful." He turned to the bartender to place the order.

Locke offered me a seat. He leaned in close. "Thanks for coming. My father would have been insulted if you had declined."

I dipped my head in agreement.

His mother sashayed from the elevators. She had changed into a navy suit, a string of pearls that probably cleared out the entire Indian Ocean, and the little dog on her arm. Her eyes scanned me from top to bottom.

"The airport lost my luggage," I said.

She forced a smile and tipped her head. The corners of Locke's lip curled upward.

"Here you are," Locke's father said as he handed me a stein of beer and passed his wife a flute of champagne.

She frowned at the beer. "Dear, have the bartender pour another flute of champs for Tinklee."

"Thanks. I'm good," I answered.

That was not the right answer. She looked at me as though I had served macaroni and cheese in a caviar dish.

"Is our table ready?" she asked with a masked sweetness and plastic smile.

On cue a server answered. "Yes, ma'am. You can leave your drinks and we will bring them to the table. This way."

"Lovely, could you dispose of one of those steins and bring two glasses of the champs for the ladies?" She patted the air near, but not too close, to the waiter as she walked away

Oh my God. Was she for real?

The server rattled off the specials and placed our napkin on our laps once we were seated. Locke's father ordered for the table and disappointment flushed through me when he didn't order pretzels. No beer. No pretzels. What kind of Germany trip was this anyway? My champagne arrived at the table. I wanted to refuse it out of spite but I had a feeling this dinner would be the kind that required alcohol.

I picked up the glass and drank it. The entire glass. It went down like a glass of soda with the same effect. I needed something with a bigger burn and quicker reward. Locke lowered his head to keep from laughing. His mother's mouth pinched tight.

"I can imagine flying must be quite dehydrating," his father said and waved for the server to fill my glass.

"Yes, sir," I answered.

"How did you decide to become a military pilot? I have to say I am quite intrigued," his father said.

"My father and my brother were both Air Force pilots," I said. "I got hooked at an early age. I never wanted to be anything else."

"Interesting. Do they still fly?"

"No, sir. My dad retired from the military and my brother passed away."

"How terrible. You have my condolences."

"Was his passing flying-related?" his mother asked leaning forward suddenly interested in what I had to say.

I wished the conversation would turn back to my wardrobe. "Yes."

"Well," Locke's mother said as her gaze moved to Locke. "I hope you are listening. Perhaps now you will understand how ridiculous this career choice is."

"Please, don't start." Locke sighed.

"You did your time. It was respectable. Appropriate. But now you need to come to your senses before something like that happens to you. Tell him, dear," she said.

His father nodded. "I agree that it is not wise for you to be entering into someone else's conflict. Perhaps it is best to come back to the British force."

"I made a commitment to our allies, and I stand by it and them," Locke said.

"Well, hopefully entering into this skirmish won't tarnish your image," his mother scoffed. "It is not well supported internationally."

Tarnish his image? Was she bagging me?

"The Americans have always tried to do the right thing even when it wasn't the most popular," Locke said.

"Sometimes it's better to mind you own business," his dad answered. "Choose your battles, if you will."

"And sometimes you must stand up for what you believe in," Locke said.

Awkward. I wanted to close my eyes and pretend I wasn't sitting here.

"You must move back to England. Finish your law degree from Cambridge, it is time you make your move into Parliament," his mother said.

"I'm where I want to be. You need to respect that," he said.

"Well, at the very least, perhaps you will consider returning to our military. In a more appropriate position for someone of your… commitments and station." His father spoke as though he attempted to be a voice of reason. Locke wasn't listening.

"Excuse me." I pushed back my chair to offer them privacy. "I need to use the restroom."

Locke and his father stood.

"I need to powder my nose as well. I'll join you," his mother said with a fake smile. She folder her napkin and handed the little dog to her husband.

Damn it.

The bathrooms were far from the table. She didn't speak as we walked, preferring the *click-clack-click* of her heels to punctuate the stare I felt boring into the back of my skull. I reached for the bathroom door. She pulled it closed behind her.

"You need to stay away from my son," she said, her tone icy.

I turned. She met my gaze.

"I don't know what you are talking about," I said.

"I wasn't born yesterday. I see how he looks at you."

"He's my instructor," I said.

"Which means it's inappropriate for many reasons. None of this is right for him."

"He's a grown man. I think he can decide what is right for him."

"It is a common enough practice. American girls are fascinated by the accent and aristocracy. Always dreaming of being a princess."

"You've found me out," I said and rolled my eyes.

"Perhaps you are a challenge to him, but we must be practical. A female military pilot? It is unseemly for someone of his breeding. He has responsibilities and a reputation. You are little more than an unnecessary distraction."

The romp through the nineteenth century was fun, but I was tired and had enough of the insults that she had directed toward both me and her son. I considered laying loose, maybe dumping her tea in a nearby river, but she *was* Locke's mother.

"Pass my apologies to your husband," I said. "I am unable to stay for dinner. I suddenly lost my appetite."

A smile crept across her face. "I will pass along the message."

She made my father look like parent of the year.

* * * *

I might be an Air Force pilot and an American, but since when did that translate to a speck of dirt on the bottom of her shoe?

Why did it even matter to me what Locke's mother thought anyway?

Screw her, and her furry little dog too.

I pulled off my shoes and pulled out a pair of sweats from my bag. The tiny pouch from Lyric was sitting on top. I dropped the stone into my hand and rubbed it, then pulled out the card.

Tinklee,

My gift might be silly and more for my peace of mind than yours, but it will make me feel better knowing you have it.

Jade offers protection and will keep you from harm. (Yay!) It will attract harmony, good luck, love and friendships. (Awesome) It stabilizes one's personality by soothing the mind and releasing negative thoughts. (Be happy) Referred to as a "dream stone", it can bring insight into your dreams. (maybe even the hot and sexy ones) Most importantly, Jade encourages you to become who you really are. (You're already fantastic!)

When all else fails, throw it at the enemy. Ha! Ha!

Stay safe.
Love, Light and Happiness,
Lyric

Her letter made me smile. I collapsed back on the bed and squeezed the stone. There wasn't a jagged edge or snag over the whole rock. I breathed in through my nose and out through my mouth. I took another deep breath then glanced down at the rock. It was broken. Negative thoughts about Locke's mom still ran through my mind.

Someone knocked. The savory aroma of buttery pretzels hit me even from the hall. My mouth watered. I set the jade on the table.

I unlatched the chain and opened it. Locke held up two steins and a paper bag. I reached for the pretzels before letting him inside. I ripped open the bag and tore off a piece, popping it into my mouth.

"I wasn't sure you'd want to see me," he said handing me a beer.

"You were smart to have brought beer and pretzels." I stepped aside to let him in then closed the door quietly.

"What did she say that made you leave?" he asked.

I shrugged and handed him the bag. "It doesn't matter."

"Just ignore it. Anything she said." He tore off a piece of pretzel and handed it back to me.

"I felt a bit like Cinderella before she went to the ball." I sipped my beer.

God, it tasted good.

He shook his head. "Her *title* is not what she makes it out to be. It's only important to her and her circle of friends."

"What are you?" I asked.

He laughed.

"What?" I smiled at the sound of his laugh. I missed it.

"It just sounded funny. What am I?"

"I mean *your* title and stuff. What does it mean?"

"My father is an Earl of a small region," he said. "I am given the courtesy of his title. Technically, I am an Earl."

I thought about his call sign. Duke. Duke of Earl.

"Now you're smiling. What's so funny?" he asked.

"Your call sign finally makes sense," I said.

He shook his head and grimaced. "And now you know why I never want to use it."

"And your tattoo on your ankle…the family crest." I air quoted.

"You really are bad with accents. That sounded Swedish."

I laughed as I grabbed the rest of the pretzel from him and sat on the floor.

"What did my mother say to you?" he asked again sitting down across from me.

"To stay away from her precious little boy."

He scowled and took a swig of his beer. He looked like he needed more than one. "What did you say?"

"The truth. I said you were my instructor."

"I really hope you specified the instruction was limited to flying the jet."

I pinched a piece of pretzel and threw it at him. It bounced off his chest.

"I told her that her son was a royal pain in my ass."

He smiled.

"I have a few questions," I said.

"Oh boy."

"You studied *law* at Cambridge?" I paused and waited for his nod. "And it's clear that your family is loaded." He shrugged but agreed. "And you have a position in Parliament that could pretty much be handed to you."

He rolled his eyes and sighed.

I continued, "So why are you doing all of this?"

"Careful or you'll sound like my family," he said.

"I am just trying to figure it out. Are you still in some sort of rebellious, piss off your parents stage? Or is this something you really want to do?"

"It's something I believe in," he said.

Of course it was. Locke was noble and a man of integrity.

"And aggravating your parents is an added bonus," I finished with a teasing smile.

"Something like that."

Locke was becoming less of a mystery but I wanted to know more.

"Your dad seems…nicer."

"Father is a humble man with a more realistic outlook on life. He's actually the one who holds the title and fortune, but Mother has a stronger personality. Father learned to choose his battles."

I snorted. "A wise man. Your mother reminds me of Kassie."

He erupted in laughter. "I wish you had said that to her at dinner."

"Why?"

"My mother considers Kassie to be our family's dirty little secret. Her mom got pregnant by a Catholic American and was disowned by our family. The family doesn't even acknowledge Kassie. Mom hates that I do."

"Never thought Kassie and I would have something in common," I said.

"Kassie really isn't so bad once you get to know her." I opened my mouth to argue but he continued speaking. "Think about how you would feel if you were abandoned by your family simply because of your dad's religious affiliation. That has to have some sort of effect on you."

"I guess," I replied with a shrug. "But I would consider them ignorant and move on."

"Don't forget, her mother lost a large inheritance and title. She might not care, but Kassie does," he said and smirked. "She retained the entitlement though. Just like my mother." He glanced at his watch. "Speaking of which, I need to go say good night to my parents."

He reached out his hand to help me to my feet. My hand fit perfectly in his palm, and in a natural reaction, I rose up onto the balls of my feet and leaned forward. My lips brushed against his, just the barest hint of pressure. He backed away.

"What about the tailspinning out of control and all the other crap, not to mention, the shampoo bottle you threatened me with?" he asked.

"Maybe it's easier knowing your family is as messed up as mine."

"Yeah, well, you can't choose your family, so you have to find a way to love them, flaws and all." He shrugged. "I'm glad my mother told you to stay away from me."

I flushed as my heartbeat thumped against my chest. I'd gone too far. The rejection and disappointment stole the breath from my lungs.

He reached for my cheek. "Because you love to do the opposite of what people tell you." His lips returned.

Oh my God. He was toying with me. I swatted him and he grabbed my hand, pulling me closer. I wanted more of him. Much more. I ached so badly inside without him.

He lifted me easily, carrying me to the bed.

"I want you more than I've ever wanted anything," he confessed in nearly a whisper.

His lips pressed against mine.

"Show me."

A devilish grin crept across his face as he tossed away his shirt, his lips lowering to my navel. My skin tingled where they touched. I arched my back, needing and begging for more.

His tongue explored the flushed skin between my breasts as his hands lifted and removed my shirt along its way. My nipples hardened in anticipation of his touch.

He kissed me right below my ear.

"You are so beautiful," he whispered softly as he kissed my neck causing my body to shiver. The sincerity and desire in his voice made me believe him.

He traveled lower, teasing my nipple with the tip of his tongue until he caught it between his teeth. I ground my nails into the bed as he pulled.

I let out a low growl as goose bumps rose over my skin.

"Who knew an aristocrat could be so improper?" I teased, my voice raspy.

He chuckled, his breath setting my skin ablaze. He cupped my other breast—squeezing. Claiming. My breathing became more rapid as my body quivered. His hands gripped me tighter, pulling me closer. He returned his lips to mine and pressing firm, demanding more.

"Bloody hell, I need you," he whispered in between breaths.

I lifted my hips, pressing harder into him.

"Take me, Locke." I breathed heavily, unfastening his pants and dragging them off his hips.

He was perfect. His gaze warmed every part of me. His smile was hungry, and he slipped off my panties with a promising kiss. I gasped as he joined me and we molded into one. He was mine and I never wanted to let him go. He held me as we glided with a craving desire. I dug my nails deep into his shoulders. He stared at me, as if he studied me, memorized me, and pushed in deeper as my breaths became raspy and shallow. My vision darkened and I buried my face in his neck to keep from screaming.

"It's okay, Tinklee. Let go. I have you." He pulled me closer, deeper, until finally fireworks erupted like the night we had met.

He whispered in my ear, "I'll never leave you."

Chapter 26

I was afraid to move or breathe. It was easy to get into this position and harder to get out. Locke's arms held me tight against his chest. I listened to his heart beating. I wondered why my heart raced faster than his. His arms held me, and my throat closed. As his words rang out in my mind. I backed away, trying to catch my breath.

"Are you okay?" Locke asked as he smoothed my hair back.

No, I wasn't. His words fell short. He couldn't promise that he would never leave me and I wanted to protect myself from ever caring or ever being hurt when it happened. But instead I was falling in love and even worse, with the man who was going to prove the jet wasn't responsible for Colin's accident.

I needed him to leave. I needed to be alone.

"Tinklee, what's wrong. Are you hurt?"

How did this happen? I grabbed a loose sheet from the bed, wrapped it around me and I got to my feet. I heard the rustle of his pants, then he was back, hands on my arms.

"Why aren't you saying anything?" He turned me around and forced me to hold his gaze.

"I need you to go," I said.

Hiding my emotions from people was not the same as not having them. I was such an idiot. I was falling in love while my brother was rotting in a grave. He would never have the chance to love. It wasn't fair.

"What? Why? Am I missing something?" he asked. His every word pounded in my head.

"Just go, please."

"Talk to me. What's wrong?" he asked.

I handed him his shirt.

"Are you bloody kidding me?" His voice was still deep. Raw. "I can't believe this. Why are you doing this, after what just happened between us?" His expression softened. "You felt something between us. It frightened you, and now you want to run."

"I'm not afraid of anything. Locke, I'm sorry, I just want you to go."

He reached for my hands. I kept them firmly gripped on my sheet. His fingers grazed my arms. Tender. It was too much.

"It's okay. I feel the same way," he said moving closer. "I love you."

No. This couldn't be happening. How did this happen? A lump in my throat threatened to choke me.

I wiggled from his touch and walked toward the bathroom. I needed to be alone.

"You're afraid of being hurt, but you can't stop caring inside because you say it on the outside." His voice softened. "Stop running. Just be you and allow yourself to feel."

The calmness of his voice overwhelmed me. I spun around.

"Damn it, Locke. Can't you see? This is me. The *real* me. The whole fucking, broken, messed up package." My voice shook.

"Let me help you," he pleaded and ran his hands through his hair. "I don't want to lose you."

His eyes were soft and gentle. I wouldn't break.

My voice lowered. "You never had me."

No one could ever have me. Too much of me died in that crash with Colin, and just like him, it was never coming back.

I held the door open. He stared at me but didn't argue. My words said enough for both of us. I looked away, unable to watch him leave. The door shut. The click of the latch brought me to my knees.

* * * *

Falling in love with Locke wasn't an option. I couldn't feel that way for him. I would never get close to anyone or set myself up to feel that pain ever again. I couldn't handle it, nor did I deserve it.

I ignored the knock at the door. We said all that needed to be said. But the knocking didn't stop.

"Go away," I mumbled.

"It's Stitch. Open up."

I wanted to be alone.

He banged harder, adding a kick to the knocking. "I'm not going away until you open up."

I pulled myself to my feet. Stitch's eyes widened as I opened the door. I tugged the sheet tighter against me.

"Are you coming in or what?" I barked.

He sat at the table, looking away, as I pulled on my shirt and sweats.

"Sorry, I didn't mean to snap at you. It's been a rough night," I said with a sigh as I sunk into the chair next to him.

"Duke, huh?"

My pulse quickened. How did he figure it out? This was bad—really bad, but this was Stitch. He loved me like a sister but would he protect my secret? What if he accidentally let it slip to someone else?

"How'd you know?"

"We were coming down the hall when he walked out of your room," Stitch said.

Shit.

"Who else knows?" I asked.

He grimaced, giving me the bad news. "All of us."

"Great." I sat down and put my head in my hands. "Now what?" Not only did I lose Locke, but we were going to lose our wings. I'd screwed up everything.

"No one will say anything."

"How can you be so sure?"

"Because you're one of us. We protect each other. Besides, half of us already suspected, and the rest will probably be too drunk to remember anyway." I dropped my head back down onto my arms.

"Do I need to kick his ass?" Stitch asked.

He was serious.

"No, I was the asshole," I mumbled into the table.

"I don't believe it."

"Because you don't want to see me that way," I said. "But the reality is I'm screwed up, and I'm an asshole."

"Every person I know is screwed up in some way." Stitch leaned back in the chair. "And who isn't an asshole sometimes?"

Lately it was becoming a habit for me.

"You know, you fight against being happy harder than anyone I've ever met," Stitch said.

He wasn't helping. "I just told you I'm screwed up."

"Then we need to find a way to unscrew you."

I scrunched my eyebrows.

"What does that even mean?"

Stitch chuckled as he pulled me into a bear hug.

"I'm trying to be philosophical after drinking a vat of German beers. How in the hell do I know?"

I laughed through my misery.

"Colin always described you as a firecracker. It would crush him to see you've extinguished your spark because of him." He patted me on the shoulder.

I sighed.

"I didn't douse it, I lost it. That girl's gone."

"No, she isn't. I've seen glimpses of her over the last few months. You need to stop pushing her away."

I didn't answer. I didn't know what to say.

"No matter how hard you try, you'll never be able to change what happened. It took me a long time to realize it myself." His voice cracked and as I looked up into his eyes, they turned misty. "He loved you and he would want you to live again."

I knew he was right. No more tailspinning. I needed to find a way to gain control.

"I think I need to go to sleep." He yawned. "You okay?"

"I will be," I said.

He squeezed me one more time and headed to the door. He picked up the jade stone on the way. "What's this?" He asked.

"It's a jade stone. My friend gave it to me."

"Looks like Kryptonite," he replied and tossed it back to me.

I caught it and glanced down, rubbing the polished face between my fingers.

"For the record, I think Duke's a good guy," he said.

Yeah. Me too.

"Tink." His voice was soft and I was surprised when I looked up into his wet eyes. "Colin would have thought so too."

I bit my lip struggling against the rock wedged in my throat.

He shut the door behind him and I laid my head down on the table. Stitch was right. Colin and Locke would have been instant friends. So many things about Locke reminded me of Colin. Their commanding eyes, how they owned a room, their natural talents and how they both loved me, differently, yet unwavering.

Having feelings for Locke frightened me, but pushing him away wasn't working. It was impossible. The feelings were there whether I wanted them to be or not. And Colin wasn't coming back, no matter what Locke discovered.

I really messed things up. Again.

Chapter 27

By the time we landed, everyone's faces matched the sickly green of our flight suits. A weather front had rolled in halfway through the grueling flight to Africa and we struggled against it most of the flight.

The flight line was in a full frenzy and several medical personnel lined the runway. No one in our group had alerted an inflight emergency so it had to be from something unrelated.

Bright yellow lights flashed all around as crackling radio calls mixed with the sound of jet engines.

"What's going on?" I asked Mojo once he was in earshot.

He shrugged. "I don't know. Nothing came across my frequency. T-Rex told me to go to the van. There were some F-22's that landed. He was checking it out."

"I wonder what's going on," Freak asked as he jogged to reach us.

"Mojo said the F-22's were up," I said. "Do you think something happened to one of them?"

Our instructors had gathered and one of the F-22 pilots approached. He shook their hands with a deep-set frown. He gestured with his hands as he spoke. Something wasn't right, and the unknown churned in my gut. Locke broke away from the group and greeted Bodhi. A long moment passed before he looked back at me. His eyes found mine. My heart begged him to forgive me. I needed his strength, his love, but his expression shadowed darker than the clouds churning overhead.

"Let's go inside," he said.

"What's wrong?" This was about more than last night.

"Did a plane go down?" Stitch asked.

Locke shook his head, looking ill. "Special Forces took heavy fire. There were injuries and a casualty."

Ash…I sucked back a breath.

"They're waiting for the black hawks. We're to get inside and wait for orders," Locke said.

"I'm waiting here," I said.

Locke didn't argue. I didn't look around me, but I was certain no one else moved either.

The chopping of whooping propellers erupted over the hillside. The flight line frenzied with first responders as the first helicopter touched down. The team ran against the forced wind, grabbing and lifting a stretcher. I stepped forward, struggling to see. Locke grabbed my shoulder. A cold chill traveled down my spine as two more were removed. Everyone was shouting orders as a medic squeezed an ambu bag over someone's mouth as he ran along side.

"Who's on the stretchers?" I asked trying to steady my voice.

"Don't go over there. Let the medical team help," Locke said.

Three of the Special Forces team members jumped from the first helicopter. Locke squeezed my shoulder and pointed. Ash. He jumped from the helicopter and his face twisted in pain. He was bloody and covered in mud, but he was alive. I glanced up at Locke and he nodded. I broke into a sprint and ran across the line.

"Ash!" I shouted.

His gaze stayed hardened and dark until I shouted again. The lines on his face softened as he recognized me. Without thinking, I wrapped my arms around his neck.

"Oh my God! I'm so glad you are okay!"

His free arm wrapped around my waist and he lifted me. He groaned, and my feet crashed back to the ground.

"You're hurt." I searched over his arms and chest for any injuries.

"I'm fine." He reshouldered the strap on his weapon. "You looked like an angel running toward me. I thought maybe I hadn't made it after all."

"You need a doctor," I said. I whistled and waved to get the attention of two airmen.

They ran to Ash, dumping his weapon into my arms and pushing me from their path. I followed as they helped Ash to walk.

"We have him, ma'am," one said. "You can meet us at the medical building."

I nodded and Ash forced a smile through his wince as they loaded him into the van. Ash closed his eyes and leaned against the headrest as they drove away.

Locke's face was sullen as he removed the weapon from my hands and handed it to another airman. I hadn't seen him approach.

"Is he okay?" he asked.

I nodded. His arm wrapped over my shoulders. I leaned into the warmth.

His hand fell to my back and he led me away. "We'll go to the medical building."

I looked up at him, forcing him to hold my gaze, "He's my friend. I care about him."

"I know. I'm glad he's fine," Locke said, "I wish I could say this was unusual, but it's not. The casualties and injuries of our comrades is a reality of war." His voice was as gentle as the warning would allow.

I tried to swallow, but my throat had gone dry. This was a hell of an arrival.

* * * *

Ash waited for me in his recovery room. He had tossed the blanket from the bed, but he couldn't sit up to push it beyond his knees. One of his pant legs was cut midway up, and his calf was bandaged. A large dressing wrapped over his ribs. Blood was seeping through.

"You're still bleeding," I said and pointed to his chest.

He glanced down and shrugged. Tear stains streaked his cheek.

My stomach knotted. "Are you in pain? Let me…." He was too much of an alpha to ever cry. He had to be hurting.

"I'm fine," he said swiping fresh tears from his eyes. "We lost Sully."

I took his hand. "I'm so sorry."

"His wife is expecting their first baby. A little girl." He gritted his teeth.

"Push it to the back of your mind and shut it out."

His eyes narrowed. "Sully and I have been friends since training."

"You'll only torture yourself if you think about it," I said.

His jaw flexed.

"I loved him like a brother," he said.

"I know, but you can't change what happened. Don't put yourself through that hurt." I wouldn't wish that sort of pain upon anyone.

His brows creased. The heart monitor hooked to his chest beeped faster as he reached for my cheek.

"Not thinking about it would be a dishonor to his memory and sacrifice. I need to think about him. I need to remember him so I can be certain his unborn child knows him the way I knew him. It hurts like hell, but I am blessed to have had him as a friend."

He wasn't thinking clearly, but I wasn't going to push him.

"Tink, sometimes you have to hurt to heal."

Was he offering me comfort? What the heck was happening? I needed to find his doctor to change his bandage. I stood to get away from his confident sadness. It freaked me out.

"You're dressing is leaking."

He was silent as I escaped to find a doctor. Bodhi and Locke were talking only a few doors down. I fist bumped Bodhi.

"Ash needs his dressing changed," I said.

Bodhi flagged down a passing tech and issued the order. He didn't let me leave.

"Can we talk?" he asked. He guided me to a chair.

Locke walked toward Ash's room.

That was not a good idea. They had recently kicked each others asses. I opened my mouth to argue but Bodhi raised his hand.

"It's fine. They need to clear the air," he said then cleared his throat. He continued, "I've been helping with the investigation of your brother's accident. Reviewing medical records."

I wasn't expecting this, but I nodded. He lowered his voice.

"Do you know if your brother was struggling with Post Traumatic Stress Disorder?"

No, he was okay. I craned my neck to hear if there was anything breaking from Ash's room as I shook my head.

"They're fine," Bodhi reassured me, then sat down next to me. "How was he when he came back from the war? Did he ever talk to you about any of it?"

"I don't know." I struggled to remember when he came back. We were overjoyed—treating him to breakfasts in bed and tripping over ourselves to help with his laundry and cleaning. "He was different, I guess, but still Colin. Was he being treated for it?"

"No, there weren't any records of it, but he may have kept it hidden or he may have asked a doc to keep it off the records. I thought you might be the best person to ask."

I bit my lip before I answered. "He would keep it from me. He was my big brother, he would never tell me if he thought it was a weakness."

"It's not a weakness."

I tilted my head. "I know. I'm just saying Colin would have viewed it as one. He was prideful."

"What are you saying?" My pulse raced as anger consumed me. "Do you think Colin killed himself?"

He shook his head rapidly. "No. Not at all."

I retreated from attack mode.

"I think he may have been suffering from conversion disorder," he explained.

I wrinkled my eyebrows.

"Hysterical blindness," he clarified. "Have you heard of it?"

"It's something about anxiety creating a physical symptom?" I asked.

He nodded. "Like blindness, paralysis, or even blacking out," he said. "This is just a theory."

Locke walked out of the room. No busted lip or blackened eye. It must have gone well.

"Everything okay?" he asked cautiously.

"I guess we could ask you the same," I said.

"He wants to say good night to you."

I couldn't determine Locke's expression. If he were playing poker he would fool the world with his veil.

"So what happens now with the investigation? How do you find that out or even prove it?" I asked Bodhi.

"I need to dig deeper, but I wanted to keep you in the loop," he said.

I wasn't sure if I felt better or worse. Could Colin have been crying for help and we missed the signs?

I nodded and went to say good night to Ash.

The tech was injecting something for discomfort into his IV fluids when I came in. He moved his legs over and patted the bed for me to sit.

"You don't have any more injuries, and Locke came back out in one piece. So I guess you made some sort of truce?"

He smiled. "We're good."

"What did he want?" I hesitated. "Or you can tell me if it's none of my business."

"He told me he was sorry about Sully, then we apologized in a guy sort of way for our fight." I rolled my eyes and he smirked. "We talked about your brother."

"Why would he talk to you about *my* brother?" My hands gripped defensively.

"Can I speak freely without risk of you hating me?" he asked.

I wasn't sure if I could ever hate Ash, but I raised a cautionary eyebrow for him to tread carefully.

"Did your brother ever talk to you about the war when he came back?"

Why did everyone want to suddenly talk about this tonight?

"I was a new member on the team during his deployment," he said. "I didn't know him very well but I knew of him."

Why didn't he mention this before?

"I was on one of the missions that he was a part of. It was considered successful, but at the same time, we thought it was an epic fail."

I listened.

"We knew where they were stashing weapons and combatants. The plan was to destroy the target with airpower. We waited on the ground to take control of anyone who got out," he said his voice scratchy.

I stood and poured him a glass of water and handed it to him. He took and sip and I sat back down as he continued, "The mission was going according to plan. The fighters flew in, locked on target, and unloaded but at the same time, a radio call came in. They said children were used as shields. We tried to abort, but it came too late."

My heart dropped into my stomach. I remembered hearing about it, but I didn't realize it was a mission that Colin or Ash had been involved in.

"The local media used it as propaganda. Said our forces had targeted a school," Ash finished and took another sip from his cup.

"But why would Locke be talking to you about any of this?" I asked.

"A lot of us were haunted by what happened. We never had solid proof of any of it, but the propaganda…those images stick with you. It's hard to take any human life, no matter what the cause. But to think you could be responsible for the death of innocent children…." Ash swallowed hard.

"…it's unbearable." I finished.

He nodded. Colin loved children and I knew how it would have affected him even if he weren't responsible.

"But how did he fall through the cracks. How did everyone else recover?" I asked.

"I don't think anyone knew how affected he was. He put on a good front," he said. "Like you."

Ouch. Ash thought I was a fraud. I tried to pull my hand back. He held it tighter.

"You're afraid to show weakness. But loving someone isn't a weakness."

I yanked my hand harder.

"Duke is a good guy. He's crazy about you as much as you are for him."

"Why are you saying this? Why would you try to push me to him?" I questioned, searching his eyes.

"Because you care about him. And you can't make any of those feelings go away, even if you think you can," he paused and tilted his head slightly as he continued, "Just like you can't stop loving your brother or keep from hurting because you want to. It doesn't work that way."

I forced myself from showing emotions while the pain devoured me inside. It was killing me knowing his words rung true. I had gone about things all wrong.

"You're stupid," I said.

His eyes widened.

"You're stupid and stubborn. Good thing you're hot." Ash chuckled.

"I'd kick your ass, but you're in a hospital bed," I said.

"I'm sure there will be plenty of future opportunities." He reached out his hand and I scooted up to hug him. I cared about Ash even though my heart belonged to Locke.

His face looked drawn. He was in pain, even with the meds they shoved at him. The dark stubble on his chin made his pallor even more noticeable. He had been under fire, his friend was killed, and somehow, Ash was comforting me.

"I'm really sorry about Sully," I said.

"Me too. He was a great man. So was your brother. They deserve for us to continue loving them," he said.

I bit my lip and nodded.

His voice softened. "Promise, Tink."

I didn't get this way over night. I couldn't fix it that fast either, but at least I was ready to try.

Chapter 28

I had to figure things out with Locke or let him go. I watched him silently as his head leaned against the wall with his eyes closed. I had been awful to him, yet he still came back for more. I pulled him through a tornado of detachment, and it wasn't fair.

His eyes slowly opened and held mine for a moment.

"Are you hungry?" he asked.

"I should be."

"Me too." Locke pushed himself up from the bench. "Let's see what we can find."

We walked outside the hospital wing and toward the large mess tent. The perimeter of the tent was lined with containers full of brown plastic bags. The center was filled with rows of tables.

"Nothing like a tasty processed Meal Ready to Eat," I said, turning up my nose.

"Take the macaroni and cheese. You can kill the taste with the hot sauce." Locke handed a bag to me. I took two bottles of water.

"Let's sit outside," I said.

The weather cleared, but several dark clouds shaded the moon. I loosened the laces on my boots. My feet screamed for freedom.

"Bodhi and Ash told me about my brother."

He didn't respond. His lip drew into a thin line and his Adams apple bobbed. I couldn't read his expression or his silence, so I asked, "What do you think?"

Locke ripped open the MRE packs and activated the heating elements. He didn't answer the question.

"I promise not to bite your head off. I want to hear what you have to say," I assured and snatched the M&Ms from the package.

"I think he was struggling," he said.

"But what do you think about Bodhi's theory?"

"Your brother had multiple reports of environmental concerns with the jet, all of which turned up negative after extensive investigations," he said. "If he were having anxiety type episodes they could have been mimicking a lack of oxygen."

"So you think he was suffering from PTSD."

"It would make sense," he said nodding.

The sweet M&Ms suddenly tasted bitter. "How did we miss the signs? What kind of family are we?"

"A good family. A loving family," he said.

"How can you say that? You've seen us together. We're a disaster." I sipped my water and thunked my head against the wall.

"You're a disaster because you feel helpless. You've lost a vital piece of your puzzle and you can't figure out how to put it together again."

"A puzzle is ruined without all of its pieces and we're missing our vital piece—the heart. Colin was the one who reminded us how to love each other." I tucked a loose strand of hair behind my ear.

"Sure, it looks different, but it can still be beautiful, you just need pull the pieces together a little tighter and maybe add a little glue," he explained and tilted his head as he watched me. His blue eyes warmed me like a blanket.

"But every time you see it, you know something is missing."

"And every time you see it, you will honor it by remembering how beautiful it was and by reminding other people how special it was," he said.

My voice was flat. "But what if it's your fault that it's gone?"

"It's not your fault."

Locke reached out to touch me but retracted, as if his hand passed too close to a flame.

I closed my eyes as Ash's words resurfaced in my mind. I swallowed hard then slowly moved closer to Locke. "I was there the day of his accident," I said quietly.

Locke's eyes softened allowing me to move at my own pace. "Colin seemed out of it. I asked him if he was sick, but he said he was fine. There was something about his eyes. Something different."

"Did he say anything?" he asked cautiously.

"No, but he wouldn't. I was his little sister, and I was there to see him fly the jet I begged him to fly. The jet *I* wanted to fly more than anything. He never would have disappointed me."

I pushed against the bridge of my nose to keep from crying.

"Tinklee, you can't blame yourself. He was keeping it hidden."

"I should have seen it. Mom mentioned to Dad that she thought something was wrong. He ignored it. I ignored it, too. There was...."

I stopped speaking. There were too many memories to filter through. Everything and nothing might have warned us about a problem.

"Everyone missed it," he said gently.

I nodded then turned my head toward him.

"Locke, I'm so sorry about last night."

His fingers stretched out and touched mine beside him.

Clash ducked from the tent. "If you two aren't careful, people are going to start to talk."

I retracted my hand worried what he'd seen or heard, but his expression gave away nothing more than arrogance. Clash was the last person I wanted to see.

"We landed in the middle of the Special Forces return. We just finished visiting," Locke responded but didn't hide the dismissiveness in his voice.

"I heard they lost one today," Clash said with a shrug. "You better get some sleep. We have an early brief tomorrow."

I squeezed my water bottle in my hand, popping the lid. He was such an insensitive bastard.

Clash grabbed his food and stalked away.

"How are you friends with that guy?" I asked.

He shrugged. "He's changed."

"He hates me almost as much as he hated my brother," I said.

"Clash was jealous of your brother and I think you remind him of it."

"I'm glad." I pushed to my feet.

Locke smiled.

"His ego's gotten worse now that he has had a taste of leadership," he said.

"Then I wish someone would burn off the asshole's taste buds."

Locke laughed. "Let's get some sleep before you get court-martialed."

* * * *

Our room consisted of a large tent full of cots. They kept me with my squadron so I bunked beside all the guys. My stuff waited for me on my bed when we walked in.

"How's Walker?" Mojo asked. He and a few of the guys were playing cards. He was losing.

"He'll be fine physically. He's torn up about Sully," I said pulling off my boots.

Freak shook his head. "It kills me man. He was a good dude."

I nodded. I didn't know him very well, but he was one of our boots on the ground.

Stitch held up a bottle of water. "Here's a toast to those who have gone before us."

Everyone in the room raised a hand and called out, "Hear, hear."

The tent fell silent for a few minutes then the normal mutters began to return.

I fidgeted with the zipper on my duffle.

"You want us to throw some sheets up or something to give you some privacy?" Freak asked glancing over his cards at me.

"No way, man. She may be the only pair of tits I see the entire time I'm here." Mojo teased.

I drilled my boot in his direction.

"That's gross, dude. She's like our sister," Freak said.

Mojo winked. "Duke doesn't seem to have a problem with it."

I launched my other boot and this time it clipped him in the head. He shouted.

"Shut up, Mojo, I'm trying to sleep," Woodstock yelled from the end of the row.

I grabbed a pair of sweats and a towel from my duffle so I could take a shower. It was a long day and I needed to find a way to unwind. I slipped my feet into a pair of flip-flops and smacked Mojo one more time on the way out.

The girl's showers were a bit of a walk from our tent but I didn't mind the alone time. I needed it.

The new theory about Colin spun around my head.

How did I miss the signs of his personal battle? Guilt tugged at my belly. Did he even recognize what was happening or was he hiding the pain beneath his smile?

Acting.

"This is my little sis, Airman Wilson. She'll be in the jet soon." Colin said as he shook the airman's hand and kept the other one wrapped around my shoulder.

He reached out his hand to greet me. "Nice to meet you, ma'am. So you'll be learning from not only your brother, but the best of the best."

"I'm so excited to be this close to everything. It makes me want to jump in the cockpit now," I said.

Colin laughed.

"Soon enough. Tink does everything with full force. She'll pass me up on day one," Colin said.

I stood back and watched the airman strap him in. He explained a few things in the cockpit. My heart raced with exhilaration. I couldn't wait to be sitting in his seat.

"Staff Sergeant Hansen is taking her to the tower," Colin said. "Can you make sure she gets to him?"

"You okay, sir?" Airman Wilson asked, frowning.

Colin rubbed his forehead with the back of his hand. "I'm good. The humidity is rough today."

"You want some of my water?" I asked.

He took a drink and handed it back to me. His head was lined with beads of sweat. I was warm but comfortable. Then again I wasn't wearing all the equipment he was.

"Better?" I asked.

He blinked his eyes a few times before a warm smile lit up his face.

"Couldn't be better. Ready to see what this jet can do?" he asked.

"Colin...."

"Come on Tink, I set this up just for you. Let me hear some excitement. Are you ready to see what this jet can do?" he shouted with excitement.

He went through a lot of trouble to set this up for me. I didn't want to ruin it.

I forced a smile.

"Hell yeah!"

"Let's do it."

He lifted both fisted hands over his head in a warrior-like movement and I mimicked.

A burst of cold water blasted through the showerhead jarring me from my memory. I shut off the water and shivered as I reached for a towel. The forgotten image burned in my mind.

Something seemed off, but not enough to question it. Or was it and I chose not to? Airman Wilson. I hadn't realized he was the crew chief that day. My Staff Sergeant Wilson. I remembered him from the funeral, but I didn't remember him from that day. I had blocked most of the event from my mind.

I dressed and rolled dirty clothes in a ball with my towel. Mostly everyone was asleep when I made it back to the tent. Locke stayed up, reading on his tablet in his cot. His body tightened, shifted, as he watched me pass. Sharing a tent this close and under the surveillance would pose a challenge.

I pulled out my tablet and blocked out the air conditioning with my headphones. I clicked the familiar video. Colin's accident lit the screen. A message popped up in front of it.

Don't.

It was a text from Locke.

Don't what? I typed back.

Watch the video.

Don't. I typed.

Don't what? He answered.

Tell me what to do.

I hit send and sat for a moment trying to suppress a grin. I'd felt even more connected to him after opening up to him about Colin. I leaned forward and glanced toward Locke. He was watching me with the half lifted lip grin that drove me wild. I had to look away or we would both be in trouble.

I shut off the tablet and pulled out my earphones. My tablet buzzed and lit up.

Good night XO

My heart fluttered.

* * * *

Morning came too fast. I rubbed sleep from my eyes and yawned. I rolled out of bed, and Mojo ruffled my hair.

"G'morning sleeping beauty," he teased.

"I don't do mornings, Mojo, and touching me is a sure way to lose a limb."

He laughed and handed me a bottle of water.

"Coffee. I need coffee," I mumbled as I rummaged through my bag for a flight suit.

"Drinking coffee before you fly is awful," Stitch said.

I raised an eyebrow. Try me.

"Fine. I'll get you coffee and meet you at the brief. Anything else?"

"Protein bar," I answered.

"I'm coming with you, bro," Mojo said. "She isn't kidding when she says she doesn't do mornings."

I glared.

"We had them set a shower and bathroom area next door. The shower is only solar and the toilet is portable but at least you won't have to go so far," Stitch said.

"Thanks," I responded.

I usually didn't want special treatment, but this I would accept without argument.

The morning air was muggy and it felt good to brush my hair and pull it into a ponytail. I fell into a chair next to Stitch and almost kissed him when he handed me a Styrofoam cup of coffee.

Locke was in the front of the tent with his sleeves rolled up reviewing a map with T-Rex. There were two sets of four-ships going up this morning to perform surveillance on some suspected terrorist camps and to get familiar with the new terrain. It was decided we'd go up one student to instructor.

"You're with me and Stitch is with Duke," T-Rex said. "Stay on our wings. It should be a routine surveillance mission but we have to stay alert. Got it?"

"Yes, sir," I answered.

Once we finished the brief and grabbed our gear we made our way to the jets. The flight line was buzzing with jets and fuel trucks. Ammo and weapons airmen were securing live munitions onto several of the jets. I tried to blink the image of the Black Hawks landing yesterday and pulling out stretchers. My mind flashed to Ash lying in a hospital bed.

"Stay on my wing." T-Rex pointed at me.

I nodded, and he split to make his way to his jet.

Sergeant Wilson saluted me and I returned the gesture. He frowned. "You okay, ma'am?"

His words hit me as I recalled him asking the same thing to Colin.

My throat was thick and I could only nod. I climbed into the cockpit and stretched as best I could as he strapped me into my harness.

I pulled on my helmet and forced a smile.

"Ma'am?" Sergeant Wilson's face paled.

I nodded.

"Ma'am. Are you sure? I think…." His voice was shaky.

"I'm good."

He stared at me, but didn't argue.

The canopy lowered and the jet came to life.

"Shooter check!"

"Two! Three! Four!" came the sharp response from the flight.

"Any issues?" T-Rex asked.

"Everything is in the green," I confirmed.

"All right, let's taxi."

"Shooter flight, you're cleared takeoff, Runway One, two, right. Switch to departure," the tower advised.

"Shooter flight cleared for takeoff, switching," T-Rex responded.

I taxied to the runway and followed T-Rex. I adjusted the air inside the cockpit as sweat dripped between my breasts.

T-Rex ordered minimal verbal chatter. Within seconds I was in the air. My body shook with adrenaline.

It's just surveillance. Pull yourself together.

My breaths shortened, and I concentrated on slowing the rhythm. T-Rex's wing stayed in my vision on my radar.

I tightened the strap on my helmet and adjusted the rheostat on the airflow. Something blocked in my throat. I swallowed hard. It only made it worse. Shit. Something was wrong.

"Shooter flight, one's coming to a heading of one, two, zero," T-Rex radioed.

"Two," I choked trying to gag out the words.

"Three," Locke called.

"Four," Stitched answered.

"Two. Everything okay?" T-Rex asked.

I swallowed hard trying to force the tickle from my throat. Fear chilled my blood and my eyes watered. My brain turned fuzzy.

"Affirm," I forced. I released the transmit button and coughed hard.

Come on, Tink. Breathe. Stars twinkled in my vision and my arms felt heavy.

"Shooters, suspect ground track bearing one, eight, zero. Three miles, hook right!" T-Rex shouted.

T-Rex's wing snapped and I followed instinctively. The weight of the G's slammed me into the ejection seat causing the blood to drain from my head. The world started to go black as my vision tunneled. I felt as though

I had left my body and was watching myself from a movie theater seat. Nothing seemed to make sense.

What was happening?

"Shooter…shh…Two…" T-Rex's mumbled voice echoed.

Where was I? I wondered disoriented.

"Tink." The word rang soft and familiar. "Tink!"

"Karma!" Stitch's terse voice screamed across the radio.

I quickly scanned my instruments. Six hundred and fifty knots. I separated from the fight to the west in slight descent. I was Karma. He was calling to me.

Shit! I was in my jet. In the air. Flying. Panic smacked me in the face causing my arms and legs to shake.

"Shooter Two is extending west." I replied.

My head ached.

I checked my instruments again and leveled the nose of my jet off the horizon. Holy hell! My heart pounded against my chest, and I fought the urge to tear off my helmet.

I was closer to T-Rex's wing then I should have been. A second later and I would have crashed right into him.

"Two update status," T-Rex radioed. Trying to assess.

"Shooters, I have a slight engine malfunction," Stitch called. "I need to head back to the base."

"Copy Three. Shooters, let's return to base," T-Rex answered.

I focused on T-Rex's wing and followed his route back to base.

We taxied in. My blood pulsed. Sweat dripped down my back and I fought to control my shaking. I wanted to rip off my helmet and oxygen mask. The cockpit closed in on me making me feel claustrophobic. I needed more airflow. I focused on my breathing. I didn't want my tapes to reveal that I was losing it. What had happened?

I resisted clawing at the canopy when the jet stopped. I was a caged animal needing to escape. As soon as the fresh air hit me I ripped my helmet free and struggled to unstrap. I needed my feet planted to the earth. The crew chief pushed the ladder closer and his eyes widened when he saw me already free from the harness.

"Ma'am?" His voice wavered.

I swung my legs over the side and rushed down ladder.

My legs were uncertain but I forced them to move as I ran toward the camp. Once I made it to an isolated area, I lowered my head between my legs so I didn't pass out.

"Shit, shit, shit!" I whispered.

I almost died. I could've died. I pulled my hands against the back of my neck. How would my mom have survived if that car drove up her driveway again? I looked up at the sky and blew out a deep breath shaking my hands.

Oh my God. Is that what Colin went through? Shit. My body turned cool and my arms and legs shook uncontrollably. I wrapped my arms around my knees trying to gain control. If Stitch hadn't call out my name that last time I may have suffered the same fate as my brother.

But what happened? My eyes darted as if searching for the answer.

Was I tired? Was it the turn?

I swiped away a drop of sweat from my brow and wrung my hands together. No. Something wasn't right. Something was different. I felt like my head was spinning and full of cotton at the same time.

A hand touched me on my back. I jumped.

"Breathe." Stitch knelt down and rubbed my arms.

I nodded. He didn't need to say it.

"Damn it, Stitch! Does everyone know?" I asked not recognizing my own voice.

He shook his head. "I think just Duke. He told me to find you."

Stitch pulled me into his chest.

"They're going to ground me," I said.

"That's not important now. The important thing is, you're okay." He let me out of the hug, examining me.

"It was odd. I can't explain it," I said.

His hands shook as he ran his fingers through his hair.

"I almost lost my fucking mind up there," he said. "I was so scared when I didn't hear you respond to the radio call."

He squeezed me into another bear hug, crushing me.

I gave him a few minutes before I tried to speak.

"I can't breathe." My voice was muffled.

He let go and chuckled as his ears turned red. "Sorry."

"Don't be sorry. You saved my life today," I said.

He frowned.

"Just say it," I nudged him.

"It's nothing."

"It's something. You should see how squished up your brows are right now," I mimicked his grimace.

"Don't think I'm crazy," Stitch said.

I nodded.

"I felt like something alerted me that there was something wrong." He paused. "Like a sixth sense or something."

I hugged him tightly then glanced up at him and touched his cheek.

"If there is such a thing as a guardian angel, Colin would be the first to volunteer, and he would have called out to his best friend to help him save his little sister." My voice cracked.

He looked down at me and nodded as a tear rolled down his cheek.

"Are you okay?" Locke's voice startled me.

I spun around. The muscles in his cheeks tensed.

"I'll leave you two alone," Stitch said.

"No, we need to make sure we are on the same page," Locke said. "T-Rex is suspicious. I told him I thought you were both nervous, but everything would be fine. He wants both of you flying again with him and Shatter."

My heart thumped in my chest. I was still too freaked out to even consider it. For the past half hour, all I wanted was to get the hell out of the cockpit. The thought of going back in was fuel for a nightmare.

"Do you think that's a good idea?" Stitch asked.

"What happened?" Locke demanded.

Stitch cleared his throat. "I got the story down. I'll see you guys later."

Locke didn't respond as Stitch brushed past him.

"You scared the bloody fucking shit out me," he said sitting beside me.

I swallowed. His face was red. This was the most un-in control I'd ever seen him.

"I freaked the bloody fucking shit out of myself, if it makes you feel any better." I leaned my head on his shoulder not caring if anyone saw. I needed to feel that I was still alive.

"It doesn't make me feel better at all." He laced our fingers together. "What happened exactly?"

"I don't know. I lost it and couldn't recover. When we pulled into the G's, I was gone," I said. "Just gone. Somehow Stitch's voice brought me back."

"Are you tired? Did you eat enough?"

"I mean, I'm tired. I ate what I usually do." I started to giggle.

Locke didn't find it amusing. He frowned, staring me down.

"I'm sorry, I don't know why I'm laughing," I said. "It's just that…this is so stupid. Why am I laughing?" I wiped my face. "It just felt like there was something wrong with the environmental system."

"Tinklee, this isn't funny. *That* isn't funny," he said. "Why do you think it was the oxygen system?"

"Because I couldn't breathe. I needed air and it wasn't enough," I said.

"Do you really think it was the environmental system?" His voice was hard. "We'll have the system looked at."

"No," I said. "I don't know what happened, but I understand why Colin thought something was wrong with the jet."

It was another answer taking me one step closer to understanding what Colin was going through. My cheeks tingled remembering the uncontrollable panic.

I bent up my knees and buried my head. What the hell?

He smoothed my ponytail along my back. It soothed me, calming my breath and knowing I was no longer fighting this battle alone.

"What do you think?" he asked quietly.

"I think I experienced what Colin did. But right now I don't know what that is," I turned my head to look at him. "All these theories about Colin and the memories flooding back to me. It's messing with me."

"I think I should find a way to get you off the schedule tomorrow and let you rest," he said. "You need to give yourself a little recovery time."

"I feel ridiculous," I said.

"Don't. You're going to be fine."

"How can you be so sure?" I asked.

"Because you're a survivor," he answered.

I sighed. Or as usual, I could pretend to be.

Chapter 29

Locke managed to get me off the schedule in the morning by claiming the complexity of the mission required instructors to fly. He also set up a time to talk to Sergeant Wilson. I went back to the tent and was asleep before my head hit the pillow. Mumbled whispers woke me, and I rolled over. Ash?

"Hey," Ash said. I blinked trying to focus on his face. "Sorry, I didn't mean to wake you. Freak was looking for paper so I could leave you a note."

Freak shrugged and left us alone.

I shifted my legs and rubbed my eyes, "Are you supposed to be out of the hospital?"

"I'm fine. I wanted to go to Sully's sendoff," he said his shoulders drooping.

I reached out and squeezed his hand.

"You okay?" It was a dumb question but it needed to be asked.

"I will be. I heard you went up today, your first flight of the war. Was it epic?" he asked.

"I guess you can say that."

He raised an eyebrow.

"It was fine. Just a surveillance run," I only partially lied. It was an improvement.

"Are you flying tomorrow?"

"No. I think I'm getting sick. I'm going to take the day to recover." Damn. That was a full lie.

Ash's jaw tensed. "What aren't you telling me?"

"Nothing," I said and faked a chuckle.

"You are a horrible, horrible liar," he replied and exhaled. "Tell me when you're ready."

"When are you going back out into the field?" I changed the subject.

"Tonight," he said.

My eyes widened. "Are you kidding me?"

"It's a war. They need all able feet on the ground," he said.

"But are you able?" I asked.

"Oh…I'm able," he winked.

I shook my head and laughed. He was impossible.

He jerked a thumb over his shoulder. "I'm going to grab something to eat. Want me to bring you something back?"

"No, thanks. I'll wander over in a bit and grab something," I said.

"It sounds funny to say, I'm glad you're here, even if it is a warzone." He took my hand. "You helped me more than you'll ever know last night."

"I'm glad I was there too."

He leaned over and kissed me on top of the head. "Hope you feel better." He winked before walking away.

* * * *

The smell of jet fuel flooded my senses and it reminded me of how much I used to love the jets.

Used to.

I wasn't sure how I felt about any of this anymore. I sat on the ground at the flight line perimeter and watched the jets taking off and landing. From the moment I was born, the military was a part of my life. As much as it was an honor, it had been a hardship of sacrifice. I loved serving my country. I couldn't even imagine doing anything else. But the flying? Did I still want it as much as I used to?

I lay back on the ground and stared at the stars. How would my mom have reacted if the uniformed men knocked on her door again, and this time, said her daughter was gone? Would she feel like she was no longer a mother? Would the empty ache in her heart destroy her? How would my dad react? Judging by my send-off, I knew I had to do anything I could to come back home to save our family.

I was tired. Tired of fighting everyone and everything including myself. I didn't even know who I was anymore and frankly I was getting sick of myself. Things needed to change. Starting with the jet. I needed to remove myself from the cockpit.

I sat up and put my head between my knees. I was a fighter pilot. A JSF pilot. It was my dream. Could I walk away? I made a commitment to the Air Force, my squadron, and this war, but if I wasn't comfortable in that cockpit, none of those things mattered. Flying with my head screwed up was dangerous, not only to me, but everyone I cared about. But I didn't know how to breathe in any other skin. Could I figure it out?

This was frigging insane.

If I walked away, I knew I couldn't come back. This would be a permanent decision. I pushed myself to my feet and stared into the distance as one of the JSF's took off. I had to walk away to survive. The flame from the afterburner branded the decision. I was done flying. And I was done with the JSF.

* * * *

I woke up unrested but determined to still do my part, only with my feet firmly planted on the ground. My heart tugged for me to reconsider and I shook off the feeling. I would have to find Shatter and tell him before they put me on the schedule to fly again. I'd request to stay here and work with mission planning.

"How are you feeling this morning?" Locke asked walking up behind me.

"Good," I said.

I had felt fine until I heard his voice. I knew he would not support my decision.

"Where are you going?"

"Just checking in to see what's happening," I said biting the cuticle on my thumb.

"Do you think you feel up to going on the schedule tomorrow?" He was keeping his steps in stride with mine.

"I guess," I said as I shrugged. "I'll see where Shatter wants to use me." I tried to keep things noncommittal.

"Shatter? Shatter isn't even involved in scheduling." He reached out for my arm and stopped me. "What's going on?"

"Nothing. I'll check with whoever's running the schedule."

"I'm working with the schedule," he said still holding onto my arm.

"Oh," I said with a nervous laugh.

He pulled me to the side of a tent. "What's going on?"

I looked at the ground and kicked around a stone with my foot. "You'll make a bigger deal out of it than it is."

"Maybe. But tell me anyway."

I fidgeted. He placed his fingers under my chin and lifted until our eyes met.

"Tell me," he said.

"I don't want to fly anymore."

The words sounded odd, unfamiliar and tasted like a betrayal, not only to me, but to everyone who believed in me.

His eyes widened.

"Never again or just not yet?" His voice rose from a whisper.

"I'm done. I don't want to fly anymore."

Good. That sounded more confident.

"You don't mean that. You're freaked out. Hell, I'm still freaked out. You don't have to fly yet, but you will fly again."

"This is why I didn't want to say anything. You're not listening. I had an epiphany last night. I'm done."

He shook his head. "No."

Stay strong, Tink.

"You don't have a say in this," I said.

"Yes, I do. I'm *not* letting you do this."

That did it. I folded my arms and narrowed my eyes. Let me?

"You listen to me carefully." He gripped my arms. "I am not letting you give up. I'm bloody telling you it won't happen. No bloody fucking way."

I didn't speak. He ran his hands through his hair, hesitating while a few people passed by.

"I'll put you on mission planning," he said. "For now. Give it a week or two, then I'm going up with you. I'll stay on your wing. You lost your confidence. I'll get it back."

I knew I wouldn't change my mind. But what he proposed seemed like a reasonable compromise.

"Fine," I said.

"Fine?" He questioned and lifted his eyes in surprise. "Fine, yes?"

"Fine, yes. For now."

He grabbed my arm and pulled me into a hug. It only strengthened my decision. Without the jet standing in our way, I could freely accept Locke's arms around me.

"Thank you," he whispered into my hair. "I'll fix this, I promise."

"Why are you so keen on fixing me?" I asked as I rested my head on his chest.

"I said I'd fix *this*. Not you."

"It's the same thing."

"No, it's different," he said.

I looked at his eyes. He smirked. It was the same. He brushed his lips to mine, stirring a hunger in me.

"What if someone sees us?" I whispered.

"I don't care anymore." His lips lingered, and I longed for the taste of him. "I love you." He murmured the words against my lips. My heart pounded loudly in my ears as my eyes traveled up slowly until they met and held his. His eyes softened as a sweet and reassuring grin crept across his face. I reached up and touched his face to be certain I wasn't dreaming. The corners of my lips curled. His arms wrapped around me lifting my feet off of the ground as his lips crushed against mine. "I'm ridiculously and completely in love with you, Tinklee and I don't care who knows it." Never had anything ever sounded better or tasted sweeter.

His love has always held steadfast even as I faltered. This time I wasn't running. I was planting my feet because I loved him too, but returning to a life with emotion was a work in progress. Luckily Locke understood me and seemed willing to wait.

I rested my head against his chest and he rubbed his hand on my back.

"Thank you."

* * * *

I worked with mission planning for the next week. It didn't seem to raise too many eyebrows, but T-Rex knew. He watched me, asked how I was doing every time I saw him. I knew deep down under his tough exterior he would protect my secret. Unfortunately for Locke, each passing day only secured my decision to stay out of the cockpit. We both knew the longer I was away from it the more dangerous it would be to climb back in.

"I have a line for us," Locke said, sitting on the stairs outside the meal tent.

His announcement shadowed the sunny mood that I was in over the fresh food delivery this morning. I squeezed stale MRE peanut butter on my apple and avoided eye contact.

"Day after tomorrow. Morning run. There is a two-ship line scheduled to do a scout mission. It will be the perfect chance to go back up."

I bit into my apple and shrugged attempting to be non-committal until I figured a way out of his plan.

"Is that a *yes* shrug?" he asked watching me.

I sighed. He wasn't going to make this easy.

"I don't want to return to the cockpit," I said. The words still sounded foreign to me.

"If you stay off the schedule again next week people will ask questions. Sneaking in one line will take some of that pressure off," he recommended and tossed his fork back into the bag. "I don't want to push you."

I tilted my head and raised my brow.

"I don't. But the longer you stay on the ground, the more difficult it is going to be to get back in the air."

It was difficult to argue against the truth especially when it came for the man that I loved.

"I'll think about it." I stood.

It was best to change the subject before he changed my mind. "I have to go finalize plans for the mission you're going on tonight."

"I'm on crew rest, but I'll be over a little later," he said.

I nodded and turned around almost running into Ash. I braced myself on his abs.

"Whoa, sorry," I said.

"Watch it, you might hurt yourself on this steel."

A devious grin spread across his face. Somehow Ash could make cheesy lines work. I smacked him and winced.

"See," he said and chuckled.

I shook my hand and glanced back at Locke. His jaw clenched. He wasn't as charmed but he did manage to make jealousy look sexy.

"Why haven't you been flying?" he asked.

"I was sick," I said.

"You don't look sick." He tilted his head as his eyes scanned me. "You don't look sick at all."

Locke cleared his throat.

"I have to go," I said. "I'm mission planning."

Time to go before we had a repeated scene from my front porch.

"Glad you're feeling better." Ash waved as I walked away.

He had no problem calling me out.

Chapter 30

My eyes blurred as I reviewed the intricate details of tonight's mission. Intel confirmed a location for one of the top ten leaders of the LRA Special Forces. The ground team was going in to secure the enemy and their compound.

The desert mountains and canyons of northern Algeria would be challenging. The vertical terrain made it tough for the team members to climb and move quickly. Every canyon was deep and indistinguishable from the next. It was difficult to get the exact target and proper weapons effects. The ground team's plan covered every possible scenario, but you could never be certain what would happen.

I squeezed my eyes shut and stretched my arms over my head.

"That bad?" Locke asked. His voice washed away my tension.

"It's going to be interesting." I pointed to the intended target.

"Where is everyone?" he asked as he picked up the map and leaned against the desk.

"They went to get coffee. It's going to be a long night."

I tucked a loose strand of hair behind my ear. I hoped I didn't look as exhausted as I felt.

"Visibility is going to be reduced to a mile because of the wind and dust. It will be a challenge." He tossed the paper aside.

"Did you get any rest?" I asked trying not to react to how close he was sitting to me.

"It's hard to sleep when your scent lingers. I wish we didn't have twenty other guys sharing the tent." His leg brushed mine and my thighs flooded with heat as my eyes traveled up his body and back down again.

"Careful you don't start something you can't finish, sir." I leaned back and unzipped the top of my flight suit. A satisfied grin traveled across my face as Locke's eyes widened and mouth hung open slightly.

"Don't throw challenges out there if you don't mean them, Lieutenant." He pulled my chair forward and leaned over me. Every nerve ending lit on fire as his breath warmed against face.

This was a dangerous no-fly zone.

I licked my lips as his eyes hooded with desire. He leaned forward and caught my bottom lip between his teeth. A low purr rumbled from my lips. His hand tangled in my hair and pulled me closer as I pressed my lips against his. It had been way too long and I couldn't resist. I dug my fingers into his hips. His tongue tickled my lips before it swept inside. I lifted my body closer, needing more of him.

"What the hell?" Shatter shouted in a raised shocked tone, smacking his hand on a desk.

I flinched, knocking my teeth against Locke's.

"Shit," I hissed and grabbed for my teeth praying they were still there. After two years in braces and diligent retainer wear, they had better be.

Locke licked his lip as a tiny speck of blood formed.

As the shock dissolved and realization set in. I stood, my knees shaky.

"Sir, I can explain." Locke's tone was sharp and serious.

The heavy feeling of remorse dulled my chest. My wings might not be an issue anymore, but Locke's were.

"Not now," Shatter's sharp tone cut through me. "Later. Right now, I need to focus on the mission."

"Yes, sir," Locke answered, tense.

I wished I knew what he was thinking.

"Karma, you might want to comb your hair before the brief," He glanced up from the map and shot me a glassy stare obviously annoyed.

"Yes, sir."

I smoothed my hair back into a ponytail as a rush of heat flushed my cheeks.

Locke avoided eye contact. This was probably his first black mark on a perfect record. What were we thinking?

We weren't. That was the problem.

I rushed from the room.

"Duke, stay. I need your input on something," Shatter barked.

I turned the corner. Shit. Would it matter if I no longer flew and he was no longer my instructor? But what if they somehow blamed him for my decision to quit flying? The government losing a million-dollar investment was not going to go over well. They would want answers.

After dragging a brush through my hair, I twisted my ponytail into a bun. The taste of Locke still lingered on my lips. As much as we craved each other, we needed to get it together. Too many people knew about us already. Thankfully Shatter was too distracted to deal with us at the moment and hopefully, he would cool off before he called us to the mat. My unease settled a bit though the mortification still held a strong presence.

"What's wrong?" Ash joined my stride as I hurried back to the brief.

"Nothing? Why?" I asked.

"You get a wrinkle right here when you stress," he said, pointing between his brows.

His assessments of my moods were always spot on, probably a gift of being the youngest in a large family. But he didn't need to know about this.

"The mission tonight looks tricky," I said.

"Brief says in and out, no problem." Sarcasm laced his words.

"You don't agree?"

"Nope. I think we need to plan for the worst and hope for the best."

He pulled the flap back from the tent and I walked in. Always the gentleman. He joined the rest of the Special Forces on the right side of the brief. Stitch nodded to a chair beside him and I slid into it as Clash, Shatter, and Woodstock moved forward to speak.

Shatter reviewed the flight plan to provide coverage for the ground team. Their mission was to get in and out, securing any documents, equipment, and combatants they came across. The F-35 JSF would be ready to provide coverage as needed.

"There should be limited hostiles within the compound, no air threats, no quick reaction force," Shatter said. "In and out prior to sun-up. JSF's shouldn't even need to hit the tankers."

"If the information we are looking for is so valuable, why would they leave it unprotected?" Locke asked.

Clash straightened his stance. His lips drew into a straight line. "We have good intel," he answered.

Locke frowned. "How recent is it?"

"Recent." The word was short. Clash didn't expect any further questions. Ash leaned forward instead.

"What's the source of the intel?" Ash asked.

Clash narrowed his eyes. "Reliable."

Ash continued his line of questioning. "Sir, no disrespect, but if this is a goldmine of important information, how confident are we of the intel suggesting it is unguarded? Shouldn't we go in a little heavier in case anything unexpected happens?"

"No one suggested it is *unguarded*, Captain. It is lightly guarded." Clash's air quotes highlighted his arrogance and stupidity.

My blood boiled. What gave him the right to speak to Ash or any of these guys with such disrespect? They were Special Forces for a reason.

"It is what it is. We are always flexible and ready for real time changes," Clash finished.

It was like repeatedly walking into a brick wall. Clash obviously wasn't going to discuss this any further.

The brief ended, and Locke approached the ground team, discussing the plan with their lead captain. Stitch caught me before I joined them.

"When are you going back up?" Stitch asked.

I shrugged.

"The longer you wait the tougher it will be."

It was not the right time to tell him my days in the cockpit were probably over.

I nodded.

"Can I do anything to help?" His hand rested on my shoulder.

"I'm fine. They're heading out. You'd better go."

"Next mission is you and me, Tink," he said.

"Let's concentrate on one mission at a time." I forced a smile, avoiding a lie.

Stitch reluctantly nodded, willing to end the conversation. For now.

Chapter 31

I had too much nervous energy. It would be at least an hour before everyone else was in the mission-planning cell but I went there to wait for them anyways.

I sat on a chair and took the jade stone out of my pocket. I never left without it anymore. I loved how smooth its surface was and tossing it around kept me distracted.

I slid it back and forth along the old worn table changing the distance each time. The gemstone was a similar shade in color to Colin's room.

I remembered how his room reeked of stale beer from the piles of empty cans that lay around his room during his last visit and how he lived out of a duffle when he usually hung and divided his things by color within an hour of being home. I squeezed my eyes tightly shut. The signs were there if only I'd looked closer.

During that trip, he shrugged me off when I tried to get him to go for one of our usual jogs, instead sleeping late and barely leaving his room. I thought he was probably tired from the long hours he'd been putting in at the squadron, but now I know that it was more.

If I'd only paid more attention to the small signs of his suffering and added them up maybe we could have gotten him the help that he needed.

Wrapped in guilt and frustration, I stared at the stone in my hand and threw it hard at the door just as Mojo flung the door open, and it pelted him in the chest.

"Shit!" Mojo buckled. "What the hell was that for?"

The stone bounced across the floor. He scooped it and squeezed his hand.

"Give it back," I said and extended my hand.

"Yeah, right. Like I'm an idiot," he replied. "What's wrong with you anyway, you look like you saw a ghost."

I shook my head not wanting to relive the memory again and reached for the headset. I needed to concentrate on the mission right now. Everything else was going to have to wait.

Mojo set up in the mission-planning cell with several other airmen that had come in. I plugged my headset into the control station and snatched my stone from the table and dropped it in my pocket when Mojo wasn't looking.

The three monitors in front of me displayed computer-generated tracks of the various aircraft flight paths and friendly positions on the ground. As I slewed my cursor over the different tracks a small pop up window displayed critical information. I had the same flight products as the mission team as well as the slides from the briefing. Within minutes the satellite radios crackled with chatter.

"Be advised Jackpot is ten minutes out and looking for a situation update," the helicopter called.

I held my breath, anxiety crushing my chest. Ash thought *Jackpot* was a lucky name for the chopper delivering his team to the objective. I hoped he was right and luck was on their side.

"Jackpot, Roller, objective area is clear. Zero hostile activity." The command aircraft answered.

"Objective area clear," Ash's voice rose over the radio. "All players be advised from Pit Boss—Double Down."

Pit Boss was Ash's team—a lucky *and* clever nickname. I hoped he was as confident about the objective as the call signs they devised.

"Roller copies Double Down," Locke answered.

My heart fluttered anxiously hearing his voice. The mission was a go.

Everything in the mission room was still. Only my breaths pumped from my microphone to my ears.

"Jackpot, thirty seconds!" the chopper advised.

My chest tightened.

The helicopters made their final approach call to the landing zone.

"Roller, this is Jackpot, heads up we have some sort of activity to the Northwest of the objective."

"Roller copies, be advised it looks clear to us," Locke responded.

The radio calls tensed as the special ops team prepared to leave the helicopters and begin their assault on the compound.

Ash's voice came across the radio. "Pit Boss is boots on the ground."

His breathing quickened as much as mine. Popping sounds crackled in the radio.

"Troops in contact," he shouted sharp and quick. "Troops in contact. We're taking fire from the north."

Shit. I clutched my hands

"Jackpot hit! Egressing south!" the chopper call erupted.

"Roller Four missile launch from the north, defending west!" Locke ordered.

The other radios exploded in chaos as everyone transmitted at once.

I jumped to my feet as Mojo adjusted his microphone.

"Roller, this is Pit Boss!" Ash's voice garbled as the feed picked up interference. "I say again, we are taking direct fire from multiple positions to the north. We are pinned down and need immediate support."

"Pit Boss, stand by," Locke answered his tone cold and fiercely focused. "We have multiple enemy missile launches and heavy anti-aircraft artillery fire. Rollers, ambush and defend to the west and rejoin south!"

"This is Pit Boss, I have multiple wounded. Can you circle back and pick us up?" Ash shouted as popping and explosions boomed in the background.

"This is Jackpot, we'll try and make it back in there. We've been hit, but all systems are still functional. We're taking heavy fire."

More explosions erupted as gunfire popped. Locke's voice broke through the radio chatter.

"Roller Three, rejoin the flight to the south. Take Two and Four. Attack the northwest enemy position. Jackpot, I'm rejoining with you and will escort you, Pit Boss. Hit them as hard as we can and get everyone out of here, now!" His words were commanding, his voice controlled, yet I knew him well enough to hear his concern. I pulled my hands across my brows.

"Roller Three copies, commencing attack!" T-Rex barked.

"Jackpot, Roller One is rejoined, let's press north."

"Pit Boss is taking more fire! They have us pinned down. We need assistance or we're going to be overrun."

"This is Roller One, I'll be in on those hostiles in thirty seconds, keep your heads down."

"Pit Boss copies. Let 'em have it!"

"Roller One is off target, two bombs away!"

The explosions were deafening in the background. I could barely make out their voices as I paced back and forth.

"Good hits, Roller! Good hits! Jackpot, how far out are you?" Ash questioned. His breathing turned rapid. They were on the run.

“Jackpot is thirty seconds out, be ready for a hot pickup!” shouted the helicopter pilot.

“Pit boss is ready, bring it in.” He gasped. “Roller Three, good hits on the Northwest target!”

My heart raced though we seemed to be regaining the advantage. I wiped the beads sweat from my lip.

Locke’s voice cut through the radios and gripped at my chest. “Jackpot, you are taking fire from the east now. Heavy fire from the east!”

“Roller One, we see the team, we need more time.”

“Jackpot missile launch to the east, it’s on you!” Locke yelled in warning.

“We’re unable to defend!”

Fear crashed into me and the hair on the back of my neck stood.

“Jackpot, you have more missile launches from the east, I’ll try to decoy them off you. Roller Three, attack that missile sight. Now!”

“Roller One, negative,” Woodstock yelled.

My blood ran cold.

Locke didn’t answer.

“Roller One, negative. Copy.” T-Rex shouted. “Don’t.”

Chapter 32

I had fallen into another nightmare.

Large explosions rang in my ears as a surge of blinding panic flushed through my body. I closed my eyes and held my breath shaking my head rapidly.

"Roller One is down."

My full body trembled and as a primal scream rang inside my mind.

T-Rex's voice radioed in a shocked calmness.

I opened my eyes slowly and scanned the computer screen. Roller One was missing.

No, this couldn't be happening.

The room was deafeningly silent.

Not again. Please. Not Locke. I prayed without a sound, uncertain if I was pleading with God or Karma. My knuckles blanched from my death grip I had on the table. Please don't take him from me. I couldn't lose Locke. My heart begged with whoever would listen.

"Any signs of ejection?"

"Is there a beacon signal?"

"Mark the crash sight on GPS."

"Can a ground team get visual?"

The room erupted into a controlled chaos and I could hear their voices asking questions, questions that I needed to know the answers to, but it was like I was staring through a looking glass, watching someone else's horror.

"Karma?"

I couldn't answer all I could do was stare.

"Confirm Roller flight." Mojo shouted into a headpiece.

"Karma?"

"Roller One," Woodstock shouted trying to radio Locke again.

"Roller Three," T-Rex's voice was almost unrecognizable as he confirmed his location.

Stitch joined the chatter, his words cracking. "Roller Four."

"Roller Three," Woodstock radioed, his voice strained.

Roller One remained silent. My blood iced over with fear.

"Karma?"

Mojo snapped in my face and pointed to my headset.

I turned my head, feeling like it had been disconnected from my body. I'd been here, done this before.

Bury the hurt to survive the pain.

I'd had my heart being ripped from my chest before, only this time it was different, it was gripping at my soul. I couldn't lose the deep tearing pain that was shredding me apart.

My mind scrambled to capture the remembrance of his scent, the warmth of his touch, the sound of his voice. Only it didn't need to, I remembered everything about him. Locke was burned deep enough within me to last me forever only he was so much a part of me that I was uncertain if I could survive without him. Or if I even wanted to.

"Switch to ground frequency." Mojo pointed and shouted at me. "Slots One and Two are five minutes out. Get your shit together, Karma. Ground troops. Now!"

My heart forced blood through my unwilling veins. Everyone was shouting. Moving. Running. I blinked disoriented that life was still happening around me.

"Roller Two. Any visual?" Mojo asked.

"Pull up!" T-Rex barked.

Explosions erupted. They were taking more fire. Mojo reached over and hit a switch on my headset.

"I'm five hundred feet. Have visual on wreckage."

Devastation crushed the air from my lungs. It was Ash. He was on the ground headed toward the impact site. Gunshots pounded in my ears.

"We need air coverage!" Someone ordered.

My stomach knotted as the nightmare continued.

"Roller Two. Ground call for assistance," Mojo said.

Shatter grabbed the headset next to me and pulled them on.

"Slot flight is two minutes out." He held up two fingers.

More explosions rang into my ears.

"Wreckage is surrounded by hostiles." Ash grunted into the radio.

"Get on the chopper, Pit Boss."

"Not until we locate Roller One." A sliver of hope shot through me.

"Jackpot needs to lift off. We can't hold them," the helicopter radioed.

My pulse quickened. Maybe he survived. I knew the chances were minimal. But I wouldn't give up hope. I couldn't. Blood pumped wildly in my veins as I came back to life. A shimmer of hope that he'd ejected safely flickered wildly.

"Hostiles moving," Ash confirmed.

If they were moving, then Locke wasn't in the wreckage. He had ejected. I silently prayed that they wouldn't leave him to be captured or worse. I searched frantically for another headset.

Please Ash, don't give up.

"Move out, Pit Boss" An officer beside me ordered.

"No," I shouted and spun to face him. "You can't leave him."

The officer didn't look at me. "We can't risk losing twenty men to save one. One that we aren't certain survived."

Shatter dragged his hand across his face. He nodded to Mojo. "Bring 'em back."

My voice cracked. "No. Don't. Sir, you can't leave him, please." I begged.

Shatter nodded again.

Mojo's shoulders dropped. "Rollers, bring it home," Mojo said, his voice pained as his eyes held mine begging for forgiveness.

I shook my head. No way in hell. I reached for the control switch.

"Stand down, Lieutenant," Shatter ordered.

I stared him down. "How can you leave him?"

"Slot flight disengage. Mark coordinates and return to base," Shatter said. His face creased in anguish. He reached for my arm. Nothing he would say would justify his decision to leave Locke behind enemy lines. I pulled away, tearing off my headphones and throwing them into the console. I pushed my way out of the room needing distance.

The warm air burned my lungs. How could I be standing front row center watching another man that I loved be ripped from my life? I couldn't do this again. I couldn't lose Locke, like I had lost Colin.

Was fucking Karma still not satisfied?

Gravel crunched beside me and someone dropped to the ground. Mojo's aftershave hit me. And even though he was only following orders, I was still pissed at him.

"We'll find him. He's a survivor," he said.

"Go away," I growled.

"We're a team. We need each other."

My eyes narrowed as I lifted my head.

"Some team," I seethed. "He sacrificed himself to save everyone, and how do we repay him? We left him."

"It wouldn't have been a sacrifice if we lost the rest of team going after him. It would have been a massacre."

Mojo was right, but it didn't bring me comfort.

"We'll go back. They are already formulating a plan," he said.

He was trying to help but nothing would erase the pain and fear until we brought Locke home. Until I could see the spark in his eye, touch his warm skin, and feel his unwavering love.

"They won't give up until he's back," he said.

"How can you be so sure?"

"Because you'll be a pain in their asses until they do," he answered as his lip curled into a hesitant grin. He stood and extended his hand to me. "Come on, let's go wait for the guys and figure out how to find him."

I wanted to roll into a ball and hide, but I couldn't.

I wouldn't fail Locke. We had to get him back one way or another.

* * * *

Find your will to survive. My mom's words rang through my mind. Locke was my will and I wouldn't give up until we found him.

Woodstock stormed into the briefing room and shoved a chair against the wall before falling into it. Stitch followed T-Rex, their expressions twisted and tortured with deep-set brows and thinly drawn lips. The ground team filed in with faces streaked by dirt and sweat. Some of them were bleeding. One of the guys let out a roar and punched the wall, breaking through the wood.

Ash was one of the last in. My heart raced. His stare burned wild. He sat in the back. Alone. I needed to ask him what he found, but Mojo stopped me.

"Give them a minute to unwind."

"What do you have?" Shatter pushed his way into the room with Clash.

"We walked right into a damn trap. They were ready for us," one of the ground team members said.

"Did we recover any documents or intel?" Clash asked.

I gripped my fists and didn't look up, painstakingly close to assaulting a superior officer.

"Are we able to confirm anything about Duke?" Shatter asked.

I wanted to tell him he that he didn't have the right to speak his name, but I was more concerned with what the team discovered about Locke.

"He wasn't in the cockpit," Ash's voice was hoarse from yelling. A light-hearted feeling of hope fluttered through me. "But that's all. We couldn't get close enough." The flutter crashed and burned landing in the deep pit of my belly.

"Did we recover anything?" Clash repeated.

My lips drew into a thin line.

Ash glared at him. "We got our asses smoked and almost killed. If it weren't for Duke, our entire team and helicopter flight would have been overrun. And you left him out there."

I wasn't going to have to kick his ass, Ash was ready to do it for me.

"Stand down, Captain," Clash warned.

I almost laughed. Did Clash have a clue who he was dealing with?

"Great fucking intel, by the way," Ash said.

Bodhi and a team of airmen rushed into the room bearing medical supplies and bottled water. They rushed to the wounded, but Bodhi reserved a glance for me. His face paled. I knew he wanted to know about Locke's status just as much of any of us.

"What's the plan?" T-Rex asked.

I returned my attention trying to shake off the feeling of doom and refocusing on my determination to bring home the man I loved.

"We need to get back out there," someone said.

Yes, thank God, they were willing.

"The jets are being refueled. I'm ready as soon as they are," Woodstock answered.

"Ever hear of a plan?" Clash asked.

"We're ready. That's the plan," Mojo said.

"So are we," Ash shouted.

Roger that. The cockpit haunted me almost as much as never seeing Locke again. I had to get over it. Locke needed me.

"Half of you are injured, and we are short on rested instructors at the moment," Clash said. "I suggest we regroup in the morning."

"He won't make it that long," I blurted. "He could be injured. They were already searching for him. We need to find him first."

Clash turned toward me. His lips drew into a thin line. "We aren't certain he survived. We would only be putting more troops at risk. For *one* man. It doesn't make sense."

That *one* man had called Clash a friend.

I slammed my hands on the desk. The searing pain matched the blinding rage taking over my mind. "What the hell is wrong with you?"

"Karma, sit." Shatter snapped and pointed at me. "Clash, I've got this. Why don't you go gather intel?"

Someone behind me scoffed.

"Better yet. See if there is any sign of communication from Duke," he said.

Clash's eyes darkened as he walked from the room.

"Fantom, compile a team. Previous instructors only. Get together with the ground troops and coordinate. Time is of the essence, but we can't risk a team by going in blind and without proof of life."

I needed to be on that rescue mission to bring Locke home, I couldn't be a bystander any longer. The fear and my will for survival that had pushed me away from the cockpit were suddenly pulling me back in.

"Rollers, Slots, go get some rest. It's been a shit night," Shatter said.

"My team too," the Special Forces commander said. "After Bodhi checks you out, go recharge."

"Karma, upfront." Shatter snapped his fingers.

My eyes burned. I tensed my jaw to prevent any more outbursts, deserving or not.

"You do *not* speak to a superior officer that way," Shatter said. "I realize this is *sensitive*," he whispered his last word as he looked around, "But this is still the military, and there is a code of conduct."

"Yes, sir."

"Given the situation, you will not be flying on any of the missions involving Duke's recovery."

"Sir," I raised my voice, not believing my ears.

"Final decision," he said.

I knew I couldn't argue, but how could I be certain they wouldn't give up?

"Are we clear?" He eyes held mine.

I swallowed my frustration before answering. "Yes, sir."

He nodded and walked away. He stopped and glanced over his shoulder. "Karma?"

I looked up not wanting to hear anything more.

"We'll bring him home."

* * * *

I had been sidelined in the battle for survival. I had to make certain the right players would still be fighting for us.

Bodhi tended to Ash's wound. He had burst open most of the sutures from his previous injury.

"Are you okay?" I asked.

"Are you?" He scowled as Bodhi pressed on the wound.

"You can't answer a question with a question," I said.

"No, I'm not okay. We owe Duke our lives and we left him." He pushed Bodhi's hand away. Bodhi didn't seem insulted.

"You didn't have a choice," Bodhi said as he gathered the old bandages. "He's tough. He'll make it."

He walked away with his shoulders slumped. No fist bump.

"I'm sorry," Ash said, avoiding looking me in the eyes.

"It's not your fault."

He threw a roll of leftover tape with a grunt. "We should have kept some feet on the ground."

"It would have complicated things even more."

"How are you so fucking calm?"

My heart beat strong and slow.

"I'm not," I said. "I'm dying inside."

"Well, that's at least an improvement."

I questioned instantly on the defensive, "What is that supposed to mean?"

"You answered one of my questions," he said as I simmered down. "Honestly."

I softened my posture. Talking to Ash was comforting. He was always honest and at this point, I was done lying to others and myself.

"Do you think he made it?" I asked quietly.

Doubting his survival felt as dangerous as doubting the jet.

He took my hands in his. I swallowed the lump in my throat.

"If anyone could, it would be him," he said.

I prayed he was right.

"You're in love with him."

I nodded.

"We'll find him, Tink. I promise, I'll bring him home." He paused. "Now that you're being honest, do you want to tell me why you're not flying?"

I tucked a loose strand of hair behind my ear. "I don't want to fly anymore."

His eyes widened.

"Ever?"

I shook my head.

"Why? I don't understand."

"I don't want it anymore." I shrugged. "I hate my jet."

"You sound like it's a person."

"She's consumed so much of me, she probably could be," I said.

"Typical woman. They take every part of you, then chew you up and spit you out."

I grimaced, it was not time for a smile.

"I'm teasing. I want you to be happy, Tink. And if it's with Duke, so be it."

"Thanks."

"Don't thank me yet," he said.

I tilted my head. Now what?

"I'm not going to leave you alone until you get back in that cockpit," he said. "You are a survivor. You are a fighter pilot. You can move past whatever happened. You need to find that drive. Teach that bitch who's boss."

My lips curled in a half-hearted attempt of a smile.

"You need to get back in the jet. We need pilots like you."

"Like me? I don't think so."

"Like you. Fierce. Determined. Stubborn." He winked. "Hot."

And though it felt unnatural, I forced a slight smile.

"You have to, Tink."

"Shatter said I couldn't fly on these missions."

"Good."

I frowned.

"Cause when someone tells you no, you'll do it anyways just to prove you can."

Chapter 33

There were no signs of Locke. The numbness from the initial shock of losing him had been replaced by my fortitude to find him.

I wandered from room to room anywhere discussions were being held about his recovery mission. When I wasn't eavesdropping, I neurotically checked beacon signals for signs that Locke was trying to make contact.

"This is the best possible scenario according to his last coordinates," T-Rex pointed the directions on a map.

I scooted closer to where he stood with Shatter and craned my neck to see.

"Most likely he would be here, here, or here." I reached between then and tapped the map.

Shatter glanced back at me with his jaw firmly set.

"You said I couldn't fly," I said. "You didn't say anything about me helping with mission planning."

"She's right. Those would be his best chances for survival." T-Rex nodded. "Duke has advanced training in survival. He'd head for the mountains."

"Fine. Share it with the ground troops." Shatter looked me over. "Have you slept at all?"

I didn't answer and he frowned at me.

"We need you rested even if you're not flying."

"I'm fine, sir," I lied.

"None of us are fine. But we have to rest to function," he said. "Have you eaten?"

I shrugged.

"I'm ordering you to grab something to eat and get to sleep."

I opened my mouth to argue. He cut me off.

"If you can't sleep, then close your eyes. I don't want to see you around here for at least six hours. Mission brief starts at 1600."

"Yes, sir."

My stomach growled, but the thought of food made me want to puke. I moped all the way back to the tent, hoping that they were right about Locke heading to the mountains. I prayed he was physically able to. I knew, if he was alive, he was running short on time. Oh God.

As I entered the tent, all the guys were sleeping so thankfully I didn't get the awkward stares wondering if I was going to go off the deep end.

I unlaced my boots and wiggled my toes as I pulled off my socks. I stared at the faded scar on my foot. The memory of his touch, his taste, his everything, crushed me like a weight on my chest. I needed him here with me more than ever. He would have the precise answers of what we should do and he would know exactly what to say to make me feel better. Only he couldn't, because we'd lost him.

And I never even told him how much I loved him.

* * * *

Roadblocks weren't an option. These men would blow up anything in their path to bring their comrade home and so would I.

Everyone had their heads buried in maps, jaws clenched. When T-Rex briefed, I listened, ready to add any information that may have been overlooked. But he hit every detail with fine precision. The ground team was ready to burst from the room with caged adrenaline.

"As long as the weather cooperates, we should be ready," Clash said from his seat.

I glared, despising every thing about him.

"We'll be ready without its cooperation," Woodstock answered without hesitation.

"We'll be ready for everything and anything they throw our way. Screw Mother Nature," Fantom said.

Chills trickled down my arms. They were ready. And for the first time since the crash, I was suddenly hopeful. If Clash were smart, which I seriously questioned, he would keep his negative comments to himself.

The door swung open and a young captain rushed to the front of the room.

"Sir, you need to see this."

A shiver skated down my spine.

Shatter took the tablet from her hand. Something was streaming. I couldn't hear much, but it looked like some sort of video.

The color drained from his face. He stood and walked out.

No one spoke. No one moved. I wanted to vomit.

Was it news about Locke? Or was there another crisis that would divert his attention? My chest filled with daggers desperately needing to know.

Twenty minutes passed. It felt like twenty days. He came back with the tablet. He handed it to T-Rex then whispered something into his ear.

"Karma, Stitch, come with me."

I pressed my lips together to keep me from questioning him about what the hell was going on. His jaw tensed. Everyone stared. My legs froze. I couldn't move. This was bad news about Locke. I could feel it.

"Stitch," he repeated.

I felt a hand rest on my elbow. I wanted to pull away, but then I remembered my mother the day she stoically opened the door to the two men in uniform that had arrived to tell her that her only son was dead. I pulled from her strength and her courage. I stood, raised my chin, and walked stoically from the room.

* * * *

Our footsteps were the only sound. We followed Shatter to a building next door. He sat us at a bare table.

I laced my fingers in front of me and sat taller.

Shatter ran his hand through his hair then scratched his cheek, as if struggling for words.

"Sir," I said.

He exhaled loudly before starting to speak. "We have a video that we believe shows Duke has been killed in action. We are waiting for confirmation."

A shocked pain gripped and twisted at my chest as I tried to grasp what he was saying. My brain processed video, Duke killed and waiting for confirmation. My entire body tingled.

Stitch touched my shoulder. I shrugged him off and attempted to keep it together.

"It hasn't been confirmed?" I asked.

"Not officially, but it's enough to call off the search and rescue."

I wanted to scream. I wanted to vomit. My pulse raced as my mind searched for something to convince him otherwise.

"What was on the video?" I asked mustering up all the strength that I had.

He looked at Stitch and frowned.

"Sir, what was on the video?" I repeated.

"I think it's better…."

"Sir, what is on the fucking video?"

Shatter winced. "Enemy combatants dragged his body down a street."

I sucked back a deep breath, nearly choking on it. I needed air. I couldn't breath. I shoved back my chair and stumbled. Stitch gripped my arm, but I yanked it away. This could not be happening.

What the hell did they do to him? Bile rose in my throat and I slapped my hand across my mouth. Locke was dead.

"Let's go back to the tent," Stitch said softly. "We can figure out everything else later."

I dropped my hand from my face and held my stomach. "Did you see his face?" I ignored Stitch.

Shatter shook his head. "There was a bag over his head, but he was in a flight suit. They held his helmet and torn parachute."

"It could be someone else. They could be using it as a propaganda video." I shook my head as quickly as I spoke.

He unfolded a paper and handed it to me. I stared at the enhanced image of a jet-black helmet. The shield was cracked and a bloody handprint was smeared along the insignia. My hands trembled. The helmet was definitely Locke's. He continued to wear his helmet from his old squadron. His was black and ours were dark gray.

His damn helmet didn't prove anything. Locke was strong, brave, and a warrior. *My* warrior. He wasn't gone. He wouldn't leave me. He promised me and I allowed myself to believe him. I needed to believe him. I had to believe that Locke loved me too much to leave me. I touched his handprint on the paper and closed my eyes.

Except it was a promise that no one could keep. This was life and this was what life did to you. Why had it chosen to do it to me again?

I shook my head and crumpled the paper in my shaking hands.

He couldn't be gone. I loved him and I never told him. Why hadn't I told Locke that my heart belonged to him, forever? Maybe he would have fought harder to come back to me. It would be a regret that would haunt me.

Shatter dragged his hands down his face and let out a long puff of air before speaking. "There's no sign of life. Nothing from his radio. The body appears to match his build and with his helmet and his parachute." He paused. "It might be all we ever have. We may never get more evidence."

"Tink," Stitch said.

I wanted to scream, to run, to fly to the gates of hell and strike a deal with the devil. Anything to would bring him back to me. I gripped the chair and threw it over. My breath grated as I exhaled loudly and pressed my hands to the top of my head.

“Did they kill him, or was he dead when they found him?” My voice shook as my eyes met Shatter’s.

His eyes filled with tears. “We don’t know. We may never know. They’ll tell us whatever they want.”

I hooked my hands around the back of my neck and pulled forward. “We need to get his body.” I swallowed hard to keep from heaving.

“We’ll try,” he said. “Duke was a hero.”

My breath caught as a deep hollow ache burned in the cavity of my chest. He swiped tears from his eyes. Stitch’s teeth dented his lip and he blinked rapidly as his arms wrapped around me. I buried my face into his chest feeling empty.

Locke was gone.

Chapter 34

My body was numb from the pain of having my heart torn from my chest. Stitch walked me back to the tent so I could rest. I lay on my cot staring blankly at the ceiling.

All I could think of was getting him back to his family. Locke deserved a proper burial and I needed to see him. I needed to touch him.

Though I barely knew them, my heart ached for his parents. And Kassie. I couldn't stand her, but she loved Locke. I didn't wish this pain upon anyone. What about Bodhi? Had he heard yet?

My head throbbed and my eyes stung.

I hung my hand over the side of the cot and pulled my bag from underneath. I needed something to wipe the beads of sweat from my brow. My hand brushed something soft—Mom's handkerchief. I grabbed a T-shirt and wiped my forehead then tossed it to the side tracing the embroidered names with my finger. Colin and Tinklee.

Why was this happening all over again? I buried my head into my hands. The lingering scent of vanilla hung onto the handkerchief.

I refused to talk to or see anyone after I left the tower that day—after I left without Colin. The silence followed me. Everyone stared. The hush of sorrow was as haunting as the accident's explosion.

The pain never went away. I could hide it from everyone except myself. Time was supposed to heal, but so much time had passed and I still felt as broken as that day. Maybe there was too much guilt mixed in with the pain to recover. I asked Colin to fly the jet. I missed the signs that he needed help. He went up the day of the accident for me. He loved me, and I failed him in so many ways.

"I miss you so much," I whispered. "I am so sorry I couldn't help you. I'm sorry I didn't understand."

The memory of his smile and the sound of his laugh rang in my ears. I remembered the words were spoken about him at his funeral. He was a man of honor, strength and integrity. A kind, gentle soul, yet a skilled airman.

"I promise that your sacrifice and your spirit will never be forgotten." My voice sounded stronger. "I'm sorry it has taken me so long to tell you that I love you."

I wasn't sure if I was speaking to Colin or Locke. They both deserved to hear my words. It had taken me entirely too long to tell both of them.

I fell back onto my pillow and my head thumped against something hard. It was my tablet. My hands shook as I turned it on.

I closed my eyes taking a deep breath. When I opened them, I typed *Dead Military Pilot in Northern Algeria* into the search engine. A link to YouTube listed first. My chest pounded as my trembling finger tapped it.

Men with rifles were jumping, celebrating and screaming into the camera. Behind them, a truck dragged a body in a green flight suit with a torn parachute wrapped around it. Tears formed in my eyes, but I forced myself to keep watching as the camera panned to the top of the body. His head was covered with a bloodied burlap sack.

I stared in horror as another one of the men shook his helmet. The one from the photo. Another shook his boots causing my stomach to lurch. His feet were cut and bruised as his body bounced along the uneven ground. I gagged. Oh dear God. What had they done to him? I covered my mouth with the palm of my hand and forced myself to keep watching. The pant leg of his flight suit rode up his calf, catching along the graveled path.

My lip trembled and my throat burned with rage. Locke didn't deserve this. No one did.

I stared, horrified at the image.

I focused in on his leg. His ankle. His left ankle. His left ankle was smooth.

Smooth.

Unmarked?

"No family crest. There was no family crest. No tattoo." I whispered loudly to myself. "Oh my God, it's not Locke." I shouted.

The man in the video wasn't Locke! My heart raced and my legs shook as adrenaline rushed me. I jumped to my feet and blinked hard trying to focus.

They couldn't call off the mission. This wasn't Locke. Locke could still be alive.

I shoved the handkerchief into my pocket on top of my stone then ran from the tent, pumping my arms.

A crowd of airmen stood outside the mess tent and I pushed and shoved them from my path as I bounced around like a pinball. Once I finally broke through, I picked up my pace and leapt over busted sidewalk. The tent was up ahead. My lungs burned and my muscles twitched as I ran up the stairs, gripped the handle on the door. I burst through the briefing door, gasping for air.

"You're here," I gasped, grabbing onto to the wall for support. "Thank God, you're still here."

"Tink?" Ash said calmly as he stood.

"It's...not...it's not him." The words burned like fire as the spilled my lips. I reached for my throat, trying to swallow.

T-Rex's eyes widened. "Someone get Bodhi." He snapped his fingers and pointed to the door.

Ash was in front of me with his hands on my arms.

"Tink, calm down. Breathe."

I was trying to, but I'd broken a frigging world record sprinting here.

"The mission. Call it back on. It wasn't Locke in the video," I said still panting.

"Let's go get some water. Come on." Ash tried pulling me toward the door.

"Listen to me! I'm not crazy."

Even though I'm sure that I looked it.

Someone handed me a cup of water and I knocked it to the ground.

"She's in shock," Clash said. "Someone get her out of here."

"Damn it!" My voice roared back. "Listen to me, it is not Locke. I can prove it."

Bodhi tore into the room. He pushed Ash out of the way to get to me.

"Bodhi," I said. "Thank God. Do you remember in Australia? The night you got Locke drunk and talked him into getting that tattoo?" I grabbed his arm.

He nodded, but frowned.

"Bodhi, tell them. Tell them where he got the tattoo."

"I don't remember. Some sketchy hole in the wall." He shook his head, his eyes bloodshot.

Ash reached for me. "Tink."

"No," I hollered and pushed him away. "Where? Where on his body did he get the tattoo?"

"His ankle."

"Yes, his ankle. His left ankle," I shouted. "T-Rex, pull up the video."

T-Rex's eyes were hooded as he watched me. He didn't move.

"The man they are dragging doesn't have a tattoo on his ankle. It isn't Locke!"

Shatter came into the tent.

"What the hell is going on?" he asked.

"The chick's losing it and everyone's watching." Clash leaned back in his chair.

Woodstock reared up and tipped the chair over, knocking Clash head over foot. Clash scrambled to his feet knocking the chair out of the way. Woodstock was puffed and ready to go. Fantom shoved back the table eager to join in.

"Knock it off. Someone tell me what the hell is going on. Now," Shatter ordered.

"Sir, we're all about to find that out," T-Rex said.

He hit play and the video came to life on the screen.

"Forward it," I said.

He pointed at the screen.

"There. Stop it. Right there."

He paused. The man's dark olive-skinned leg froze on the screen. The green flight suit pant leg was pushed up to his shin revealing the smooth, inkless skin of his left ankle.

"Dude, you're right," Bodhi gasped drumming on the table in front of him. "She's right."

"Right about what?" Shatter asked looking confused.

"Sir, Locke has a tattoo on his left ankle," I said with a slight grin. "Look at the left ankle." I pointed to the screen "There is no tattoo. That isn't Locke."

"I guess you'd know," he muttered.

Ash grabbed me and squeezed my shoulders.

"Hot damn! Let's go get our guy," T-Rex shouted.

The room erupted in cheers and pounding on the tables.

"I hate to be the one bringing up touchy subjects," Clash said. "But this still doesn't mean he's alive."

"We also don't know that he isn't," Woodstock argued.

"We still don't know where to look, and bad weather's rolling in. We should wait until it passes and go in tomorrow."

"We can fly above them. Only drop down if we're needed. We should still go tonight," Fantom said.

I didn't have to argue. They were doing it for Locke.

"The weather report…." Clash began.

"You're not even flying. It should be up to us." Woodstock pointed to the Special Forces team. "And them."

"We're ready," Ash said.

Thank God. This was wasting time. Time that Locke didn't have.

"Get an update on the weather report. Call to ready the jets. Go get me an update on last GPS coordinates and any updates of sign of life," Shatter snapped off orders.

He lightly patted my arm as a small gesture of hope and left the room.

"We'll bring him home," Ash said squeezing my shoulder.

* * * *

We can't. Those two words shot through my heart like a lightning rod. My hearing betrayed me. It was the only answer.

Shatter stood in front of the room, his face creased with anguish as he delivered the crushing news. "The risk versus benefit is too great. We can't risk all these men to rescue one. One that we don't have sign of life or location. The weather is too severe. "

"We volunteer. You're not asking us," Woodstock argued.

"It doesn't work that way." He shook his head.

"Sir, his chances of survival greatly diminish after twenty-four hours," Ash said.

"I know the statistics. My hands are tied. I'm not the only one making the call here. Headquarters has ordered us to stand down unless it's an emergency or we have definitive proof of life. We may get authorization if we get proof of life. The jets will remain cocked and ready to go. Fantom, Woodstock, T-Rex and Clash will be in the jets at twenty-one hundred for ground alert."

I needed to change his mind. Their minds. But I had nothing and it was maddening. Anything that I said would be dismissed in the same way they were dismissing Locke's life.

"I'm sorry." He avoided my eye contact with me as he exited.

Fantom stood up and flipped the table then walked from the room.

"I don't know why we're waiting. We could sit in the jets all night waiting for authorization, then it could be too late. We should just go," Woodstock said, punching the wall as he left.

T-Rex hung his head. He folded up the maps before leaving.

Mojo, Freak, Stitch, and I remained seated.

"I usually shut up and color, but this is messed up. Seriously messed up," Freak said.

"Isn't there something we can do?" Mojo asked.

There had to be. I just couldn't figure it out.

"Maybe we can convince them to go in without us." Stitch nodded to the ground team.

They were in deep focused conversation. Ash glanced my way, winked and gave a thumbs-up. I hitched my brows. What were they up to?

"Screw them. We should steal a jet and show them what the newbies can do. Who cares about a stupid storm anyway?" Mojo kicked the table.

Ash waved me over.

"We're still going," Ash said quietly. "Tonight. Actually now. If the storm is as bad as they are saying and he's injured, he might not make it through the night."

My eyes widened, shocked and grateful for their decision to go after Locke.

"We're going too," I said.

If they were going to risk everything for Locke there was no way in hell that I wasn't going to join them and help cover them from the air.

His eyes widened and he leaned forward like he hadn't heard me.

"What?" he whispered loudly.

"The four of us. The jets are ready and waiting. The instructors won't be out there for two more hours. We can be gone before they realize what happened."

Ash surveyed his guys before moving me away from the group. His voice stayed low.

"You're talking a court martial, Tink. I was telling you so you'd know we weren't leaving him. I'm not asking you to put yourself at risk too."

"You don't have to ask. I'm telling you we're going. At least I am."

"I am too," Stitch said.

"Me too," Mojo answered.

I turned to Freak. He nodded.

"There is one problem. The four jets are scheduled for ground alert under four different pilots' names. The crew chiefs will know the difference," Freak said.

He was right, but I had a plan. At least I hoped I did.

"We have access to the system, we can change the plan. Stitch—swap our names in the scheduling program, Mojo—put the flight plan into the system and Freak—grab our gear then meet us at the flight line. We should have thirty minutes to get into the cockpit and out of here before they figure it out," I said.

The guys rushed into action without hesitation.

I turned to Ash and wrapped my arms around his neck.

"Thanks, Ash."

"Are you sure?" he asked.

"Hell yeah, I'm sure. Let's do this."

He handed me a paper and I glanced down at it. The number 070.40 and the code name 'True Grit' were scribbled on it. It was the communication frequency on the radio that he wanted us to use.

"True Grit?"

We usually used gambling references. We were going without squadron approval so it was probably a good idea to use something unrelated, but I didn't understand their choice.

"The Duke. John Wayne. One of greatest movies ever, True Grit." Ash looked insulted at my lack of recognition of his brilliance.

It was the wrong Duke reference, but whatever; if Locke was out there we would find him.

Chapter 35

I sprinted to the flight line to make certain the jets were ready. Staff Sergeant Wilson was securing one of chocks on the jet.

He glanced up then snapped to attention. "Hi Ma'am. There's been a lot of changes to the schedule tonight," he said.

Awesome. We were one step closer.

"Ma'am?" He raised a questioning brow when I didn't answer.

I didn't want to lie to him.

"The weather's been causing chaos," I walked around the jet trying to avoid his stare.

A Senior Master Sergeant jogged up holding a clipboard in his hand.

"Sergeant Wilson, what are you doing? These jets are only on ground alert," he shouted over the engine noise.

Shit. Our plan was going to go up in smoke before we even struck the match.

"Yes, they were sir. But the updated schedule has it pushed up to a 1930 takeoff." Staff Sergeant Wilson flipped through the paperwork.

"Was this authorized?"

"Yes, sir, it was signed off by Major Rex."

He pointed at the clipboard. The Senior Master Sergeant looked over the document, nodded, and hurried away.

Great Mojo. Add forgery to our list of crimes.

Adrenaline pumped wildly through my body. My hands shook as Sergeant Wilson walked over to me.

"The jets are ready when you are, ma'am."

"Okay. Thank you, Sergeant Wilson."

I couldn't look him in the eye.

"Yes, ma'am. The helicopter is long gone," he said. "And ma'am, I'd make it a quick takeoff."

I glanced up and he winked.

Stitch, Freak and Mojo rushed over to me. They pulled our gear from two large duffels, and we quickly dressed.

"How'd everything go?" I asked.

"So far so good," Stitch answered. "We need to hurry."

"Stay on frequency 070.40. Code word True Grit," I said.

A grin spread across the others' faces. Men. They got it.

"No chatter until I radio. I'll take one. Stitch—two, Freak—three, and Mojo—four."

"True Grit flight's a go," Mojo said. "Let's do it!"

I climbed my ladder and strapped my helmet on. Sergeant Wilson snapped me to the seat.

He gave me a thumbs-up and I nodded. There was no turning back.

The canopy lowered and the jet awakened along with my nerves as I taxied to the runway. I thought my days of being in this cockpit were over but right now, I needed her. And Locke needed me. I shifted my focus onto him. His lightning blue eyes bore into my memory with linger of his touch. He was mine, and they couldn't have him. I couldn't save Colin, but I had to try to save Locke.

My cheeks were tingly and I adjusted the air, sucking in a deep breath.

Keep it together. You've got this.

Something poked me in the chest under my straps. I shifted but it dug deeper. What the hell was it?

I reached into my pocket. My fingers brushed something cool and smooth. The stone. It was for clarity, confidence, and good luck. If I ever needed it now was the time. I gave it a rub, said a quick prayer, and dropped it back into the pocket.

As I took the runway, I gripped the stick and pushed forward on the throttle, forcing myself back into the seat and easily soaring into the air.

I swallowed the large lump in my throat. We made it into the air. I prayed Sergeant Wilson would be okay. It was going to be chaos when the instructors stepped to the jet. Maybe we should have told Woodstock so he could've run interference, but the fewer people who knew the better. We were all going to lose our wings over this. And more than likely go to jail, but I didn't care.

Locke was worth the risk.

We would have to go off the original plan. And we had no tanker if we needed to fuel. There was no room for error. The closer we got to the mountains the bumpier the flight got. I gripped the stick tighter. The other three held tight to my wing.

Once we got within range, I flipped to the frequency. I could hear small ground chatter.

"True Grit One, flight ten minutes out," I said.

"True Grit Two."

"True Grit Three."

"True Grit Four."

"Boots already on ground, we're on the move," Ash reported and followed with his current coordinates.

I punched them into the map. My jet jerked as a large lightning bolt erupted in front of me.

Shit! That was close.

Thunder erupted and my wings rocked. I gripped and steadied.

"The weather's kicking our ass," Ash radioed.

"We need to keep pressing and see if it starts to thin out. If anyone see's a break in the cloud deck, sing out so we can get under the weather and put eyes on the objective," I ordered.

I listened, my heart pounding louder than his call.

"Copy, be advised, we were able to determine the location of the objective's radio. Someone from home base sent us his last coordinates. They were time stamped thirty minutes ago, nothing since," Ash said.

What the hell? Home base? Thirty minutes ago?

"Can you confirm who sent the coordinates?" I questioned.

T-Rex's voice cut through the radio chatter. "True Grit, those are the best coordinates that we have. Do your best."

Holy shit. It was T-Rex and Locke's radio was active. The good news was there was sign of life. The bad news was the cat was out of the bag at home base.

"We're proceeding toward old coordinates, but he may have moved, or worse, it may be an ambush. We need you to search the area from the air and get eyes on the objective. Be ready to respond if this is a trap." Ash's orders resonated in my head.

A sliver of hope jittered in my chest. Please, let it be Locke.

"True Grit, we're five minutes out from the old coordinates, what's your status?"

Ash sounded calm. Then Karma reared her ugly head.

"Son of a bitch! We need support. Taking fire," Ash shouted as explosions boomed through his radio.

Anti-aircraft artillery came arcing through clouds like fiery water hoses followed by larger caliber rounds slicing the sky like lasers. Large popcorn explosions detonated all around. The ethereal glow of surface-to-air missiles launches erupted from their sites in the distance.

Shit. It was an ambush and we had walked right into it.

Chaos erupted on the radio. "Two has missile launches to the west. They're on me!"

"True Grit, the coordinates are empty, I say again, he *isn't* here. We're taking direct fire. Need immediate support!"

"Holy shit. Bandits!" Mojo's voice cut through everyone's chatter.

"I'm painting two hostile fighters on radar inbound toward our position. They're haulin' ass and trying to get a lock on us," Freak shouted.

"True Grit, we're outnumbered. We need support. What's your status?" Ash yelled over the explosions.

This was my fault.

I had to end this and get everyone out before more people got killed. I disobeyed orders and had no business being up here. I adjusted my airflow. I couldn't breathe. The fate of everyone was in my hands—my wings. My body choked over each breath.

Please let me get everyone out of here.

I gripped my stick. I could do this. I had to. That's when I heard it. The faintest radio transmission mixed in with all of the other communications.

"Karma?" a voice murmured. It was weak and I wondered if my mind was playing tricks on me.

"Duke?" I strained to hear.

"Karma…" the voice was whispered and thin. I instinctively turned west toward the explosions and missile launches. "Karma, it's Duke, can you read me?"

"Yes, Duke, I hear you," I radioed through the chaos.

"One, you're taking fire! What the fuck are you doing?" yelled Mojo.

"Everyone zip it! I got him!" I answered.

"Say again?" Ash radioed.

Gunfire pounded in the background.

"I said I've got him! I've got Duke," I shouted. "Duke, what's your status?"

"Holed up, enemy activity, nonambulatory, require medevac." Locke's voice clipped his words. Like he was winded. He was wounded.

"One, we need to confirm that's him. It could be another ambush." Freak cut in. "Enemy fighters are closing fast. We need to get out of here!"

It was him. There was no doubt, but I needed to prove he wasn't under coercion.

"Duke, tell me what I did to you on the night we met?" I blurted out, desperate to prove it was him.

"What?" It was the collective response from Stitch, Freak, Mojo, T-Rex, and Ash.

"You beat the bloody hell out of me!" Locke whispered back in that accent and I could picture a smile on his face.

A smile gripped my face. He was alive and nothing would stop me from bringing him home.

"It's him! True Grit Three and Four split off and get rid of those bandits! Two and I are going below the weather to get eyes on his location. Let's get him out of there."

"Roger that!" It rang in unison.

"Duke, we need a fix on your position," I radioed.

"From old coordinates, I walked from my house to yours...about four kilometers," Locke rasped.

He was four kilometers to the east. We had to hurry.

"Ash…."

"Got it. We're on the move," Ash interrupted.

"True Grit Three's engaged with bandits. Let's take them out!"

I had to get below the weather. I searched desperately. Off in the distance in the middle of all the fireworks was a small break in the cloud deck. Perfect.

"Two, there's a break in the weather to our Northwest, let's go."

I wrapped the jet around and the G's crushed me back into the seat. I put the small hole in the clouds on my nose and jammed the throttle into afterburner.

"One, wait! That hole's closing in on itself and we don't know what's on the other side. Abort!" Stitch yelled.

Never.

"Karma, you could be flying right into a mountain. Abort!" T-Rex wailed from home base.

I could see the clouds collapsing on themselves as they highlighted and glowed with explosions. I had no idea what was on the other side, but I had to do it. I had to go in blind.

I squeezed my eyes tight as the jet punched into the clouds. The swirling darkness enveloped the jet, and every bump and dive of turbulence created another series of beeps and warnings from my screen. The seconds slowed to a stop. My heart struggled against the G-forces. This wasn't a storm. This was an eternity.

Then, finally, I broke out, underneath the cloud deck. My stomach lurched. If I thought the world was ending above the clouds, it was Armageddon below. Tracers arced up into the sky as explosions went off everywhere. The mountains climbed up into the clouds as lighting and gunfire mixed.

"Two, I'm below the weather. Stay up there and cover. There isn't room down here for multiple jets."

"Copy."

Stitch's words blew with forced air. He had been holding his breath.

"I'm getting too old for this shit," T-Rex growled.

I searched from the old set of coordinates toward the east.

"Karma, this is Duke. I can hear you." His voice was even weaker than before.

"Duke. Hold on. We're on our way. We'll get you out."

"Not to complicate matters, but I need medical assistance as soon as possible." His voice rasped and gurgled like he was choking on blood. A sense of urgency raced through me. I had to get to him. Now.

I dodged enemy fire trying to keep Locke on the radio.

"Duke, just hold on. We're coming." My wings rocked violently. I gripped my stick firmly. "I need eyes on your position. Can you help me?" I asked.

A small strobe light lit up on the horizon.

"I've got eyes on," I shouted. "Ash keep going east. You're about two kilometers away."

"Roger that," Ash huffed.

"True Grit Three, splash the lead bandit!"

Stitch, Freak, and Mojo fought off the hordes above so we could rescue Locke.

My eye's swung back to the strobe light. Flashlights. Hundreds of small flashlights swung back and forth rushing toward the strobe.

"Duke, cut your light!"

The strobe disappeared.

"Duke, cover up as best you can. This is going to be a little close."

He responded by clicking the microphone. They were near him. Determination jolted through my chest. We were too close to lose him now.

I swung the jet to the east and got ready for my bomb run. The flashlights were steadily marching toward Locke. They would be on him any second.

I ignored the bullets arcing toward my jet and lined up on the largest group of enemy forces, releasing the bomb right in the middle of the group. I slammed back in the seat racking the jet back around to the west. Readying for another pass. Explosions ignited the valley.

"Keep your head down, Duke."

The mike clicked.

The explosions were so close to my jet that their shock waves rocked us as small peppering metal grazed the jet. All systems were functional. The silence was deafening.

A few of the flashlights reappeared and started moving faster toward Locke's direction. Ash's strobe was still too far away. They needed more time.

"Ash, you're about one kilometer away. I'm coming around for a second pass."

"Copy, one klick out," Ash confirmed.

I lined up the jet as I radioed Locke, "Duke, hang tight for two minutes. Prep your gear for pickup."

My blood chilled when he didn't answer. The flashlights were closing in. I didn't have a choice. I had to stop them before they were on Locke.

I ripped all three of my remaining bombs and pulled a high G roll back to the west. The explosions shook me violently in the cockpit.

The ground was dark except for a single strobe. I tried to control my breathing but too much adrenaline was rushing through my veins. I gripped the stick tighter. The radio silence tore at my chest.

"True Grit. We have him!"

It was Ash. He had Locke.

"Let's get the hell out of here."

I blew out a hard, shaky breath and hollered.

The rescue helicopter dashed in from its holding area and hovered. Ash's team scrambled to load into the helicopter and egress out of the ambush area. Freak and Mojo took care of the enemy fighters as we climbed high out of the area. We had made it through the first battle, but we had no idea what we would encounter when we returned.

Chapter 36

Our guys had Locke and they were bringing him home and regardless of the consequences, I would have done it again.

The jet's wheels touched down on the runway. Lights flashed yellow and red awaiting my arrival. There were medical *and* security vehicles.

The three F-35's were parked in different spots then usual. I could see T-Rex standing with folded arms next to Clash whose expression looked fervently ravenous like a wild coyote.

Would they have enough handcuffs for all of us? My mind was frantic to find away to accept full responsibility.

The canopy lifted and the fresh air smacked me in the face as I pulled off my helmet. I shook my head and my hair fell loose from its tie. Should I lift my hands in surrender? Toss the gun strapped to my survival vest? Lie on the ground? Being arrested was new territory for me. My dad was going to lose his mind when he found out. Too bad he wouldn't agree that any publicity was good publicity. An awkward giggle escaped me and I choked it back with a forced swallow.

"Ma'am, are you okay?" asked Sergeant Wilson.

My eyes widened. He wasn't cuffed.

He leaned over and unstrapped me.

"Don't say anything," he advised in a low voice.

I nodded.

My feet met the ground unsteadily. I gripped the ladder for a second longer as I drew in a deep breath. Clash and T-Rex stood next to Freak, Mojo, and Stitch. Clash looked half-crazed. The others were calm. Expressionless.

What the hell was going on? The impulse to ask fought wildly inside of me. I held it back, trying to play it cool as I took my place beside Stitch.

The thumping of the helicopter almost brought me to my knees. Holy hell this was intense. The lack of food and sleep was finally catching up to me. Stitch glanced sideways at me. His body shifted. I shook my head, signaling him not to move. One by one the team members jumped from the Black Hawk. A medical team stood by with a stretcher as we waited.

Where was he and where was Ash? I was dying inside.

Two more men jumped from the edge, covered in dirt and smeared with blood. They assisted another two men equally dirtied and bloodied. Their hands were strapped in front of them. Combatants. Prisoners. They shuffled them to the side.

I needed to see Locke.

A member of the ground forces jumped quickly from the edge and snapped around to face the entrance. I caught a glimpse of his profile. It was Ash. The medical team moved forward and Ash raised a hand signaling them to stop.

What was he doing? Why had he stopped the medical team? Light blond hair caked in mud came into my view.

Locke. I bit my lip fighting not to show any outward sign of how desperately I'd missed him, needed him, and loved him. I would be eternally grateful that I was given a second chance to see the sparkle shining brightly in his eye. He was alive. A sweet, metallic taste spread as I bit harder.

He leaned from the helicopter as someone steadied his arm from behind. He was ghostly white. Ash assisted him as he stepped from the ledge. He winced and stumbled slightly. I stepped forward and Stitch gripped my arm. Ash did the same to Locke. We both tensed. He stood upright his face laced in pain.

They stood shoulder to shoulder. Fierce. Strong. Warriors. Two good men. Correction, two *great* men.

I blinked my eyes. The image would be a snapshot in my mind forever.

Locke's eyes met mine. His lip lifted into the half grin that drove me wild.

A smile spread across my face as my body warmed with certainty that it was worth it. He was worth it. Locke promised to never leave me and he didn't. I didn't lose him. He came back to me and he would be mine to love forever.

His face drained as his eyes rolled back. He collapsed to the ground and shook uncontrollably. Ash dropped beside him in shocked horror.

"Locke!" I lurched forward and broke free from Stitch's grip.

My legs felt heavy and I seemed to be running in place as the medical team rushed around him. Not now. Not after we had done it. Not after he was back and safe. I'd given my freedom to save him. I'd give my life too.

His body convulsed then lay still. Ash stumbled backward than scrambled to his feet, his face distorted.

"No!" I screamed. My voice was unfamiliar and barely audible above the muddled sirens and engines.

The medical team ripped open Locke's flight suit and cut his shirt, stripping it from his body. Ash rushed to me, gripping my waist holding me back.

Locke's chest had a large wound that seeped blood. His skin was gray.

I yelled, struggling to break free as each shouting command from the medical team tugged harder at my heart.

"He has a gunshot wound to his chest!"

"No sign of an exit wound!"

"I lost his pulse!

"He doesn't have a pulse!"

Fight Locke. Don't you leave me.

"Hold pressure on the wound!"

"Hook him up!"

"Hurry."

The medics frenzied then froze when the machine pitched a high squeal. A robotic voice called, "Analyzing rhythm. Please stand clear."

I held my hand over my mouth. Afraid to breathe and not wanting to without him.

"Shock advised. Charging."

Oh my God. His heart stopped. I couldn't lose him.

"Everyone clear!"

The machine beeped. And I feared my heart would stop too.

"Clear!"

His body jerked. He returned to stillness as blood trickled down his side.

Ash pulled me closer to him. His chest pounded in my ear.

I waited.

Closed my eyes.

Squeezed them tightly.

"Analyzing" the robotic voice advised.

"Detecting rhythm. No Shock advised."

"He has a pulse. There's a pulse." The words sounded jumbled as they ricocheted through my mind.

My knees buckled. Ash held me tighter.

"He's lost a lot of blood. Let's move. Now!"

The team moved with a blur.

My fingers and limbs tingled as the emergency vehicle zoomed away. I buried my face into Ash's chest and squeezed my eyes shut. My body trembled.

Ash's voice whispered into my hair. "Get it together. The shit is about to hit the fan."

* * * *

We won the battle only to have to face a firing squad. Clash ordered everyone to the debrief room. He stormed out in front of us.

Once he was out of earshot, T-Rex smacked Mojo in the head. "Your signature looks nothing like mine."

Mojo chuckled and T-Rex smacked him again, silencing him.

Clash didn't give anyone a chance to sit before his voice bellowed against the stillness of the hall.

"There is a total lack of respect for authority. Shit, I don't even know how it would be presented in a case. It's too far-fetched. The mission was cancelled with *good cause*."

I fell into a seat and rested my aching head into my hands. His voice sounded like an adult from a Snoopy cartoon and I wished someone would turn off the damn volume already.

"Four airmen and a team of special forces basically gave us the finger and went out anyway." He turned and pointed at T-Rex. "And you, what was your role in all of this? You don't even look surprised."

"Screw off, Clash. The last I checked, you weren't anywhere on my chain of command," T-Rex said.

"I'm in everyone's chain of command," he shouted.

Wow. And just when I didn't think he could get any more arrogant.

"What about her?" Clash poked his thumb in my direction. "What about her obvious inappropriate relationship with Duke? It's been happening right under your noses. How are you going to skirt around that?" He turned to me and glared. "You're done."

"Are you threatening her?" Ash voice chilled the room.

"Stay out of this, Walker. You're in your own world of shit without butting into our squadron issues." Clash pointed at Ash then turned toward me. "She's an attention seeker like her brother. Too bad she didn't burn like he did."

"What the fuck?" Stitch shot to his feet quicker than my face lit fire.

Before anyone could say another word, T-Rex had his forearm to Clash's neck pinning him to the wall. I didn't move. The entire room stood. He had crossed the line.

"Apologize, you piece of shit," T-Rex threatened through clenched teeth.

"They're renegades and I say it like it is," Clash said.

T-Rex pushed harder.

"Fine," he coughed. "Sorry."

It was an empty apology. Honestly, I didn't care. His opinion meant nothing to me. Colin was a good man, and Clash was nothing but jealous of him. I wouldn't desecrate Colin's memory by arguing.

"Karma?" T-Rex turned to me.

Off with his head, I wanted to answer, but I resisted. I couldn't say anything derogative to a superior officer, even if he was a classless dick.

"Let him go," I said. "It's an honor to be compared to my brother. You can't hurt me or his memory."

I took the high road. T-Rex released Clash, who stumbled.

"Hopefully his memory will keep you warm in prison," he muttered as he rubbed his neck.

Shatter broke into the room with the Special Forces commander. A second later and Clash would have been scooping his teeth up off the ground.

"Everyone take a seat," Shatter snapped as he rushed to the podium. "Clash, I see you're continuing to make friends. We are going to debrief the mission. From start to finish. I want a full account of everything."

"Debrief?" Clash interrupted, his head jerked back like he had taken a blow to the face.

Shatter's jerked his head toward him. "Did I stutter?"

"Sir, they stole military property, disobeyed a direct military order, brought home two enemy prisoners of war and we are going to debrief?" Clash questioned as he gestured wildly. Shatter's eyes narrowed and Clash dropped his hands to his hips as he continued, "With all due respect, shouldn't you be reading them their rights before anything else?"

"Why would I read them their rights?" Shatter barked.

I hated to agree with Clash on anything, but we did do everything he had mentioned.

"Are you kidding me?" Clash wiped his mouth as his words sprayed.

"Clash, have you ever considered for a moment, just a single, fucking moment that you don't know *everything*?" Shatter mimicked Clash's whine.

"Sir?"

"Do you think any of my pilots or Slap's ground team would for one second disobey their commanding officer's orders?" Shatter asked.

I sank deeper into my chair. Was this a trick question?

"I don't understand."

"We knew about the mission. We approved the mission. Just because we didn't ask your approval doesn't mean anyone did anything against orders."

"No, there's no way. Why are you covering?" Clash's voice shook.

"Are you questioning my integrity, Major?" Shatter raised his eyebrow.

Clash's lips drew into a dauntingly thin line. "No, sir."

"Good then. That will be all for you. Go get me an update on Duke's transfer."

Why were they transferring him? I needed to see him.

I shifted in my seat. Shatter shot me a sharp narrowed look that kept my feet planted where they were. Clash stormed out.

Once the door slammed, Shatter continued. "Duke is unconscious. Critical, yet stable condition. He'll be transferred in the morning to a military hospital in London per the request of his military and family. You got him just in time. Nice job." Shatter paused and I settled in my chair. Locke was alive and I wasn't going to jail.

Shatter slammed his hand against the podium. I jumped. "This is where I want to lose my shit. But if I do you will all be in jail and the rest of us would be out of jobs." His face turned crimson. "Rules are in place for a reason, whether we like them or not. This time was a success, but next time could be a disaster," he said jabbing his finger against the wooden stand.

I dropped my shoulders and listened as he continued, "Our jobs are difficult and unpopular decisions need to be made at times. As future leaders you need to balance thinking rationally, without emotions. Remember it is always mission first people," his eyes landed on mine. "Always. This turned out to be the right action done in the wrong way."

We had reacted without thinking. Thankfully, it saved Locke and got me back into the cockpit. But his words resonated. They were the advice from an admirable leader. One that was willing to stand up for what he believed in. Us.

"This was a covert operation. God knows why in the hell I chose all the prior students to carry it out but regardless it went off pretty goddamn amazing. It will be marked as highly classified. It will never be discussed or shown on record that it happened. No one will ever be able to speak of it until long after your retire."

I couldn't believe it, but it sounded good to me. No jail time and a secret story for the grandkids.

The Special Forces commander reiterated Shatter's sentiments and shared a few of his own. They were both in agreement this should go down as the mission that should not be named.

The debrief was quick and painless. Turned out the two enemy prisoners of war were fairly high-profiled. One was second in command of the LRA and singing like a canary. There were more missions planned for tomorrow and everyone was ordered to rest, which I would welcome, happily.

Right after I saw Locke.

Chapter 37

I rushed to the hospital wing, searching, unable to go another second without touching him. After a few misses, I heard Bodhi's voice. I hovered by the door, listening.

"He's lost a lot of blood. We gave him a transfusion, but the bullet needs to be removed."

"We were given strict orders not to operate, only to stabilize him for transport."

"It's too risky."

"It's out of our hands."

Shit. I was so sick of people saying *no* without good reason.

I knocked on the door.

"Come in." Bodhi called.

I walked into the room. Locke was hooked up a ton of wires and machines that beeped. He was still pale, but not as grayish in color. The other doctor nodded to me on his way out.

"How is he?" I whispered.

"He's stable, but you don't have to whisper. He's unconscious not sleeping. I would prefer him to wake up." Bodhi scratched the stubble on his face.

"Why won't they let you operate?" I asked. He creased his brow. "Sorry, I overheard."

"British military orders," he said. "Family wishes."

"Red tape sucks." I moved next to the bed and took Locke's hand into mine. It was warmer than I'd expected.

"Yeah, no wonder some people just rip through it."

Frustration dripped from his words.

I traced my finger along the back of Locke's hand.

"What are the risks?"

Bodhi pushed a chair to me.

"If the bullet shifts or his condition changes during transport it could be bad. Really bad."

I sat, clutching his hand.

"Can you steal me an operating room?"

I glanced sideways.

"I'm joking. Geesh, Tink. Your expression. You'd do it, wouldn't you?"

I shrugged. I would do anything for Locke.

"It wouldn't do us any good. I'm not a surgeon." He adjusted a dial on one of the machines. "I was wrong, you know."

"About what?"

"When I said you two shouldn't be together. I was wrong."

"Or maybe you were right."

"No way. I wish I had what you do. You risked your life to save him. He's lucky he has you."

"I'm the lucky one. Besides, it was Ash's idea to go after him. He and his team did all the work."

"They went after him because of what Locke did for them. But let's face it. I don't think Ash would have gone against orders if it weren't for you."

I stiffened. Some classified mission. I thought we were out of trouble.

"I was in the control room with T-Rex and the others," Bodhi said. "You had a full audience. Everyone heard how you crushed it. Your four-ship put a major hurt on the enemy and Locke and the ground team wouldn't have made it home if it weren't for you."

"I don't even know what I did. It felt like I was on autopilot."

"Well dude, your autopilot is pretty fucking ballsy."

"Or insane," I said with a chuckle.

"It's probably good to have a touch of both." He patted me on the back. "I'll leave you two alone. I'll be outside if he needs me."

* * * *

No one could fully prepare for the horrors of war nor predict how you'd change when you came out on the other side.

My pride of fighting for a good cause was overshadowed by the image of Locke lying in bed, hooked to wires, wrapped in bandages, and stapled back together. He'd been through so much, both physically and emotionally. Thankfully Locke was strong. But then again so was Colin.

I leaned forward resting my head on my hands that were still gripping his. His bandaged foot peeked from underneath the sheet. I let go of his hand and slid up the fabric, uncovering the intricate design of his family's crest tattooed on his ankle. The marking saved his life.

Something golden in the middle caught my eye. A tiny delicate circle interlaced an intricate emblem shaded similar to my favorite stone. I touched my neck. The sphere reminded me of my necklace. Unlatching the chain, I leaned over to match the tiny circles. They were identical in size and shape.

Lyric had mentioned the circle was the symbol for Karma.

My brows knitted.

"You're beautiful even when you're glowering."

His voice was low and rough and my heart leapt in reaction thankful for the chance to hear it again.

"Locke!" I gasped. "Oh my God. You're awake. Let me get Bodhi."

"No," he whispered. "I just want you."

I wanted him, too.

"Bodhi needs to know you're awake."

"How about for once you let me call the shots." He smiled weakly. "You can't do it. Can you?"

I shook my head.

"Fine. Go get him," he said.

I rushed from the room. Bodhi was somehow awkwardly asleep on his feet.

"Bodhi. He's awake!"

He stumbled and gripped his stethoscope.

"Locke is conscious," I repeated.

He rushed past me toward the room.

"Make it quick, Bodhi. No offense but you're a bit of a third wheel at the moment," Locke said.

"I get it dude," he answered and shined a light in his eyes. "Are you in any pain?"

Locke chuckled softly.

"I know it's a dumb question. But do you need anything stronger than what we're giving to you? I'd rather keep you alert to monitor but I don't want you suffering until your transfer."

"Transfer?"

"You need surgery and it's been requested that it happen in England."

"By whom?" He rolled his eyes. "Never mind. I know by whom. Give me the paperwork. I'm not going anywhere. I've got everything I need to recover right here."

His eyes met mine. I wasn't going anywhere either.

"Your vitals look fine. Except for the bullet, I think you're doing remarkably well. I'll get the paperwork ready."

He hurried from the room.

Locke didn't watch him go. His eyes never left me. "Why are you standing so far away?"

I shifted. "You need to rest."

His brows furrowed. I didn't want to upset him.

"I'll stay, but you need your strength, Locke. You need to recover."

"I'll be fine. I'm not going to die." I flinched at his choice of words. "You went through too much to rescue me. Which, by the way, was bloody reckless."

He reached out for me. His hand was warm and comfortable in my own. I loved him so much it terrified me.

"Awesome choice in mission name. True Grit."

Now I had to rent the movie.

"How much trouble are you in?"

"None."

His eyes widened.

"Shatter and T-Rex covered for us."

"Thank God," he said and squeezed my hand. "Can I ask you do something for me?"

I would do anything for him.

He brushed his hand against my cheek and I closed my eyes welcoming his touch. When I opened them he was watching me intensely.

"Anything," I replied and truly meant it.

"Talk to me."

I knew what he was asking, but I didn't know what to say. I harbored guilt, fear, and grief, yet they were all there, mixed with a tremendous amount of love for this amazing man. Everything was muddled.

He sighed.

"Not now, Locke. You don't need the added stress."

"Not knowing what's going on in that head of yours is stressful. So if you want me to rest, you'll need to tell me. It's my best chance for recovery."

The left side of his lip lifted. I was done for.

"You were right about what you said in Germany. I'm afraid. Everything about you, about us, frightens me."

He held my hand, allowing me to go on. I took in a deep breath.

"I don't ever want to hurt the way I did when I lost Colin. I didn't think I would survive. When they told me you were gone, the raw emotions flooded me again. Only this time, I couldn't shut it off. The pain, the hurt, or the *guilt.* It would have killed me this time. Losing you would have finished me."

"The pain and the hurt are normal. But why do you have guilt? I don't understand why you blame yourself for Colin's accident. Whether it was the jet's environmental system or whether it was PTSD, it was not your fault. You can't carry that burden."

"It wasn't the jet. You know that. And I know it now. I may have always known it deep down." I let out a long drawn out sigh. Locke rubbed his thumb along my hand as I continued, "I think I was blocking it out because I didn't want to face it, to accept the signs were there and we missed them, ignored them. I wanted something to be wrong with the jet because I was hoping that if the jet went away, maybe she would take my memories and pain with her."

Locke never let go of my hand. "Your brother kept it hidden, *very* well hidden. We can see everything in hindsight, because we were searching for the answers."

"But I convinced him to the fly the JSF. He didn't want it. He went up the day he died, for me."

"The one thing I discovered about your brother is that you and he were very similar."

I cocked my head and nodded for him to continue, even if I knew where he was going with this.

"No one could make him do something he didn't want to. And if someone told him no, he pushed harder. Neither of you ever showed any signs of weakness."

Yeah, well, we could thank my dad for that.

"It's okay to be vulnerable. It's okay to care. It's all right to love again."

After everything I was still unwilling to accept what he was saying.

"You don't believe it," he said and frowned when I hesitated. "Just say what you're thinking, Tinklee."

"You'll think I'm crazy."

"You stole a jet and blew up half of Northern Algeria. Nothing you can say will ever tip the crazy meter beyond that one."

He had a point. It was time to come clean.

"I think I have bad Karma."

Judging by the look on his face, the meter just broke.

"You know, Karma? It's when bad things happen to you because of the bad things that you've done," I explained.

He paused, grimacing as he attempted to adjust his position. "So, it also can mean *good* things can happen because of the *good* things you've done also. Right?"

"Yes, but I have the bad kind. And I think that's why you got hurt."

He chuckled and winced. I pulled my hand back and he tightened his hold.

"I'm not laughing at you. I promise. I'm laughing because the reason I got hurt is that I went into a warzone where people shot at me, then I flew into the middle of the frenzy. It has nothing to do with luck. It was choice."

"It's Karma, and I don't think it's the same as luck. They're different." I held up my necklace for him to see.

"Why were you holding this on my leg?"

"It's the symbol for Karma. It matches the circle in your tattoo."

"That's kismet," he said.

"Or bad Karma."

He laughed.

"Would you stop? If there is any Karma involved, it can only be the good kind."

"How can you say that? I nearly knocked you out the first night we met and I've been nothing but problematic ever since."

"I've had my share of daft moments. I'm thankful your bottle met my noggin that night. I'm willing to take my chances with your Karma. Good or bad."

I'd never felt more blessed. He lifted my chin until our eyes met. The familiar entrancing blue gaze was full of love and desire.

"I love you, Tinklee," he said and pulled me closer until our lips brushed softly.

He was everything to me and I would never lose the chance of telling him again.

"I love you, too." The words felt as natural as breathing as they whispered from my lips and I would never go another day without telling him or showing him just how much. Our love saved both of our lives.

He leaned back and brushed a strand of my hair from my face.

"I fought to stay alive so that I could hear those words."

"I fought for our lives so that you could hear them," I breathed.

My lips met his with a new desire, fueled not only with passion but deepest love. I carefully snuggled next to him, resting my head on his shoulder. He had broken through my walls, opened my heart to love and my will to live again. Our breathing fell into a comfortable rhythm as we drifted to sleep.

Chapter 38

I blinked, familiarizing with my surroundings. Bodhi fidgeted with the lines attached to Locke.

"Morning dude," he reached out and fist-bumped me as I wiped the sleep from my eyes.

"What are you doing?" I yawned, glancing back at Locke.

His chest rose and lowered at a peaceful pace. I carefully slipped from the bed.

"They're still requesting transfer."

"What do you think? Is it safe?"

"His vitals are much stronger. I would prefer the surgery be done here but I'm not as concerned. He had a good night. I suspect you had something to do with that."

"Yes, there was a happy ending," I said and the second the words were out, my cheeks warmed.

Bodhi chuckled.

"You know what I mean."

"Oh, I know."

I rolled my eyes.

"He's not going to be happy about the decision." I tousled my hair and smoothed it into a bun.

Bodhi shrugged. "His embassy's involved. We don't have a choice."

"Oh bloody hell. Where's a damn butter knife? I'll flick the bullet out myself," Locke muttered.

I laughed, but he glared in frustration.

"It's not the bloody embassy," he paused. "It's my mother."

The Countess of Huntingdon was a much more challenging obstacle.

"Well, whomever it is they won't budge. The decision's made."

"Maybe it will be for the best," I said.

He raised his eyebrow, studying me.

I squeezed his hand.

"I'm certain the environment will be more suitable to surgery and recovery than it is here."

I imagined Locke in a castle with a staff catering to his every need.

"Why are you grinning?" he asked.

"I was envisioning the Earl's royal treatment," I replied and curtseyed.

He shook his head and chuckled.

"I'll be back." Bodhi laughed as he walked from the room.

"Seriously, Locke. As much as I don't want you to go, it would be better for you long-term."

"What about you?" he asked.

"What about me?"

"I hate leaving you here."

"It's my job. It's what we do."

"I know, but it's different. You're also the woman I love."

"And you're the man I love, but we're fighter pilots. That hasn't changed."

"So you're fine with going back up in the jet?"

I nodded.

"What's changed?"

"She saved everything that was important in my world. I have a new respect for her."

"Crazy women."

"What would you do without us?" I teased.

"I don't ever want to find out. Now get over here and kiss me."

"Yes, sir."

I leaned forward and pressed my lips to his. He felt warmer, stronger. His hand rested in the small of my back and his tongue explored my mouth, I pressed harder wanting more. The machine beeped loudly and I jerked away trying to catch my breath.

Bodhi rushed into the room toward the machine. His eyes darted between the tone then toward us. He folded his arms with a frown.

"Really?"

I covered my mouth with my hand trying to hide my guilty grin.

"Come on Bodhi, lighten up," Locke said. "Where's that guy from Australia who…."

"He's trying to keep his partner in crime alive."

"I can't wait to hear more about these crimes," I kidded.

"Then let our friend heal. When this is all over we can create our own sordid affairs. We'll invite Lyric to come along," Bodhi said, smirking.

I laughed. "It's a deal."

Suddenly my life was full of hopeful plans for a future full of friends and love, something my brother would never have. A pain tugged at my heart.

Locke glanced at me with questioning eyes.

I sighed as the guilt lingered. "I feel bad Colin will never experience any of this."

"He was loved."

I nodded.

"And I'm certain he loved you too."

"I want to do something to honor him."

"That's a brilliant idea."

The idea lifted my spirit. I would find a way to preserve Colin's memory and help others.

Bodhi's hip buzzed and he reached toward the sound.

"Your transport's ready."

* * * *

I stayed with Locke as they transferred him to the flight line. A private jet waited at the edge of the runway. The entire squadron, Special Forces team, and all crews lined a path, standing at attention as we passed. Though it was a silent goodbye, it spoke volumes.

I glanced over at Ash as he stared forward. I would never forget what he did for me.

Two nurses clad in white uniforms and traditional hats stepped down the entrance stairs. A man dressed smartly with a white jacket nodded to Bodhi and accepted his paperwork.

"Good morning, sir," the man said as he dipped his head to Locke. "How are you feeling?"

"Good morning, Doctor Oldham," Locke replied. "I'm not pleased with the transfer, but I'm certain I'll have to take that up with my mother."

The doctor nodded with a hint of a grin.

"This is Dr. Fisher and Lieutenant Pinkerton," Locke said. "They'll be joining us until it is time to depart."

He nodded. "Yes, sir. Nurse Cooper and Nurse Morgan will escort you inside."

A few men in uniform assisted in lifting the stretcher onto the plane. I followed inside.

Holy crap. The jet was elaborate. The wood was warm and the seats richly trimmed in emerald green and gold fabrics. It felt like someone's living room, not the inside of an airplane. They transferred Locke into a plush bed already equipped with monitors. The nurses began attaching his leads. A dog yipped and I silently cursed knowing who would follow the sound.

The fragrance of expensive perfume filled the air as Lady Snooty Pants entered with a forced smile. She was wearing white gloves and a pillbox hat that reminded me of Jackie Onassis. Everything seemed awkwardly out of decade.

She strolled over to Locke and touched his cheek with a frown that matched mine. "Oh dear God. You're a mess."

"Hello, Boody. Good to see you again." She flicked a fake wave of her hand.

"Bodhi," Locke corrected.

"Yes, of course. And, you." Her glance at me lingered longer than I liked. I still had on my flight suit from yesterday, covered in sweat and dirt. Her disgust brought me gleeful satisfaction.

"Do they not expect you to bathe in the hospital wings?"

"It's optional," I responded and smiled sweetly.

"She's joking, Mother," Locke said. "Tinklee risked her life to save me yesterday. She never left my side. You should be offering your appreciation rather than issuing insults."

His mother's expression looked conflicted like she'd just swallow a handful of sweet and sour candy. Thankfully, Locke's father strolled in while he was speaking.

"We will forever be in your gratitude, Miss Pinkerton. Good Morning, Bodhi, it's a pleasure to see you again."

Bodhi accepted his handshake. I nodded in acknowledgement. His dad played nice at least.

"Well, thank you for escorting our son. It was lovely to see you again." His mom dismissed us.

"I would like to say goodbye to my friends. We can discuss my annoyance of the situation later. Please give us a moment alone." Locke wasn't having any of her bad behavior.

"Yes, darling. But be quick, I'm sure your friends are eager to get back to what they were doing."

I wanted to smack my head. Actually I wanted to smack her head, but I strained a smile instead.

"Good to see you both again." Locke's dad flicked a tiny salute.

The dog yipped again as they walked through a hallway.

Locke rubbed the IV in his hand. "I apologize for my mother. There's no excuse."

Bodhi chuckled. "She's all sorts of scary."

I rolled my eyes.

"Well, dude, it looks like you're good to go. Let me know if you need anything."

He leaned down and hugged him. No awkward one-armed bro-shakes. It was the real deal. And, even in the midst of the hug, Bodhi checked Locke's monitors. He'd be a wreck until we received word that Locke's transfer went well.

So would I.

Bodhi promised us some privacy waving for the nurse to follow.

I faced Locke. I ached for the moment alone, but the beeping of his machines interrupted anything I wanted to say, and the sterile, antiseptic smell masked his earthy scent of sandalwood. I ached for him—both for his wounds and for *him*.

"I'll be back as soon as I'm cleared." He must have read my mind.

"You have a bullet inside of you and fractured bones. That may be a while."

"I hope the conflict ends soon," he said.

"Yeah, me too."

I bit my lip. Saying goodbye was much more difficult than I'd imagined. The too-fresh ache of missing and needing him burned in my chest.

"Play by the rules. No more rash decisions," he said reaching for my hand. "I can't lose you."

"I'm not the one who sacrificed myself."

His brows drew together.

"Tinklee, promise."

"I'll try. Can you have someone let me know as soon as you're out of surgery?"

"Only if you promise."

He wouldn't let it go.

"Fine, I promise."

"Sir, we need to be going." The doctor peeked his head into the cabin.

Locke nodded raising his finger to request a moment longer.

"I'll miss you," I said.

He pulled me near until our lips met. My heart tore apart. He captured my lip between his teeth and pulled.

"God, I want you so bad," he whispered.

The memory of his lips exploring my body set my skin on fire. My nipples hardened as my thighs tingled. I shifted uncomfortably.

"Something the matter, lieutenant?" he questioned with a smirk knowingly, making things worse.

"You're so bad," I said softly, my voice hoarse.

He winked his enchanting blue eyes mesmerizing me.

"I love you so much," I breathed the words.

"I love you more."

Chapter 39

I had been so worried about Locke that I hadn't even had the time to consider what Ash was going through. He lost his friend, was shot at, and tore open himself more times than I could count. I needed to find Ash, make certain he was okay, and most importantly thank him.

I began searching at the mess tent. The tables were empty. I followed the path out back and peeked between several buildings until I finally caught the glimpse of something bouncing in the air. A football. It had to be Ash.

"Hey there." I raised my hands and nodded toward the ball.

Ash spiraled the ball in my direction.

"What's up?" he asked.

"I was looking for you." I replied as I caught the ball and tossed it in the air a few times. "Did you get checked out by the medical team?"

He nodded. His color looked good, but I could see he was favoring his right side.

"How's Sully's wife doing? Have you heard anything?"

"She had the baby. She named her Cori. After him. It was his given name." His jaw flexed.

"Cori. I like it."

He shrugged. "Did Duke make it back okay?"

"Yeah, they're supposed to do surgery in the morning."

I tossed the ball back to him. He caught it without a word.

"What you did means more to me than you'll ever know," I said.

His knuckles blanched as he squeezed the ball. "It's my job."

"It was more than that and you know it," I replied. I lifted my hands to request the ball before he punctured it with his grip. "Yesterday was a bit crazy."

He shook his head. "I can't believe what you did. I guess love makes you do some pretty fearless shit."

I spiraled the ball back to him. He snagged it with a wince.

"You okay?"

Clearly he wasn't, but he nodded.

I walked over toward him but he tossed the ball, stopping me.

"I'm fine," he snapped.

I raised a questioning brow, but didn't push.

"It was intense. I was scared to death but when I heard your voice I knew what I needed to do. I couldn't stop until I had done everything to protect *both* of you." I tucked the ball under my arm. "Ash, I don't want things to be awkward. I care about you and don't want to lose you, but if being friends isn't what you want, I don't want to hurt you either."

"I get it. You love us both, but you're not in love with me. God Tink, you have some of the lamest let-down lines I've ever heard."

"Those are your words not mine." At least I was trying. I spun the ball hard at him. He easily snagged it.

"It's what you were going to say?" He pointed the ball at me.

"No, it wasn't."

"Wasn't it?'

It was.

"Oh, shut up. You're so frustrating."

He smirked then slid down the wall and rested against the building. I sat down beside him and he wrapped his arm around my shoulder. "I meant it when I said I want you to be happy. It just sort of stings to see you with him."

"I know," I replied as I leaned back against his chest. "I'm sorry."

He rested his chin on top of my head. "I'd rather have your friendship than nothing at all."

"That's good because when someone says no, it makes me try harder." I tilted my head back to look up at him. He chuckled.

"And don't I know it. God, Tinklee Pinkerton, you're something else, you know that?"

"Is that good or bad?"

"A mixture of both."

* * * *

We were drones that ate, slept, planned, and flew. Nothing more.

All outside communication had been cut off for four months. The LRA tapped our communication and it was too risky to have it vulnerable. At times it felt like there was nothing else happening in the world besides this conflict. It became all we knew.

Our isolation had become maddening and it killed me not to be able to communicate with Locke. The last e-mail I had gotten before they shut us off to the outside was that his surgery went well, though it would be a drawn-out recovery. Our reunion was what motivated me to keep going.

I dragged myself out of bed, showered, dressed and laced my boots. My hair hung well below my waist and I was tempted at times to lop it. The season returned to an intense heat and I pushed sweat beads from my brow. I sauntered into the briefing room.

Shatter and T-Rex stood at the front of the room. Stitch was bouncing a ball against the wall as Fantom squeezed a handgrip. I plopped into a seat and clicked lead from my pencil. I doodled on an outdated map. The members of the previous mission rolled into the room, spirits higher than usual.

Shatter waved to the last man to shut the door. I glanced around the room. Where was Ash? Our schedules had somehow shifted and I rarely saw him anymore. My gaze stopped on a figure leaning against the wall. It was Ash and he had a University of Colorado shirt resting on top his head and partially covering his face.

Shatter began speaking and I turned around. "The cells have been broken, the factories have been destroyed and Algeria, Tunisia, and Morocco have regained control. What this means folks is that you did a damn good job and we're going home!"

Whoops and whistles filled the air.

Yes! We were going home—finally! Hot showers, real food, jogs on the beaches, cold beers and Locke.

I was going to get to see him again and be able to hold him. My heart bottomed out. I missed him so much that I ached. There was nothing that I needed more than to touch him, feel him, *taste* him. The memory of our bodies sliding along each other, molding into one made my thighs heat.

"I'm not sure I should interrupt," Stitch said.

My ears burned and my hand shot to my mouth making sure drool hadn't run down my face.

"I was just thinking about how good a cold beer at Krusty's is going to taste." I tried to cover.

"Your nose does a little twitch when you lie. Whatever it was, it seemed better than a cold one a Krusty's," he whispered with a nudge.

A hot Brit making love to me definitely ranked higher than a beer at Krusty's.

Tingles shot through me again. God, I needed to stop before I fell apart in the middle of this room. Stitch chuckled as he walked away.

I jumped to my feet and turned toward Ash. He had disappeared.

Chapter 40

Home sweet home. I lifted the flowerpot and grabbed the spare key. It was an odd way to return. Nothing like you'd see in the movies. No welcomes, no pomp and circumstances, nothing. Everything was so covert that I'm not even sure the majority of the world knew what we were doing or how long we had actually been gone. Without the ability to communicate, our families were unaware of our homecoming. I thought it was better. A gradual, peaceful integration into society was easier than being smacked in the face with normalcy.

I dropped my bag and flipped on the air conditioning. The sun was setting but the heat still drenched me. I glanced at the clock. It was 1930. I hadn't a clue what day it was. I unzipped my flight suit and let it fall to the ground. I wanted to run naked into the ocean, but being arrested and caged within the first hour of my return squashed the impulse. I grabbed a pair of shorts and pulled them on. They fell lower on my hips than usual. Could someone get this girl a burger and fries? I chose my favorite honey lager from the fridge instead. Liquid calories would have to suffice.

I reached for my tablet. A wifi signal never looked more amazing. I tapped on my e-mail. A prompt read, "Retrieving messages." That could take a while.

I grabbed my beer and went outside, jumped the banister and landed on the warm grains of sand. An early moon already danced along the water. I waded up to my ankles, the waves crashing against my legs.

The haunting images and taxing hardships of war swept from me as the familiar scents and security of my homeland welcomed me home. I would never forget the memories of the horrors I had witnessed, yet somehow I felt strong enough to move forward and live, letting them go.

"Ever hear that the energy you put into the universe will come back to you?" The voice spoke behind me.

Locke? My body tensed, afraid to turn around in case he wasn't real.

"It has been exactly three hundred and sixty-five days. We've come full circle and are standing in this same spot the night that we met."

I squeezed my eyes shut and prayed that he was real. His hands rested on my hips as his lips brushed against my neck. My body trembled as he spun me around pulling me into him. The moonlight shimmered from his face. His familiar blue eyes sent chills dancing through my spine.

"The night I hit a stranger in the head with a bottle?"

He took the lager from my hand, tossing it in the sand.

I smiled.

"The night I knew my life would never be the same." He brushed his lips to mine.

"But how? How did you…."

"Someone must have some bloody awesome Karma working on their behalf," he replied as his lip lifted into a half-lifted grin. "I heard you were coming."

His hands cupped me lifting me off the ground. I wrapped my legs around him. His lips pressed firmly against mine and I pressed harder needing to be closer.

"Oh my God, Tinklee. I've missed you so much," he growled.

His tongue swept into my mouth and the taste of him unleashed me.

"Maybe you should show me." My voice was rough, breathless, needy.

He lowered me to the beach, hovering over me, his eyes dark with a craving desire. He pressed his hips closer to me and every nerve ending inside me went wild.

Fireworks exploded into the air and I startled at the sound, my heart pounding wildly in my chest.

"You okay?" He asked.

"I love the lights, but I think it's too soon for the explosions."

His lips swept against mine. "Let's move our celebration inside."

He swooped me from the ground and I shrieked in shock.

"I didn't even know it was the Fourth of July."

"Yeah, well, you've been a tad bit busy fighting for everyone else's freedoms."

Another explosion of lights erupted, followed by the explosion. I couldn't stop my body from tensing. Locke understood and rushed toward his house.

I'd never been inside of his home before.

He reached for the back door and pushed it open.

"Close your eyes."

I scrunched my brows. His lips brushed each of my eyelids.

"Close them."

His house had his familiar earthy scent.

"Good, you're smiling."

How couldn't I be? I was in the arms of the man of my dreams, and hopefully he was carrying me into his bedroom.

A familiar scent of vanilla verbena mixed in the air.

"Keep your eyes closed."

I squeezed them tighter. He lowered me to my feet. The suspense was killing me.

"Okay, open them."

I gasped delightfully surprised. Hundreds of candles flickered all around the bathroom. A large beautiful soaking tub filled with bubbles and sprinkled with delicate petals overlooked the moonlit ocean.

"Oh my God, Locke. This is incredible." I glanced back over my shoulder as his hands rested comfortable on my hips. "When did you do all of this?"

"I got in this morning. Kassie caught word you were coming home."

I disliked her a little less.

"Are you going to join me?"

"No."

I pouted. He laughed.

"I have something to do. This is your time to relax."

"I don't want you to leave."

"I promise, I'll be right back."

A huge eruption of lights lit the sky, luckily without the accompanying boom.

"It's soundproof. Enjoy the display."

He kissed my neck and I reached back, keeping him tight against me.

His tongue traced along the side to my collarbone and explored along my shoulder. Heat traveled south and I pressed back against him. He wanted me as much as I wanted him.

"Locke," I breathed.

"Yes, darling?"

"Don't go." My voice was a whisper.

He reached under my shirt and easily unsnapped my bra with the flick of his fingers. His hands moved around to my breasts and he rubbed them as his kisses traced back along my neck and to my ear.

He gently squeezed my nipple with one hand as his other hand slid into my panties.

"I'd been dreaming of this moment for four months," I said drawing in a deep breath.

"Me too." He whispered as he nibbled on my ear.

His fingers found their way inside and moved in comfortable rhythm as his thumb gently massaged.

"Reality is definitely more satisfying," I rasped.

He growled as his teeth scraped my neck and he squeezed my nipple hard. I arched my back and the explosion of lights erupted in perfect unison with my body.

"Welcome home, Love."

* * * *

Holy hell. The Brits sure knew how to make you feel welcome. I wanted to offer him the same pleasure but he stopped me from unbuttoning his pants. Instead he undressed me and helped me into the bath. He kissed me and vanished from the room.

Okay, he was right. This was pretty freaking amazing and something I definitely needed after months of cold showers in the dirt. What was so important that he wouldn't join me? Another eruption of lights filled the sky. I couldn't believe how much had happened in one year.

I lathered, rinsed and repeated as I tried scrubbing the lingering filth of war from my skin. Locke had bought my favorite shampoo and shower gel and as the water drained I returned to my scent. I wrapped my hair in a towel and picked up the monogrammed robe that was lying out for me. A glass flute sat on the sink along with a covered bucket of ice. I wasn't really a champagne type of girl, but he had gone through the trouble.

I lifted the towel and smiled. My favorite honey lager was chilling in the ice. I twisted off the lid and took a sip of the cold sweet liquid. This homecoming was more perfect than I could ever have imagined.

Locke promised he would be back. Where did he go?

I followed the path of twinkling candles and flower petals into the bedroom. It was exactly what I would have expected it to be. Masculine woods with earthy tones with floor to ceiling windows that continued from the bathroom to the sky. Sparkling light flickered in the room as I walked along the edge of the bed tracing my fingers along the expensive threads. My jersey cotton sheets and old down comforter paled in comparison. The bed was elevated and it made me wonder if I would need a running start to leap inside.

I took a sip of my fluted lager and turned back around. Locke was standing in the center of the room. My insides flipped with excitement as his licked his lips. He was overdressed in a pair of pressed khakis and light blue shirt that matched the shade of his eyes. I couldn't wait to wrinkle him. I grinned at the thought and he reached out his hand. I sat my glass on the nightstand and went to him, ready to finally have him.

He took my hands into his and rubbed the top of them with the back of his thumbs. His palms were clammy and his jaw tensed as he swallowed. My heartbeat quickened. Something was wrong. I focused on his eyes and as he took a breath his gaze softened.

"The first day I met you, I knew there was such a thing as love at first sight. I watched you standing in the moonlight in the ocean and I was drawn to you, consumed by you. We may have gotten off to a bumpy beginning and even with all of the stumbles you became a part of me deep inside."

And he became a part of me.

"You say I was trying to fix you but I was simply fighting for my life. You are my life, my breath, my soul. I am not complete without you."

Goosebumps erupted on my skin as my heart fell deeper in love.

He knelt down and my pulse raced and my knees weakened. I was probably the only girl in the world who had never dreamed of this moment so I was even more unprepared of how it would feel.

He pulled a tiny black box from his pocket and opened it holding it before me. The stone sparkled in the candlelight like thousands of twinkling fireflies. I'd never seen anything more elegant or magnificent.

I reached my shaking hand to my mouth trying to process what was happening. He removed the ring from the box and held it before me.

"Tinklee Pinkerton, would you do me the honor of becoming my wife?"

My eyes blurred as euphoric bliss consumed me. Locke refused to give up on me and somehow he fixed me. Maybe not to perfection, but I remembered how to love and, more importantly, I *wanted* to. Tears streamed over my cheeks. I was too overwhelmed to move or to speak.

He stood as a look of concern spread across his face. He reached up and swiped away the tears.

"I hope those are happy tears."

I swallowed the lump, preventing me from speaking as more tears streamed down my face.

Locke pulled a handkerchief from his back pocket and dabbed my cheeks.

"I'm sorry," I lifted my shaking hand to my mouth. "I..." my voice choked and I buried my eyes into my hands. "Oh my God, this is the worst acceptance to a proposal ever." I shook.

Locke removed my hands and bent down to look into my eyes.

"Are you saying yes?" he asked hesitantly.

I nodded swallowing hard trying to find my voice.

"Yes," I smiled through my tears. "Yes, I will marry you."

He pulled me tightly into his chest holding me.

"Bloody hell, you had me worried. I'd never seen you cry before."

I pushed the tears from my face. It had been so long since I had been able to cry. I felt less broken. More like my old self.

"I'm sorry, I'm a hot mess," I said with a laugh still shaking with nerves.

"Always hot. Never a mess."

Locke took my hand and slid the delicate ring onto my finger. His smile spread he lifted my fingers to his lip. It was like igniting a flame on a torch. My body burned craving for his touch. He felt it too. Love transitioned to a lustful hunger in his eyes.

He untied the belt to my robe and it fell open. I unbuttoned his shirt, pulling it from his shoulders. His muscles tensed as my fingers traced along his perfectly defined chest.

My fingers paused as they reached a pink scar. It was barely visible to the eye but vividly evident and symbolic in my mind.

"I was so afraid I had lost you," I whispered.

"You could never lose me. I'm yours for eternity."

"And I have the ring to prove it," I said with a gentle smile.

"Damn, that looks so sexy on your finger," his voice growled as his lips brushed against my neck and he pushed the robe from my shoulders. His kisses traced along its path.

In a fluid movement, he lifted me from the ground, his lips never once moving from my skin. I melted into him, so consumed by love and desire that I no longer knew where his lips ended and my skin began. He laid me back on the bed as his tongue traced the valley between my breasts. His lips curled over my nipple. He gently tugged as I moaned and arched my back, wanting, needing more.

I wrapped my legs around his waist and into the small of his back. I pushed my hips into his, pulling him closer. His lips moved along my stomach and further south between my legs. He kissed my thighs and a tidal wave of heat flooded between my legs. His tongue traced along my skin and I lifted my hips to beg for more. His tongue explored as he caressed me. My breathing intensified. I needed him. All of him. Now. It had been way too long.

"Locke," I begged.

His pants fell to the ground as his body slid along me. The friction created more heat.

Our eyes met.

"Tell me, Love," His voice was rough, his expression fierce.

I tried to hold it together but I was clearly falling apart.

"I want you." My voice was breathless. "I need you."

He pressed his lips roughly against mine and my nails dug deeper into him as he gave me what I craved. He thrust against me in a steady rhythm. Deeper, harder, demanding more each time. I buried my head into his neck and squeezed my eyes tighter as my nerves came undone. My heart pounded wildly from my chest. Bright sparkling lights exploded in my vision as my body rippled uncontrollably. He pulled me closer and held me tight as his body erupted.

I was no longer afraid. Locke was mine. Forever.

Epilogue

I still had moments in the jet that consumed me, yet I managed to find a way to battle through each struggle. I took it day by day and each hurdle molded me into a stronger pilot and person. The jet wasn't responsible for my brother's death, neither was I, or my father—it was the trauma of war. I understood it now and Colin's case had finally been closed with the correct answers. It didn't make my pain disappear, but it made it understandable and more manageable

I leaned against the banister, opened my tablet and flipped through the pictures from today. Every member of Colin's squadron attended the grand opening of The Colin Pinkerton Center and paid tribute to him. The large sandstone structure was surrounded by a calming backdrop of flowering cherry trees that overlooked a large pond. My father and I hand planted each one of them, together.

The center was the perfect way to honor my brother and to offer aid and assistance to military members suffering with Post Traumatic Stress Disorders and their families. The process of working side by side with Locke and my father, to bring it to life, was healing. I knew Colin would be proud of our work.

I slid my finger across the screen causing the tablet to slip from my grip. I juggled it in the air trying to keep it from falling off the deck and into the sand. That was close. I squeezed it tightly as I stared at the screen. A familiar image paralyzed me on my feet.

Colin's video.

I hadn't watched it since before the war. I remained frozen staring at the screen. My heart pounded forcefully in my chest. My hand trembled as I reached toward the screen and tapped.

Are you sure you want to delete the video?

Meet the Author

Jamie Rae is a New Adult and Young Adult author, orthodontist, literary agent, Air Force veteran, military spouse and mother of three. Jamie was born in Uniontown, Pennsylvania and is a graduate of Laurel Highlands High School, West Virginia University and University of Nevada, Las Vegas. She is an avid reader and animal lover. Jamie writes with one goal in mind…create stories that will linger in your mind and tug at your heart.

Follow Jamie on Twitter @JamieRaeWrites
Also check out her website at www.jamieraewrites.com
for updates on future stories.

CPSIA information can be obtained
at www.ICGtesting.com
Printed in the USA
FSOW02n1141091115
13150FS